A TALE ETCHED IN BLOOD AND HARD BLACK PENCIL

They first met at primary school, Martin, Colin, James, Eleanor, Karen, Robbie, Boma, Helen, Scot, Joanne. Together they were taught the alphabet and their tables, some of them fought each other and they all learned how to recognise the laws of the pack—the strong, the weak, the bampots. Through puberty and adolescence they progressed through the system, their relationships shifting, sometimes coalescing, often fracturing.

Then twenty years later one of them is dead, one is in intensive care and another is in custody charged with murder. And on the fringes of the investigation are others from that original class—the detective inspector, the lawyer, the local hard man and the pub owner. Is there some nugget in their shared experience which explains the messy murder scene in the hills outside Glasgow?

A TALE ETCHED IN BLOOD AND HARD BLACK PENCIL

Christopher Brookmyre

WINDSOR
PARAGON

First published 2006
by
Little, Brown
This Large Print edition published 2006
by
BBC Audiobooks Ltd by arrangement with
Time Warner Books Ltd

Hardcover   ISBN 10: 1 4056 1454 4
             ISBN 13: 978 1 405 61454 2
Softcover   ISBN 10: 1 4056 1455 2
             ISBN 13: 978 1 405 61455 9

British Library Cataloguing in Publication Data available

Printed and bound in Great Britain by
Antony Rowe Ltd., Chippenham, Wiltshire

For Gerard Docherty and Allan McGuire.

And in memory of David Welsh.
Twenty years on, I'm not missing you any less.

Contents

Prologue

ST ELIZABETH'S
Primary One

Primary Three

Primary Four

Primary Five

Prologue

Friends Reunited

'Are they deid? Jesus Johnnybags, are they both deid? Fuck's sake, man, answer us. Fuck's sake.'

'Naw. Wee Elastoplast an they'll be fine. Whit does it fuckin look like? Ye any aspirin?'

'Aspirin? Whit, is that gaunny fuckin revive them?'

'It's for ma heid. It's fuckin thumpin. Cannae think straight.'

'*You* cannae think straight? Fuck's sake, how d'ye think I'm feelin? Whit a mess, man. Whit a fuckin mess. Whit the fuck happened? I mean, for fuck's sake, that's . . . that's . . .'

'I know who it is.'

'Well in the name ay the wee man, I know you liked him aboot as much as me, but you're no tellin us ye . . .'

'I'm no tellin ye anythin. Ye're free tae draw your ain conclusions, but the fact is, the less I tell ye, the less ye can tell any cunt else.'

'So why the fuck did ye ask us tae—'

'I need help. Ye gaunny give us a hand, or whit?'

'Or whit? Or you kill me as well so I cannae tell any cunt?'

'Don't be fuckin stupit. I'm desperate here. Does it no look pretty fuckin desperate tae you?'

'Naw, it looks like I missed desperate and came in well past dia-fuckin-bolical. Jesus God. Whit the fuck?'

'Aye, well, the worst's yet tae come. That's how I need your help. If ye cannae dae it, I understand. It's no like I'm askin for a loan ay your lawnmower

3

or somethin. All I'd request is ye keep your mooth shut. Your shout. Stay or go, but if it's go, go noo.'

'I'm stayin. I'm stayin. I am. I just need a wee minute here, but.'

'We've no got a wee minute.'

'Naw, right enough. So whit is it ye want us tae dae?'

*　　*　　*

'Detective Superintendent Gillespie, looking the picture of elegance and poise, as ever.'

'Aye, you'd best get that in before I see the bodies. I tend not to be so elegant when I'm poised over a lavvy bowl. I always know I'm in for a treat when I spot you Forensics boys walking about wearing face-masks.'

'I love the smell of corpses in the morning.'

'Funny nobody ever asks if you're single, Alex.'

Karen is standing under a small cluster of trees, offering relief from the light drizzle. It gets more heavily wooded further ahead, where Alex's cybermen are resplendent in their coveralls, making the scene look like cheap BBC sci-fi. It's a *copse* of trees, she thinks, but the word wouldn't come earlier, because it was too close to 'corpse', and she doesn't want to cement the association. Doesn't want to create another word or sight that can only ever after make her think of human remains. There's no end of beauty spots and isolated idylls of tranquillity that have been utterly ruined for you if you're in the polis.

She's not kidding about the face-masks, but, on the whole, Alex is nonetheless a welcome sight, because he's good at reminding you it's just a job.

The thought lasts for a wee while, at least; though probably works better for him. He's a pathologist. He sees meat and evidence, and while she's talking to him, so does she. But afterwards, she's the one who's got to put the pieces back together until they form a picture of a human life, one that ended in the worst possible way.

'Story I heard, you were offered the chance to pass on this one, let Keith Fox handle it, and yet here you are.'

'This is my old native soil, Alex.'

'You're from Carnock?'

'Naw, naw, Braeside,' she says, looking down the valley to where the town she grew up in sits hugging the foot of the hills. 'Couldnae resist the lure of the home fires.'

'Apposite choice of words, Detective, under the circumstances.'

'Crispy critters?'

'Double body-barbecue, aye. That's what attracted the farmer's dog. Buried bacon, probably still warm when Rover smelt it.'

'Buried?'

'Aye, but not very deep. I'd say your killer dug a shallow pit to burn the bodies in, then ran out of time, or petrol, or both. Dawn's breaking, maybe. Whatever. Doesn't want the smoke spotted. So he just fills it in and fucks off. Job's definitely only half done. I mean, no much chance of an open-casket funeral for either of this pair, but your boy wanted more than to ruin their looks.'

'Tried to make them unidentifiable. Did he smash the teeth?'

'No. I think he had his sights set on complete obliteration, no evidence of remains whatsoever.'

5

'What? Just by burning them in a pit?'

'Aye. I said that's what he set his sights on. I didnae say he was any good at it.'

*　　　*　　　*

'Right. We've got tae get rid ay these bodies. We need tae get rid ay that fuckin BMW fae ootside as well, but that can wait.'

'Whit aboot Tempo's motor?'

'That can stay. It's meant tae be here.'

'Is emdy due here that would be lookin for him? Whit aboot the rest ay these lodges? Whit if there's a bookin? Whit aboot a cleaner, mibbae?'

'The cleaner's no due unless the lodges are in use.'

'How d'ye know.'

'I just know, awright?'

'Whit aboot bookins, but?'

'Don't know. Never bother. We've got time tae work, but we've no got time tae waste, ye get me?'

'Aye. So whit are we daein wi the bodies? Gaunny bury them somewhere?'

'Naw. Are ye fuckin daft? Bury them? Dae ye no read the papers? Some cunt oot walkin his dug ayeways finds them when bodies get buried. Or some cunt sees ye cairryin a shovel, an that's you fucked again. Nae danger. We've got tae make sure they're *never* found, an the only way tae guarantee that is tae make sure there's nothin left tae *be* found.'

'Aw fuck, man, you're no talkin aboot choppin them up an bungin them through a mincer or somethin, are ye? I couldnae handle that.'

'D'ye think I could fuckin handle that? Are ye

forgettin who these cunts *are*, lyin there? Naw. I'm talkin aboot dissolvin them.'

'Dissolvin them? Where the fuck are we gaunny get somethin that'll dae that?'

'I'm no quite sure, but I thought we'd gie B&Q a try.'

*   *   *

'Fuck, man, it's no workin. Stinks tae high heaven an aw.'

'Need tae gie it mair time.'

'Mair time? It's been two hours an aw we've gied them's a fuckin rash.'

'At least that's mair than the first stuff we bought did tae them. Thank fuck we kept the receipt.'

'Well, we cannae go back tae B&Q a third time. It'll be shut by noo. This stuff isnae workin.'

'Mibbae need tae leave it overnight.'

'Overnight? Whit, so oor next move's in broad daylight? Come on. If this stuff was gaunny dae the biz, it would be fizzin an bubblin like somethin oot *Doctor Jekyll*.'

'Well whit else dae ye suggest? Mibbae there's a big cheese-grater through-by we can use.'

'Stop actin the cunt. I'm tryin tae help here.'

'Sorry.'

'See, whit we need is, hingmy, yon super-acid . . . Mate ay mine used tae work at Redhill Plastics, an he says they had this fuckin nasty stuff they used, called ololeum.'

'Linoleum? Whit, we gaunny wrap them up in it?'

'Naw, no linoleum: ololeum. Any cunt got a wee splash on them an they were straight doon the

7

burns unit.'

'That sounds mair like it. You still got thae wire-cutters?'

'Back at the hoose, aye.'

'Whit we waitin for, well?'

*   *   *

'See, he just lay down the bodies and the clothes in here, poured on the fuel and chucked in a match. As a result, the undersides are undamaged; well, unburnt. Or, rather, that's not true either. They *are* burnt, but by chemicals, not flame. Superficial blistering, almost certainly sustained post-mortem. I can test for specifically what was used when I get them back to the lab, but from what I've seen right here, I'd wager your man's first attempt at getting rid of the evidence was a shot at the old Crippen jacuzzi.'

'Yuck,' was all Karen felt like contributing.

'But whatever he used didn't do the trick. Unsurprising, really. The chemicals required aren't exactly the kind of thing you've got lying around in the garage, you know?'

'Crippen?' asks one of the local Dibbles. Karen would say he was hanging about like a bad smell, but that particular role has already been adequately filled by what's inside the Forensics tent. McGowan, she thinks the Dibble's name is. 'Is he the one that dissolved the bodies in acid?' he goes on.

'Correct, Constable,' says Alex.

'It's just that, for what it's worth, there were two eejits apprehended the other day, breakin intae Redhill Plastics, over at the Nether Carnock

8

industrial estate. I'm pretty sure I heard somebody say they were tryin to steal oleum.'

Karen stares at him. 'My Higher Chemistry was a long time back. Remind me. Oleum?'

'Super-concentrated sulphuric acid,' the Dibble tells her.

Alex nods. 'The very dab.'

'Who was it? Do you still have them?'

'Cannae remember the names. I think they were released late yesterday evening.'

'Get on it. Now.'

* * *

'You awright?'

'Just aboot. Never been shittin maesel so much in a polis station; no even the first time I got put in the cells. Jesus fuck, man.'

'But ye never said nothin?'

'Aye, I tellt them the lot. That's why they let us walk right oot, ya fuckin tube.'

'Just thinkin oot loud. Fuckin bad score, but. Thought they could see right through me, man.'

'Whit did ye tell them?'

'I stuck tae the story. Says I've a blocked drain and I heard this stuff would save us a plumber.'

'Me as well. Your drain, obviously. It was savin on a plumber that sold it, I reckon. Could see it in their faces, thinkin: "Aye, right enough, thievin bastarts thae plumbers."'

'Whit d'ye think we'll get?'

'A fine. If it's anythin custodial, it'll be a jakey sentence.'

'Aye, well, we better get a shift on if we don't want somethin a bit longer, eh?'

'Nae kiddin. And nae fuckin aboot noo. Whit time's it?'

'Hauf nine. Bastarts hud us in there the whole fuckin day.'

'At least it's dark. That'll help.'

'Whit's the script?'

'We get back an clean up the lodge. That shite we bought at B&Q does at least have wan decent use: it bleaches the fuck oot ay carpets, so we can cover up the bloodstains.'

'Whit aboot, ye know . . .'

'We get them intae the boot ay the motor, take them up the braes, intae the woods. Dig a wee pit an burn them in it till there's nothin left but ashes.'

'Will some cunt no see the fire?'

'No if it's deep in the woods. Come on. First stop's the garage.'

'Whit for?'

'Ten Regal an a scud book. Whit d'ye hink? Petrol, ya daft cunt.'

*   *   *

'Two of them, then,' says Alex, watching the Dibble walk briskly away, dialling his mobile as he goes. 'Makes sense, I suppose. Hard to imagine one person being capable of so much stupidity on his own. To be this incompetent would require a pooling of efforts.'

'Gives us a timescale, though,' Karen observes.

'Indeed. If they were released late yesterday, we can back-extrapolate their movements prior to arrest. Puts the murders at Tuesday at the latest. Then once they got out—practically dancing with relief, I'd bet—they had to work fast on plan B,

10

which was to get up here with a can of petrol and try a spot of DIY cremation. Have you any idea what kind of temperature is required to consume human bone, DS Gillespie?'

'About as much idea as these two.'

'Quite. So I'm picturing the pair of them with the jerrycan empty, the sun coming up and their victims still medium-rare. They've got no choice but to fill in their wee hole and run away before anybody wakes up and clocks them leaving the area. Off they pop, along comes the farmer and his faithful companion, and *voilà*, that's where we come in.'

'What about the victims? Are we looking at a dental records job? You said they didn't smash the teeth.'

'Yes, the teeth are intact. Like I said, I believe they thought they could completely destroy the bodies. By the time it came to considerations such as rendering them unidentifiable, it was too late. That's if it even occurred to them at that point.'

'So is there anything you can tell me about the victims right now?'

'Oh yes. Both shot execution style, close range, single tap to the head. Younger one to the right temple, older one through the forehead. Both male, as you know; both white. I'd put the younger one at thirty-six years old—'

'Thirty-*six*? Not "mid-thirties"?'

'Thirty-six,' Alex reiterates. 'And a Taurus, in fact. Dark hair—'

'Tau . . . Right, you're taking the piss.'

Alex smiles. 'Not at all. See, they set fire to the victims' clothes, but they forgot to pat them down first. I told you we were dealing with a unique level

11

of incompetence. There was a heavy-duty leather wallet among the remnants of a pair of jeans. His condoms are probably past their best, but the driving licence is still perfectly legible. His name was Colin Temple. Liked his designer gear, by the look of it. He's got a store card for . . . DS Gillespie, are you all right?'

She nods, swallows. Okay, yeah, this was always a possibility. Probably why she wanted the case, if she was being honest. It still feels pretty heavy, takes a second or two. 'Sure.'

'You knew him?'

'Not for a long time, but we were at school together. What about the other one?'

'Not quite so generous with their clues this time, but they left him all his jewellery. He's got the initials "JT" on a ring. Could be the missus, of course, but—'

'Johnny Turner,' says another of the local plods. Spiers, this one is called.

'What's that?'

'We found his motor all burnt oot, up the dams yesterday. Rang up to tell him but naebody was home.'

'Johnny Turner,' she repeats. 'Rings a bell.'

'Bampot,' says the plod. 'Hard man turned drug dealer. Runs things around Braeside for the bigger boys over in Paisley. Sons are bampots, too. Auldest yin's inside for murder. Next wan doon won't be long behind him, if somebody doesnae murder him first.'

'And what can you tell me about Colin Temple?'

'No much. Runs a hotel in Paisley and owns some lodges by the fishing loch a couple of miles the other side of the hills. Never in bother wi us is the bottom line, and if he was linked tae Johnny Turner, it's news tae me.'

'And Johnny Turner? Age, height, build, anything that can help give us a quick positive?'

'Mid-sixties, medium height, stocky build,' says Spiers.

Alex nods, but shrugs to convey that it's hardly distinguishing. 'Anything else?'

Spiers looks to Alex. 'Big chunk oot his skull where some bastart hit him wi a hatchet way back when?'

Alex barely suppresses a grin as he nods affirmation.

Spiers gets a call on his radio and takes a couple of steps away to hear the message better. There are a few long, garbled volleys on the remote end of a one-sided conversation, with Spiers' contributions limited to 'okay's and 'really?'s. Alex shakes his head in mild amusement.

'What?' she asks him.

'Good job he said that. Saves me trying to work out where that particular wound fits into the bigger picture.'

'No, that'll be my treat,' she tells him.

Spiers has turned back around and is looking impatiently at her. He's got news. He waited deferentially for her to finish speaking but the inverted commas were already coming through his lips.

'DS Gillespie, maam, it's the oleum pair. Constable McGowan called the station and they sent some officers out. They've got one in custody, but the other is . . . Well, they've got him, but he's been stabbed umpteen times and has apparently got a six-inch blade through his skull. Ambulance is taking him direct to the Southern.'

The Southern General. Major neurosurgical centre. Not good.

'Did you get the names?'

'Yes, ma'am. Both members of Braeside Nick's Frequent Flyer programme. Sergeant Reilly at the station suggested you'd know them better yourself as Noodsy and Turbo.'

'Noodsy and . . . Christ. Which one's in the ambulance?'

'Turbo.'

'More Friends Reunited?' Alex asks.

'Yeah. They were both in mine and Colin Temple's class at school. But that's the lesser of the connections here.'

'What's the biggie?'

She nods to Spiers for him to break it to the pathologist.

'Turbo is Johnny Turner's youngest son.'

ST ELIZABETH'S

Primary One
61 Ursae Majoris

Tears and Other Spillages

There is a smell of apples. Not fresh, not the smell when you have one in your hand, which disappears when you bite into it and the taste takes over inside your nose. It's something more fusty and a wee bit yuck: apples that have been left too long somewhere dark, maybe one of the desks with the lids that open. The smell itself isn't bad, but Martin is a wee bit uneasy when he smells it, so he thinks it's the smell he doesn't like, when in fact it's how the smell makes him feel. It reminds him of Gran's pantry, where she keeps her carrots and sometimes cooking apples, which are huge but don't taste as good as normal apples. He took a bite of one once when he was in there looking for biscuits. You're allowed as much fruit as you like because it's good for you and doesn't rot your teeth or make you fat, but you get a row if you start eating something you don't finish. Gran says your eyes are bigger than your belly when you don't finish something you asked for, and she laughs, but Mum gets angry 'because it's a waste and there's black babies who are starvinafrica'. The cooking apple was sour and Martin knew he couldn't eat another bite of it, but it was the biggest apple he'd ever seen, the size of Florence's head on *The Magic Roundabout*, and he knew Mum would give him into huge trouble for not finishing it, so he put it back under some other apples and turned it so that the bite was facing the other way. You got worms in apples, so maybe when Gran found it

19

she'd think that was what had taken the bite. But he'd worried about it because he knew it was naughty, and you got into even bigger trouble if you were caught later than at the time, because Mum said being sleekit was worse than the naughty nurse itself. So every time he was at Gran's house after that, he went to the pantry hoping to find that the apple was gone, but it wasn't, and that was when the pantry started to smell of it. Even once the bitten apple was finally away, the pantry still smelt of it, and it always made him feel funny inside.

Today, however, is the last time the smell will remind him of anything else. From now on, though it will always make him feel the same, it will remind him only of this place.

He squats on the floor, along the wall beneath the windows, facing the door on the other side of the room. The wooden desks are arranged in several rows, all facing the front, but nobody is sitting at any of them. The majority of the children are lined up alongside him, but some are still standing around the door, not letting go of their mummies. Most of these are crying, and those who are not soon begin to once their mummies unclasp their hands and wave bye-bye. Quite a few of the boys and girls along the wall are crying too, which makes Martin think that he ought to, like it is the correct response under the circumstances. He didn't cry when his mummy went away, though strangely he thought for a moment that *she* might. She left him at the gates and wished him luck, then went back to her car and drove off before she was late for work. He didn't cry because he didn't feel sad and nothing was sore. He used to cry sometimes when Mummy left him at playgroup, but that was when he was really totey. Now, though, he's starting to wonder if it's expected of him, as his gran advised him yesterday to watch the other boys and girls and do as they do if you're ever a bit confused.

He is about to join in bubbling when the boy next to him begins speaking. He doesn't know the boy; doesn't know anyone in the class, in fact. All the children he knew at nursery are starting at Braeside Primary instead. He doesn't know why he has been sent to a different school, but didn't really think about it until today. The only boy he knows who is supposed to be starting at St Elizabeth's is Dominic Reilly, whose mummy is friends with Martin's mummy so they sometimes play at each other's house. Martin prefers it when they play at Dominic's, because he has a Matchbox Motorway and Dominic's mum lets them have orange ice-lollies made of Tupperware from the freezer. But Dominic isn't in this class, and he didn't see him outside, so maybe Dominic's mum changed her mind and sent him to Braeside Primary with the others.

'Hullo,' says the boy. He looks friendly. 'What's your name?' he asks.

'Martin,' Martin replies.

'I'm Scot. I'm not greetin. My da says I hadnae tae greet. How are you no greetin? Did your da tell you no tae as well?'

Martin thinks about this, can't remember his dad giving any advice for school other than to work hard and not get the belt. Mummy told him off for saying this, but in a happy way, so Martin knew Daddy was making a joke.

21

Martin likes the look of Scot. He is smiley and seems unperturbed by his new surroundings. Martin wants them to be friends and decides this would be helped along if they have something in common, so he fibs and says, 'Yes.' Then he adds: 'And not to get the belt.' Martin doesn't actually know what this belt is that his daddy was talking about, but thinks it will make Scot like him if he sounds as though he already knows something about school.

'Aye,' Scot agrees. 'Tsh, tsh, aiyah,' he says, giggling and doing some sort of action with his hands that Martin doesn't follow, though he grasps that pain is involved.

A little later, the mummies have all finally gone and all the crying seems to have stopped. The teacher announces that her name is Mrs Murphy and gets them all to say, 'Good morning, Mrs Murphy.' Then she reads out everyone's name from a sheet of paper, to which they each have to say, 'Present, miss,' and put up their hands. Martin understands that 'present' is another word for 'here', so knows the teacher won't be giving them parcels. He is not sure all the other children know this, however, as some of them looked very happy when they heard the word.

There is a girl nearby who is rocking from side to side as she sits cross-legged. Martin noticed her because she wasn't one of the ones who was crying. He suspects that maybe she needs the toilet.

The teacher reads out the name 'Helen Dunn' and the rocking girl shoots her hand up, saying, 'Present, miss,' with gleeful enthusiasm. Martin notices that there is another girl further along the wall who also has her hand up. She seems like she

22

wants to say something but is too shy. The teacher looks at her and she starts to appear very worried, probably about to cry.

'What is it, dear?' the teacher asks in a soft voice. The girl's eyes fill up and she starts to bubble. 'Come on, you can tell me, pet. There's nothing to worry about. We're just all getting to know each other's names. What's yours?'

The girl sniffs, trying to get her words out through the greeting, which Martin knows is hard, especially when you're a bit feart. 'Helen Dunn,' she says.

The teacher turns to the other girl, who still has her hand up, still looks very happy, like she really did get a present.

'And you're called Helen Dunn, too?' Mrs Murphy asks, looking at her sheet of paper.

The girl now looks a bit worried. 'No,' she says. 'I'm called Karen.'

'Why did you put your hand up when I said Helen's name, Karen?'

The girl's cheeks go red. 'I couldn't wait, miss,' she says.

The teacher smiles and covers her mouth. Martin suspects she's laughing. The ladies at playgroup sometimes did that. Mummy said this was because it was rude to laugh at people when they make mistakes. None of the children laugh. Martin doesn't know if this is because they are being polite or because they don't realise Karen has made a mistake. He hopes it's the first one, because then he won't have to worry that they'll laugh at him if he does something daft, too.

The teacher goes through all the names, then starts over again, but this time when your name is called, you have to go and sit at the desk she tells you. Martin jumps to his feet when his turn comes, and climbs quickly on to the seat, which is connected to the desk by big metal pipes. He lifts the heavy wooden lid and looks inside. It is empty apart from a few wisps of pencil-shavings underneath a round hole at the very front. Martin looks at the desk next to him to make sure it is the same and that the hole is supposed to be there. He doesn't want the teacher thinking he broke it, in case he gets the belt. Daddy was joking about this, which meant he didn't think it was very likely, but that meant he'd be all the more angry if it actually happened.

Martin watches the others take their places one by one, seeing the next row fill up. To his right is a girl called Alison, who was crying when her mummy left and still looks very feart. He had been hoping to end up next to Scot, but he is two rows away on the left, his name having been among the first ones called.

Once they have all been given a desk, the teacher talks for a very long time, and Martin has to try hard to keep listening, like at Mass. Mummy says to listen because the priest is telling a story, but it never sounds like a story to Martin, just boring talk, talk, talk. The teacher's voice is nicer than any of the priests', though. They all talk in a kind of half-singing voice, which Martin thinks must be because they are talking to God, as nobody talks to normal people like that, not even on telly.

When she is finished, she opens a cupboard and produces a pile of blue books which she calls 'jotters'. Then she asks the girl in the front row, nearest the teacher's table, to go round and give one to everybody. The girl is called Joanne. She is bigger than Martin and a bit plump, and wasn't crying before, so Martin thinks she must be five already. He won't be five until November. He watches her hand out the jotters, eagerly taking hold of his. There is writing on the back, blank white pages inside, and on the front a box with three rows of dotted lines.

While Joanne is doing her rounds, there is a knock on the classroom door, and a man in blue overalls enters, carrying a big orange plastic crate.

'Good morning, Mr Johnston,' says Mrs Murphy. 'Children, this is Mr Johnston, our janitor, and he's got something special for us. Say: "Good Morning, Mr Johnston."'

They all say it, that Karen girl really shouting it out. Joanne stops where she is, like she's forgotten what she's doing, and has to be told by the teacher to return to her task. Everyone is trying to see what is in the crate. It looks like white triangles.

'And what special thing do you have for us, Mr Johnston?' the teacher asks him.

'School milk, Mrs Murphy,' he says. He smiles.

Martin has never heard of a janitor before, but he knows there are sometimes two names for the same job: a normal one and a fancy one, like joiner and carpenter. He has now worked out that janitor is the fancy name for a milkman, and looks forward to telling his daddy this tonight when he gets home from work.

Once the janitor has gone away again, the teacher sits at her table and once again begins calling out everybody's name. This time it takes ages, because when it's your turn you have to bring your new jotter to her and get your name written on it. Then you are allowed to pick up a carton of milk and a blue straw and take it back to your desk to drink it. Martin's name is called, and as before he immediately follows a boy named Gary Hawkins. Gary passes him on his way back from the crate, clutching his triangular carton and already eagerly stabbing at it with his blue straw. Martin notices varying levels of success in extracting the milk as he progresses towards the front: some contentedly sipping away; others comparing with their neighbours for clues as to piercing the container; while a girl called Zoe is tugging at the edges as her straw lies in wait upon her desk.

Mrs Murphy writes Martin's name on one of the dotted lines, then points to the line below it and tells him that if he is a good boy and pays attention, he will soon be able to write his name underneath by himself.

Martin gets scared and excited at the same time when she says this, because he can already write his name and he wants to tell her but is a bit feart that the teacher will be angry with him if he says he can do it then doesn't get it right, which sometimes happens because the letter 'M' is tricky. He remembers his mum telling him he should never hold back from trying something or giving an answer just because he is afraid it might be wrong, but she also told him not to talk back to the teacher unless she asks a question first, so he doesn't really know what to do.

He has just about decided it will be safer all round simply to keep his mouth closed when Mrs Murphy points out to him that it is already hanging open. 'Is there something you want to say, Martin?' she asks. 'Don't be afraid.'

'I can write "Martin",' he tells her. 'But I sometimes make a mistake with the "M" at the start.'

'Well, that's excellent, Martin. Why don't you show me?' And she hands him a pencil.

He feels a bit sick now and wishes he had said nothing so that he could already be away back to his desk with the carton of milk.

Martin takes a deep breath and grips the pencil extra tight, concentrating hard and hoping the 'M' comes out right. It doesn't. He looks at the one above, written by Mrs Murphy, and sees it doesn't have as many wiggles. He stops and looks at her, feeling himself getting ready to greet.

'I'm sorry,' he says. 'I know how to draw a "M". I just don't know when to stop.' And then he does start crying. He just can't help it.

'Never mind, Martin. That's almost there. Let's see you do the rest, shall we?'

Martin wonders if the 'shall we?' is an escape option, a chance to say 'no' and retreat from the chance of further disaster, but can tell from a feeling in his throat that it will make him cry all the more if he takes that route. He nods and sniffs back some tears and snotters, then applies pencil to paper once again.

'Very good,' Mrs Murphy says. '*Very* good, Martin.'

Martin is happy again, the choking, crying feeling instantly gone. He lifts his jotter and clutches it like a prize, so proud of it that he is already halfway back to his desk before Mrs Murphy reminds him that he has forgotten to take his milk.

He climbs on to the bench again and examines the carton. Turning it over in his hands, he notices a small circular indentation with a thin film of plastic stretched across its base. He stabs it and a small jet of milk spurts from the top of the straw, which he instinctively covers with his mouth. He hears a giggle and turns to his left. There is a boy across the row and one seat back grinning.

'That came oot goin' the nineties,' he says approvingly.

Martin smiles back and feels as pleased as he did when he was able to demonstrate to Scot his knowledge of the belt.

Mrs Murphy calls out Helen Dunn next, and some of the children look to that girl Karen to see if she will come out at the same time. She doesn't, but she looks like she really wants to.

Martin hears a tut and looks forward, where a few desks in front Zoe is still struggling with her carton. The teacher looks up too, and says: 'No, no, dear, you need to jag it through the wee hole. Dear, pet, don't pull the sides or you're going to . . . Pet, dear, hello . . .'

But Zoe is concentrating too hard on her task to realise the teacher is talking to her, and Mrs Murphy can't remember her name. The teacher looks at her list and calls out, 'Zoe!' just as Helen Dunn is approaching Zoe's desk. Helen stops in her tracks, maybe not sure now whether it's still her turn after almost being usurped the last time. Zoe, meanwhile, gets a fright at the sound of her name and in her surprise flips the carton into the air. It spins the few short feet across the aisle to land on another girl's desk, where it bursts open with a milky splat, some of which hits Helen. The girl goes to jump out of the way but bangs her knees on the underside of the desk, then slaps an elbow into the puddle.

There are screams and shrieks from all around. Zoe, Helen and the splattered girl all start greeting, and so do a few others around the room. Martin wants to laugh but thinks his mum would say it's wrong, like when someone does a pump in church. He thinks the teacher will say it's wrong too, as she doesn't look very pleased. He hears the breathy, muted sniggering of someone who is trying to keep it in but just can't help himself. Martin looks around and sees that it is the boy who giggled before, and once they have seen each other it becomes impossible to stop.

The teacher says 'shhh' a lot and tells everybody to calm down. 'There's no use crying over spilt milk,' she says, and Martin notices her smile a wee bit as she does so. He now knows it's all right to laugh, knowledge that strangely makes the giggles subside. The crying doesn't stop, though. The three girls involved are all bubbling away, but not as much as that girl Karen, who is doubled over her desk, shuddering and taking big loud gasps of breath in between. It is only when she lifts her head and suddenly stops that Martin realises she wasn't crying, she was laughing, but he doesn't understand why—or indeed how—she has so instantly ceased.

Then the girl behind her, Joanne who gave out the jotters, shoots her hand triumphantly into the air and makes everything clear.

'Please miss, please miss, please miss, Karen's peed herself.'

29

Martin looks to Mrs Murphy to see whether it's all right to laugh at this one, but he doesn't think it will be, because he hears her saying a prayer, and prayers are never funny. She closes her eyes for a wee while, and when she opens them again she is staring upwards, like the priest sometimes does during Mass.

'Jesus Christ Almighty, give me strength,' she says.

Concept Execution

There's no more space in the clearing, so Karen leaves her car tucked in as far off the track as she can manage without pranging a tree and walks the short distance to the late Colin Temple's woodland lodges. She doesn't know whether it normally accommodates block bookings, but today it looks like the place is hosting a small-scale polis convention. Alex and the other men in white coats appear to be in charge of the asylum, their activities centred on one lodge, second from the far end of the shallow arc of buildings. Karen has to laugh at the sight of one particular Dibble earnestly engaged in applying police tape to the exterior. This is not the kind of place you're likely to find a lot of curious passers-by. It's about five miles from the nearest pavement. Karen grew up in Braeside and was only vaguely aware the fishing loch existed, far less where to find it. She kind of wishes she had; it would have been a great spot for a picnic, the ideal destination for a walk with her pals on one of those precious few summer days worth the description. On the other hand, had that been the case, it would now be about to get crossed off: another romantic location forever violated by other people's horrors.

She stops and looks around for a few moments, trying to filter out the sounds of radios squelching from open car doors and jacket pockets. She wants to picture the place without polis motors and Forensics vans, see it as it looked to the people who died here and to those who walked away.

Of those, Turbo's immediate destiny is in the hands of a surgeon at the Southern General, while they've got Noodsy safely locked up in Braeside nick. She's going to interview him later, but not before she's developed her own picture of what they're dealing with, in order to see how his version holds up; and not before she's let him sweat a while. Noodsy never was much good under pressure back when she knew him. He was so used to getting caught that the mere sight of an authority figure accusing him was usually enough to elicit a resigned acceptance of his fate.

Alex emerges on to the wooden-decked patio at the focal lodge's entrance. He notices Karen's approach and gives her an amused smile. More criminal masterclass stuff to be found within, then. He hands her a spare face-mask, but mercifully not for the reason she anticipated. The fumes hit her as soon as she steps on to the decking.

'Sainsbury's must have been fresh out of Shake 'n' Vac,' Alex says. 'They've been using drain cleaner to get rid of the bloodstains from the carpet.'

'Should I pick some up the next time I spill red wine?'

'Does the trick, aye. As long as you don't mind your carpet looking like this.'

Alex ushers her inside with a wave of his left arm and she gets an instant eyeful of what he means. There's no obvious trace of blood, but the otherwise brown carpet looks like it's gone down with a bad case of vitiligo. The largest of the bleached—nay, scorched—patches are both in the centre of the floor, though there are plenty of others between there and what she learns is the door to the bathroom.

'I'd posit that they had a go at dissolving the bodies with the drain cleaner and then used it on the bloodstains some time after they had their change of plan. Covered up the fact that the stains were made by blood, but not exactly inconspicuous, is it? Specially if they were hoping to make it look like this Temple guy just disappeared.'

'How do you know it was drain cleaner? Can you tell just by the smell?'

Alex gives her that smile again. 'Found the receipt. It was folded over umpteen times and twisted back and forth—by the fingers of a very nervous individual needing to keep his hands occupied—but it was perfectly legible. Dates, times, it all fits. B&Q Darnley—for all your corpse-disposal needs. Typical DIY store, though. The stuff you buy never quite does the job when it's not in the hands of a professional. And these were definitely not the hands of a professional. The receipt was in the bin, for Christ's sake.'

'The bin?' she asks, barely able to believe the criminal ineptitude until she casts her mind back and remembers the only thing either Noodsy or

Turbo was good at was getting into trouble.

'Amazing, isn't it? In my experience, it's the mark of the true numpty that he can create almost as much new evidence in his attempts to cover his tracks as he actually removed from the scene of the crime.'

'Which will be your way of saying you don't have a weapon.'

Alex shrugs apologetically. 'Or shell cases.' He laughs a little. Found out. 'It's early days, but I'd have expected to find some rope fibres by this stage too,' he confesses.

'Rope fibres?'

'Aye, going by the locations of these two big stains. They were both shot point blank in the head only feet apart in the same room. Can't see how you can do that to two people without restraints. One, sure, element of surprise, but not two.'

'That's assuming they were both killed by the same gun.'

'Which we are going to be lucky to establish without bullets.'

'Well, as you say, it's early days.'

Alex shakes his head, then points to fist-sized marks in two of the walls. 'Something's been dug out of those and the holes filled in with Polyfilla. Also on the B&Q receipt, by the way. They've obviously watched enough telly to know to get rid of the dramatic stuff. The plan must have been to make the victims vanish and dispose of the ballistic evidence. Not entirely stupid in theory, just badly lacking in the concept-execution part.'

Karen looks again at the filled marks and the stains on the carpet. 'I don't know about concept, but I think Johnny Turner and Colin Temple might

33

argue they managed the execution part just fine.'

Coins

It's playtime and Colin is on the loo, something he had been looking forward to since shortly after drinking his milk. He had asked Mrs Murphy if he could go out to the toilet, like a few of the other children had been allowed to after that skinny girl Karen wet herself, but had been told just to wait because it would 'soon be the interval'. He didn't know what the interval was, though it sounded like that thing his mum had gone to Glasgow for recently. Mummy had been really pleased when she came back, so it must have been something good, but he didn't understand why you wouldn't be allowed to do a pee before it. Fortunately, the bell rang a wee bit later to signal playtime, so he had the chance to relieve himself before whatever the interval turned out to be.

He had seen toilets like this when his dad took him to the baths. As well as the normal toilets and sinks, there was a row of white things stuck to one wall, like teardrops cut in half. These were what Dad peed into, standing up, but Colin wasn't big enough to reach, and the one time Dad held him up, he went all over his trousers and they had to go right home to change instead of to the canteen for chips. The same thing had happened at home when he tried to do it standing up. His mum had told him he'd have to wait until he grew a bit and got trousers with flies, and Dad said he'd soon have flies on all his trousers if he kept getting pee on them. The teardrop things at school were much lower down than at the baths and Colin wouldn't need lifted up to use one, but elevation hadn't helped at the swimming, and he really didn't want to end up with pee—and flies—all over his trousers. Lots of people had laughed at that girl Karen and she'd had to wear a spare skirt that the teacher got from a cupboard, with *no pants*!

Colin had gone straight to the toilets as soon as the teacher told them they could leave the classroom, and found himself the first one there. This was just as well, as there were only two cubicles to have a sit-down in like at home. It felt good, like that time they'd been in the car on the motorway and he had to hold it in for ages until they got to Uncle Jim's house. There wasn't as much wee this time, but the feeling of relief was just as great.

Another boy comes in just as Colin is exiting the stall. He looks about the same size as Colin, so must also be a Primary One, but Colin didn't see him before, so maybe he is in the other teacher's class. He goes into the cubicle next to the one Colin was using and locks the door. Colin walks over to one of the sinks and turns on the taps to wash his hands. He usually only gives them a quick skoosh if it's just a pee, but he likes the look of the big pink blocks of soap that are next to each basin.

He is drying his hands on the blue roller-towel thing when a load of bigger boys—Primary Twos and maybe even Threes—come tumbling into the room, laughing and bumping into each other. Most of them go and pee into the teardrop things, but two of them just take a drink from the water-fountain. It is one of this pair whose interest is suddenly taken by the cubicles.

'Heh, somebody's in there daein a shite,' he announces with a joy that Colin finds odd, and a hint of malice of which he instinctively knows to be wary, something compounded by the use of a bad word. Now finished peeing, several of them approach the cubicle. None of them washes their hands, not even a quick skoosh. One of them bangs on the door.

'Are ye daein a big huge toley in there?' he shouts.

'Big broon shite,' laughs another.

'Big smelly keech.'

'Mingin big plops.'

There is no response from within. Colin, having been seated in the next stall only moments ago, can vividly imagine why not.

He remains confused, if darkly fascinated. What's so unusual or remarkable about doing a poo? Are they making out they don't, or something? Surely not washing your hands is far more deserving of ridicule, if smells are the issue?

Then one boy, who had not joined in with the shouting, steps forward among the small gathering. He is taller than the others and looks a bit fierce. 'That'll dae, yous,' he says. 'Stop it. That's a fuckin sin. Lea the boy alane. Just a wee Primary Wan. Staun back.'

They do, allowing him to approach the door, which he knocks gently.

'Wee man? It's awright. Mon oot. Naebody's gaunny touch ye, okay? It's awright wee man. I'll look efter ye.'

There is a long, silent pause, then Colin hears the lock being slid back on the cubicle door.

36

'Mon oot, wee man,' the tall boy repeats. Brian, one of the others called him.

The Primary One emerges cautiously, looking scared. He's not greeting, but he's not far off it, either. The tall boy puts a hand out like grown-ups do when they want you to come with them or trying to stop you being feart. The Primary One takes it and steps fully away from the stall, now in full view of everyone.

'You okay?' he asks.

The wee one nods shakily.

'Did you do a wee poo?'

Another nervous nod.

Then the tall boy lets go of his hand and points right into his face. 'Aaaaaaaaah—jobbie-bum, jobbie-bum, jobbie-bum,' he sings, at which all the others start howling with laughter.

The Primary One bursts out crying and runs through the door. Colin follows him. He knows he has had a lucky escape, that it could have been him, could yet be him, but he has also learnt an important lesson. Wet trousers, flies or not, he will be peeing at the teardrop things from now on and will never, ever, do a poo-poo in school.

*   *   *

Martin is talking to Scot and the boy who said his squirt of milk was doing the nineties. His name is James Doon. Martin heard this when the teacher called him out to get his name written, and noted his second name because there are two Jameses in the class. They have been wandering around the playground, exploring the place together. They have walked as far as the wall to the Big Ones' playground, then around the back of the Infant Building, past big smelly metal bins as tall as trees, and back to where they started.

There is another boy standing nearby, against a drainpipe close to the Primary One and Two double doors. The Primary Threes have their own entrance round the other side. Martin can't remember for sure, but thinks the boy's name is Robert. His desk is at the front, nearest the door, and Martin noticed he was watching him when he went back to get his milk. He looks very serious, not like Scot and James. Scot likes Slade and has a big sister who owns singles, so he can hear the songs all the time, not just when they come on the radio. James doesn't know about Slade. Scot asks him who he likes. He says, 'Celtic.'

Two girls walk by and stand at the foot of the stone steps leading to the double doors. One is Alison, who sits next to Martin, and the other is Joanne, the girl who gave out the jotters.

'We're gaunny be first when the teacher calls the lines,' Joanne announces.

Martin feels a moment of anxiety at this. It's always good to be first. He doesn't know how long playtime lasts, other than until the bell rings, but doesn't understand why anyone would want to spend it just waiting on the spot. However, as it is his first day and other boys and girls—especially those with big brothers and sisters—seem to know more than he does, perhaps there is something he is missing.

Martin looks to Scot for his response to this. He shows no intention of moving, so Martin decides he'll wait and see what advantage Alison and Joanne win from their vigil before deciding whether it's worth it in future.

There is, however, a reaction from the serious boy, Robert. He narrows his eyes until they are like slits and tells Joanne: 'You're a fuckin sook.'

'No I'm urnae,' she protests.

'Aye ye are. Giein oot books for the teacher, staunin first in line. You're a fuckin sook.' And with this he finally smiles, though it seems no more friendly than when his face was all serious. He confirms this when he turns to look at Martin next. 'You an aw,' he says. 'I saw ye oot there wi the teacher. "Very good, Martin." Fuckin sook. You'll get fuckin battered. Ma big brer says sooks get battered.'

Martin doesn't know what a sook is, but knows he doesn't want to be one if it means you get fuckin battered. 'I'm not a sook.' He searches his mind for proof of other status to offer in defence, words conferred by Mum and Dad. 'I'm a good boy. I'm clever.'

'Aye. At's whit ma big brer says. Sooks are fuckin clever. Good boys are fuckin sooks.'

Martin is horrified by having apparently supplied the evidence for his own conviction. Fortunately, Joanne comes to his rescue. 'You're a porteed,' she says shrilly.

Martin doesn't know what a porteed is either, but whatever it is, it has little impact on its target, who remains at his spot next to the drainpipe.

He has learnt a few new words today, but none with the frequency of 'fuckin'; and despite the number of times he has heard it, the context has never made its meaning clear or even consistent. The only thing he has been able to deduce for sure is that it is intended to add emphasis, but seems to be equally applicable whether positive or negative. He has been called a fuckin sook and warned he'll get fuckin battered. However, earlier Scot told him that *Gudbye to Jane* is a fuckin great song and James described the bins behind the Infant Building as fuckin giant. Elsewhere on their tour, Martin heard talk of fuckin big dugs, fuckin wee weans, fuckin fast motors, fuckin slow buses, fuckin sweeties, fuckin shoes, fuckin troosers, fuckin teachers, fuckin tellies, fuckin puddles, fuckin skippin ropes, fuckin bells, fuckin jotters, fuckin milk and fuckin Rangers.

He watched Scot put the ends of his forefingers together and invite James to 'break the wire'. James did so with a digit of his own, upon which Scot announced: 'You're on fire.' This, according to James, was fuckin funny, but according to another, named Richard, it was fuckin ancient.

In order to demonstrate something more recent, Richard had then placed a clenched fist on the palm of his hand and asked James to 'sniff the cheese'. James obligingly placed his snib close to the offered outstretched fingers, whereupon Richard punched him on the nose and shouted, 'Mousetrap!'

This, James exclaimed, was fuckin sair.

The bell rings and they make their way the few short yards to the steps, where Joanne and Alison have pride of place. The Primary Twos and Threes start forming separate lines, well versed in the procedure. The Primary Ones gather themselves in a less regimented order, gradually forming into two and then three and then four single-file queues as various new arrivals decide they like the idea of being head of the line and promptly start their own. After a few minutes, Mrs Murphy and another teacher appear. The first thing they do is tell the bigger ones to go in: first 'Miss Taylor's class', then 'Miss O'Neill's class', and so on. Then, with only the Primary Ones remaining, Mrs Murphy tells her class to form a queue on the far left and the others, Mrs Fitzpatrick's class, to line up alongside. This sudden change of circumstance strands Joanne and Alison on the wrong side of the throng, and by the time the proper lines have formed, two abreast, the pair of them end up having to go around the outside and join at the very end.

Martin doesn't quite understand why, but he finds this enormously satisfying. Then he sees that boy Robert smiling sourly to himself about it and doesn't feel so good anymore.

*   *   *

Mrs Murphy is at the blackboard, drawing letters in white chalk. Each time she draws one, they all have to copy it over and over in their jotters while she walks up and down the rows to see how everyone is getting on. She has to tread carefully around a couple of areas where the floor is still a bit damp. The janitor's mop and bucket sit by the door. Colin can smell something sharp and nasty, but it's better than the smell of wee and definitely better than the smell of spilt milk, which nearly made him sick once when a carton burst in the car and Dad said he'd cleaned it all up but hadn't, not properly.

She started off getting them to do simple circles and lines, all the same size, which Colin thought was just a boring drawing exercise, but once they moved on to the letters he understood, because they were all made of circles and lines.

They have done 'a', 'b' and 'c' and are now doing 'd'. Mrs Murphy says, 'No, dear, like this,' to the girl in the next row, and draws something for her. Colin looks across to get a glance at what the girl's mistake was, but can't see because her arm is in the way. Instead he notices through the window that some cars have pulled up outside the gates. One of them is a blue Cortina. He stands up excitedly and shouts 'Mummy!' At this, lots of the others look out of the window, too. There are now a few adults standing at the gates, which causes lots more children to get up from their desks.

Mrs Murphy tells them it will be time to go soon, but for now they have to stay in their seats until the bell goes. She says this last bit in a stern voice and everybody does what they are told, though some of them start crying.

'And before we can go, we have to tidy up,' she adds. 'Colin, as you were keen to be on your feet, you can go round and collect the jotters. On you go.'

Colin likes being given the task, particularly as it involves going right round all the desks, but is less pleased that it also sounds a bit like a telling off. Lots of children stood up, but he is the one they are all now looking at because of it, and that makes him feel uncomfortable.

He soon forgets this, however, once he begins pacing the aisles and picking up the jotters. It's like being a postman doing his rounds, trading brief greetings with everybody as he goes, except he is taking things, not delivering them, which makes it also like being Mummy at the supermarket. This reminds him of the pennies he has in his pocket. He and Mummy dropped in at Gran McQueen's house on the way to school, and Gran gave him pennies 'for the tuck shop'. Mummy said she didn't think there was a tuck shop and they should go in his piggy bank instead, but she let him keep them in his pocket anyway. Gran's always giving him pennies. It will be his birthday soon, and she's promised to get him a Dinky UFO Interceptor, like on the telly. Colin loves programmes about space. He's going to be a spaceman when he grows up.

He decides it would be fun to pay for the jotters with Gran's pennies, and places a small brown coin on the desk next to the pile of workbooks as the girl sitting there adds hers to the top. 'There's your change,' he says, which he has heard shopkeepers say to Mummy.

'Thank you,' the girl replies with a smile.

He repeats the exchange three times, saying the same phrase on each occasion. The second recipient, a girl called Alison, gets a small silver coin. The third, a boy called Martin, gets a big brown one. The game ends with the last coin, a big shiny silver one with jagged edges, which goes to James Doon.

Colin wishes there were more coins so that he can keep doing it. He thinks about asking for them back so that he can give them to the people in the next row, but he catches a glimpse of his mummy out by the gates and knows he must hurry up and finish. Most of the children have been too focused on the gathering outside to notice him doling out coins, so they don't look disappointed when they don't receive one. He says thanks to each of them as they hand over their jotters, and gets a smile back from all except one boy, who gives him a nasty look and says: 'Fuckin sook.'

*　　　*　　　*

Martin is sitting at Gran's kitchen table, where she has laid on a surprise party to celebrate his first day at school. There are sandwiches with egg, which he likes, and some with tongue, which Gran loves but Martin hates. Well, in truth he has never tasted it, but he knows it will be horrible just by looking at it. There are cakes bought from the baker's, and Gran's home-made clootie dumpling—Martin's favourite—as a special treat. Gran, Granda and Mummy are there, of course, but so is Great Auntie Peggy, Auntie Lynn, Auntie Joan, Uncle Peter and Auntie Mhairi, who is not a real auntie but Gran's friend.

Gran announces that they are going to have 'a toast', which Martin knows is about clinking glasses together like at Granda's birthday, and not an actual piece of toast. 'To Martin, the big schoolboy,' Gran says, and they all do the clinking thing, which Martin loves. 'And did you enjoy your first day at St Elizabeth's?' Gran asks.

'Yes,' he replies. 'It was fuckin brilliant.'

The Rattler

She turns over in bed and he holds his breath, hoping she's just going to roll over in her sleep. She doesn't.

Shit.

'What you doing?' she asks.

'Sorry. Didn't mean to wake you. It's okay. Just go back to sleep.'

But she doesn't. Instead, she sits up and pulls the sheet over her breasts. It's like wrapping an awkward parcel, as there's no give in the things. They're not massive, but they still seem an encumbrance, maybe because she isn't long used to having them sit there like that. He doesn't get it. Why would she do that to herself? Yeah, okay, he knows: she never made the cover of *FHM* when she was 32B. But he doesn't get that either.

'Are you leaving?' she asks.

'I couldn't sleep. I was just checking messages.'

'Yeah, right,' she says, turning on the bedside lamp.

Bollocks. This means there's going to be an argument. He's seen the script plenty of times before, with plenty of others. She has too, let's not kid ourselves.

'Suppose I should be flattered you actually turned your mobile off long enough to shag me.'

There's a self-deprecatory gag just waiting to be used, something disparaging his sexual longevity, a way to make light of it, turn accusation into flirting, flirting into foreplay. But he can't be bothered. Nothing personal, hen. He's just tired. Not tired tonight, but tired of a whole lot else. Tired of the politeness ritual that attends what's going on here, for one thing, whereby she gets to pretend that she thought this might be more than a one-night stand, and he either takes the blame or finds a way for them to part as friends in the morning.

'Look, I was checking messages, okay? It's the middle of the night and I'm not at home. I'm contractually obliged to be contactable at all times. It's why they pay me the big bucks.'

'Yeah, I've heard sharks never sleep. Doubly true of the ones in Armani.'

'And if I wasn't a shark in Armani, what's the chances a girl like you would have given me a second look?'

'I hope that's not you saying I'm shallow. Cause I'm sure you were only paying me attention because I'm such an intellectual and you were interested in my opinions on, I don't know, the Turner Prize or whatever.'

'Yeah, okay, *touché*. So we've established that neither of us was in the market for a life partner at the launch party last night. I think that means you can knock off acting surprised and offended at the idea of me leaving. Especially as I *wasn't* fucking leaving.'

'Not yet, you weren't, not physically. But your mind's been back at work since two seconds after you came, and I'm already last night to you.'

He looks at her, the bedsheet clinging to her designer tits, two-grand hairdo up top, five-grand dress draped over a nearby chair. Her *People's Choice* soap starlet award is on a shelf downstairs, beside her treadmill and rowing machine and weights. He's ten or thirteen years older than her, depending on conflicting claims about her age. She's about fourteen inches around the waist and lives almost entirely on apples, despite her chocolate-bar commercials and stories of 'pigging out' in the glossies.

'And what was I to you, Kara? Consolation prize

46

because you didn't get back with that boy-band prick? Not going to get much copy out of me, are you?'

'No, I'll tell you what you were. You were a default. A certainty. I heard people say you'll fuck anyone who's got the merest hint of fame or glamour about her. I guessed they were right, but I just thought there might be more to you than that.'

'Do I take that as some kind of compliment, or are we back to pretending you were looking for love?'

'You're acting like we just met. We've known each other for three years, Martin. Jesus. And I always liked you because I thought you were one of the good guys. When did you turn into such a prick?'

'What the fuck's this? You've had my body and now you want to save my soul?'

'No, I think it's well past saving now,' she says, turning over and tugging at her pillow. She lies flat again and turns off the lamp.

He walks out of the bedroom in just his shorts and heads down the open-plan staircase into the living area. The light atop Canary Wharf blinks at him from across the Thames through the floor-to-ceiling windows. Kara said it's one-way glass, but he wouldn't be surprised if some wee fanny across at the *Mirror* had pointed a telescopic lens at the building the odd time just in case. There's certainly something kind of unnerving about shagging in front of all that glass. Surprised it didn't inhibit Kara. She was right: he has known her for three years, and she's not the vampish exhibitionist the *FHM* accompanying copy made out. Nobody is, right enough.

47

He takes a seat on her sofa, turns on a lamp and flips open his phone. He wasn't lying: he *was* just planning to check his messages. But, that said, Kara was spot-on when she said his mind had been back at work since he came. It was worse than that, in fact: he'd been thinking about what shit he was going to spin to the BlueDay Productions people tomorrow in order to delay ejaculation.

He looks at the texts first. Nothing very interesting and absolutely nothing that won't wait until morning. He checks voicemail. David Ptrajic telling him BlueDay have read the straws in the wind and cancelled the meeting. A blank call follows, a hang-up or lost connection. Then the familiar but unexpected voice of Antonia Heston-Michaels, his old boss back when he worked at the Beeb. He needs to play it back to be sure of what she said, then again to write down the number she left. He has to go searching for a pen, finds one next to Kara's phone. The notepad is missing, though, possibly up by her bed, so he has to fish a copy of the *Evening Standard* out of the bin from a host of apple cores. He scribbles the number across the top of the front page. It's the first time he's ever seen anything worth reading in the loathsome shite-rag.

He looks at his watch. It's after two, but the message said to call urgently, no matter when. It rings five or six times. He's about to hang up and assume nobody's home, but he remembers that there are other, more civilised places where people are sleeping at this time of night, and it might take a while to get a response.

'Hello?' says a croaky, yawning voice.

'Scot?'

48

'Aye. Who is . . . Martin? Is that you?'

'Yeah. Sorry about the hour, but . . .'

'Naw, naw, honestly. Thanks for gettin back tae us. And thanks tae that Antonia lassie as well. It was the only number I had for you. It's been that long since we spoke.'

'Yeah, it's been a while. So what's up? Antonia said it was an emergency. Is everything all right? You and the kids? Helen?'

'We're fine, aye. It's Coco. Colin Temple.'

'What about him?'

'He's deid, Martin. He's been murdered.'

'Murdered? Shit.'

There's a pause. Martin doesn't really know what to say, or more pertinently what he *ought* to say. He hasn't seen Colin in twenty years, so while he's sorry the guy's dead, he doesn't get why they should be talking about it in the middle of the fucking night.

'When's the funeral?' he asks, already thinking of the reason he'll give not to go, regardless of Scot's answer.

'Dunno, mate. That's kinna problematic, due to the circumstances. That's why I called, in fact. It's Noodsy an Turbo they've got for it. Turbo's dad was murdered as well, an Turbo's critical in hospital. So fairer tae say right noo, it's just Noodsy facin the music. I was his phone call. Well, he called me, but he wanted you and he knew my number. He needs a lawyer.'

'Noodsy needs . . . ? I'm not a criminal lawyer, Scot. Haven't been for more than a decade. I work in the me—'

'I know, I told him, but—'

'And for Christ's sake, Noodsy must know more

49

lawyers than *I* do, the amount of times he's been arrested. Why the hell would he ask for me?'

'He says he needs somebody who'll trust him.'

'Trust Noodsy? What the hell makes him think I'd do that?'

'I don't know, but if I was tae hazard a guess, it would be because *he* trusts *you*.'

'Well, that's hardly the same thing, Scot. I'm sorry, mate, but I cannae help. Seriously, it's desperate, and I wouldnae even be any use.'

'He's up for murder, Martin, and he sounded like he's scared shitless.'

'I'm sure he is, but I don't see what difference anybody thinks I'm gaunny make tae the situation.'

'Look, fine, he asked me to ask ye, and I've asked ye. I guess it's fair to say the answer is naw.'

'Aye, well I'm kinda fuckin busy, what wi havin my own job to get on with, so forgive me for no droppin everythin and ridin to the rescue of some bastart I havenae spoken to in twenty years.'

'Naw, don't worry aboot it, Martin. I'll let him know. He'll be touched. Didnae sound like he was haudin oot much hope anyway, though I'll confess *I* was. But that's cause it was Marty Jackson I was lookin for, and no this prick he's turned intae.'

There are a few moments of silence. Martin thinks for a while that Scot might even have hung up.

'Naw, look, sorry, Martin, that's no fair,' he eventually says. 'It was all a long time ago. Forget aboot it. Sorry I bothered you.'

'No, I'm sorry, Scot. Tell the truth, you caught me at a bad moment. I'll call you another time. We'll need to get together, maybe if you're down in the Smoke. It's good to be back in touch.'

'Aye, sure,' Scot says, though it sounds like 'drop dead'. He hangs up, leaving Martin sitting on the edge of Kara's sofa, his bare feet agitatedly kicking the bin.

'Shit,' he says aloud. He looks at the phone in his hand and is already wishing he could rewind and have another go at that call. He shakes his head. That's twice in the past half-hour somebody's called him a prick, and what really stings is that he knows they're right. Even worse, he can't answer Kara's question about precisely *when* that was what he became. He used to be one of the good guys, she told him, but it's something Scot said that's really resonating: '*he* trusts *you*'. When was the last time anybody had honestly said that? A date prior to the one Kara's query sought, that was for sure.

There's a smell of fusty, old-but-not-quite-rotten apples from the bin. It's been filling his nose for a few minutes, since the start of the phone-call, in fact. It's an olfactory ambush, and he knows it's kidnapping him and putting him on the first plane north.

Christ, Kara, why could it not be alfalfa sprouts or fucking wheatgrass or whatever else the professionally malnourished lived on these days? Why did it have to be apples?

Primary Three
41 Arae 2

The Abandoned

Karen gets out of her mum's car just outside the gates to the Infant Building, like she has done most days for the past two and a half years. Sometimes her mum plays a game where she waits until Karen opens the door and then moves the car forward a tiny wee bit to give her a fright. She doesn't do it this morning, though, because she is in too much of a hurry.

'I'm in a right guddle,' she kept saying as they were getting ready to go out, and they were about ten minutes later than usual leaving the house. Karen is a little nervous that she might get a row from Miss Clarke about being late. Miss Clarke is a lot stricter than Mrs Murphy, who was her teacher in Primary One and Two. She is thinner and prettier, but not as nice.

Karen normally stands and waves at her mum's departing car until it disappears out of sight over the bump in the road that goes to Glasgow, but this morning she can't afford the time. She gives the briefest wave as the car pulls away and then starts running towards the entrance, where the lines go in. After the summer holidays, when she's a Primary Four, she will move to the Main Building, which has an upstairs, though it's only the Primary Fives whose classrooms are up there.

Normally there would be dozens of children in the yard, playing games before the bell goes or maybe joining the lines early to be near the front. Karen can tell the time herself now, but she doesn't need to look at her watch to know she is late, because there is hardly anyone outside. The only times she has seen it like this have been on previous incidences of sleeping in or after being to the dentist. Both of these thoughts contribute to a sicky feeling in her tummy as she jogs across the concrete, head down, one hand grasping the straps of her bag around her shoulder.

She catches sight of someone coming around the corner from the back of the building and looks up to see who else is trailing in late. She hopes it is one of the goody-goodies, like Michelle or Helen or Martin, because then she won't get so much of a row. Miss Clarke didn't shout at Kevin Duffy that time Helen was late as well, and Kevin Duffy was always getting shouted at for being late. But it is none of these. It is Joanne. She is not one of the goody-goodies. Joanne is not a bad girl either, not like Eleanor who pulls hair and says swearie-words, but Karen isn't really friends with her because she always tells lies and she's one of the ones who still talk about Karen peeing herself in Primary One. Joanne is quite fat. Not as fat as Geraldine Butler, but still fatter than anyone else apart from Geraldine, so it's just as well for Joanne that Geraldine's in the class. Karen knows you're not supposed to make fun and has never called Joanne any names, but she doesn't always feel sorry for her when others do it.

'The school's shut,' Joanne tells her, her chubby cheeks glowing red with satisfaction at being the bearer of news. 'There was a fire an it's aw burnt doon.'

Joanne is always making things up. Last week she said the whole of Primary Three were going to get the belt until someone owned up to who broke

56

the wee statue of Our Lady that used to sit opposite the boys' toilets. Zoe said Joanne was talking shh-ugar and Karen's inclination was to agree, but she'd still felt very nervous in case it turned out to be true, especially when the headmaster, Mr Monahan, came into their class. Also, whenever they had the nit-nurse, the girls got to go first, and Joanne always went back to class rubbing her arm and telling the boys it was a jag.

This morning's story, however, seems a lot more ambitious—and more immediately verifiable—than Joanne's usual fibs, so Karen holds back on her instinctive scornful response. She looks up the steps and notices for the first time that the wooden outside-doors are closed, then at the classroom windows, which show no lights on inside.

'Come an see,' Joanne says, almost breathless with excitement.

Karen follows her around the side of the building, past the entrance steps and the fire exit. More children become visible as she approaches. They are all standing around the back, none of them playing. There are no teachers.

When Karen turns the second corner, the corner where James Doon split his knee open that time in Primary Two and there was a big chunk of bone sticking out, or so said Robert Turner, she sees for herself that Joanne wasn't lying. The back of the building is simply not there, and neither is half the roof. There are just walls on three sides around a sloping pile of black stuff and wet rubbish. Most of it looks like books and jotters, and the only thing that has any recognisable shape is the big long desk from the Infant Mistress Mrs Lanegan's office. Karen has been in there just twice: once before school when she got taken to be enrolled, which had disappointingly not turned out to involve any gymnastics; and once to bring Mrs Lanegan a note from Mrs Murphy. When Mrs Murphy had called her out to ask her to take the note, Joanne whispered to her that it meant she would be getting the belt when she got there. This had turned out to be another fib, though the pleasure borne of this relief lasted only until her return to class, whereupon Robert Turner said she was a f-u-c-k-e-n sook for getting asked to go a message.

The desk now reminds her of a picture in a storybook showing a packing trunk bobbing just above the waves following a shipwreck.

'See? I tellt ye,' Joanne says, nodding in sheer triumph, her cheeks now glowing red enough to set the embers blazing again.

Karen hears a sobbing and notices that there are quite a few wee Primary Ones in the gathering, some of whom are looking very worried. The absence of adults from this particular area is normally as standard as it is welcome, but right at this moment it seems a bit strange.

'Who's going to look after us?' one of the wee ones asks tearfully. Karen is a Primary Three now and too big to be crying, but the little girl's question still strikes a chord. She and her friends often ask, 'Wouldn't it be magic if you came in one day and there was no teachers?' but now that it appears to have happened, it doesn't feel magic at all. It feels quite scary, in fact, and she begins to wonder why, especially at a time like this with the building burnt down, there would be no adults around even to tell them to stay back and not touch anything.

Able at last, though briefly, to wrench her gaze from the darkly fascinating sight of this so familiar building ripped open like a doll's house, Karen casts an eye right around the assembly and takes proper note of who is here. Her attention is caught by the attendance of several older children who should presumably right now be in class over in the unaffected Main Building. She sees a group of Primary Fours, two girls whom she knows to be Primary Fives—Helen Dunn's big sister Nicola and her friend Pauline—and three boys whom she assumes to be older still. Helen is there too, sticking close to her sister. Karen wishes she had someone bigger to stand next to as well. Also in attendance is Scot Connolly from her own class, about whom she now notices two significantly unusual details: one, that he has a bike with him; and two, that he isn't wearing school uniform. A few of the children do ride bikes to school, which they normally secure round the back at the big bins, but Scot has never been one of them, as she knows he lives right across the road on Burnside Avenue.

'Somebody'll be along soon,' Helen's big sister assures the frightened Primary One who asked the question. The girl doesn't look convinced, and neither at this stage is Karen.

'Why are there no teachers here?' she decides to ask.

'They're aw deid,' says one of the bigger boys. 'They were aw here last night havin a staff meeting when it happened.'

'Aw, naaaaw,' bawls one of the Primary Ones, before bursting out greeting.

'Shut it you, ya fanny,' another of the bigger

59

boys warns the first. 'You're upsettin the wee yins. Don't listen tae him, hen,' he adds, talking to the girl.

'Naw, I'm talkin shite,' the first boy admits. 'It was just auld Monahan that died.'

'I says fuckin shut it, you,' repeats the second, though they are both laughing about it.

'It was on the radio,' says Scot. 'During the news. They said St Elizabeth's in Braeside was closed cause of a fire and naebody was to come in the day. That's how the teachers arenae here. The Primary Fours an Fives an Sixes an Sevens have to go in the morra, but the Wans, Twos an Threes have tae stay aff the morra *and* Friday.'

'We never had the radio on,' Karen says.

'Neither did we,' adds Joanne.

'They never said anything about it on our radio,' protests Pauline.

'It was on Clyde,' insists Scot, sounding like he thinks she's calling him a liar. 'I heard it twice.'

'We were listening to Radio One,' Pauline explains. 'They never mentioned it on there.'

'That's cause it's English,' suggests one of the big boys.

'My dad always has Radio Four on,' says Nicola.

Karen didn't know there was a Radio Four—just One and Two, like the telly. She doesn't know what might be on it, but she is fairly certain if Robert Turner was here, he would be calling Nicola a f-u-c-k-e-n snob.

'Does anybody know what actually happened?' Pauline asks.

'Aye,' says one of the big boys. 'Fatty Henderson ate a whole Gregg's family-size cream cake tae herself an then fuckin exploded.'

The boys all laugh, Pauline and Nicola too, and so does Karen, even though she tries not to. Mrs Henderson teaches the Primary Fours, and is the only person in the school fatter than Geraldine. Karen looks around and happens to catch Joanne's eye, which immediately causes her giggling to stop. Joanne isn't laughing, but is nodding to herself as she files away who was.

'Did you see anything, Scot?' asks Pauline once the joke has died down.

'Naw. Ma maw an da did, but. They says there was fire engines an everythin, but I slept through it. I could sleep through an earthquake, ma maw says. I thought they were kiddin me on until it came on the radio. That's how I came ower tae see.'

'You'd think there'd be a teacher here, but,' Karen suggests. 'I'm locked oot for the day until my mum gets home. And what about these wee yins?'

'If yous need tae phone somedy, I think ma maw would let you use oor phone,' Scot offers.

This sounds like a good idea, and Karen is grateful to Scot, whom she quite likes. He is usually smiley and is never one of the ones who bring up her peeing herself that time. Then she remembers that her mum will be at work, not home, and she doesn't know the number there, so she is still going to be stranded.

'Heh, there's Harris comin,' says one of the big boys.

Karen looks towards the Main Building and sees Mrs Harris, the deputy headmistress, walking quickly towards their gathering. Karen feels the same as when she hears her mum's voice in the

61

downstairs hall on nights when she's been left with a babysitter.

'What are you all doing here?' Mrs Harris calls out as she approaches. 'Is Mr Monahan not here?'

'No, miss,' several of them reply.

'Miss, we never heard the radio,' someone explains.

'Well, let's get you all sorted out. Come up to the Main Building and I'll make some phone calls.'

There are far fewer of them left by the time they reach Mrs Harris's office. Those who knew their mums would be home simply left as soon as they, like Scot, had satisfied their curiosity with a long enough look at the wreckage.

Mrs Harris makes phone calls to parents of those in Primary Four and above, and various arrangements are made. However, it turns out the contact details for the children in the Infant Building were all in Mrs Lanegan's office. Joanne knows her mum's work number off by heart, and as a result she is soon told her granny is on the way to collect her. This just leaves Karen and three of the wee ones. Mrs Harris says she is sorry, but they'll all just have to stay in the Main Building with her until hometime. Karen doesn't like the sound of this, as she finds Mrs Harris quite scary (though not as scary as Mr Monahan) and she knows it will be a beamer if anyone finds out she ended up playing with Primary Ones and Twos all day.

But then Helen says something quietly to her big sister, and Nicola tells Mrs Harris that Karen can come home with them once their mum arrives. Mrs Harris says she'll have to ask their mum first, but Nicola assures her and Karen that her mum will say it's okay.

Karen likes Helen and is immediately excited by the notion of getting to play with her instead of going to school. She is also very curious to see where Helen lives, as she has heard Robert Turner say Helen is a f-u-c-k-e-n snob because 'she lives in a boat hoose'. Karen has only ever been on a rowing boat at Barshaw Park, and thinks it will be magic fun to explore one big enough for a family to live on.

She decides it's going to be a good day after all.

The Accused

Martin is relieved to see Scot and Colin standing near the gates when the morning bell goes, and he hurries along the pavement to join up with them. The Primary Threes are still allowed to use their own playground while the Infant Building is being demolished, but the letter his mum got said they would be taught in the Main Buiding and would have to line up at the same doors as the Fours and Fives. The Primary Ones and Twos were getting their classes in the Church Hall down the road, which only had a wee patch of muddy grass for a playground, so it could have been worse.

They all walk quite slowly through the Main Building's playground. Nobody says anything, but Martin is sure they are thinking the same as him: that the longer they take, the greater the chance there will already be a teacher at the doors by the time they get there, and thus less chance of getting a doing from the big ones. When they come in sight of the main entrance, there is no teacher to be seen, but there is the reassuring sight of Carol and Michelle at the front of a rapidly forming line, having successfully pipped their eternal rivals Joanne and Alison for pole position.

'Where are they puttin us?' is the issue being discussed back and forth along the queue.

'We're gettin split up,' announces Joanne. 'The brainy wans are goin in wi the Primary Fours an the rest are gettin took tae the Church Hall.'

This gives Martin a moment's discomfort as he considers how little he fancies the idea of being thrown in—physically or academically—with the bigger ones currently lining up alongside. Then he remembers that it's Joanne who is saying it.

'Are we chook,' says Colin, voicing Martin's thoughts for him.

Chook is the latest word to come into regular usage, exclusively to express disbelief. Is it chook, did ye chook, will I chook. He doesn't know what the word itself means or its derivation; and nor, he is sure, does anyone else. Martin has no problem comprehending the playground's neologisms, but is frustrated by how they can be unheard of one week and then common coinage to all but him the next. He suspects it must be because lots of the other boys play together away from school. Most of them live in the Braeview scheme, in the council houses where Martin's grandparents stay. Martin lives in the new houses up the hill towards the Carnock Brae.

'We're gettin put in the gym hall,' suggests Geraldine to Zoe.

'Mair like the dinner hall if she'd anythin tae dae wi it,' says Scot quietly.

They all laugh, but turn away so that Geraldine

64

doesn't know it's about her. Martin casts an eye forward along the line to reassure himself that she didn't hear. He knows it's a bit cruel, but Scot has a knack of saying things that seem all the funnier because you think maybe you shouldn't laugh. It's not like pointing and laughing at the spazzy bus, which Martin has seen the bigger boys do, and which he knew without an adult telling him was just plain bad, but maybe what his granny means when she says 'near the bone'.

Martin is surprised—and a bit miffed—that there is little discussion of the fire, and in particular its cause. He was hoping that perhaps the Braeview lot would have some stories or rumours, but it does not make the agenda, and he fears that this is because the subject has already been exhausted among them out of school. Nonetheless, he considers it well worth asking: 'Anybody heard anythin aboot how the fire started?'

Martin thinks Scot is about to say something, but he doesn't. He glances across to the Primary Four and Five lines, same as Martin did when he was anxious about Geraldine.

'My da says it was an electrical fault,' says Colin. 'He says the wiring was pure ancient.'

Colin's dad is an electricalician, which means he would know about these things. Martin is a little disappointed. He would have preferred it if there had been baddies involved. It would be more interesting that way, especially when they got caught and punished. They'd be getting the belt, no question, and from Mr Monahan too, not just one of the lady teachers. He had a few candidates in mind. Richard Ryan, for a start. He was rough

65

and always getting in trouble. He was known to hang about with bigger boys outside school, even some Primary Sixes. And then there was Robbie, Robert Turner; however, much as he'd have liked it to be so, Martin just couldn't see it. Robbie was nasty, but in a sneaky way. He wasn't brave enough to do something like that, though he did have those big brothers who were *really* scary, and they'd definitely be brave enough.

*   *   *

Check Clarke trying to get the telly out the way by herself. Magic, Scot reckons. First-rate entertainment. She had Janny Johnny in here ten minutes ago asking if she needed a hand and she told him to beat it because it's pure obvious she doesn't like him. You can tell by the way she speaks to him that she just wants rid the second he puts his heid round the door. It's the same every morning when he brings the milk. Can't get him out the room fast enough. Now she's wrestling alone with this hooded beast, like a giant bat perched on a builder's scaffolding. It's some size for a goggle-box, right enough. Biggest one Scot's ever seen, and making it even more awkward are these corrugated wing affairs it's got either side of a canopy stretched across the top. He's never known what that was all about. How come it didn't just have a screen and be done with it like any normal telly? But he does know the teacher is having a devil of a time getting them folded away, and that's before she attempts moving the thing.

They're in the utility room, which is kind of a spare classroom the teachers don't know what to do with the rest of the time, but which has now had a purpose forged for it in the flames of last Wednesday. Mrs Donnelly's class are in the library, which would have given Scot a view of his own front window had his class ended up there, but no luck. The utility room it is. Scot remembers being in it only three times before: once for a TV programme and twice for films. That's why it's the only room in the building with curtains: bowfing big green things. The programme was keech, one of those For Schools and Colleges efforts that are not bad if you're off sick but hardly up there with *The Six Million Dollar Man*. Something about a family from donkeys ago, back in nineteen-canteen or seventeen-oatcake. Mince. But nothing compared to the films. The films were total shite. One about Russian trawler fishing and the other about buffaloes in America, and both times it was meant to be a Christmas treat. A Christmas treat! Fucking trawler documentaries!

Scot had heard that at Braeside Primary they had *Bedknobs and Broomsticks* one year and *Peter Pan* another. He'd mentioned this in class once, when Father Wolfe was in doing one of his visits, because Father Wolfe had told them if they were naughty they'd get expelled and sent to Braeside Primary with all the other bad boys and girls. Scot had asked why, if it was full of bad children, they got better films at Christmas. Father Wolfe said it was because the education high heid yins gave all the best stuff to the Proddy schools and left the Catholics with the dross. Scot thought this was about as likely as Braeside Primary being full of nothing but bad weans, considering half his pals went there and weren't anywhere near as mental as some of the numpties at St Elizabeth's, and mentioned it to his da. Da offered the alternative explanation that Braeside's heidie had simply been sharper off the mark than theirs when it came to ordering the flicks, and one sight of Mad Momo Monahan would convince anybody of this theory's greater plausibility.

Then, speak of the devil, but who gives the door a wee knock and walks in? Mad Momo.

Everybody goes quiet right away. It always happens when the heidie appears. Happens as well when Lanegan or Harris pops by, but with them it's as much because the teacher's told everybody they have to be on their best behaviour. When it's Momo, nobody needs told. Everybody shites it from Momo, even the big yins, and it's not because he's the heidie. It's because he's fucking mental.

He looks, behaves and sounds like no other human being Scot has ever seen. His legs are too short for his body; that's the first thing you notice, because it affects how he walks. Or maybe it's more like his body, his big thick neck and his massive heid are too big for his legs. That's how he got the name Momo: there was a cartoon on one night, called *The Grape Ape*, with a giant gorilla in it named Momo. Nobody could claim credit for coming up with the slagging, because first thing next morning, everybody was using it. *Everybody*. The minute they saw this ape cutting about on the goggly, it rang the same bell in all their minds. Momo.

He lumbers about with his arms dangling down, and at the end of both are these clumsy great hands, like two bunches of bananas. Any time he decides to pay a visit, everybody tenses up and starts bracing themselves, because they know half the class are going to end up black and blue, with the ones he's keen on suffering as much as the villains. And here's why. Check this.

He comes through the door awkwardly, nearly sidey-ways, like the frame's not quite big enough. By this point Clarke's abandoned the telly and stood to attention, her back all straight like thon red-faced punter on *It Ain't Half Hot Mum*. She likes Momo about as much as she likes Janny Johnny, but she can't tell Momo to fuck off. She knows she's got no choice now but to stand out the way and wait patiently until he lets her have her class back.

First off he does his rounds. Up and down the rows, always picking out the same poor bastards for special attention: those unlucky enough to have big brothers or sisters, because otherwise you won't have come to his notice and he doesn't have a clue who you are.

'Aaaah, Michael. Michael Garvie, how are you doing?'

Michael is at this point trying to burrow into his desk, that's how he's doing.

'Are you working hard?'

Aye. Working hard to understand anything that comes out of Momo's slabbering gub. He talks really weird, not like anybody from Braeside or Paisley, or even Glasgow. It's a totally different accent, but not like the priests talk, because they're all Irish, apart from Father Neeson, who's from the moon. Scot's ma said Momo was from 'the islands', but she never said which islands they were. Scot reckons wherever they are, these islands must be quite far apart and only have one inhabitant each, because Momo always talks like he's shouting long-distance into a high wind.

'Yes, sir,' Mick squeaks, keeping his heid doon, but no luck: Momo sends in the banana-grapple. Mick's mouth now looks like the end of a tied-aff balloon with his lips all squinty from Momo's huge hand squashing his cheeks.

'Good boy, Michael. Good boy. Your brother Thomas is a good boy. He works hard. You work hard.'

Then he's on to Alison Taylor in the next row. Mick got off light, as it looks like his jaws are still just about connected.

'Aaah, Alison. Alison Taylor. Taylor mend my coat.' He thinks this is funny. Nobody's laughing, and not just because they've heard the same 'joke' every time he lumbers into their class. Nobody laughed the first time, because then, as now, there is a tension in the air like the whole class is holding its breath and won't let it out until the mad old monkey-walking bastard leaves.

'And are you working hard, Alison?'

'Yes, sir.'

'Good girl. And tell me, is your brother David still living?'

Seriously, that's what he says, every time. Is your brother still living? He went up the hill to St Grace's Secondary, not on a solo canoeing expedition down the fucking Amazon.

Stephen Rennie gets the same question about his big sister Charlotte, as will Zoe about her big brother Daniel. Anybody who's left the school needs their survival verified before Momo can ask after them, which always leads Scot to imagine these islands must be right fucking dangerous places.

They all get the squashed face. That's what he does if Momo likes you. And now Richie Ryan is about to undergo the standard ritual for when he doesn't. Everybody's sitting in the same rows as back in their old classroom, but the door is on the opposite side, so Momo's getting to him sooner than usual. This is probably a good thing, as Richie knows it's coming and this gets it over with. It must be worse watching the other regulars get it when you know it's coming to you next.

'Ry-an,' he says, his voice getting that bit quieter, thon breathy way. 'Ry-an. Ri-chard Ry-an.'

Richie tries his best to look up at Momo but he's finding it hard to take his eyes off the five-fingered wrecking balls dangling by the ape-creature's sides.

'And have you been a good boy?' he asks. This is a more evil trick question than any shite you'll hear out in the playground. Both possible responses produce the same result; it's just a matter of which wrong answer Richie will choose today.

'Yes, sir,' he says.

At which point Momo skelps him on the top of the head and shouts, *'Liar!'* You can hear the rap of Momo's giant knuckles on Richie's heid. It's not loud, and makes quite a high-pitched sound, but the fact that you can hear it at all makes everybody wince. 'Bad egg,' he says, or shouts is more like it. 'Bawd igg,' is what it actually sounds like. It took a few hearings before Scot clocked it properly, never having encountered the phrase before, but unfortunately Momo has provided ample opportunities for him to suss it. 'Bawd igg. Your sister is a bawd igg. You're a bawd igg.' And all the time he's either dishing out more knuckly grief or,

71

worse, grinding them against Richie's heid. Folk do it out in the playground, getting their fist tore into somebody's scalp. They call it a Jaggy Bunnet. It can be quite sore if it's somebody with strong arms, and nobody can do it like Momo.

Richie's face screws up but he doesn't greet. Richie never greets. He's the best fighter in Primary Three, and that's a fact. Okay, truth is nobody in Primary Three's ever fought him, but that tells its own story, and besides, he battered Greg Yuill at the swingpark, and he's in Primary Four at Braeside.

Eleanor Fenwick is up next. Her oldest brother is up at St Grace's, but Momo doesn't ask if he's still living. He only asks after the good ones. She gets the bawd igg bit but not the knuckles. He doesn't do that to the girls quite as much, though Scot has seen it once or twice, so it's probably not restraint that's keeping his paws off; more likely reluctance to get too close to Eleanor's minging mane. It's not nice to say it, but there's no getting away from the fact: the lassie smells, same as her big brothers. Scot wouldn't slag her to her face like some of the others, but he doesn't feel a lot of sympathy for her, either. Eleanor is a horrible lassie who reminds Scot more of a rodent than any human being really ought to. That said, there's not much she's ever done that Momo's liable to be aware of: she's getting the bawd-igg bit in respect of the crimes of Fenwicks past.

The weird thing here, though, is that Robbie gets spared. *Robbie*. Would you credit that? Robbie's got two big brothers, both heid-the-baws, which would normally be reason enough for Momo's knuckles to be powering through Robbie's noggin like a North Sea drill. But Robbie also has a big sister, Siobhan, who, according to Scot's big sister Heather, Momo rates as: 'a lovely girl, Siobhan. A lovely girl. Not like those brothers of yours. Bawd iggs.'

It could be that Siobhan's loveliness cancels out her brothers' bawd-iggiosity; or it could be because Robbie doesn't look much like the other Turner boys (or act much like them: being a sleekit wee nyaff compared to their blatant bampottery). Either way, he's been jammy enough to lurk in Momo's blind spot. He gets neither the cheek-squeezes nor the jaggy bunnets, which is just plain unfair, because he's the one child everybody else in the class would love to see on the receiving end.

Not every child with an older brother or sister gets Momoed, right enough. Scot's big sister Heather is in Primary Six, but she's obviously never made much of an impression on the heidie for good or ill, and for that he is enormously grateful. And, to balance it up, there are two kids *without* older siblings who regularly feature on the hitlist. Momo always pauses for a fistful of Zoe's face, throughout which he refers to her as Paula, which is her *wee* sister's name and probably who the mad old bastard thinks he's talking to. Zoe is always too terrified by the ordeal to open her mouth and put him right, but it wouldn't matter: Clarke usually does it for her, only for Momo to come in the next time and call her Paula again. And then there's wee Jamesy, whom Momo's heading for right now. Jamesy's got a wee sister, too. She's only four, goes to Braeview Nursery and has probably never set eyes on Momo, but the poor lassie is already doomed to official bawd-igg status whenever she makes the jump to St Lizzie's and the great ape hears her surname.

'Doon,' Momo says. He's looking all round the class with this stupid grin on his face. 'Dooooooon.' Everybody's supposed to laugh here at how funny Jamesy's surname is. It's nearly as funny as the 'Taylor mend my coat' line. 'Doon is where this one is going. Jaaames Doon.' It sounds like jams. 'Jaaames Doon. Bawwd igg.' Wallop. 'Baaawd, baaawd [grind, grind] igg. Vee-lan. Vee-lan. Do you play with matches, James Doon? Do? [Grind.] You? [Grind.] Play? [Grind.] With? [Grind.] Matches? [Wallop.]'

'No, sir,' James manages to squeak.

Momo looks round the class. 'Do you think James Doon, the vee-lan, started the fire?' he asks them all. Nobody commits either way, apart from fat Joanne, who's nodding like a wee dog on the back seat of a motor, looking fucking delighted.

A lot of stories are going round Braeview about the fire, most of them shite, probably. The one that's getting the most mileage is that Robbie Turner's brothers were involved, mainly on the basis of reports that Wullie Scoular got a panelling off Joe Turner and his mates for talking about it. That Wullie Scoular got a panelling from Jaggy Joe and his nutter pals is in no doubt, but Scot knows the reason is as likely to be that Wullie 'looked at them funny' as that he was spreading ill-founded rumours or giving away their secrets. The end result, however, has been to give the rumour running shoes while at the same time ensuring nobody mentions it around anyone close to the Turners.

For his part, Scot reckons Colin's dad's theory is

the likeliest explanation. Which makes it all the more ridiculous that Momo's acting like he thinks a Primary Three burnt down the Infant Building. Does he chook. It's just an excuse.

Vee-lan. Everybody else is just a bad egg, but wee Jamesy's a villain as well. Pure pish. Villain. Jamesy wouldn't hurt anybody, apart from himself, but that's accidental, if alarmingly frequent. Predictable and usually avoidable, but accidental all the same. Scot doesn't know why the hell Momo's got it into his giant skull that Jamesy's a bad yin, but as far as the big eejit's concerned, it's written in stone, which is what the wee man's heid better be made of if it's to survive four more years of jaggy bunnets.

Scot had felt a wee surge of optimism the other day when that Primary Six boy said Momo had died in the fire, but at the same time he was sure it wasn't true. That really nice deputy head, Miss Grainger, had left halfway through Primary Two, to be replaced by Harris, and the class had been forced to part company with Mrs Murphy at the end of the same year, ending up with Clarke. That was how it worked: the good teachers were only around a wee while but you got stuck with bastards like Momo forever.

Besides, as they say, shite doesn't burn.

*   *   *

James feels like he is coming up from underwater at the baths when the playtime bell rings and Miss Clarke says they can go. He was glad when Momo finally left the class, but his leaving wasn't enough to make him feel better. It wasn't so much his

75

head—Momo's jaggy bunnets were sore at the time but the pain didn't last, not like a boot in the balls or a punch in the belly. It was thon churned-up way he felt inside, and a whooshing noise in his head that made everyone else's voices seem like they were coming from a telly with the sound turned down. He always felt like his cheeks were pure glowing as well, and wished he could disappear so that nobody could see him.

It wasn't fair. James was hardly ever in trouble. There was just that one time, and that wasn't right, either. Lanegan wouldn't listen when he was trying to tell her the truth, and she must have told Momo about it, and with Momo, he only needed to know one thing about you and it didn't matter what else you did from then on. Lanegan hadn't listened, and in James's experience there were a lot of times teachers didn't listen, but Momo was the worst. It didn't matter how many times Miss Clarke told him Zoe's name wasn't Paula, and maybe that was why Miss Clarke never stuck up for James and said he wasn't a bad boy. He couldn't blame her, really. It was one thing saying he had somebody's name wrong, but if she disagreed when he was dishing out the bad-egg stuff, maybe she'd get a jaggy bunnet herself, or even the sack.

He walks quite slowly despite the need to be out of the room; he wants to let everybody else pile through the door and down the corridor so that nobody talks to him for a wee minute. Then when he's ready, he can go and join in a game or something, and that way they'll be too busy to bring up the subject of Momo's visit. He particularly wants to avoid Martin, even though they're good pals and Martin's always really kind.

It's sort of weird, but Martin being sympathetic and asking if he's all right makes the churning worse than somebody like Robbie giving him a slagging.

His strategy doesn't quite pay off. As he's emerging into the corridor, Scot appears from nowhere and walks alongside.

'You're a vee-lan, Jamesy,' Scot says, and James feels himself break into a smile, feels everything get lighter immediately. 'A vee-lan and a bawd igg.' It feels this way because they both know Scot is slagging Momo, not him. 'And is your brother dead yet?' Scot adds, and they both crack up laughing.

'How does he talk like that?' James asks. 'Where's he from?'

'Ma maw says he's fae one of the islands.'

'Aye,' James, says, remembering the comic-book classics he liked to flick through in the library. 'The Island of Doctor Moreau.'

They make their way through the Main Building and exit at the door nearest the Infants' playground, minimising their route through Primary Four-to-Seven infested territory. When they reach home turf, they find Martin, Richie, Gary, Paul and Robbie gathered round Colin, who is standing with his back to the fence, holding something.

'Scot, Jamesy, check this,' Martin says, and they move in closer.

Colin is holding a wee red plastic device in both hands. 'It's a killertine,' he tells them. 'Watch. Somebody gie's another cheese puff.'

'Fuck off,' Gary objects, 'I've gave up half the packet.'

'Aw, come on, don't be moolsy,' insists Richie.

77

'S'awright, there's wan on the ground that's big enough,' Gary points out, tightly clutching his poke of the tuck shop's rubbishy attempt at crisps.

Colin picks up a length of cheese-puff from the concrete and places it through the lower of two holes in the killertine, then sticks his index finger through the other.

'There's the blade. You see it?' he asks Scot and James. There is a thick white strip across two pillars of red plastic, poised above the two holes.

'Aye,' they confirm.

'Right. Check this.'

Colin plunges a handle down and drives the blade to the bottom of the killertine. It chops the cheese puff in half but incredibly leaves his finger unharmed.

'That's fuckin amazin,' Scot declares.

James is so impressed he can't even find the words at first. He just laughs with delight. 'Dae it again, dae it again,' he pleads.

Robbie walks away, followed by Paul, and then Gary. They must have seen it enough times already, though in Gary's case it might simply be to preserve his cheese puffs.

*   *   *

Noodsy lifts his head from his knees and looks at the walls so tightly enclosing him, the grey steel door and its narrow observation slit closing off all contact with the world. He feels sick. He hasn't eaten, hasn't felt hungry. He hasn't slept since they brought him here, and not much in the nights preceding, either. He keeps thinking he's going to throw up, so it's probably just as well there's nothing down there.

He's scared, really fucking scared. He wants out of here like he's never wanted anything before.

He's been in this nick—this cell and others just like it—so often it's practically his second home, but on this occasion it's different; on this occasion it's creeping him out. It reminds him of the first time, except that it's far worse than that. Sure, he was scared back then, too, just a boy, really, but full of bravado and a determination not to let anyone—polis or fellow inmates—see his fear. Today he's wearing it all on his sleeve; can't help it. It reminds him of the first time, aye, but that's not the feeling that's creeping him out. What's got him spooked, his guts churning and his eyes unable to close is the feeling like it's the *last* time. All those other arrests were for kiddy-on stuff compared to this. Fines, service, the odd jakey sentence. Occupational hazards. But what he's up for now, you're talking about the big picture. Twelve o'clock Mass.

Life.

They say it doesn't mean life, but the folk who say that have never stared down the barrel at it. Look at the best-case scenario, for fuck's sake: he's gets out in twelve, maybe fifteen—about fifty years old—and to what? No house, no wife, no kids, nothing. He's thirty-seven next birthday. Time, he knew, was running out to get hold of himself, and that was before . . . this.

Christ, what was he thinking? Well, he wasn't, that was the problem. That was always the problem, but he'd never screwed up as badly as this before; not even close. Life, for fuck's sake. He never thought about that when he was doing it,

79

when he was in the midst of all that madness, did he? That's what the politicians and journalists who are always banging on about tougher sentences being a deterrent all completely fucking fail to understand.

No cunt ever thinks he'll get caught.

The Cabaret

'Line up neatly and quietly at the door, boys and girls. We're going to the gym hall for an assembly.'

Aw naw.

Scot suspected this was coming, right enough. Clarke's been eyeing the clock every five minutes since they got back after lunchtime. Assembly does get you out the class and away from the jotters for a wee while, but it's not exactly playtime. In fact, along with school Mass, it's about the only thing that makes Scot wish he was back at his desk doing long division. It's hellish: St Lizzie's version of the Black Hole of Calcutta. Everybody from Primary Three upwards gets stowed into the gym hall to compete for the last few oxygen molecules as their arse-cheeks gradually go numb from sitting cross-legged on the hardwood floor. Numb, aye, but not quite numb enough, because something about that position seems to bring the farts out in folk; and not big raspers that you can at least get a laugh at. It's always the silent-but-violent variety, so nearby and thick in the air that they actually smell *warm*—and that's just what your nose has to put up with if you *don't* end up sitting close to Smeleanor.

All of which is to say nothing about the cabaret,

which usually takes one of two standard forms, or if you're really unlucky, both. The less frequent of the two is presided over by Harris, and begins with a wee lecture about whichever patron saint is blowing out their candles today up in heaven, concentrating mainly on the horrific manner in which they met their holy end. She usually works herself up into a mighty temper while delivering this, with the result that Scot reckons she's trying to imply that it was somehow their fault. This, however, is merely a preamble to her principal enthusiasm, which is to lead a marathon, unaccompanied hymn practice, by the end of which Scot is usually convinced the bloody martyr had it easy.

Today, though, it's the more familiar routine, the main event, the one you've not been waiting for: Ladies and gentlemen, put your bum-cheeks together for the *All-Old Momo Show*. Which would be a shite enough prospect if it *wasn't* coming on top of this morning's class invasion and random assault.

Scot catches Jamesy's eye as they troop along the corridor and see the headmaster up on stage in front of a half-empty but rapidly filling floor. They both know that it's the older weans who are most likely to be singled out during assembly, but it can depend on which classes get there first and therefore who ends up sitting nearest the front and in Momo's direct line of vision. When they were in their proper classroom, back in the Infant Building, they were usually safe, coming in at the coo's tail behind everyone else, but the utility room is only yards away from the gym hall. Jamesy's also probably thinking, like Scot, that Momo's assemblies, for no apparent reason, tend to be on a Friday, with LingalongaHarris taking the floor on Tuesdays. This is Monday, the first day everyone's back after the fire, so any bets that's top of the agenda. In a way this realisation is slightly comforting, because at least it dispels Scot's fear that Momo overheard his impression of him in the corridor earlier and is lining him up for a public belting, like happened to that Primary Six who swore at Mrs Ford.

The early arrival doesn't work out too badly. Mrs Cook's Primary Four class got in first and she has organised everybody to line up in files rather than rows. This means Michelle, Carol, Alison and fat Joanne end up two abreast at the front, leaving Scot and his pals a comfortable distance back. They are also a comfortable distance away from Smelly Elly, but as soon as he sits down, Scot can smell the same niff you get off her: sour milk and stale piss. He hears someone say, 'Awright, Scotty,' and looks to his immediate right, where he sees Matthew Cannon, who lives round the corner from him. Sitting just behind Matthew is Harry Fenwick, one of Eleanor's brothers, which explains the smell. It's a bit of a sin for Harry, really, because he's not a pure bastard like the other Fenwicks, or permanently angry and spiteful like Eleanor.

It's bucketing down outside by now and the windows all steam up as the place fills. The hall is surprisingly quiet for so many weans being in, which just shows you the effect Momo has without even opening his mouth. Sadly, that part is coming soon enough. And indeed, here we go.

'Hallo boys and gerrals,' he booms out.

'Hello, Mr Monahan,' comes the mass response.

82

Scot can hear a few 'Hello, Momo's mixed in, coming from some of the more daring or just mental bigger boys.

Momo strides back and forth, pacing the wooden boards before the wee stage at the front. Harris usually stands up there when she's subjecting them to the hymn-practice grief, but Momo likes to be as terrifyingly close as possible to his audience. He always walks like he's trying really hard to hold in a jobbie, and on these occasions his coupon adds to the effect, contorted by this uncomfortable strained gurning that it took Scot months to work out was actually his attempt at a smile.

'And are you all working harrrd?'

'Yes, Mr Monahan.'

'And are you all haaaa-ppee?'

'Yes, Mr Monahan.'

The 'Yes, Momo' chancers usually chuck it by this point, not wishing to push their luck.

'Do you know what makes me haaa-ppeee? Harrd worrk. Good boys and gerrals. That's what makes me haa-ppee. Do you want me to be haa-ppee, boys and girls?'

'Yes, Mr Monahan.'

'Do you want me to be saawd?' This illustrated by a face like a boxer dog after a swift boot in the cheenies, as well as a sudden slump in the shoulders and bending of both knees.

'No, Mr Monahan.'

'Do you know what makes me sawd?' Face still like elbow-skin, voice giving it kiddy-on crying.

'Yes, Mr Monahan,' chant about two-thirds, the remainder opting for the negative. It's the same routine every time, but not everybody is quite sure

83

of which response the auld bastard wants at this point or what everybody else said the last time. What they *are* all sure of, right enough, is every word of what's coming next.

'Lazy bones,' Momo says, coupon now all sour like he just picked his ear and ate it. 'Poor workers, classroom chitter-chatterers, daydreamers, window-starers, *bawd iggs*!' The catchprase gets fired out at high speed and maximum volume. You always see a few shoulders stiffen and straighten from the folk who've drifted off a bit and aren't paying attention. 'And do you know what else makes me saaawd?'

It's usually about fifty-fifty at this point, with Scot himself not sure whether they're supposed to be clued up and say, 'yes' or awaiting revelation and say, 'no'.

'Seeing Jesus on the cross, and the starving babies in Africa. So say your prayers, and give to the Black Babies. You'll all do that, won't you, boys and gerrals?'

'Yes, Mr Monahan.'

Aye, but we're not quite finished the wish-list yet, are we, sir? On you go, Momo. The grannies and toddlers.

'And remember, be nice to wee toddlers,' Momo implores, offering a 'kindly' expression that looks kindly enough to have any toddler bawling its eyes out. 'And when you see old ladies, help them to cross the road.'

Nae kidding. This is the script. Every time. Every. Fucking. Time. Word for word. Scot's still sure the assembly's been called because of the fire, but whatever else is on the agenda, it was always going to have to wait until this part is by with. It's like one of those dolls with a string you pull. Really, does the guy never think, Hang on, I'm actually boring *myself* here? Jeezo.

And the thing that gets Scot every time he watches Momo in action is that he's the heidie, the headmaster. You have to be clever to be a teacher, so you'd think you'd have to be extra clever to be the teacher in charge. And yet Momo comes across as one of the most stupid adults Scot has ever encountered, with maybe just Father Neeson edging him out for the all-comers' title.

It's probably just as well everybody's so bored of this as to have stopped listening, especially the Primary Sevens who've been hearing it for donkey's, because they're getting big enough to forcibly implement Momo's wishes. If they took it to heart, then Braeside Main Street would be full of old dears trying to get back to the side of the road they were happily doddering along when the St Elizabeth kids decided to do their master's bidding.

Now, though, with the greatest hits concluded, it's time for a new number.

'Boys and gerrals, there is something else that has made me sawd of late. Very sawd indeed. There was a fiyarr; a big fiyarr.' Momo says this like it's news, as if nobody's noticed the entire back of the fucking Infant Building has been missing since last week and the Primary Threes haven't realised they're all sitting in the wrong classrooms. 'And it burnt down the Infant School. And all the wee Primary Ones, the poor wee Primary Ones, and all the lovely wee Primary Twos [more balls-booted boxer-dog here] are having to go to the Church Hall for their lessons. And all the wee

85

Primary Threes have lost their classrooms as well. All because of this terrible fiyarr. Now, do you know how fiyarrs are started?'

There's close to no response at this point, apart from some dutiful 'No-o, sir's from a few of the lassies, including, inevitably, Michelle and that lot down the front. Joanne's voice comes through clear and recognisable, securing her grassing rights as ever. Momo realises he's off the hymn sheet here and decides to spotlight some solo performers. This is when it pays to be as far as possible from the front.

'David Reardon. You can tell us: how do fires start?'

There's a wee gap while this poor boy gathers himself after the shock of being suddenly picked out. 'You turn on the bars, sir?' he suggests.

A few of the bigger ones laugh, though they quickly zip it. You can tell everybody else is holding it in.

'No, not an electric fiyarr, David. A blaze. Daft boy, idiot.' David's awfully lucky Momo would have to bend down to reach him or his scalp would be getting pummelled right now. Momo sighs. Time to bring in reliable help. 'Helen Dunn,' he bellows, spotting her near the front. 'How do fiyarrs start?'

Helen, like everybody else, knows there's no single correct answer to this, and given how things just worked out for David Reardon, she sensibly takes a wee moment to think about it. There's total silence while she does, with everybody in the hall aware that Momo's temper just got turned up a wee notch. You could hear a pin drop, which means there's nobody in the hall *doesn't* hear the slightly louder noise of a wee squeaky fart from somewhere to Scot's right. It's a really tight one, a high-pitched number that sounded like whoever did it was trying their best to hold it in. A few folk giggle, and Scot can feel his face creasing up while he tries, like just about everyone else, not to laugh.

'Matches, sir,' Helen decides.

'That's right, Helen. Good girl. You must *never* play with matches,' he informs them all, wagging a stubby finger for emphasis. 'Because fiyarrs can get started by accident. Now, Brendan McIntyre, do you think *this* fiyarr was started by accident?'

Brendan, one of the Primary Sixes, pauses only a moment before replying, 'I don't know, sir,' an answer Scot admires for its astute reading of the situation and deft prevention of any follow-up.

'Well, do you want to know what I think?' Momo asks the room. 'Do you want to know what I think?' he repeats, starting to pace, giving his opinion the big build-up. He pauses for impact, letting the silence grow, and it grows just long enough for a second fart to fill it: this time louder and slightly longer, but still with enough tightness to suggest another failed bum-struggle.

Scot is shuddering now, and from all sides he hears the wheezy tittering of several weans fighting their own losing battles against laughter.

Fortunately, Momo either never heard the fart or is ignoring it and pressing on regardless. 'I think it *was* started by accident. Because, sawd as I am to say it, I think it was started by some bawd iggs at *this . . . very . . . school*. And bawd as they might be, I don't believe, I *can't* believe anyone could be so bawd, so very, very, very bawd indeed, to deliberately burn down the lovely wee Primary

87

Ones' and wee Primary Twos' and wee Primary Threes' classrooms. And that's why I'm going to give them the chance to own up. That's why I've called everyone here to assembly. If whoever did it can be as big and brave as to own up, like they thought they were big and brave when they were playing with matches, then we can put the matter behind us. They can stand up and say sorry to all the other children sitting here, then come with me to the Church Hall to say sorry to the wee Primary Ones and Primary Twos, and after that the police won't need to be told. But if they don't own up, here and now . . .' Momo paces again, shaking his head. Scot knows he's looking at a volcano about to erupt. 'Then *woe betide them*! Because they will be found. The police are clever—very, very clever—and they have machines for finding out who is telling lies. And when those bawd iggs are found, I will be taking my strap, and I will drag them round each and every classroom, from Primary One to Primary Seven, and I will *belt them in each and every classroom, for all the boys and gerrals to see*. And they will be crying [boxer-dog once more] like wee babies, crying and crying, and when they have run out of tears, I will *take them back to the first class and begin again*!'

Momo's voice echoes off the walls. There's weans with their hair practically standing on end now. It's as well the Primary Ones and Twos aren't here, because any bets they'd all be greeting.

Scot has to hand it to Momo: he makes it sound like a good offer. And if anybody believed him for a second about his end of the deal, he might even get takers. Hell, there were one or two eejits who would probably be prepared to own up and say sorry in exchange for the boost it would give their reputations to get the credit for something as massive as the blaze. *If* they believed him for a second.

'So now, here is your chance, your one big chance, to do it the easy way and own up. To say sorry. I'll give you ten seconds, and then, after that, I'll be practising with my strap. I'll be eating steak and drinking milk to build up my muscles for that strap.' And with this, he pulls the aforementioned black leather tawse from inside his jacket where it's permanently draped over his shoulder, grips it in his giant, knobbly fist and lashes it down with all his might against the stage. The crack echoes off the four walls, the reverberation felt in Scot's and probably just about everyone else's stomach.

Momo sticks the leather away again and folds his arms. 'Ten . . . nine . . . eight . . .'

Even from halfway back down the gym hall, Scot can see that the belt has left a big brown mark on the stage. Any bets it's left a few brown marks elsewhere as well.

'Three . . . two . . . one . . .'

If Scot thought there was silence earlier, then that was a riot compared to now, with every person in the place simultaneously holding their breath. You can hear rain on the windows, the purr of a car driving past out on the main road.

Then there sounds out the biggest, loudest, longest, wateriest brammer of a fart Scot has ever had the privilege to witness. Nae kidding, this is *world class*. You don't just hear it, you feel it, like when a high wind rattles the sills or an aeroplane flies low over your house. It's more than a fart; 'fart' doesn't seem a big or long enough word for this arse-concerto. It's an event, almost on the scale of the fire.

And immediately, of course, there is total uproar: a dam breaking as all that high tension collapses and everybody totally cracks up. Even the most fearful and most self-disciplined weans are helpless, their terror of the heidie no match for the irresistible hilarity of the moment. Scot is bent over where he's sitting, and even through tears in his eyes he can see some of the staff's features contort as they strive professionally to keep the smiles off their own coupons. And in the middle of it, like he's trying to hold back the tide and not get washed away, is Momo, bellowing his lungs out. 'Who was tha-aat? Who? Who made that *terrible* and dis*gus*ting noise?'

Aye, fuck's sake. Like somebody would own up to a fart like that under any circumstances, never mind to Momo on the warpath. Give us peace.

Scot has heard there is someone in Primary Five who can make himself fart when he wants to, but you hear a lot of shite like that, and thus he hadn't given the reports much credence. Scot can make himself burp (though if he does it too much it gives him the hiccups), but until now he didn't believe you could make yourself fart—or believe anyone would *want* to. But the timing of these trumpetings has just been too good to be accidental.

Momo is now walking forward among the squatting assembly like he's wading out to sea. '*Quiet!*' he shouts, but for the moment the laughter is still too infectious. '*I said quiet!*' he tries again, this time with the added visual cue of pulling the belt from his shoulder.

This has an immediate, widespread impact.

90

Everybody tries really hard to hold it in, and the noise dies right down, though there's still a lot of shoulders shuddering. Scot can see some folk nipping their own skin so that the pain stops them from thinking about how funny the fart was.

Momo holds the belt in both hands, folding it in two. 'Who made that noise?' he demands again. His eyes are blazing. His previous antics were a calculated effort in putting the wind up everybody, but since the wind came right back out, you can tell he's totally lost the place. The mad bastard's probably even forgotten all about the fire by this point. 'Who? Who?' He leans down and stares at one of the Primary Fours. 'Derek Coogan. Was it you?'

You can see this Primary Four's whole body tremble as he shakes his heid and says, 'No, sir.'

'Allan McQueen. Was it you?'

No, but if you keep this up, Momo, somebody's going to actually shite themselves, never mind fart.

Momo wades deeper, further up the hall, getting nearer to Scot. He can feel his heart beating faster, imagines wee Jamesy's will be doing double that again. He stops on the spot and starts sniffing the air. There's close to silence again now; Momo's cranked up the tension once more and put the fear back into atmos. He takes another couple of steps, still sniffing, his eyebrows bunched together like two caterpillars having a square go. Then Scot feels a horrible sensation running through him as he realises what's about to happen just half a second before it does. Momo's stopped over Harry Fenwick, his nostrils still twitching and a look on his face familiar to anybody who's just arrived in a Fenwick's immediate vicinity.

91

'Haa-rold Fenwick,' he blurts out, slavers dripping from his gub in his blind outrage. 'Disgusting boy. It was you.' And with that he reaches down a huge paw and yanks poor Harry to his feet.

'Sir, it wasnae . . .' barely escapes from Harry's mouth before greeting drowns his voice.

Momo practically drags the boy along with him, shouting, 'Out! To the front!' as he does so. He's got hold of Harry's jumper at the back of his neck with one hand and is already battering lumps out his head with the other as he hauls him forward. 'We'll see how funny those revolting noises are in just one minute,' Momo rumbles, for the benefit of all present, not just Harry.

Momo all but throws him against the wee stage as he lets go of Harry's neck, the force nearly knocking him off his feet. He puts a hand out to steady himself but his legs are all wobbly from fear. 'Get your hands out, disgusting boy. *Filthy* boy,' Momo shouts. Harry's bubbling away, shaking like a wet dog as he reluctantly lifts a hand out, palm up. He looks tiny compared to Momo, who is towering over him, trembling as much with rage as Harry is with terror. 'Both hands,' he adds, so Harry will place one hand under the other. This is so the impact won't knock the hand away and lessen the blow. Momo is a fucking bastard.

Scot feels like he shouldn't look, like there's something wrong about this being made a public spectacle, but at the same time he can't take his eyes off it. He now understands what his ma means when she says the shops were busy 'like an execution'.

'This is what happens to boys who make

disgusting noises,' Momo says. He draws the belt back over his shoulder, and, again, everybody breathes in, at which point a second superfart all but rattles the windows.

Momo's eyes nearly burst out his skull with a fury nobody has ever witnessed even from him before. He turns away from Harry to face the assembly, which is by now once again a sea of helplessly rocking weans, and stamps his right foot so hard against the polished boards it's like a bomb going off. '*Quiet!*' he roars. '*Quiet!*'

But this time there's just no holding back the tide. Momo's face is now going purple. His fists are clenched, his knuckles white and his eyeballs about ready to explode from his shuddering heid. He leans back a wee bit and then jumps in the air—both feet actually leave the ground—while screaming, '*I said . . .*' The third word was meant to be 'quiet', but as his clumpy shoes crash back to earth and shake the floor, that's not what emerges from his mouth. A top-plate of false teeth goes fleeing from between his lips and skites along the floorboards up one of the aisles between the rows of assembled weans.

A lassie screams and starts greeting. Maybe she thought Momo's heid had burst, but no luck, he's still alive. He's got one hand clamped over his gub and goes galumphing down the hall with the other one outstretched to retrieve his fugitive falsers. Meanwhile, Harris steps from the side of the stage to the middle and yells, '*Hail Queen of Heaven.* One, two, three,' and starts singing, waving like fuck to the other teachers to join in.

Some of the less hysterical weans—mainly lassies—obediently take up the hymn and just about drown out the sound of folk creasing themselves as Momo goes lolloping away up the corridor like a wounded orang-utan.

Scot looks round at Jamesy, and has never seen him happier. They even both start singing, like it's a song of triumph and not some dirge. Then more and more folk join in, singing it with a joy and enthusiasm Harris has never seen and can barely believe. But that's because they know—while she doesn't—that they've got their own version of the last line.

'Thrown on life's surge, we claim thy care,' they all belt out, big, daft grins on their faces. 'Save us from peril—and Mo-mo!'

Criminal Investigations

There is a crucial prelude to every interview, a silent exchange before the first word is spoken, which is often as instructive in getting to the truth as any of the verbal submissions that follow. That's why Karen is always nervous in the minutes immediately before her first meeting with a suspect, regardless of how many dozens of times she's done it in the past. No matter the hour, no matter how tired, no matter what other worries might threaten to cloud her vision, she has to get ready, get entirely focused for those first brief seconds when her eyes meet those of whoever is sitting on the far side of the table. It's not as though the game is won and lost in that first exchange (a deficit can usually be recovered), but it certainly helps get a result if you can be the one to seize an early advantage.

If you're ready, if you're focused, you can see a lot in that first glance. You can see fear; of yourself, of someone else, or sometimes in its sheer essence. You can see anger. You can see defiance. Regret. Desperation. Bewilderment. Defeat. Resignation. Confidence. Complacency. You can see the person on the other side sizing you up, working out tactics. And if you read it fast enough, you can evaluate every word from then on in light of this.

She's been played by a few suspects—who hasn't?—but not for a long time. It's not about instinct and it can't really be taught, other than by plain experience. In fact, it's the one thing in this job of which you could say that, early on in your career, it's possible to make too *few* mistakes. You screw up, you misread, you get taken, and you learn not to fall for the same shite twice. No amount of other cops' stories can drive it home; only your own anger can galvanise you, can make you see the same pitfall when it inevitably comes around again.

But no amount of experience makes it easier. You can't phone one in, even in what appears the simplest of cases, because somebody somewhere might be relying on you to do just that, and it might not be the person on the other side of the Formica.

She's gathering herself, preparing as she makes the short walk from her temporary office to the room where DS Tom Fisher is already waiting with Noodsy and his brief. She can feel the tingle, the charge, and the voltage today is that bit higher because of who she'll be talking to, the complicating element of their shared past. She hasn't seen this guy in nearly two decades, but beyond that there are twelve years of memories, the sum of which she will have to consider and be wary of throughout everything that follows.

But, more than ever, that first look, that first second, is going to be key. Karen doesn't know whether he'll even recognise her: and if he does, she'll need to be ready to interpret that, too. What will it be that he sees? Someone who knows who he once was, but not who he is now? A ray of hope? The benefit of the doubt? And if it is hope, then what is it that he hopes she sees in him? The wee boy she went to school with? A happy-go-lucky loser who wouldn't hurt a fly?

She reaches the door, grasps the handle, opens it with her eyes fixed on the floor. She steps inside, closes it again, turns around and lifts her head so that they can both get a good, clear look at each other. Noodsy looks up expectantly, nervously anxious to see who he's up against. She sees his eyes narrow, concentration in his face as he tries to place her. There is a brightening of his features, as though his initial impression is that wherever he knows her from must somehow make her more benign, maybe a cop who's given him a fair shake before. It's when she clears it up that she'll really get the goods.

'Hello, James,' she says, smiling.

Then he gets it. The flicker of brightness fades. He physically sags before her eyes. He looks shattered. He looks resigned.

He looks guilty.

*   *   *

96

James and Francis find Colin talking to Scot near the edge of the football field, about as far as you can get from the big yins' playground. It is afternoon playtime and James is delighted to have learnt that Francis hasn't seen Colin's killertine thing, which is why they've sought him out. While they were looking for him, James was also scouring the ground for something suitable to be chopped by the gadget, and has gathered a couple of dandelion stems.

Colin and Scot are talking about what happened at assembly, which everybody agrees was totally fantastic. James doesn't feel quite as gleeful or comfortable talking about it as everybody else, though, mainly because he was terrified throughout most of it—especially when Momo came wandering through looking for someone to blame—and is still feeling more relief than anything else. He knows it's one of those things that are much better to talk about later than they were to experience at the time, and he knows that in future he will forget the scary bits and remember only the farts and Momo's teeth coming out. Right now, it's still a wee bit too close, and he'd rather just see the magic trick again.

'Colin, Colin, can you show Francis the killertine? He's no seen it. Look, I've got these, they'll be great for choppin.'

Colin looks pleased to have a new person to impress, and reaches into his jacket pocket. He then tries the pocket on the other side, then his inside breast pocket, then back to the first one again. 'Where is it?' he asks. 'It's no there. It was there just . . . Aw flip, I hope I've no lost it.'

'Did you leave it in your desk, mibbae?' Scot asks.

'Naw, I never took it into class. I wouldnae, in case Clarke took it off us. Sugar. I hope I've no dropped it somewhere.'

'C'mon, we'll all look,' James volunteers. 'Where did you have it last? Who did you show it to?'

'I've no showed it to anybody since morning playtime,' Colin answers. 'Remember?'

'Aye. It was over by the fence near the big yins'.'

'Aw, wait, did I . . . ? I think I showed it to Gary again at lunchtime.'

'We'll split up,' James suggests. He really wants to see this trick again and can only imagine how sad Colin will be if it really is lost. Plus he'll be in big bother off his ma. James's ma never lets him take stuff into school in case it goes missing or gets broken.

James hares off towards where they were standing this morning, which is round the far side of the Infant Building from where he left Colin and Scot. The killertine was bright red, so it should be easy to see, but on the other hand, it would also be more likely to have been spotted and lifted by someone, especially if it was lying out during lunchtime. Maybe it has been handed in to one of the teachers, but if Colin's unlucky, someone's got it and will be giving it 'finders keepers, losers weepers'.

There is more space in the playground with the wee ones being away at the Church Hall, but James still has to negotiate carefully through two competing football matches, one re-enactment of Saturday's *Starsky and Hutch*, several games of tig and at least four whirling sets of skipping ropes. He reaches the site of this morning's display and examines the area patiently, pulling aside a few clumps of long weeds next to the exposed concrete bases of the railings. Then, a good bit further along the fencing he spots Robbie, squatting down on his honkers, his back to the playground and his attention focused entirely on whatever is cradled in his lap. James runs over to get a closer look and sees that Robbie's secretive and defensive stance is on account of him having the killertine clutched in his hands.

'That's Colin's,' James states.

Robbie looks up, startled, and quickly stuffs the killertine into a pocket. 'Naw it's no,' he says.

'Aye it is.'

'It's mine. I've got wan as well.'

'Have ye chook. You never had it this mornin.'

'I bought it at dinnertime wi ma dinner money.'

'Why'd you put it in your pocket, then?'

'Fuck off.' With which Robbie gets up and briskly walks away.

James takes off at higher speed in the other direction to report his discovery.

'Robbie's got it,' he informs Colin, having rounded up Scot and Francis on the way. 'I saw him.'

'Did he find it?' Colin asks, a little anxious because Robbie is the type who would claim finders keepers even when he knew whose it was.

Robbie, however, has played it carelessly, as far as James can see. 'Naw. He says it's a different wan an he bought it at dinnertime wi his dinner money, but he was tryin tae hide it soon as he saw me.'

'His dinner money?' Scot says, laughing. 'But

Robbie's on free dinners. He doesnae have any dinner money. And do they sell magic tricks at school dinners noo? Or do ye get wan free if you manage tae eat a whole plate ay that watery custard?'

James laughs, but Colin doesn't join in. It's his thing that's gone missing, right enough, so James supposes if it was his, he wouldn't be seeing the funny side either.

*   *   *

They can't find Robbie, despite scouring more of the playground than they did during the hunt for the killertine itself. Colin is feeling almost relieved. He is furious that Robbie has stolen the magic trick and obviously he wants it back, but he can see this turning into something dangerous. It's easy for the others—they're just along for the ride, and they want to see Robbie get into trouble or whatever—but Colin is very apprehensive of having to face him down. Robbie's not big and stocky like Richie, or Paddy Beattie in the other Primary Three class, but in a way he's scarier because there's this nastiness about him that never seems to be at rest. Nobody likes him much, but nobody has ever made a point of becoming his enemy, and not just because he's got those mental big brothers. He's seen arguments and scuffles break out a hundred times, felt the fear when someone like Richie flies into a rage, but that's all in the heat of the moment. Robbie looks a bit like a rodent, and when he gives you the bad eye, it's stone cold.

That said, he wants his killertine back, and

Robbie won't get away with it when everybody knows it's his.

Then the bell goes, and Colin realises that Robbie will have to make his way to the lines along with everyone else. He feels nervous because he now knows there's no avoiding it: once he gets there, the others will be expecting him to do something, and the prospect of that reminds him of just about every fight he has seen breaking out.

Robbie sees the group approaching and turns away to face the wall, where he is breaking wee stones off the roughcast with the sole of his shoe.

Colin's stomach tightens and he now understands why people talk about you shiting yourself when they mean you're scared. He doesn't know what he should say, but he knows the moment is upon him; and furthermore, Clarke or Cook or Harris or whoever will be along to take in the lines soon. This thought reminds him that adult intervention is not far away, and provides both impetus and assurance.

'Gie's my magic trick back,' he says. 'I know you've got it.'

Robbie turns around, his face all pinched. 'Have I fuck got it. I don't know what you're on aboot.'

'Come aff it. Jamesy saw you wi it. It's mine's. C'mon, just gie's it back.' Colin keeps his voice low and steady rather than challenging, trying to talk him round like it's no big deal, which it won't be if he gives it back.

'Jamesy's a fuckin liar. He never saw me wi it. Any bets he's fuckin got it an he's just blamin me.'

'I did see him wi it,' Jamesy protests. 'He's got it in his pocket, I saw.'

Colin sees Robbie place a hand protectively over

101

his jacket in response to this, and finds himself reaching towards the same spot.

'Gie us it,' he says.

'Get tae fuck,' responds Robbie, turning away in a half-pirouette.

Instinctively, Colin steps around, extending a hand towards the retreating pocket. 'Gie us it,' he repeats, then sees a blinding flash and feels a sudden jolt to his nose. The pain has barely registered before he feels an explosion of something cripplingly greater between his legs, and drops automatically to his knees, clutching his newly toed balls.

'I says get tae fuck,' Robbie hisses, slipping away towards the back of the line.

Colin's eyes are watering but he is not crying. It's weird. He remembers crying as soon as Clarke skelped him that time for carrying on in class, even though it wasn't very sore, but right now, despite his cheek hurting and his balls being in pure agony, he doesn't howl because he is still in a state of shock. It's coming, though. Jamesy and Scot help him to his feet insistently. He wants to stay down and feels the crying coming on, but they haul him up, warning that the teachers will appear to take in the lines at any second.

'I'm fuckin grassin,' Colin says, sniffing. He seldom says swearie-words because he's terrified of getting caught or shopped and his mum finding out, but he is raging now. 'He's . . . he's in trouble.' In his shaken and sorry state he found himself about to say, 'He's reported,' but that's pure ancient, Primary Two stuff, and a slagging if anyone picks up on it.

'Don't be daft,' Scot warns. 'You'll just end up in

102

bother as well.'

'But he hit us,' Colin protests.

'Teachers don't care aboot that,' adds James. 'They don't listen. If they think it's a fight, you baith get intae trouble.'

'But it wasnae a fight. I never hit—'

'Teachers never listen,' James insists, with a wounded look that Colin finds troubling.

Before Colin can make any response, Harris appears, and everybody straightens out into their lines. At this point, looking at her stern face as she doles out a warning to one of the Primary Fives, he admits to himself that Scot and Jamesy are right, to the point where he starts worrying that Joanne saw something and will grass to Harris that there *was* a fight. He keeps his head down and hopes Harris won't notice and enquire about his tears. He feels relief as she calls the lines in and he hobbles past her unaccosted. However, his anger has only increased, because it just isn't right that Robbie should get away with this. And while the others are right about teachers when it comes to things like fights, which they can't be bothered getting to the bottom of, he suspects they might look differently on something as serious as stealing. Hitting happens all the time; full fights often enough, too. But theft, that's rare, and therefore must be regarded as a bigger deal. Plus Robbie was lying. They're always being told lying about it is worse than whatever bad thing you've done. If you're big enough to do it, you should be big enough to own up to it, too: that's what Miss Clarke said herself. Lying is one of the Commandments, and so is stealing. So Jamesy is wrong, because this time the teacher *would* listen.

They all take their seats and wait for Clarke to come into the class. Colin has his hand up as she closes the door. She walks to her desk. He is sure she noticed, but sometimes she pretends not to see you and makes you wait so she knows it's important. Joanne's hand is up all the time, but Clarke knows if she makes her wait long enough, Joanne will give up or even forget what it was she was going to say. Colin, however, will not give up, and definitely won't forget.

Clarke picks up her chalk and walks towards the blackboard. For a moment, Colin fears she is going to start writing something they have to copy, which will require him to put his hand down until later. It's another successful tactic in seeing off Joanne. But before she writes anything, she looks at him and says: 'Yes, Colin, what is it?'

'Miss, Robert's stole my magic trick and he won't give me it back.'

'Miss, no, I never, he's lying,' shouts Robbie, without putting his hand up or waiting to be asked.

'Don't tell tales, Colin,' says Clarke.

'Miss, I'm not telling tales, he's took my—'

'Enough,' she says firmly, and turns to face the board. 'Right, class,' she says, 'we're going to do some handwriting exercises . . .'

Colin feels helpless, absolutely gutted. He looks across at Robbie, who stares back with complete indifference.

*   *   *

James is disappointed but not surprised by Clarke giving Colin short shrift. Teachers are always going on about how you have to pay attention; Clarke

104

has a real bee in her bonnet about it. She says it's okay to make a mistake spelling a sentence you've made up yourself or doing a sum, but it's unacceptable to make a mistake if you're copying from the blackboard, because that's 'simply not paying attention'. But when you're trying to tell them something, they don't listen, they don't pay attention; either that or they only hear what suits them. And that's why they don't have a clue what really goes on at school. Momo thinks James is one of the baddies; so does Lanegan. Ask anybody in class and they'd just laugh about that. But there's Colin telling Clarke that Robbie stole his stuff and she's acting like it's just Joanne telling the usual tales about who called who a cow at playtime. Not only did Robbie steal from Colin, but he battered him as well, so Colin probably won't get his trick back either. It's not fair. The teachers tell you to do as you're told and stick to the rules and you'll do fine, but they can't tell the difference between weans that try their best and pure bastards like Robbie.

The truth is James's card has been marked from day one—literally day one. Fucking Lanegan came into the Paki shop after school and saw him buying a Curlywurly for himself and a Fry's Crème for his ma, because he knew that was her favourite. She saw him paying with that big ten-bob coin he had been given by Colin, though at the time he didn't know the boy's name. He'd expected his ma to be all happy, because not only was it his first day at school, but he'd managed to get her a present for a surprise. But she wasn't happy. Well, she was and she wasn't. She was surprised, but not in a good way, and asked him where he'd got the money;

then she got a bit angry and said she'd have to give him money to give back to this boy, and that he must have given him it by mistake. Until this point it hadn't even occurred to James that it was the boy's money—he thought you got given it for handing back your jotter, and reckoned he now understood why his granda said you could make lots of money if you worked hard at school. After a while, though, his ma did calm down and told him it had been nice of him to buy her the Fry's Crème. The next morning, they had both forgotten about it, so she never gave him a coin to bring back, and James hadn't given it any thought until Lanegan came in and called him out of Mrs Murphy's class. She said she'd had someone's mummy on the phone reporting that a boy had stolen his money, including, she added pointedly, 'a fifty-pence piece'. James was scared at first, then a little relieved when he realised it must have been a boy in a different class she was talking about. He could explain how he got *his* fifty-pence piece and how his mum was going to replace it, except they forgot this morning . . . But she didn't listen. Didn't listen? He barely got to speak. He got as far as saying a boy in his class had given him the money and she seized upon this like the maddies in the wigs his granny watched on *Crown Court*. Banging on about 'Thou Shalt Not Steal' from the Ten Commandments and the importance of honesty, she ordered him to bring the replacement fifty pence directly to her, then she would personally return it to the boy's mum, calling this 'a satisfying conclusion', after which 'the matter would rest'. Honesty? Well, that was two lies if ever he heard them. He was wrongly branded a thief and some other boy's mum would be getting Colin's replacement ten-bob bit. Hardly a satisfying conclusion. And, as for the matter resting, nobody told that to Momo—but that cow Lanegan certainly told him everything else.

So now James is a vee-lan while Robbie gets away with everything, and poor Colin ends up losing out again, too. He starts to feel angry, the sensation similar to this morning after he'd been Momoed, something inside that was causing his cheeks to burn. He's angry with Robbie but his greater frustration is with Clarke. Robbie's a wee shite, and that's all you can expect from him, but the teachers are the ones with power, so they should show they know, show they care when something's not right.

Then he sees fat Joanne with her hand up as usual and realises it's not all Clarke's fault. It's like the story of the boy who cried wolf (though not the same as *Peter and the Wolf*, which Clarke sometimes plays to them).

Clarke responds, saying, 'Yes, Joanne,' like she's about to fall asleep, and James can tell she isn't going to listen to whatever tale Joanne tells her. But instead Joanne says she needs the toilet, and with a knackered-sounding sigh of relief, Clarke tells her to go ahead.

That's when James works it all out: what happened. Robbie went out to the toilet this morning, after playtime and just before the Daily Ten sums. He must have gone to the cloakroom on his way and dipped Colin's jacket pocket.

James knows what he must do, how he can put this right, but first of all he'll have to be patient. Clarke can be hot and cold about letting you go to the bogs, and though letting one person go usually means she can't say no to anyone else, it pays not to ask too soon. He has to wait for Joanne to come back anyway, because you're never, ever, allowed out at the same time as somebody else. James then hangs fire until Clarke has set them to a task, in this case making up sentences including the words she's writtten on the board. You've got no chance of getting the nod while she's writing on the board or talking to the class unless you're claiming you're about to be sick, and that always prompts a follow-up investigation. He watches for her settling down to mark a pile of jotters and makes his pitch, putting on his best pained face to make out he's been patiently holding it in but can't take the pressure anymore.

'On you go,' she says, 'but be quick about it.'

James runs for the door, knowing this will get him a reminder to walk, but will allay any suspicion about what he's up to. Clarke has got no reason to question his intentions, but it's not the teacher's suspicions that concern him. He makes his way quickly down the corridor to the cloakroom, which is not actually a room but an area next to the boys' toilets accommodating a row of eight double-width wooden benches, each with metal grids supporting coat-hooks between. There are also blocks of coat-hooks along the walls, forming an L-shaped enclosure. When he realised this was how Robbie had done it, James's first thought was merely to secretly replace the killertine in Colin's pocket, but his anger told him that getting it back isn't even half the battle. Showing up Robbie for what he did was important, but that wasn't the whole of the game, either. It's forcing the teachers to see what's really going on that truly matters, and he's going to do that by bringing Robbie's jacket back to the class with him. When he walks in with that in his hands, he knows Clarke will demand to know why, and then he'll be only too happy to show her.

He doesn't see Robbie's jacket, but this is no surprise. Most of the hooks have more than one coat slung over them, the top one usually hung by the hood, the facility being overcrowded by today's addition of two Primary Three classes' garments and bags. Back in the Infant Building there were specific benches allocated to each class, whereas in here it's a free-for-all. James thinks he remembers roughly which bench he saw Robbie at after playtime and begins at that end. He starts by pulling the top coats aside, and soon spots the scabby blue material of Robbie's jacket. He is about to lift it off when he remembers he'd better check the killertine is still there, just in case the sneaky wee shite has planked the goods elsewhere. The outside pockets are zipper efforts, and quite hard to get into with a heavy orange Snorkel hanging on top and getting in the way, but he tugs one open and pulls out what he's looking for.

Then he hears someone clearing their throat. Someone big. An adult clearing *her* throat.

James turns around and sees Harris standing with her arms folded at the far end of the bench. He has no idea how long she's been watching, only what she's seen.

'James Doon. What are you doing rummaging about in there?' she asks.

But he knows she isn't going to listen to his answer.

Primary Four
61 Virginis

The Most Amazing Thing Ever to Happen at St Elizabeth's

Okay, so there's something seems not quite right as Scot approaches the lines. Just a feeling he gets as he walks up, something not ringing true in what he has glimpsed, so he looks more directly at the double doors and the steps in front. Aye, definitely something the matter. It doesn't sound quite normal, either. There's always a bit of a racket from so many voices blethering and shrieking, but just now it's heightened, giddy even. Everybody's standing back from the foot of the stairs; like, a yard or two back. Normally the folk at the front will be standing on the steps and giving it king-of-the-castle right until the second the teachers come. And even more normal would be for two of those playing king-of-the-castle to be either Joanne and Alison or Carol and Michelle.

The four of them are there, of course. The bell's gone, are you daft? But it looks as if . . . no, it definitely *is* the case that they're each trying to get behind the other, trying to wrong-foot their opponents like players in the penalty box waiting on a corner.

As he gets close he can hear them speak. Instead of the usual goading, gloating, accusation and recrimination, there's a giggly, mischievous tone to it.

'After you.'

'No, we're always first. About time we let you have a shot.'

'Nonsense, we insist.'

There's much the same carry-on under way in the other lines, so it can't be some new game just between that daft wee quartet.

There's not many boys arrived yet, most of them still squeezing out the last few drops of a game of Colditz, but he sees Colin, who had cried off early to go to the bogs. He looks kind of dazed, in a bit of a dwam, or like he might be about to spew.

'Awright, Col?' Scot asks.

'Hiya,' he says, not very sure.

'Whit's goin on?'

Before Colin can answer, Joanne turns on her heel, her superpowered lugs pricked up to zero-in on a chance to break some news.

'There's a jobbie in the corridor,' she announces, with the kind of relish you normally only see on the face of Nicholas Parsons when he reveals that somebody's won a motor.

'Shite,' Scot says doubtfully.

'Aye, exactly.' Joanne beams. 'Just inside the double doors.'

Scot looks ahead. He can't see a jobbie, but the unprecedented gap between the forming lines and the steps is convincing enough.

'Did you see it?' he asks.

'Aye, it's mingin,' says Joanne. 'Aw skittery an everythin.'

'You see it, Colin?'

Colin gives him a white-faced look that fairly answers the question.

'Is there a dug in the school, then?' Scot enquires. Jai Maloney's mental red setter has rampaged through the playground on several terrifying occasions, and it only seems a matter of time before it gets indoors.

114

But Joanne now looks like the lucky contestant has bagged the motorboat as well. 'Naw. It was Harry Fenwick.'

'What, he just dropped his troosers and did it?' Scot asks scornfully. The name she has given is the obvious guess if she didn't really know the truth. It's a school-wide assumption these days: if it smells, Honkin Harry must be to blame. It's mince. Being generally a bit smelly didn't necessarily mean you were the prime candidate to spectacularly shite yourself; after all, you often saw Janny Johnny cleaning up sick, and people didn't automatically attribute *that* to Eleanor's unfortunate brother.

'You saw this?' Scot adds.

'Naw. That Primary Six boy, Bomber, he saw it. Heard him tellin his mates. He said it all ran doon Harry's legs, doon the inside of his troosers. Said it's all along the corridor an all over the floor ay the boys' toilets.'

Scot looks across to one of the other lines. Robbie's big brother Brian, or 'Boma' as he has scrawled it across several walls around Braeside, is holding court, a number of grimacing faces around him as he talks.

The lines continue to form, word excitedly passing along them as each new group of arrivals joins the rear. A number of necks are craned, which Scot finds ridiculous.

'Look at these eejits,' agrees the recently arrived Martin of the stretch-necks, all but bouncing to try and see the star attraction. 'Have they never seen a jobbie before?'

'Not in its wild state, I don't think,' Scot replies.

'Well, they'll get a close-up soon enough. We're

115

all gaunny have to walk past it to get in.'

'It'll be like thon deid punter they have on display in Russia,' Scot says. 'We can all file past slowly and pay our respects. Here lies Honkin Harry's jobbie.'

'Where is Harry?' Martin asks.

'Dunno. Aw fuck, he's behind you!'

'Whit?'

'Made you look.'

'Ya bandit.'

With time ticking on, Scot's thoughts turn to the cabaret in store when the teachers arrive. He hopes it's O'Connor. She teaches the Primary Fives, God help them, and is the most torn-faced teacher in the whole school. He really hopes his class never gets her.

But, in fact, they've hit the jackpot, for who comes loping along but Momo himself. He seldom takes in the lines, being too important for that kind of thing, and is most likely on his way from the staff room in the Annexe back to his office. He's not always the quickest on the uptake, but even Momo's radar is sensitive enough to detect something isn't quite normal about the lines. He stops in the double doorway and has a look, immediately rendering the weans quiet, though on this occasion it's as much from bated breath as obedient silence. He goggles the big gap and his big eyebrows rear up against each other like two rutting stags.

Then his nose twitches, and a moment later he looks down.

He can't speak for a second, has a couple of breathless goes at it, then finally manages his immortal words, the most memorable he will ever speak to any wean who ever attended St Lizzie's:

'God in heh-van, loowk at thawt.' He's pointing down at it, actually pointing down at it with one of his stumpy arms. It's like thon picture Scot's granny brought back from the Cistern Chapel, God giving it the big electric zap. Momo's still thinking of the divine, too. 'Mother of Chryyst, Jesus Go-hod.'

He stands rooted to the spot for a few seconds, apparently oblivious to the fact that there's now about a hundred weans in danger of peeing themselves laughing out here in the playground. It's like he's in a world of his own; or a world of just his and the jobbie's, anyway. Then he suddenly shudders from head to foot and breaks the trance, before stomping off out of sight. 'Good Go-hod, I ask you, what kind of animaaaa—'

Whump.

That's what they hear. They don't see, but they don't have to. Momo has slipped on more of the jobbie and went his kite. It is a day sent from heaven.

Maybe not so much for poor Harry, Scot reflects a wee bit later. He's heard Harry was found all balled up in the cloakroom area, crying his eyes out, and was sent home shortly after. No, not a good day for him. Nor are there likely to be too many for, well, as far into the future as Scot can possibly envisage. The poor bastard is going to have to pilot a mission to Mars, cure all known diseases and score the winner in the World Cup Final before he's got any chance of being remembered for anything else.

Primary Five
Chara

Debts

Martin can see Noodsy through the wee wire-meshed window into the interview room. Whenever he runs into someone from his childhood days, he's normally struck by their appearing much smaller than he remembers. Teachers, in particular, seemed to have been put through a harsh shrinking mechanism during his university years. Noodsy, however, was someone in that exclusive schooldays echelon of being shorter than Martin, so his stature seems to be pretty much as Martin remembers it. He looks older, though; and not just twenty years older than back then, but like those twenty years aged him more than they aged his beholder. His eyes are glazed and heavy, missing that guile-free twinkle, that boundless, innocent energy. Poor bastard looks like he hasn't slept in days, which is probably about right.

Then the polisman unlocks the door, allowing Martin to walk in, and two decades briefly fall from Noodsy's face. There's a flash, a glimmer of the wee boy Martin once knew, before age and circumstance all but extinguish it again. All but, because there's still something burning in there somewhere.

'Marty!' he says, and, to Martin's shame, tears form in Noodsy's eyes as he speaks. He wipes them away with an embarrassed sniff and extends a hand to shake.

Martin is a little relieved, as he thought for a moment Noodsy was going to hug him. He's not shy of the physical contact; it's the being a two-

121

faced hypocritical cunt part that would have made him uncomfortable. He doesn't deserve this welcome, and nor is there much he imagines being able to do subsequently to earn it.

'You came, man. I don't believe it. Thanks, man. Fuckin amazin. Thanks so much. Brilliant tae see ye.'

'You too, Noodsy, though the circumstances aren't exactly . . .'

'Naw, I know. Near as bad as bein back in O'Connor's class, eh?'

Martin smiles, but it feels inappropriate to laugh, even politely. 'You're lookin at a bit more than two of the belt, Noodsy.'

Noodsy nods solemnly. 'I know. That's how I'm so grateful you've came, man. I want—'

'Noodsy, before we go any further, I've got to put you straight. I'm no a criminal lawyer. I mean, I was for a wee while, but that was ten years ago, so I—'

'Aw, naw, it's awright, man. I've already got a brief. Polis werenae gaunny sit aboot while we waited tae see if you showed up, were they? Didnae even have a number for ye. I got some Legal Aid dude. He's awright, considerin he's aboot twelve. Had worse.'

Martin takes a breath, referees a bout between a dozen different reactions to this news, most of them, well, prick-ish. He knew about the other brief, because in order to be allowed to see Noodsy, he had to tell the desk sergeant he had been asked for specifically and was therefore here as a replacement. However, this doesn't sound like he's replacing anybody, not even a Legal Aid dude who looks about twelve.

'I'm sorry,' Martin says. 'I came up on the first flight soon as I heard . . .'

'S'awright, man. I didnae ask for ye cause you're a lawyer, Marty.'

'So, what . . . ?'

'They've got me for murder, man. *Two* murders. And I swear on my mother's grave, I had nothin tae dae wi it. I'll put my hand up tae the conspirin tae pervert, but that's aw I did. I just helped get rid ay the bodies. They were baith deid when I got tae the lodge efter Turbo phoned us.'

'Scot said you needed somebody who would believe you.'

'My brief believes me, Marty. Briefs get paid tae believe ye, whether they believe ye or no. But my brief's no gaunny find oot whit really happened, and neither's the polis. Polis are just like the teachers used tae be. No interested in whit actually happened, just want the quickest solution to gie themsels a quiet life. But the only way I can get oot ay this is if somebody can work oot whit happened in that lodge afore I arrived. *That*'s how I asked for you: you're the brainiest guy I know, Marty. Brainiest guy I *ever* knew. Much brainier than that Karen Gillespie wan anyway.'

Martin nods but says nothing, concealing his emotions. This is even more desperate than Noodsy or Scot thinking he could do some Clarence Darrow act. Flattering, in a tragically naïve kind of way, but still desperate, and flailingly so. In his efforts to bum Martin up, Noodsy has misremembered: it was always Helen and Michelle who were his competition in those stakes, not Karen, but then from Noodsy's point of view, half the class must have seemed comparatively brainy.

'I might no be as brainy as you think,' Martin tells him. 'This isnae like me helpin you wi your homework or somethin.'

'Naw. It's mair like me goin up on that roof thon time,' Noodsy says, his face now as stony as it is scared. 'I helped you that day because I knew I was the only wan that could.'

Aye. The bugger didnae misremember *that*. Martin nods. He takes out his mobile, sets it down on the table and switches it to voice-memo mode. 'You need to tell me everything you've told them,' he says.

The Laws of the Game (Part One)

'I've got to tell you a secret,' says Paul.

It's lunchtime and they're playing football on the school pitch, carrying on the same game from morning playtime. Colin's team are losing 17–15, but they've caught up four goals from earlier and don't even have Stephen Rennie back from lunch yet (though, saying that, the others don't have Matt Cannon either). The pitch is not as busy as playtime, because a lot of the boys are still in school dinners. Colin takes a packed lunch, which means you get more time to play, because you just sit down and eat it then leave when you're done. If you go to dinners, you have to line up, and if you're not quick out of class you can end up in second sitting, after which there's hardly any time before the bell goes.

Colin loves lunchtime, loves how you can feel like ages have passed since the bell went or before it goes again. If you're playing sodies or Flash Gordon or something, you can really lose yourself in the adventure. These days it's football he likes best, though, and lunchtime is when it feels like you're playing in a proper game, with ebb and flow, not a wee kickabout that's over before it's got going. Colin always goes in goals. That was where he was put when he first started joining in games, because he wasn't very good at kicking the ball. He wasn't much cop at stopping it or catching it either, but nobody seemed to find this sufficient reason to offer to take his place, and so in goals he stayed. But that was when the games were up in the playground, on the concrete. Once you're in Primary Five and above, you get to use the pitch at playtimes. No one is sure whether this is a rule created by the teachers or the pupils, but the reason for it is pretty obvious when you see how mobbed the grass can get, with sometimes three separate games taking place at once. When you're in Primary Four, you don't much fancy getting caught up in that, so there is never any chance of the smaller ones being motivated to contest the restriction.

Today, though, there are only two balls on the pitch, because recently the Primary Fives' and Sixes' games have merged, leaving just the Sevens to a match of their own. Despite there being lots of Primary Sixes in both teams, Colin's position between the posts is no longer dictated by his stature. The bigger boys still demand that he plays in goals, but these days it's because they reckon he's good at it. And that's fine with Colin, because in goals is where he enjoys playing, as long as it's on grass. It's the diving that makes the difference.

You can't dive on concrete, which means most of the saves you make in the playground are just a matter of sticking your leg out and letting it rebound off your shin. So, by the time they start playing on the pitch, it doesn't occur to most kids to do anything else when a shot comes in; nor, as it's always the weest and rubbishest ones that get put in goals, is much else expected of them. But one of the first times Colin joined in on the school pitch, Stephen Rennie, the best player in his year, hit this long shot, hard and straight, towards the bottom-right corner, and, having struck it clean, he wheeled away with his arms up to celebrate in front of an imaginary Parkhead Jungle. It was September, the grass was long, the ground was soft, and Colin had been thinking about Gordon Stewart, 'The Safest Hands in Soccer', in *Roy of the Rovers*. Colin threw himself full length across the goal and got his right hand to the ball, deflecting it round the post.

It was, according to absolutely everybody, the best save they'd ever seen. (Absolutely everybody, that is, except Stephen Rennie, whose disbelief that Colin could have stopped his shot was only overcome because it was his own team-mates who were telling him.) He then cemented his newly acquired status by diving again, this time outwards, to cut out the resulting corner-kick, catching it in both hands as he landed comfortably on his side.

Thereafter, there was no question of him playing outfield, and it was a source of private pride during team-picking disputes to hear the likes of Stephen Rennie argue his opponents couldn't have Matt Cannon on their side if they also had Colin in goals. The greatest compliment, however, is that he usually gets to stay in when it's a penalty. Normally the best players tell the wee guy they've forcibly installed between the sticks to get out and let them take over at such crucial moments, because saving a penalty is even more impressive than scoring one, and they're not passing up the opportunity for such glory. This still occasionally happens, but not when the scoreline is tight, as Colin's ability—or maybe just his preparedness—to dive makes him much harder to beat. Being honest with himself, he knows it's more the latter. Diving saves are the easiest thing about being the goalie. Nobody can hit the ball that hard from much of a distance, not even Stephen or Matt, which makes landing on the grass a less painful prospect than getting in the way of someone leathering it straight at you from two yards in the midst of a goalmouth stramash.

It's quite cold today, early December, and the ground is hard but dry. They tend not to play on the grass if it's wet, because you end up with soaking trousers if you fall down, and that's no joke if it happens at morning playtime and you won't be going home to change until four o'clock. Colin's got his anorak on, with insulated padding, which means he can still dive, though there haven't been many opportunities since the lunchtime break got under way. The balance of play, or, rather, the imbalance of players, has seen most of the action confined to the other end, where the majority of the boys on the park are swarming around the ball. You sometimes see Jamesy or Francis standing on their own, away from the morass, screaming for someone to pass because they're in space. This is usually followed, once possession has been lost with no pass attempted, by equally loud accusations that their team-mate is 'a ball-greedy bastard'.

The only others isolated from this roaming frenzy are Martin, Paul, Robbie and Colin. Martin is not much of a player and has therefore spent his own share of games between the posts (or jackets), but when playing outfield he is one of the very few to assign himself the role of defender. This, as he has confided to Colin, is because he has learnt that with both teams made up almost entirely of strikers, you get more chance of a kick at the ball by hanging back in defence. Another reason for his chosen position is that he and Colin are pals and can have a chat and a laugh during the long periods when play never leaves the opposing penalty box.

Robbie, who is playing for the other side, is here because he is a mooching wee bastard. Mooching is hanging around the other team's goals in the hope that the ball breaks forward away from the pack at the other end, offering the chance of a sneaky shot without first having to negotiate your way through two dozen opponents and as many team-mates trying just as hard to get the ball off you. Robbie is a persistent practitioner of this, despite it earning him almost as much resentment from the guys on his own side as his opponents. It also frequently prompts Matt Cannon to shout 'offside', but as nobody other than Matt knows what this term means, it has no effect on play.

Paul is on Robbie's side, and though he is also, technically, mooching, this is neither a common tactic for him nor the real reason he's in Colin's goalmouth. He's there to chat, having just returned from school dinners, and will most likely rejoin the action proper later. The three of them have been talking about *Logan's Run* on the telly, though Martin has seen the film at the pictures and says it was much better and you even got to see a woman's bare bum. Colin loves telly and films about space. He doesn't want to be a spaceman anymore, though, because he's seen the real space rockets in books and they look pure rubbish compared to the ones in stories. Plus they can only go as far as the moon, which is nothing. He's got books about stars and the universe, and he knows the names of all the planets; some of the constellations as well. It's called astronomy. That's what he's going to be when he grows up: an astronomer. He's asked for a space telescope for Christmas, so he can look at the stars every night.

Robbie is a few yards away, nearer the edge of the box, hoping for a punt up the field. Paul has had a wee look to estimate Robbie's distance and earshot before venturing that he has this secret to tell them.

'What is it?' Martin asks.

'You've got tae promise no tae tell emdy, right? Cause it's dead secret and I'm only tellin yous because you're good mates.'

'I promise,' says Martin.

'Aye, me too,' agrees Colin, eager to know what it is, and hoping it's in the same league as Kevin's revelation last week that he'd seen Zoe Lawson's fanny when she stayed the night in his room because their parents were all having a party.

Paul has another wee look towards Robbie, which prompts Colin to check further upfield to confirm the ball is still pinging around the other penalty box. Then he tells them: 'I'm really fae another planet.'

Colin's first instinct is to look to Martin for a reaction, but Martin doesn't look back; in fact, his eyes are fixed on Paul.

'My whole family. We had tae come here tae hide oot because there's folk after us.'

Martin now sends a glance Colin's way, a very serious and concerned look on his face, like he's seen Paul fall over and hurt himself rather than just tell them something really daft. That's Martin, though: he's never a bastard, which is probably why Paul has sought him out for this. Colin's heard similar, knows the deal. They all have. It's like a game, usually, except you're pretending it's not a game, and you never acknowledge that. Jamesy once said he had the power to turn invisible but could use it only when his life was in danger. Colin himself remembers, a little uncomfortably, telling people he had a pilot's licence and could fly a plane if the owners would let him. But this was Primary Three stuff. Okay, maybe Primary Four at the latest, but definitely a pure slagging now, in the wrong hands. Colin and Martin both know this. Colin understands why Paul's chosen them to tell, but still can't believe he's saying it. Besides, they're not playing together: they're in the middle of a game of football.

Paul was off school for a couple of weeks recently. Colin overheard his mum say quietly to his dad that the McKees were getting something called a 'D-Force', which he thought might be a new car until his dad replied that it was 'a shame for the weans'.

'We've all got superpowers back on our home

130

planet, but we cannae use them here in case folk find oot and the baddies come and catch us. The planet's called Star X Z Five. It's dead far away. Further than Spain.'

Colin looks forward again to check the proximity of Robbie, but his attention is caught more pressingly by the sight of Richie Ryan hoofing the ball from the edge of the opposing 18-yard box. Richie's got a hard kick on him, and he's caught it a cracker, on the half-volley, causing it to soar high and far towards Colin's penalty area. It lands midway into their half, well ahead of the pursuing stampede, carrying plenty of momentum after the bounce. Robbie runs out to meet it. He makes an arse of trying to kill it with his foot after the second bounce and it ricochets away to the left, just inside the area. Robbie is still nearest as it slows almost to a stop, though Martin has gone out wide to close him down. Behind them, the rest of the mob are charging up the pitch like Viking invaders, leaving only goalie Mick Garvie and Robbie's mooching counterpart Gary Hawkins in the other half of the field. They're still too far back to intervene, though, despite the front-runners shouting on Robbie to 'play it back for the shot, first-time, Robbie, first-time, come on'. Colin would welcome this, because an effort from that range would be just perfect for diving at, but he knows there's no chance. Also shouting, and a far nearer option, is Paul, who would be clear through on Colin if Robbie played, as he is desperately appealing, a 'square baw, Robbie, square baw'. Colin knows there is no chance of this, either. Instead, Robbie goes for glory himself, stepping around the ball so it's on his right foot and giving it a big dirty toe. By this time, however, Martin's right on him and the ball deflects harmlessly off his knee before bouncing out for a shy.

'Ah, ya wee ball-greedy bastard,' Paul moans, the sentiment quickly echoed by several of the new arrivals preparing to set up camp in Colin's penalty area.

'Fuck off,' Robbie replies, eyeing Paul rather than any of the other complainants; inevitably given that Paul is the smallest of them. More surprising was Paul's own outburst, his anger getting the better of his caution. It's going back a bit now, but Colin has not forgotten how coldly brutal Robbie was in responding to his own moment of challenge.

Colin understands Paul's frustration, however. Paul isn't one of the good players but tries really hard and absolutely loves it when he converts a rare opportunity to score. Okay, strictly speaking, Paul had been mooching when that chance came, but he still put himself in the right spot and Robbie should have played the pass.

Big Richie takes the shy. He's nothing like the first one there or particularly noted for his throwing ability, but his team-mates defer to him on the dual grounds that it was his terrific kick that started the move and that he can batter just about anybody else on the pitch. He holds off for a wee minute as he has spotted Matt Cannon returning from the dinner hall and it's wise to wait until their star player has made his way across the pitch. The delay also allows just about everybody else to take position around the touchline and the right-hand side of the penalty area. Only Paul and Dominic distinguish themselves: Paul by moving back to the edge of the 'D' to anticipate a clearance; Dominic a straight marking job on Paul, with the added incentive of a possible head start for a break-away attack if the ball gets cleared.

Richie throws the ball to Matt, who shimmies, twists and sometimes just shoulders his way past several challenges as he progresses into the box. Colin doesn't like how this is shaping up, as Matt looks like soon being in his preferred striking position for his preferred striking method: less then four yards out for a full-blooded, point-blank blooter which Colin would prefer to go past him rather than off him. Matt skips past another obstacle and draws back his foot, at which point the only dive Colin is considering is out of the way. Instead, however, Martin suddenly lunges between them and gets a boot in the way before the ball has travelled two feet, deflecting it at high speed towards the edge of the area, left of the penalty spot, where Paul and Dominic are hovering. They both react, but Dominic is quicker and gets to the ball first. He misjudges, though, the spin and it comes away from his foot, allowing Paul to nip it off his toes with one touch and go past him. It looks brilliant, like Paul has turned him and left him for dead. Paul glances up, sees he is on his own and gives it an almighty arse-winder from almost the full eighteen yards. He meets it sweetly, hard and true.

Colin can tell from the moment it leaves your foot whether it's a toe, a sclaff, a daisy-cutter, a dipper or whatever, and he knows this is something rarer. Paul has met it perfectly, at pace, right off the laces, and it's flying fast at an unwavering eighteen inches off the deck, straight across him

133

and into his bottom-right corner. However, eighteen inches is the perfect height for diving at, and the ball still has plenty of distance to cover, which is why Colin is already airborne. There's no way he's getting his body behind it—it's too fast and always moving away from him—but with his arms outstretched he is able to get his fingers to it, just as his (thankfully jacket-clad and thus well-padded) shoulder hits the turf. There's too much power behind it, however, and though Colin's hand deflects it up, its momentum is still taking it forwards. He looks up from the deck to see it loop over him and bounce once behind his head before spinning on with more than enough pace to take it over the line.

About an inch before it does so, Robbie steps past Colin and toe-ends it as hard as he can through the goals, then goes running off with his arms in the air making crowd noises, regarded as the just reward of all goalscorers. Colin can't believe it. Even as the ball dropped close to Paul and Dominic, he had heard Martin receive unaccustomed praise for a 'brilliant tackle, well in wee man' upon the normally unstoppable Matt Cannon. Then Paul had pulled off a nice piece of skill and balance to set himself up for a shot from a distance only Matt or Stephen would normally attempt, and justified his audacity by unleashing a peach of an effort. This in turn had brought out a dive of unprecedented scope and bravery on the part of Colin, one they would all no doubt remark upon despite it proving insufficient to prevent Paul's once-in-a-lifetime thunderbolt from finding its well-earned and rightful place in the back of the imaginary net.

And then that wee shite had just nicked in and ruined everything by thieving all the glory.

Robbie, however, is not the only one who's running. Paul is now haring after him with an urgent sense of purpose that Colin suspects has little to do with wishing to congratulate him on a clinical piece of close-range finishing.

'That was ma goal ya fuckin prick,' Paul shouts at him, causing Robbie to stop and turn round.

'Naw it wasnae. Colin saved it.'

'It was still goin in.'

'Was it fuck,' Robbie insists, albeit half-heartedly. He turns as though to walk away rather than face down Paul's argument, and he looks far from defiant.

'Aye. It. Fuckin. Was.'

Each of these last short bursts of speech is accompanied by Paul booting Robbie up the arse, the fourth kick seeming to lift Robbie clear off the ground, though this is as much a result of his attempted leap out of the way.

'It was Paul's goal,' rules Matt Cannon, putting a hand on Paul's shoulder, which seems to assure him of his status and restrain him from sending Robbie on another short-range flight. 'Good goal, wee man,' he adds. 'Cracker ay a shot.'

Paul smiles a wee bit but Colin can tell he's still raging. Though he's been awarded the goal, the moment is over. He can't go doing the hands-up run now, and that's the best part. However, Colin believes Paul, in his state of anger, is missing the bigger picture. In the last couple of minutes, something has happened that will have a far greater impact on his standing than merely scoring a stoater of a goal, and this is soon borne out as more and more boys rejoin the game from the dinner hall.

'What's the score?' Colin hears Paddy Beattie ask Anthony Hughes, one of the Primary Sixes.

'I hink it's nineteen-fifteen.'

'Eighteen-fifteen,' insist a few voices.

'But never mind that,' Anthony says. 'Paul McKee battered Robbie.'

'Paul battered Robbie?' Paddy asks. Pleasure and disbelief are equally measured in his voice, but his volume is not. Robbie is not nearby, but close enough, it would appear, to have heard.

'Aye. Robbie mooched his goal and Paul took a pure eppy and battered him.'

'Naw he never,' Robbie insists, walking closer to state his case.

'What you talkin aboot?' Anthony laughs. 'He booted your arse umpteen times and then Matt jumped in and saved you.'

'Saved Paul, mair like. He hardly touched us. I was ignorin him.'

'Ignorin him? Is that a new word for shitin yoursel?' Paddy asks.

'Fuck up,' Robbie says, the delivery notably lacking his usual viciousness.

'If he never battered you, why don't you claim him, then?'Anthony inquires.

This makes Colin uncomfortable. He doesn't like it when folk try to instigate fights between people, and he fears for Paul if this gets pushed through to a conclusion.

'Nae point,' replies Robbie. 'He'll shite it. He knows I'll batter him, so he'll no turn up.'

'Sounds like you're the wan shitin it,' says Paddy.

'Fuck up,' says Robbie again, and walks away.

Colin fears for a moment that he is going to head straight for Paul to claim him after school or to settle the matter more immediately, but instead he just wanders away to stand on his own in his favoured mooching zone around the penalty spot. And that's when Colin understands why Robbie won't be claiming Paul now or later, and why he didn't fight back when Paul booted him. He was scared. He was scared then and he's scared now, despite what having been officially battered by Paul will do to their respective reputations.

Robbie stands for a moment, his eyes drawn more to Colin and Martin than to where play is under way, and frequently beyond them to the steady stream of boys making their way to the pitch and playground from the dinner hall. Then he screws up his face in that pinched way of his and begins trotting across the pitch towards the new arrivals. Colin guesses he's intending to start spreading his own version of events before they hear it from anyone else, but he can't see the point. It will only make it worse when they hear the truth.

Careers

'There's somebody would like a word, Mr Jackson,' says the polisman who is waiting in the corridor outside the interview room.

'Who would that be?'

'The Detective Super in charge of the investigation. Just follow me.' He leads Martin along the hall towards the security barrier and the reception lobby. 'Just there,' he indicates, gesturing towards a tall woman in a dark suit, standing with her back to him as she chats to the desk sergeant. She clocks the other polisman's approach and spins around on one sturdy heel.

It takes Martin a long second to realise that Noodsy misremembered nothing. 'Detective Superintendent Gillespie,' he says, standing as straight and tall as he can. She still seems to tower over him. She's probably got only two or three inches on him, but they made their mark indelibly when these things really mattered.

'Mr Martin Jackson. What a pleasure to see you again, and in such a beautiful suit. Must have cost more than my last car. Of course, they do say there are few more impressive sights than a Scotsman on the make, and you certainly look the part.'

'I always liked you in uniform. Shame you're in plain clothes.'

'Step into my office, please. And don't push your luck.'

She ushers him into a stuffy fire hazard of a room, strewn with folders, loose paper and polystyrene cups. He thinks of his own dual-aspect corner suite in Holborn and wonders why he's the one feeling juvenile and a little intimidated. Karen pulls out a swivel chair for him then takes her own seat on the other side of a desk so marked with coffee rings it could have been the sketch pad of the guy who designed the Audi and Olympic logos.

'So, Detective Super,' he says. 'I didn't even know you were in the polis, let alone . . . Guess you must be the one with all the gen on what happened to everybody. Or the bampots, at least.'

'Not so much. I've not long transferred to this division. Haven't been to Braeside before now. I'm

138

catching up fast, though. Of course, if I wanted to know what happened to you, I'd just need to pick up a copy of *Heat* magazine.'

Martin sighs. He feels a blush coming on, which pisses him off, because he does *not* want to look remotely bashful about this. 'One photograph, once,' he says. 'One fucking photograph. And they didn't even get my name right. I was *Matthew* Jackson, if I recall correctly. But *everybody* bloody saw it.'

' "Showbiz lawyer Matthew Jackson" was, I believe, the caption. And are you still seeing . . . ?'

'I went out with the lassie for less time than it took to develop the snap. I'm sure if you read *Heat* more carefully, you'd know who she's with now. What about you? Are you married?' He glances at her left hand; there's no ring, but you never know, especially with women in male-dominated professions.

'Divorced. Nobody you knew. But don't change the subject. What the hell is a showbiz lawyer doing here? Especially given Noodsy already has a brief.'

'He asked for me.'

'Oh, I know that. I don't think anybody expected you to actually come, but I was intrigued. That's the only reason the desk sergeant let you see him, by the way. I know why Noodsy asked—he's desperate and he's daft. What's beating me is why you answered, and what you think you can do.'

'Have to admit that's got me struggling a bit as well,' says Martin. 'So far, the best argument to come up is that I still owe him for something he did in about Primary Five.'

'I still owe you for something you did in Primary

Seven, but it doesn't mean I'm going to cut you any slack if you become any kind of nuisance to this investigation.'

'At this stage, I don't even know how to go about being a nuisance to your investigation. How's Robbie, by the way?'

She grimaces. 'Not good. He was in surgery for about seven hours; now in intensive care. Sounds like a frenzied attack: multiple stab wounds, and there would have been more but that the knife got stuck.'

'Have you got any suspects?'

'You mean apart from the obvious?'

'Who's obv . . . You don't mean Noodsy?'

'He's already involved in two murders, one of them Robbie's dad.'

'Aye, but come on, this is Noodsy we're talking about. He's admitting his part in trying to get rid of the bodies, but can you honestly see him killing anybody? Robbie, different story. He was always a psycho. Murderer would have been what his careers adviser recommended. But Noodsy?'

'It's been twenty years, Martin. How well do you know Noodsy these days? And how well did any of us know each other even then? We're not children anymore. We're none of us who we used to be.'

Martin can't answer that one. He used to be the brainy kid, but right now he's clueless. He used to be impeccably behaved, a walking bundle of conscientiousness and honourable intentions. Now he's a shark in a suit. Or just a prick, to put it more succinctly.

'We're going to have Noodsy's clothes analysed to see who the bloodstains match. If it's all three, it'll make my job a lot simpler.'

'That's what he wanted me for.'

'I'm sorry?'

'He was concerned that the police already had their minds made up and would reach whatever conclusions made their job simpler.'

'I'll reach whatever conclusions the evidence compels, Martin,' she says, stung.

'I wasn't casting any aspersions, just saying this is what he thinks I can do: find out what really happened before he got there.'

'That will be the focus of our investigations, I can assure him. It's just the "before he got there" part we're not ready to accept on merely his word.'

'So you think he did it?'

'All three? I've already said, I—'

'Any of them. Alone, or with Robbie.'

'I don't have enough evidence to think anything yet. What makes you so certain he wouldn't, other than you thought he was an okay guy at school?'

Martin laughs, a little embarrassed, to concede the point. 'I've got nothing but his word. Though Noodsy's never lied to me.'

'The stakes are a bit higher just now.'

'I know. I'm flailing here, I admit it. But the look on his face when I showed up: it was more than just surprise to see me. It was like a glimmer of hope, like he was relieved there was someone here who would believe him.'

'Aye, but that probably says as much about what Noodsy thinks of you as about anything else.'

'You saying I'm a mug?'

She smiles. 'I'm sure you're nobody's mug these days, Martin. You're a lawyer, a media lawyer at that: you could no doubt outstrip us all in the cynicism stakes. But you weren't always so

141

streetwise. Noodsy hadn't seen me in forever, either, but do you know what I saw in his face when I walked in to interview him?'

'What?'

'Despondency. Defeat. Now, I've known the guy as long as you, and I'd have expected his eyes to light up if he thought *me* being the cop meant there was a greater chance of him being believed. Instead, it looked like someone who'd known him so long being the cop meant precisely the opposite. Noodsy's a career criminal, Martin, and quite the wee fly-man. You should see his sheet. He learnt the hard way how not to get the blame. He knows how to play his angles.'

'And you reckon I'm one of them.'

'I'm keeping an open mind. That's my job. Your job is three-hundred-odd miles away. Don't forget that.'

'It's fairly prominent in my mind, I promise you. But I told him I'd try. I gave him my word.'

'And is that worth much these days?'

'It's worth something *to*day.'

She gets up to show him out, walks him to the front entrance.

'It was good to see you again,' he says, with as much sincerity as he can muster.

'You too, Martin. I just wish . . .'

'Yeah, I know.'

They shake hands and he walks down the short outside steps. He's at the bottom when he hears her voice again.

'Martin?'

'Yeah?'

'That Primary Seven debt. You bring me anything you find out, and I'll keep you in the loop my end.'

She looks roughly as sincere as he had hoped to appear a minute ago. He smiles and nods. 'I only did it because I fancied you,' he says. 'But I'll take what's on offer.'

Cursed

Colin sees the ball disappear into a cluster of players near the centre of the park but has little chance of following the play at this point. Everybody is back from lunch, meaning both games are in full swing, most concerningly the Primary Seven match which is right now crowding out his penalty box. It's hard enough to see up the pitch through the ruck of bodies, but his eye is drawn more to the Primary Sevens' ball anyway, and the possibility that it could be driven very hard in his direction at any moment. His task, should that happen, will be the opposite of his bigger counterpart, in that Colin will be leaping to get out of the way of the ball while the Sevens' keeper tries to block it, to say nothing of evading death by stampede should it end up loose in a crowded goalmouth. Martin has sensibly taken up position in front of the eighteen-yard box, with the unspoken understanding that he'll give Colin a shout if play looks like heading their way. Simultaneous attacks on the same goal are Colin's most dreaded scenario: not only can there be as many as three balls to keep track of, but diving even for the tamest of shots is fraught with the danger that you'll launch yourself straight into a sturdy pair of legs that weren't there a split second ago. His greatest fear is hurling himself into a full, mid-air dive while the Primary Seven keeper does the same thing from the opposite direction. It hasn't ever happened, but he can vividly imagine the results, having seen the mess when Jamesy and an older boy, following the flights of different balls, ran into each other and clashed heads. That said, the number of such simultaneous attacks is surprisingly few. This is partly down to the size of the pitch and the time the ball therefore spends in the endless savannah grasslands of midfield, and partly down to the Primary Sevens' tendency just to blooter the smaller boys' ball out of the park any time it gets in their way.

Hearing no warning from Martin, Colin takes a prudent step back behind the goal line as the six-yard area suddenly floods with Primary Sevens. The ball gets hooked away by a defender before the keeper can make his way through the scrum to grab it, and falls for one of the few attackers with the presence of mind to take position a bit further back. He gives it a right welly, but catches it a wee bit too high up the leg, which dampens the impact and kills some of the pace. Despite this, it still runs nicely off his shin and along his foot in a ski-jump effect, giving it enough loft to clear all the bodies between him and the target. The ball hits the underside of the bar on its way in, which makes the goal look even better. The scorer runs off to celebrate as everyone acknowledges it to have been a cracker, though Colin knows it would have been judged as 'well over' had the game been up in the playground, where anything passing between the jackets at more than shoulder height is the

144

subject of dispute.

The goalmouth clears as the attackers retreat and await the kick-out, the mass of players dispersing just in time for Colin to see his own game's ball sent up the wing for Jamesy to chase. Jamesy is one of the best dribblers (or most ball-greedy bastards, depending on whether his efforts come to anything) and likes to take the ball out wide where there's space to generate some momentum. He's having a pretty good game today, and has been instrumental in a few goals as well as scoring two, but there's no way he's getting to this ball before Martin. Normally Colin would be calling to Martin to pass it back for him to pick up, but there are still a few Primary Seven stragglers who might get in the way or even take a gratuitous swipe at it.

'First-time it!' he shouts instead.

Martin judges the bounce and runs on to it, swinging his leg for the big punt up the park, or at least that's where it would have gone if Martin didn't have a foot like a ten-bob bit. He gets a meaty enough dig at it, so it's not lacking in range, but it slices well wide to the right, off the pitch and clear of the high perimeter wall.

'Aw, shite,' is the most popular response, mainly after the checking of watches and realisation that the bell is going to sound well before the ball makes it back on to the pitch.

This probable timescale is bound to be prominent in Martin's mind, too. Colin remembers how much he was crapping it when he managed to send a drop-kick over the outside wall, and that was without the added pressure of a ticking clock. You're not allowed to go outside the school

145

grounds during school hours, and you're particularly warned off going over the wall because the adjoining enclosure is a derelict wasteground. From what Colin saw of it when he was searching for the stray Mitre, there was nothing more dangerous about the place than some broken glass and jaggy nettles, but in the teachers' eyes it was littered with unseen deathtraps and therefore utterly forbidden to enter. How else you were meant to get your ball back, they neglected to say (and there was certainly no recorded instance of one of *them* bothering their arses to go and retrieve the situation, especially as they had a flakey if you ever so much as chapped the staff-room door during a break), but their position on the matter was underlined by the threat of the belt if you got caught doing it. That was what Colin had been scared of when he had been forced to scale the wall, far more than any accident that might befall him in the act of climbing or in traversing the Cursed Earth beyond.

Thinking about it, he couldn't remember anyone ever getting caught, what with it being well out of sight of the staff room, but the chances of being spotted by a teacher were massively increased as soon as that bell went, which it duly did before Martin had even got a leg-up.

Sometimes folk play on for a wee while after the bell, banking on the teachers taking a few minutes before calling in the lines, but this risks Harris having one of her periodic crackdowns. The Primary Sevens thus keep playing; but, with their ball out of bounds, most of the Fives and Sixes cut their losses and head for the lines. Only Colin, out of solidarity, and Graham Wilson, whose ball it is,

146

hang around to wait for Martin.

Colin looks back and forth from the wall to the playground at the other side of the pitch. The lines are forming, steadily fewer Sevens still playing their game of brinkmanship with the teachers. Every second raises the stakes. Being missing from the lines is big trouble, to say nothing of the clearer line of sight to the wall afforded from the top of the steps where the teachers stand to take in the classes. Suddenly Colin hears a thump, and with an accuracy sadly lacking from his earlier attempted clearance, Martin hoofs the ball back over on to the grass. The waiting Graham catches it cleanly and immediately starts haring towards the lines. There's another agonising wait before Martin finally reappears, his eyes fixed on the Main Building doors as he clambers over the wall. He jumps rather than drapes back down, visibility being a far greater concern than physical safety, landing on all fours. Colin offers a hand to help him up the slope, then they both sprint towards the playground.

Their pace slackens as they near the concrete, the sense of urgency suddenly diminished as soon as they can see that there are no teachers there yet, and far fewer folk already in the lines than it looked to panicked eyes. They even start to catch up with some stragglers from their own game, confident about their comparative safety even from Harris as long as there are still Primary Sevens playing on the grass. One of them is Paul, who seems to have the attention of four or five other boys. News travels fast, Colin thinks. It's probably less than half an hour since the incident, but he's already got folk who missed it gathering round to hear about him giving Robbie a doing for stealing his goal.

Colin hurries again, wanting to hear a bit of this—and the reaction to it—before the lines get called and they all have to be quiet. Everybody knows Robbie is a sneaky wee shite, so they're bound to be lapping it up. But as he nears the group he can tell something is wrong. Paul is trying to walk away, but they keep moving to surround him. Then he hears what's being said.

'Come on, Space Boy,' says one. 'Tell us whit planet you're fae again.'

'Naw, better no annoy him,' cautions another. 'He might use his special powers on us.'

'Have you got a ray gun in the hoose, Space Boy.'

'Does your mammy run ye tae school in a starship?'

Paul finally breaks through their circle and escapes to the relative obscurity of the class lines, but the reprieve will only be temporary. Colin knows that this is merely the beginning. He looks along the line and sees Robbie, the boys next to him glancing conspiratorially at Paul. That's what he had run off to tell the new arrivals, what he was busy telling everybody. Down on the pitch, he didn't appear to be paying attention, but the sly wee bastard must have heard every word, and had put it to devastatingly effective use. His doing from Paul was all but forgotten, and certainly relegated down the gossip agenda. It was now just a daft dispute over who scored a goal, whereas this, this was serious slagging material. Just as he had on the pitch, Robbie had nicked in at the last moment and stolen from Paul with a decisive final touch. And

148

this time, there would be no adjudication from a senior figure to put it straight.

The Laws of the Game (Part Two)

Martin comes around to the sound of water running, somebody having a shower in an adjacent room, to which the door is ajar. He opens his eyes, takes in his unfamiliar surroundings, remembers where he is. Remembers what he's doing here. What he *did* here.

Aw, Christ.

*   *   *

Karen is playing Chinese ropes with Helen, Alison and Michelle, just outside the shed in the girls' area of the playground. Joanne is hanging about between the poles, just out the way of where Zoe and her pals are playing balls against the inside shed wall. Joanne's face is tripping her because she's just got back from lunch and found Alison already joined in someone else's game. Joanne is, of course, welcome to play Chinese ropes too, but she doesn't want to because she's pure rubbish at it. She's all right at normal ropes, as long as you do it shoo-shaggy, which is just back and forth, or if you're doing it fullsy-roundsies not too fast, but Chinese ropes is different. It's not really a rope at all, but a long chain of interlinked and different-coloured elastic bands, and you don't swing it: two of you hold it up, higher each time, and the other girl has to get her leg over it and pull it down so

149

she can step across. Karen is good at it because she has long legs, but Michelle is even better despite being shorter, because she's double-jointed. She does gymnastics on Saturday mornings at the sports centre and can stretch her leg dead high. Alison isn't as good at it as Karen or Michelle, but she's got this twisting jump technique that looks amazing, like a ballet dancer or something. Karen sometimes pulls the chain that bit lower if it looks like Alison's leg isn't going to make it over, because she likes to see the wee bow Alison does when she succeeds. Helen is the weest and can't do above shoulder height, but she loves playing it anyway. It's her ropes, in fact, so it's not that she's just joining in because she can't get a game at anything else.

Joanne stands nearby, kidding on she's not bothered, like she just happens to be passing, maybe on her way to joining in the hopscotch game down at the far end, but inside she's fizzing. She will join in eventually, Karen knows, though only after she's made a few failed attempts to get everyone—and especially Alison—away to play something else. But this isn't just because Joanne doesn't like Chinese ropes. She'd be fine about playing it if it had been her and Alison's game and she could then say who was allowed to join in. This, however, is Helen's game, and with Alison already a part of it—to say nothing of Karen being involved, too—Joanne's nose is well out of joint.

Joanne and Alison have always been friends, going right back to Primary One, but of late Joanne seems to have become very defensive about her playing with anyone else. Joanne always wants to be playing with Alison alone, though she'll settle for a game with a select few others as long as she and Alison are in charge. Well, you hear her saying she and Alison are in charge, when really it's only Joanne who is, but she likes to stress her and Alison's togetherness. Alison isn't bossy and she doesn't share Joanne's enthusiasm for cliping on people; nor does she seem so bothered these days about claiming first place in the lines. It tends to be the case that Joanne drags her along to the steps as soon as—and sometimes well before—the bell goes, just as it tends to be the case that Joanne will immediately seek out Alison wherever she is in the playground, but Alison will never make a point of seeking out Joanne. This is something Karen has started to notice since she and Alison started playing together more, and it doesn't appear to have slipped Joanne's attention either.

It's weird and annoying. Michelle and Carol are best friends but neither of them gets all pushy if one of them starts playing with somebody else. Nor have they got anything against Alison playing with them even though they have this long-standing rivalry about the class lines. Helen and Karen have been special friends since that time they played round at her house on the day of the fire. They play at each other's house now on some weekends and quite a lot over the holidays, but sometimes they can go for days without joining in the same stuff in the playground, and that doesn't mean they've fallen out.

Joanne, however, seems to think that if you're friends with one person, you can't be friends with someone else. Or at least that Alison shouldn't be. Joanne has never looked favourably on Michelle, given their epic battles to front the lines, so Alison

151

being involved in a game of Chinese ropes with her is betrayal enough, but it's Karen's presence that has really got her chubby cheeks aglowing.

'You're trying to take Alison away from me.' That's what she said to Karen last week when Joanne tracked the pair of them down to the grass banking at the far side of the football field. The banking slopes down quite steeply to the high wall at the bottom, and it's a quiet place to go if you just want to sit and talk. You get to sit on grass instead of concrete, plus, unlike the flat grass at the other side of the pitch, you are in little danger of getting hit by a ball, because if you sit well down the banking, it usually goes over your head. Alison had suggested they go there 'for a picnic' because she had an apple and a poke of crisps left over from her packed lunch and it was unusually mild and sunny for the time of year.

'You want Alison tae be your friend? Well, she's *my* friend, *right*?'

Karen had been baffled by this outburst, and from the look on Alison's face, it was clear she didn't entirely follow the logic, either.

'I'm not trying to take her away. We're just having a picnic.'

'Aye, well, you'd better not, right? C'mon, Alison. The bell's gaunny go any minute.'

'I want to finish my apple,' Alison argued, while Joanne stood over her, glowering.

'That Carol and Michelle will be on their way to the steps already,' Joanne warned.

'Well, we'll end up second anyway, then, won't we?' countered Alison.

Whether she would have stayed and defied Joanne, Karen never discovered, because the bell did ring at that point. For Joanne, though, this sacrilegious sentiment was enough to set off her alarms and to confirm Karen as an undesirable influence and her new worst enemy.

And now Alison is playing Chinese ropes with her!

Joanne stands and watches for a while longer, then inevitably makes her bid. 'Alison, I'm finished my lunch now. Comin to play houses?' she suggests. It's a confident and cunning gambit, subliminally suggesting to Alison that she was, whether she knew it or not, only doing this to kill time until her true friend was ready. It also contains a less subliminal insult to her competitors and how they choose to fill their precious playing time. It almost deserves to succeed for its sheer audacity, but alas, Joanne has concentrated too much on strategy and not enough on timing. It's Alison's turn to jump, and she's on a roll. If she was standing holding one end, she might be tempted, but not while she's feeling confident of breaking that chin-height threshold for a new personal best.

'I'm playing Chinese ropes,' she responds, betraying just a little impatience at having to state the obvious.

'Okay,' Joanne accepts. She plays it poker-faced, only a tightening of her folded arms indicating an increased determination after this rebuff.

Joanne gives it another wee while, waiting until Alison tries—and fails—in her next attempt, before informing her that 'There's a brilliant game of hopscotch goin on over there, really, really good. Come we'll join in?'

'It's my turn to hold,' Alison explains, an

obligation towards her fellow players offered by way of letting Joanne down gently. 'Why don't you have a game? Can Joanne have a game?' she asks Helen, whose game it officially is due to rope ownership.

'Yeah, come and join in, Joanne,' says Helen, who is always far nicer to everybody than a lot of them deserve.

Joanne has a look on her face that suggests she'd rather go and lick the railings, but she knows she can't walk away now without losing face. 'Aye, okay. But don't make it too high.'

Joanne waits until Helen has had a shot and then takes her turn, with Karen and Alison holding. They start the chain at kneesies, which even Joanne can manage, then move up to hipsies (or bumsies, as they call it when they're feeling giggly). Joanne's cheeks seem to expand with effort and determination as she takes a wee runny-up and hurls an ankle on top of the chain. Her foot gets over but her trailing leg is slow, and the elastic snaps upwards again between her thighs. It tugs her pleated skirt and shows her knickers for a few moments before she grabs the rope with both hands and untangles herself.

Alison says, 'Woooo!' at the sight of her exposed underwear. Folk always say, 'Woooo!' or do that wheet-whee whistle if you accidentally show your pants. Sometimes you get a beamer, but it depends who else is around; you usually just laugh if it's only girls. They all laugh on this occasion, including some of the girls playing balls in the shed. All, that is, except Joanne, who looks furious. She takes a short couple of steps nearer the shed and jabs an angry finger at Zoe, who is still

154

bouncing balls off the wall and, as far as Karen can tell, may not even have been paying attention.

'It's just lassies that saw it,' Joanne says indignantly. 'An it was just pants. At least I never showed aff ma fanny tae Kevin Duffy.'

Oh, God, this one again, Karen thinks. And Zoe wasn't even among those laughing.

The story had gone round in whispers a couple of weeks back and nobody was much inclined to believe anything Kevin Duffy said, but Joanne had seized upon it like it was a ten-bob bit in the gravel. She was always looking for something that was 'a pure slaggin' for some poor soul, and which could be used to encourage others to say they weren't friends with whoever it was, as being friends with certain people was a pure slaggin, too. Poor Eleanor was the ultimate example. She might be tolerated to join in games, but nobody wanted to be officially friends with her because she was smelly. Karen always felt guilty about how Eleanor was treated, and tried to be nice to her whenever the occasion arose, but the sad truth was that Eleanor wasn't very easy to be nice to. She was always sour and suspicious, and Karen knew that no matter how hard she tried or how much she felt it might be the right thing to do, they weren't going to be friends. However, nor would she ever join in when people were being horrible to her, such as calling her Smeleanor, or when they played bugsy touch, about which Eleanor (it was perhaps wrongly assumed) was oblivious.

As well as Eleanor, there was, of course, Geraldine, who physically couldn't even join in most of the games, at least not with enough effectiveness as to make it worthwhile. Lots of the girls were friends with Geraldine, but she was still on the end of a lot of slagging and therefore relegated to this social subset that Joanne was always looking to add to. It didn't take much. Helen was an attempted target, her pure slagging being that she once called the teacher Mummy back in Primary Four. In Karen's case, as well as mistakenly identifying herself as Helen on her first day, she had, of course, peed herself when she got overexcited at Zoe bursting her milk. Fortunately, as the years passed, fewer and fewer children saw any profit in raking it up again. Karen got the impression Joanne was disappointed that the incident hadn't had a permanently blemishing effect, as though she believed it should have been widely regarded as forever putting her on a par with Eleanor, wet pants for life.

Now it was Zoe she thought could be eternally disgraced by the shame of a boy claiming to have seen her private parts.

'I never showed him anything,' Zoe protests.

'That's no what *we* heard. You were stayin at his hoose and you pulled up your nightie an everythin.'

'Get tae France.'

'Come on,' appeals Alison, everyone having already seen this picture a few times. 'It's your turn to hold, Joanne.'

Zoe turns around to resume bouncing her balls, advised by her friends to 'just ignore her'. Joanne, still visibly fuming, takes hold of the chain from Michelle.

Michelle starts from hipsies and makes it as far as nosies before failing at head height. This is an unusual setback, but may have something to do with Joanne holding her end almost at full stretch above—rather than on top of—her head. Michelle rolls her eyes at Karen as she steps aside, aware of what happened, but she doesn't say anything. She knows she'll get another turn when Joanne's not holding, so it's not worth making a fuss. It pays off, too, as Joanne simply gets on with it for a while and restricts her remarks to complimenting Alison on having the best technique.

Karen expects Joanne to repeat her antics when she is making her own bid at head height, but she keeps the rope where it's supposed to be. Karen hitches her skirt up a wee bit to allow her legs the maximum stretch, but she doesn't make the jump. Joanne's eyes are bulging and she looks like she's bursting to contain her glee as she observes Karen's failed attempt. However, to Karen's surprise, she says, 'Hard luck,' and even offers to stay holding and give up her own shot so that Karen can try again. She can be nice when she tries, though it probably helps that right now she sees it as the best way of keeping in with Alison.

Karen gives it another go. She can sometimes do head height, sometimes not, but she was really close with that last attempt. She bounces on the spot instead of a runny and swings her right leg up as high as she can. She can tell she's made it because she feels the elastic tug on the right side of her ankle. But just as she's twisting her hips to complete the jump, she feels the chain shoot up between her legs and sees Joanne yanking it as high and as hard as she can. It's not sore and it doesn't trip her over or anything, but it pulls her skirt up like happened to Joanne, and exposes her knickers. Knickers that Joanne must have caught a glimpse of before, hence her eye-popping, hence

157

her generous offer, and hence her wheeching the rope up her skirt.

'Ah-ha-ha. Check the colour of Karen's pants. They're all bluey. They've been washed wrang. Ah-ha. Bluey pants. That's a pure slaggin. Karen's mammy doesnae wash her pants right. That's a pure slaggin. Imagine wearin pants that havenae been washed right. Probably means they're smelly as well. Poo-ee.'

'Right, you're not playing this game anymore,' decides Michelle, even though it's Helen's game. 'Go on, get. You're bein horrible to Karen. Away and play with somebody else.'

Joanne doesn't contest this, nor is she likely to see it as any great loss, as she's not getting Alison to herself anyway. She stomps away in search of, Karen is sure, a more receptive audience for this monumental piece of news.

'Just ignore her,' Michelle says, echoing the advice Zoe received a few minutes ago.

Karen nods and says she will, but she can't get Joanne's look of triumph out of her head, can't shake the fear that this time she's got something she can really work with. Anything that gets your underwear on to the playground agenda is potentially damaging, but add the issue of cleanliness and, well . . . Truth was you didn't add the issue of cleanliness in these things—you *multiplied* by it. And while it didn't have any impact on Karen's standing with Helen, Michelle or even the coveted Alison, it wasn't Karen's friends that Joanne was hoping to influence.

Sparring

It's last night. He's in the Railway Inn to meet Scot, to catch up; on each other and in Martin's case on twenty years of Noodsy. The Railway was Scotty's call. Martin is checked into the Sheraton in Glasgow and would have preferred to meet somewhere in town. Scot was working in Paisley, however, and anyway still lives in Braeside, though not exactly in his old neighbourhood. Not in the 'new hooses', either, but in one of the big Victorian places right up on the brae itself, bordering farmland. The Haunted Mansions, they used to call them when they were weans, because few dwellings in the town predated the Second World War, and not even the private modern houses had any such imposing stature. Martin is kind of curious to see round the place, but figures he might have some making up, never mind catching up, to do before Scotty is likely to extend an invite. He is curious to see Helen, too. He missed the wedding because he was on holiday in Australia at the time, and that was fifteen years ago. He's never seen the kids, the oldest of whom must be— *Jesus*—thirteen.

He actually thought Scot's choice of the Railway might be part of his penance for the other night. Martin has only ever been in it a couple of times before, having left town by the time he was old enough to go drinking. Indeed, being of a legal age to drink would have made him a comparative coffin-dodger among the Railway's contemporary clientele. It was the place everybody boasted about

159

getting served in when he was at St Grace's; basically a school disco with a licence. Staff must have been under orders not to bother about ID and the polis must have been on back-handers. It was a garish kaleidoscope of metallic colours inside, the surfaces thus presumably easier to mop clean of blood and sick. Wall-to-wall with blootered underage neds and blootered underdressed lassies, clutching glasses of Pernod and blackcurrant as they danced under a glitterball to the latest Stock, Aitken and Waterman prole music. There was a special shuttle service to Paisley at closing time, straight to the Royal Alexandra, blue light all the way.

From where he's sitting now, it's hard to believe it's the same place. Brass pumps stand proudly along the lacquered hardwood bar. The floorboards are stripped and polished, broad beams once hidden beneath floor tiles and lino, and thus protected from the indignities of a thousand teenage spews and as many burst noses. The vinyl-upholstered benches are gone, high stools hugging shallow wooden shelves around the walls, framed black-and-whites of Braeside past hung a few feet above the pints and ashtrays. Not only is it difficult to imagine how the same room used to look; it's hard to imagine it ever looked different from this in the century since the inn first opened for business.

He normally drinks bottles of Dos Equis or, at the scruffiest, Becks when he's out in London, but he orders a pint of Eighty Shilling because it seems appropriate. It goes down quickly, partly because it's good and he's well ready for it under the circumstances, and partly because he's on his own and there's nothing else to do. He's about finished it when his mobile rings. It's Scotty, to say, redundantly, that he's running late at work. Martin finishes the pint and is about to get up for a refill when one is placed down on the table in front of him, along with a glass of red wine.

'This one is on the house,' says their bearer. 'We don't often have somebody famous in the place, so I thought we should make the most of it.'

She pulls up a chair and sits down next to him. He'd been served by someone else, a bloke, and had only caught a side-on glimpse of her at the bar. He'd noted the skirt suit with some approval, though it was an approval he tended to accord to any woman who had managed to reach her mid-thirties without doubling the size of her arse; and within that there was an equally broad subset of those dressing at all more stylish than a char-woman going on-shift. Kara wasn't wrong about him fucking anyone with a hint of fame and glamour; she'd just overestimated how much glamour was required to meet his minimum.

She seems familiar, and is clearly very sure of his identity, but he can't place her. She's got long, straightened black hair, dyed but stylishly so, framing a face that he considers passably attractive but which nonetheless is pricking a more repellent instinctive response. She's bringing him a drink, she's smiling and he's already cursorily given her the thumbs-up on his personal, semiconscious 'would you?' test. Yet something is telling him to be wary. Something is telling him he doesn't like her.

'Have you forgotten who I am, Martin?' she asks, enjoying her advantage. 'Or do you know fine and you're blankin me?'

'A bit of both,' he says, poker-faced, his unease making him reluctant to turn on even the auto-charm. 'I can't quite place you. It's been a long time.'

'Tell you what, I'll take it as a compliment.' She's smiling still, but it's not entirely warm, and nor is she in a hurry to give up what she's dangling over him.

He thinks of a cat playing with its prey. Then it hits him. 'JoJo,' he says.

She nods slowly, looking very pleased with herself, as well she might. No wonder he couldn't place her. She slimmed down a bit in her teens, but he'd have expected her to blow up again later in life. Back when she was Queen B (for bitch) of the trendy crowd, he used to picture her a few years down the line with a couple of chubby kids at her feet, an arse wider than her garage and tits bouncing off her knees. She's not skinny; she doesn't have that emaciated over-compensatory look of the obsessive slimming zealot. Instead, she's just well proportioned, allied to a confidence about her movement and poise suggesting her more streamlined shape isn't something she has recently acquired. He remembers somebody saying she had the kind of face that would be pretty if she lost weight, but at the time he never bought it because he couldn't divorce the face from the person. Now, he'd have to admit they had a point. There's still a cruelty to her visage, however. Okay, maybe that's too harsh, but an archness, at least, suggesting even if she wasn't cruel, she wouldn't be particularly merciful, either.

'You're looking . . . different,' he says, about as

162

much of a compliment as he can bring himself to deliver.

'Not the same you, either, is it? Look at this suit. Clocked the shoes, too. Quite the metropolitan these days, aren't you? Of course, I suppose you always have to be at your best in case there's a photographer about to jump oot and snap ye.'

Christ. 'Yeah. I also do a bit of legal work,' he says tiredly. 'Yourself?'

'Well, sorry to disappoint. I know you'd love to hear I'm a career barmaid, but I own the pub.'

'Why would that disappoint me? What, are you still calling me a snob because I'm a brainy kid fae the bought hooses?'

'Oh, come on,' she says, stalling the wineglass halfway to her mouth. 'You tellin me you never have a wee smug thought to yourself about how much better you've done than all the folk who gave you a hard time?'

'Cannae say it's prominent in my mind when I'm locked in contract negotiations, no. That's such a small-town way of thinking.'

'Aye, I suppose. You couldnae wait to get oot the place, leave all us nobodies behind.'

'When did I ever say . . . You know, JoJo, the irony is, I always got called a snob, when I never actually did or said anything snobbish. You were the one who looked down on me. You made simplistic assumptions, thought there was nothing more to me than being the brainy kid.'

'And you assumed because you were brainy that everybody else was thick.'

'I never looked down on anybody, JoJo.'

'Perhaps not when you were at St Lizzie's, Martin, but you did later on. By God, you did. You

163

were just too right-on to admit it to yourself.'

'Christ, free drinks *and* psychoanalysis. Service in this place is fantastic, though I'll maybe just take a poke of crisps with my next pint.' He looks at his watch, cursing Scot for his choice of venue and doubly so for the bastard still not being here.

'You here to meet Scot? Cursin him tae, I bet.'

'How do you—'

'Naebody else you could be meetin. I know why you're here as well. '

'Bad news travels fast.'

'Aye.' She nods. 'Nae surprise that Johnny Turner got himself murdered. More a shock aboot Colin.'

'Nae surprise aboot Robbie either, I guess. More a shock aboot Noodsy.'

'Mmm,' she says, but she doesn't look so sure. 'I'll tell you this: if that Karen Gillespie wants to know a thing or two aboot this toon, she should ask me. Cannae see it happenin, though, can you?'

'You two were never exactly a mutual appreciation society. I don't remember the details, I stayed well clear and took no sides.'

'No sides, naw, but I bet you wish it was her instead of me sittin here the noo.' She grins, lapping up his discomfort.

'So what should she be asking you about?' he says, just the first thing he can think of to head off where she's taking this.

'Anything. I'm a big Nosy Parker that runs a pub.'

He laughs politely. 'I think what you've done with the place is amazing, by the way.'

'Aye, I'm very proud of it. Not in the same league as the swanky places you and your celeb

164

mates hang out in doon in London, but it'll do us small-town thinkers.'

And that's how it goes on. They sip their drinks and spar. There are polite smiles on their faces but neither of them says anything that isn't laced with bitterness. Every statement is guarded, barbed, conceding no territory in a retrospective battle for the moral high ground. But it's compelling too, a contest neither wants to lose or abandon.

Martin doesn't know how long has passed when his mobile rings again: this conversation could have been ten minutes that felt like an hour or vice versa. It's Scotty again. Whatever's up at work is no nearer resolution. He apologises, says they'll meet tomorrow, which is Saturday, after all.

JoJo needs to hear only one side of the call to know the situation. She's looking at him when he hangs up. 'So,' she says. 'You for the off, or can I get you another?'

Violence

Karen considers it testimony to how highly Joanne values her new pure-slaggin material that she has relinquished first place in the line—even without competition today from Carol and Michelle—in order to spend more time spreading the big news. Her comparatively late arrival also affords her a spot in the queue better positioned to broadcast it further, as up front would have presented a buffer of unsympathetic parties between her and fresh ears.

She doesn't get a unanimous response, as plenty

165

of the girls are doubtless also the shame-faced owners of twin-tub casualties and either uneasy or simply unconvinced about its stigmatic status. But there are still enough who are happy to latch on to it for the sake of their favourite bloodsport. Predictably, the most squealingly delighted is Geraldine. These days she has to endure far less taunting herself, since the discovery that her bulk could be a source of intimidation as much as ridicule, but she still knows how she is generally regarded and is therefore seldom slow to embrace anything that makes somebody else the target.

Thus encouraged, Joanne is going for the ultimate test of a slagging's substance by attempting to transmit it across the great divide into the boys' line. This is an undertaking with a very low success rate, given that these are two cultures trading in entirely separate currencies, but she evidently reckons it's well worth the risk of failure for the potential pay-off.

'Have yous heard?' she asks, having finally grabbed some of the boys' attention. 'Karen's pants arenae washed right. She's wearin mingin pants, bad as Eleanor. Mibbe it's actually been Karen that smells all along and we've been blamin Eleanor by mistake.'

Karen wants to ignore it, let them assume it's just the latest dribblings from Joanne's incessant gub, but she senses the danger. The Eleanor comparisons are damaging enough, but putting doubt in folks' heads as to who the source of the smells is could have long-term consequences.

'She's talkin mince,' Karen says, trying not to sound too angry, because it's unwise to let your classmates sense your buttons have been pushed.

'They just got a bit dyed cause they were in the twin-tub with a blue T-shirt.'

'See?' Joanne responds triumphantly. 'She's even admittin herself her knickers arenae washed properly.'

'They're washed fine. They just—'

'Ah-haaa. Cannae be washed fine, you just said so yoursel.'

In the main, the boys' eye-rolling indifference is the standard indicator that the news hasn't made the leap. Only one of them appears to be interested, though worryingly it is Scot Connolly, who has what Karen's gran would call 'a wicked tongue in his heid'. 'So Karen's knickers went funny cause they went in the wash with somethin else?' he asks Joanne, smiling and glancing along the line at Karen, too. She feels a lump in her stomach. 'Well, at least naebody can say that aboot you, eh?' he adds.

'Too right,' she affirms with a smug nod.

'Naw. Cause your mammy can only fit your knickers in the machine wan at a time.'

Karen now has a new hero. This decisively ends Joanne's foray across the void and serves as a warning shot to Geraldine, too. Karen offers Scot a smile by way of thanks, but he has already turned away to lap up the laughter of his mates.

Joanne's response to this rebuff, however, is simply a renewed effort to consolidate her successes on the girls' side. This one is too good to be allowed to slip away, and she looks fiercely determined—desperate, even—to capitalise fully. Everybody has heard Scot's remark, which threatens to shift the focus, so she needs to act quickly, and she does. With the teachers still not back to take in the lines, she skips a few places along the queue and touches Eleanor on the shoulder. 'Bugsy touch!' she whispers as she skips away, waving her right hand in the air.

Bugsy touch is kind of like tig, where you have to touch somebody else to get rid of it, but whereas tig is just a harmless game, there is something nasty about bugsy touch, because it's supposed to be Eleanor's bugs that you've got. The spiteful element of it doesn't stop there, either. Unlike tig, it tends not to take place in the wider range of the playground, but during the lines, where there is limited scope for movement, and with the added suspense that the teachers may appear at any second, at which point everyone must stand still, leaving someone with the bugs. That person then gets treated by the others as if they were truly smelly, and it's an excuse to come out with things even the worst of them wouldn't say directly to Eleanor, though she is likely to be in earshot.

Joanne knows well that Karen is one of the girls who won't join in. This sometimes leaves Karen with the bugsy touch because she refuses to pass it on, but other times someone else will touch her in order to get the game going again among those who want to be involved. There is a cluster of such refuseniks towards the front of the line, causing the game to restrict itself to Joanne's immediate vicinity and greatly reducing the chances that it will be Karen who ends up tainted. However, the very fact that Joanne does not seem frustrated by this is what really has Karen worried, something not eased by Joanne contriving to end up with the bugs when the teachers appear.

It's Mrs Cook and Mrs Henderson, who teach

the Primary Fours. The Fives will therefore get sent in first, as the teachers will send their own classes in last and accompany them to their respective rooms. This means that there is no adult escort as they make their way inside and up the stairs to Miss O'Connor's class. Consequently, Karen is able to continue chatting to Helen and Michelle, and has forgotten about the threat from Joanne by the time she reaches the classroom, already turning her worries to whether she'll remember her Catechism answers that she tried to memorise last night.

The Catechism is a wee green book full of things that are like prayers, in that they are all about God and Jesus and all that, except they come in the form of questions and answers, whereas prayers are a bit more like poems. Miss O'Connor assigns them three or four Catechism answers a week, to be tested on Thursday afternoon. The problem with this is that if you memorise them too early in the week, you can have forgotten them by Thursday, and if you leave it until later, you can forget to do it altogether. This has happened to Karen a couple of times, and it is an utterly horrible sensation when you realise as you walk in after lunchtime; but sometimes even though she has learnt the answers, she forgets bits when it comes to reciting them, because Miss O'Connor is quite scary and makes her nervous. Miss O'Connor asks at random, so you can be lucky and get asked after a few other people, which refreshes your memory. But if you get the answers wrong, you have to copy them all out ten times for the next day. This itself is not a particularly arduous sanction, but the tongue-lashing that comes with it is far worse. What's on Karen's mind as she approaches their class is that Miss O'Connor has been in a horrible mood all day, and that's without anybody doing anything to make her angry.

Karen is rehearsing her answers in her head when Joanne suddenly appears at her side, taps her on the shoulder and declares: 'Eeeew! That's Karen got Eleanor's smelly bugs *and* her own. Double bugsy touch! Eeeew!'

Karen goes to her desk, trying to shrug it off, but some of the girls filing past are holding their noses or doing wafting gestures in front of their faces. She glances at Joanne as she sits down two rows along, and sees her grimace like she's about to be sick, though all the while her eyes are indicating how much she's loving it.

Karen feels this exasperated rage thrill through her. It's not a hurt, not a recoil from being singled out, but an offended certainty that she just shouldn't have to be putting up with this. She can hear Helen once again advise that she 'just ignore her', but while she finds Joanne's antics pathetic, she really grudges her the pleasure she's taking, and wants very much to stop it. She looks to the open door and listens carefully above the low-level chatter of the class taking their seats, searching for the sound of Miss O'Connor's approach. You can always hear her coming because she wears these high heels that go clack-clack against the stairs as she comes up them. Karen hears no such sound, so there is time to act. She doesn't want to lower herself to the level of the bugsy touch game, but equally she doesn't want Joanne to have the satisfaction of sitting there mugging at her all afternoon.

Karen gets up and runs not to Joanne, but to Geraldine, who has just squeezed herself into the otherwise ample space between her desk and the connected bench. She brushes the top of Geraldine's head and then makes her way quickly to Joanne.

'Well, if I've got the double bugsy touch,' she says, 'you can have the double tubby touch,' and slaps her on the upper arm.

Joanne grabs where Karen has just hit her and cowers her head into her chest, shrieking and moaning in a manner massively disproportionate to the force Karen used. It seems a ridiculous— even potentially embarrassing—reaction, until a voice sounds shrilly behind Karen and turns her insides to ice: 'Karen Gillespie! Get away from there and go to my desk, *at once*!'

Karen turns to see Miss O'Connor standing just outside in the corridor, next to the other Primary Five teacher Mrs Robertson, from whose class she has apparently just emerged.

Karen barely breathes as she makes her way to the desk. Miss O'Connor closes the door with a room-silencing slam and then redundantly calls the class to order. Then she walks slowly to her desk and sits down, waiting a few seconds before looking at Karen, who can feel herself physically trembling.

'I won't tolerate violence in my classroom,' she says. 'Go directly to Mrs Harris and tell her I need to borrow her belt.'

*　　　*　　　*

It takes ages for Karen to return. Feels like ages to

171

Martin, anyway, and must feel much longer for Karen. They're doing the Catechism Inquisition, as Scotty calls it. O'Connor makes out she picks folk in random order, but Martin knows that's pish. He never gets picked until near the end because he never forgets to learn the answers, and the more folk who come out with the right responses early on, the easier it is for those who are called later to pick them up. This just proves she's more interested in catching folk out than in them learning the Catechism, because otherwise what would it matter if a few kids picked up the answers from hearing their classmates? The end result would still be that they knew their stuff.

Everybody hates O'Connor. Folk think you must like the teacher if you're clever or if you never get into trouble, but they're wrong. Martin thinks it's the other way round: that he hates her more than most because he's giving his best and still gets met with a sour-faced scowl from a woman who seems to be in an eternal bad mood. It's not because she's strict; Clarke was strict, and he didn't hate her. Teachers ought to be strict if they're doing their job properly (Mrs Ford is known as a push-over, and any time Martin's seen her class when on an errand, it has looked pure murder). But O'Connor's nasty streak belongs more among the weans than the staff.

Sending Karen to fetch the belt herself, for instance. That's just sick. And she always does it, too, though it wouldn't surprise him if she had her own belt and sent folk anyway. Scotty got it a few weeks back. He said going to Harris's office and bringing it back was far worse than the belting itself. This was something she was undoubtedly aware of, seeing as she went on enough about the Romans' cruelty in making Jesus carry his own cross.

Well seeing O'Connor never asked Joanne if she was all right. She knew fine Joanne was acting it, but O'Connor's been in a horrible mood—even by her standards—all day, and was just looking for someone to take it out on.

It's a disgrace. If anybody deserves the belt, never mind a wee slap on the arm, it's that cow Joanne, and he's not just saying that because she's nasty to him and calls him Professor Brainbox. Martin knows you're not supposed to be cruel about people's appearances, but he can't help thinking Fat Joanne has never looked so ugly as she does right then when Karen finally walks back in carrying the belt. Her face is a truly unflattering mixture of delight, satisfaction and cruelly eager anticipation.

Poor Karen. You can tell she's suffering and has spent all of her gloomy errand trying with all her might not to cry. She's not blubbing, but her eyes are moist and Martin can see streaks on her cheeks. He hasn't really paid her any particular attention before. The boys don't talk much to the girls, so you usually notice only the ones that for whatever reason stand out or make themselves the centre of attention. Karen isn't super-brainy, like Helen, or thick like Margaret-Mary. Nor is she dead pretty, like Michelle, or pure horrible like Eleanor. But standing there, helpless as she hands over the instrument of her imminent punishment, she's suddenly got Martin feeling all funny inside and wishing he could come to her rescue. He's daydreaming there's some way he could lie to take

173

the blame, and all that would come with it. Wouldn't that be amazing? And then she'd want to kiss him.

*   *   *

There is a reverent hush as Karen is directed to a spot in front of the blackboard and reluctantly puts up her hands, but Colin suspects he's not the only one who is secretly delighted, as he is any time O'Connor decides somebody is for the belt. You feel a bit guilty when it's one of your pals, but it's still an exciting spectacle. The teachers like it, too. Otherwise they would do it out in the corridor, wouldn't they, like he's heard one teacher does at Braeside Primary. Like it? *Love* it. That's why they make the whole thing into an exhibition, with O'Connor even giving it the maximum build-up by sending the victim to Harris for the hardware.

This is the first time it's ever been a girl, though, and it's making him feel a little weird. Good weird, though. O'Connor is the worst teacher they've ever had, and everybody hates her, but there's something about those long black boots she wears that makes him think of the ladies in pantomimes. She's got long black hair, too, like the Wicked Queen in *Snow White*.

Seeing O'Connor—or any of the women teachers—using the belt gives him a feeling he never gets when it's Momo (even though he is the scariest and hits the hardest), and now the prospect of O'Connor giving it to a girl seems to be multiplying whatever it is.

He feels a tightening between his legs and realises he has a stauner.

Robbie hopes she greets. He loves seeing folk get the belt; loves it more when it's someone who's never had it before. He'd fucking love to see a fucking snob like Helen get it. She'd greet, definitely. Or Martin. He'd greet as well. Or Colin. Robbie battered him in Primary Three. Poof. Fucking snobs.

O'Connor brings it down. Hear the swish, hear the crack. Robbie's been told it used to be fours and sixes, and sometimes they'd insist it was the same hand. That would be fuckin *yes*. Just when they're in pure agony, they've got to stick their mitt back up for some more, until it's red-fucking-raw. But the most you ever see now is two, and usually on different hands. Karen's getting two. Clarke only ever gave one, but O'Connor always gives two. She hasn't cried at the first one, but O'Connor's making her wait a wee minute between strokes, giving her time to think about the next one coming, and that might set her off. He really hopes she greets. Come on, greet.

Crack, it comes down again.

Karen doesn't greet, though. Her eyes are all filled up and her throat's pure swollen, but she keeps her face straight as she walks back to her seat.

Then she greets.

Fuckin yes.

* * *

Martin turns over in the bed and sees his clothes

scattered on the floor, the jacket and trousers he worries so much about getting crushed when he pulls on a seatbelt just lying abandoned on the carpet. He instinctively puts a hand to his head, but there's no hangover, and thus no inebriation to mitigate what has happened.

Christ.

He hung up that same jacket, that shirt too, in his wardrobe, the first time he went to bed with Becky Soleno, whose rocketing public profile occasioned that inescapable bloody photo in *Heat*. Two nights ago, he'd at least taken the time to drape his clothes delicately over a chair as he and Kara undressed one another. Last night, however, there had been no room in his thoughts for anything beyond the extremely immediate.

Jesus Christ.

He's had grudge fucks before. Or rather, he thought he had. That floor manager Maria at Carlton, with whom he had all those run-ins; that acid-tongued harpy Emelia on the Sky News legal team. Rechannelled tension, a physical catharsis of selfish, angry sex. There was something almost healthy about that.

Last night, though: *that* was a grudge fuck, thirty years in the making.

How was it possible to have such a good time with someone you hated so much? How was it possible that the mutual dislike and resentment itself should be what made it incomparable?

God almighty. It had been animal. It had been ugly. It had been the absolute antithesis of 'making love'. *Jesus*, even the way they talked to each other was still full of spite and mistrust.

He remembers pulling her bra off, her kneeling

back from him for a second as he looked at her tits.

'Droopy enough?' she asked accusingly. 'Aye, I bet Becky Soleno's don't look like this, though they might do a dozen years and two weans doon the line.'

Martin's response had, in fact, been anything but disdain. They weren't gravity-defying pneumatics, which was definitely no bad thing, but it was needlessly harsh to invite him to agree with the term 'droopy'. If anything, he preferred how they looked—and certainly how they felt—to most of the girls he'd slept with of late. For a start, it was a relief that there was some give when you squeezed them. It even half-occurred to him to say as much, to tell her she would look better than Becky Soleno if there were thirty people working on the photo-shoot for her, too. He didn't, though. When it came to it, he didn't want to sound solicitous or anxious to please. He felt like it would come across as weakness, and that she would in that same moment silently declare victory for herself.

He hears the shower being turned off. Seconds out, next round, the really tough one: facing each other in the daylight. He sits up and gets his bearings. They're at her place, above the pub, a surprisingly sprawling maisonette, testament to the days when the inn offered accommodation to travellers.

He looks at the clock as JoJo emerges, wrapped in a towelling dressing-gown. It's eight-fifteen. 'You're up early,' he says, compelled to say something.

'Aye. Need to be sharper if you want to sneak oot before *I* get up. Kids could be back any time.

177

Well, Alison could. Jason's half-man, half-mattress these days since he hit his teens. But still.'

The details come flooding back. The kids are fourteen and twelve. They stay at their dad's most Fridays, Tam McBride. Martin didn't know him. He was a couple of years older and went to the High. They've been apart for six years. JoJo got the weans and the pub in the divorce.

'It's okay,' he says, swinging his legs out of the bed. 'I know "get out" when I hear it. I don't want to put you in an awkward spot. I'll get my stuff and you can skip to the part where you pretend this didn't happen.'

JoJo shakes her head. 'You really don't think much of me at all, do you? But that's nothin compared to how little you imagine I must think of you. Well, you're wrong. I wasnae very nice to you once upon a time, boo-hoo. A lot of people werenae very nice to me, either. Do we write them off for good? Who the hell wants to be judged for life on how they behaved as kids?'

'Well, Noodsy's putting a lot of store by it,' he replies, buttoning his shirt. 'But otherwise, point taken.'

'We're not the people we were, and we didnae know those people very well, either. Look at Eleanor. All we saw was the wee, smelly, angry lassie. We'd no idea what was behind that. Even Robbie. He was horrible to everybody, but nothin like as horrible as his father and his brothers were tae him. Bad weans don't necessarily turn intae bad adults. And the same goes for the good yins.'

No kidding, he reflects.

On his way out, he passes an open door into JoJo's son's bedroom, catches an eyeful of an

178

image-bedecked teenage wall. There's a St Mirren crest, some yellowing sports-page clippings, posters of Blink 182, The Offspring, Bowling for Soup, Green Day, and a few *FHM* girly pull-outs. Yup, Kara's up there. Jason's wanking off to her when the door's shut.

Martin's had the real thing and Jason's mammy on consecutive nights.

It's appropriate he's at the Railway Inn. His life right now is a fucking train-wreck.

Trespasses Unforgiven

Afternoon playtime lasts only ten minutes, officially, though it can be anything between twelve and fifteen depending on when the teachers decide to bail out of the staff room. It's still not a lot, especially for a game of fitba down on the pitch, where it can sometimes take ages for the ball to make it from one end of the park to the other, and Jamesy is keeping an anxious eye on his watch. He's scored two goals today, both during lunchtime, and is confident he's considered to be having a good game overall, especially that jinky wee run where he got the cross in and Matt Cannon scored with a header. It looked pure gemmie, and Matt didn't forget Jamesy's due, saying, 'Some baw, wee man.' But he'd love to score three, to be able to say he'd got a hat-trick. He'd done it a few times up on the concrete, but the space was smaller and there was always hunners of goals in those games: forty-eight-each affairs. Goals were harder to come by down on the

179

pitch, and it felt more exciting when there were proper lines on the grass, not to mention posts and a crossbar instead of jackets or drainpipes. They were playing with an old brown tube today, too, which made a pleasing 'whump' when you booted it, and was easier to control because it didn't ping around like a plastic ball or even a new leather one. Plus, it never hurt when it got stoated off you, because it was old and all the enamel had come away, leaving only soft leather underneath.

They've been doing a lot of defending because Matt Cannon got kept behind by his teacher. Not only has this weakened their team, but the other lot have had that wee bit of extra purpose as they try to get back from now only two goals down. It's funny how that happens. You can be getting pure scopped and you just play on, not bothered about the score, but then you get a couple back and suddenly everybody's trying harder because there seems something to play for. It's at times like this you need somebody on the park to rally your team, but with Matt absent, nobody really carries enough respect.

Time is leaching away. Worse, they've swapped ends since lunchtime, so the opposition are kicking into the end away from the buildings, which seriously adds to retrieval time after a goal or if it goes behind. The other end is close to the Annexe, the modern one-storey bit joined on to the Main Building, which houses the Primary Sevens and the staff room.

He really wants that third goal. Nobody's scored for his team this playtime, with the other team clawing back their lead, so not only would it complete his hat-trick, but it could be the goal that stops the fightback and ensures victory. The ball has been booted clear a few times, but right over his head, bypassing the midfield and going right to the other end, and that's no use because the only player they've got up there is Robbie. Moochers only mooch because they're shite and they've got no chance of scoring otherwise, so they always get robbed of the ball; either that or they try for goal themselves. Same difference: the ball ends up back in the keeper's hands.

Then, for once, Mick Garvie manages a decent drop-kick and Jamesy picks it up out wide, where he likes it. He goes past a couple of players and heads for the box. Folk are shouting, 'wee baw, wee baw,' for the pass inside, but there are too many players around them for there to be any point. They're just shouting like they do any time their own team-mate has it. A few call him a ball-greedy bastard but he knows he's right to keep it and make for the byline—then it'll be worth a pass. Besides, if he passed it now, one of the eejits would probably try for glory, despite everybody knowing you seldom beat Colin with a long shot. Colin always milks it like fuck, and dives around making it look spectacular when he could as easily stop a shot with his feet, but he's still a good goalie, no denying it.

Jamesy sees Martin coming out to meet him as he nears the byline. Martin beat him to a ball at lunchtime when he blootered it into the Wasteland, but that one had been much nearer Marty, and this time Jamesy has the ball under control. He jinks past him and looks up, sees loads of folk pouring forward into the box. He takes a swing and makes sure he gets his foot under it,

181

sending it in high and hoping somebody sticks the noggin on it. Most of them shite out of it, and of those who jump, all but one get their timing wrong and it goes over their heads. Gary Hawkins is the exception, clearing the danger with a glancing header to send it out for a corner. It's hard to tell if he meant it, but it looks good anyway.

Matt normally takes all the corners and free-kicks, no matter what area of the park, same as Stephen Rennie on his team. They both take all the penalties too, even if it's you who got brought down (though sometimes, if they're winning comfortably, they'll let one of the hard-cases take it, just to sook up to them, or maybe the guy whose ball it is). With Matt not playing, it's up for grabs, or rather it's up for grabs to the best fighter out of all who want it.

Jamesy doesn't want to take it. He wants a goal, and you don't score from corner-kicks, despite Matt and Stephen always trying since they saw a Brazilian do it on the telly.

Graham Wilson gets to take the corner. He's not a good fighter or anything, but it's his ball. He takes a runny and gives it a big welly into the area. Colin jumps for it, but there's too many folk in his way. He does well to get a touch, but doesn't get close to catching it. The ball drops behind him, on the edge of the six-yard area, falling just in front of Paddy Beattie. He only has to side-foot it in with his left and it's the decisive goal to end the fightback. Jammy bastard, Jamesy thinks. But instead of just stroking it home, Paddy decides to take a touch so he can change foot and pure leather it in with his right, because some folk think hitting it in dead fast from six yards is somehow impressive. He blooters it as hard as he can, but by this time wee Marty has dived in. Most folk think Martin's a poof and a shiter because he can't fight, but the same folk would be jumping out of the way of a shot like that. Martin *is* a bit of a shiter, to be honest, in other ways, but at football, he never does less than he possibly can, no matter the score. The ball skites off him with so much speed and loft that it clears the bar in a split second, before continuing to climb and loop right up on to the Annexe roof.

'Aw, fuck,' everybody agrees.

There is less accord over what will happen next. Nobody is going to dispute that it's a corner, but getting the ball back in order to take it is a trickier matter, and the question of whose problem that is, trickier still.

'You'll need tae get that,' Paddy is insisting.

Martin looks worried, but in this case marginally more by what retrieval would entail than by crossing the otherwise extremely intimidating Paddy.

'No I shouldnae. It came off me, but you're the one that took a big blooter at it.'

'Aye, an if you hadnae got in the way, it would have been a goal instead ay up on the fuckin roof. You're no gettin oot it, ya wee poof. Go an fuckin get it.'

'Aye,' agrees Richie Ryan. 'It came aff you last. On you go.'

'Aye, get on wi it,' chimes in Charlie Russell, who sits next to Richie.

Jamesy has often heard folk say, 'The baw's on the slates', meaning something's ruined and can't continue. He understands where it comes from, but in his experience, as slated roofs are always sloped, the ball going on to one only has this result if it gets stuck in the gutter rather than rolling clean off. The low-rise Annexe, however, is a flat-roofed affair (an architectural decision even his nine-year-old mind finds baffling, given the average rainfall), and in his opinion 'The baw's on the bitumen' has a far more final ring to it.

Janny Johnny is supposed to go up there if a ball gets stuck, or at least that's what the teachers say when you tell them, but the lazy bastard seldom does. As a result, at best the owner can be waiting weeks to get his ball back, but more likely the local big boys will nick up there in the evening or over the weekend and fuck off with it.

Still, this is regarded as a known risk to anyone who chooses to bring their ball into school (the corresponding benefits including taking the odd corner and very occasional penalty). It is expected that you climb over into the Wasteland if you put the ball over the wall, but up on the Annexe roof is different. The appreciable threat to life and limb, in combination with the thought of how mental the teachers would go, means that it is normally regarded as a lost cause.

Right now, however, folk are suddenly acting like this isn't—and hasn't aways been—the case. They're all starting to gang up on Martin and making out that it is expected that you go up there, which is total shite. The rules haven't changed. None of *them* has ever been up there, unless it happened when Jamesy was off sick, which he doubts. They're just doing it because Martin's never in trouble and they think he's a poof. They were probably all hoping he'd get caught going

184

over the wall at lunchtime because he's never had the belt. They know there's no chance of him doing it, but that barely matters because it's a slagging for him if he cries off, which is a result for them, too.

It's a pure sin. Martin never does anything to hurt anybody. It's not right that they all gang up on somebody because he's nice and not a bastard to folk. Jamesy wants to help, wants to head this off. He also wants that hat-trick, and with time running out there's only one chance of getting it. 'I'll go up,' he announces.

'Don't be daft, Jamesy,' says Paddy. 'Let that wee poof get it.'

But Jamesy is already running, his mind made up. He considers himself a good climber, and has already been on a higher roof, back during the October Week holiday, when he and his pal Stewpot were playing along at Braeside Primary.

'Somebody keep the edgy and give us a shout if any teachers come,' he says, then heads around the back of the Annexe. He thinks about using the big bins to get up under the gutter, but there's a sturdy iron drainpipe that will do fine. It's perfect, in fact: the joins, brackets and offshoots providing footholds as his hands grip the white-painted metal. The wall is roughcast, too, which gives good grip against his trainers. There's a wee heart-attack moment at the top as he gets both elbows over the edge and feels himself sway backwards for just a sec, but it passes and he makes it up okay.

He can't see the ball at first. The roof is mainly flat, but there are these big see-through plastic pyramid efforts, six of them, sticking up to about waist height. Jamesy keeps one eye on the doors to

185

the Main Building as he scuttles along between the two rows of pyramids, then spots the ball nestling against the base of one of them. He has a swatch down as he passes the first pyramid, and can see into one of the Primary Seven classrooms. It's different from the ones he's always been taught in: they have wide tables and plastic chairs in wee groups instead of individual wooden desks. There are Formica worktops around the walls, too, and the floor is carpeted instead of wooden. It looks dead flash and modern. Primary Seven must be gemmie.

It would be quicker to walk upright, but he can see into the girls' part of the playground from up here and doesn't want to be noticed by a tell-tale like Fat Joanne, so Jamesy proceeds on all fours, staying between the rows of pyramids for cover. He gets the ball and kneels up so he can give it a decent throw and make sure it gets down first time. It does, bouncing once on the bitumen before disappearing over the edge to where someone will be waiting for it. He just hopes they've got the decency to wait for him before taking the corner. And if there's a penalty, he definitely deserves to be taking it. He turns to make his way back, and as he does so takes a wee swatch down through the pyramid the ball was resting against.

He sees more carpet, a table, a teapot, a plate of biscuits, six or seven mugs, two newspapers. And several adult faces staring right back at him.

'Aw, naw.'

*   *   *

Martin is walking home with Helen. They're going

186

round the outside and are just passing the rebuilt Infant Building. They often walk home together because they live on the same street. Folk say they're going with each other, because that's usually the only way a boy and a girl would be walking and talking, but they're not. Helen's nice but Martin doesn't think about going with her. He thinks Michelle's pretty, as does everybody else, but the truth is he's never really thought much about going with anybody. Not until today. He'd really like to go with Karen now.

Helen's talking about Karen and everything that happened, but she's not talking about the important stuff like Karen getting the belt: she's filling him in at length about all sorts of other mince to do with Chinese ropes. Girls witter on about this kind of guff all the time: who said what to who, who's fallen out with who, who's best friends with who. It's so endless and trivial, going on like a budgie. That's probably why he's never given much thought to going with any of them. It would be different with Karen, though. He could tell her about *Jaws*, because he's seen it at the cinema, and they could talk about that. Or *Top of the Pops*.

It's hard to think about Karen while Helen is wittering on about Fat Joanne, so Martin finds himself thinking instead about Jamesy getting the belt, which makes him sad and a bit angry, too. Jamesy saved him, and look what happened. It wasn't right. He had been relieved when Jamesy said he would go, but anxious at the same time because it was dangerous and unnecessary. You couldn't blame O'Connor this time for giving the belt, but that just underlined why nobody should

187

have demanded that somebody go up after the ball. He knows fine if Paddy had booted the ball up there without a deflection, or Stephen Rennie, or Richie, nobody would have suggested going after it, not even Graham, the Primary Six whose ball it was.

Helen reels him back from his contemplation by mentioning Karen's first-hand response to getting the belt. 'She said it was quite sore, but not sore enough to make her cry. She said it was being out in front of everybody that—'

Martin hears Helen make a weird spluttering noise and is suddenly aware of something rushing past him. He turns to look at her and sees that there is brown stuff coming out of her mouth, more of it smeared around her nose and chin. She wobbles dizzily for a moment then bends over and spits. Martin hears laughter and looks ahead. He sees one of Robbie's big brothers—Brian, he thinks his name is, though he is always known as Boma—and another Primary Seven, both standing a few yards away and laughing. Boma's right hand is filthy, dripping mud from his fingers.

Martin has some hankies in his pocket. He hands them to Helen, who bats him away at first because she's still trembling with shock. Then she takes one tentatively and begins wiping away the mess, spitting more dirt as she does so.

Boma and his mate are still standing there, pissing themselves.

Martin feels an anger like nothing he has ever experienced before, something that needs to be vented or his head will explode. 'Ya fuckin dirty fuckin evil fuckin bastards,' he screams at them. Martin seldom—almost never—swears, because

188

it's a sin and you have to tell the priest at confession, but he needs these words, knows nothing else will express the depths of his fury.

They both keep laughing; all the more, in fact.

'Ya fuckin pricks,' he yells again. 'Fuckin big hard men daein that tae a wee lassie. Fuckin *wanks*!' This last he bellows so hard it seems to scrape his throat on the way out.

It has an impact on Boma, too. His laughter subsides and he walks towards Martin. He looks huge. He has a face like a skull: hollow and gaunt, with his hair cut really short, almost down to the roots like Slade in that poster on Uncle Tommy's bedroom wall. Martin always thought he was the scariest-looking of the big boys, even when Boma was only in Primary Six and there were bigger hard-men in the year above. He looks even scarier than Joe, the oldest of Robbie's brothers. And now he's walking towards Martin with his teeth bared and nostrils flaring.

Martin knows he's in trouble, but the rage inside still has him in a kind of oblivion. He throws himself at Boma, his fists balled and swinging. He then feels an explosion of pain in his stomach and doubles over, his useless hands now drawn into his middle. From the edge of his blurred vision he sees Boma's shoe drive towards him, then a flash of white as it connects with his face.

He feels his nose burst, too. He's not crying yet; like Helen, he's still too much in shock.

'An you better no grass, ya wee cunt,' says a voice.

Martin hasn't heard this insult before, but he knows instinctively that it is a swearword. He can tell by the viciousness with which it is issued.

He wouldn't have told anyway. The teachers never care about things like that, even less if it happens after school hours.

*   *   *

He tells his mum he got hit by the ball. He is able to embellish convincingly about the praise he received for stopping a goal, before comfortably heading off the subject by relating how Jamesy got the belt for going up on the roof.

By bedtime the pain is far less and his nose all cleaned up, but around his eye is starting to swell. He can't get to sleep for ages because he starts worrying that Helen will tell Harris or somebody what happened, and if there's any follow-up, Boma will think he grassed. He worries about getting a keeker too, because everyone will notice and it'll get talked about, and it would be just his luck if this was the one time a teacher decided to investigate.

By morning, he does indeed have a big keeker, swollen and starting to discolour. Everybody asks about it. Everybody except O'Connor. He's relieved, but he hates her for it, and he knows he's right to hate her for it.

Primary Seven
Beta Hydri

Making a Name

It's bucketing down with rain, so they're having what the teachers call a 'wet playtime', which means they all have to stay in class. They can talk and sit at different tables and they can eat their sweets and stuff, but 'shite playtime' would be a far better way to describe it, Martin reckons. The windows are all steamed up, so you can't see outside, and the whole place stinks from the damp jackets placed on radiators because everybody got drookit coming in this morning. Last year, the jackets would have been soaking. Now they're drookit. Same as things don't get dirty or manky anymore, but mockit. Mockit is even more recent. Things were still manky when Martin got the flu and had to stay off for a week and a half. They were mockit upon his return. Many, many things were mockit, in fact; you could tell a treasured new word had entered the playground lexicon because folk were liberal to the point of incontinent when using it. Perhaps it was a case of practising in order to get into the habit, because some new words became not so much alternatives as outright replacements, and using the outmoded version was asking for a slagging. Stating 'Is it dick', for example, having been state-of-the-art scorn in Primary Five, would now finger you as out-of-touch and a pure wean, not to mention a snobby poof for baulking at the swear-word required in the new Primary Seven vintage: 'Is it fuck'. State the utterly prehistoric 'Is it chook' and you'd be best asking for a transfer to another school.

Martin was increasingly aware that the longer Primary Seven went on, the more everybody seemed to seize upon anything that could single you out. It used to be you had to endure some kind of memorable embarrassment before anyone reckoned they had slagging rights, but these days they were getting like piranha, snapping desperately at the merest morsel. Such thoughts always caused St Grace's to loom forebodingly in his future. He had heard it was far worse up there, and it wasn't all the shite you heard about folk getting their heads flushed down the lavvy by Second Years that scared him. Scotty's big sister Heather had told him, for instance, that simply taking a sealed Tupperware cup of juice along with your packed lunch was enough to get you called a poofy mummy's boy. This had troubled him not simply because his mum *did* tend to pack precisely such an item with his lunch, but because it would never have occurred to him that it was a potential source of abuse, and thus there must be dozens of other potholes just waiting for him to walk into once he made the big move up the hill. He already knows he'll get it for being good at his work and seldom in trouble, so starting off in deficit means he can ill afford to concede any other social points.

Harris comes in again and tells them all to pipe down. That's the second time and she's threatening punishment if she has to come back a third. They're only talking, and no way is it that loud. It's just because the Primary Seven classes are in the Annexe alongside the staff room. Plus, if they all sat there in silence, the old boot would be shattered. She likes nothing better than shouting the odds and making out she's disappointed in them when inside she's loving it.

Everybody hates Harris now much more than they hate Momo. They're still wary of him, but he doesn't cut the same intimidating figure he did when they were younger. He seemed to get smaller every year, and went gradually from this giant ape to just a strange old man. It took a while, but one day Martin became aware that Momo was actually shorter than quite a few of the other teachers, all of whom were women. And the next thing he noticed, though they tried to disguise it, was that the teachers clearly thought he was an eejit as much as the weans did.

The younger kids still think he's the bogeyman, and after the bell goes he'll no doubt be battering lumps out of a few Primary Three or Four noggins on account of their older siblings, but it's Harris who really casts a cloud over Martin's year. And that's not because either she or Momo has changed, only that the kids now see them through older eyes. Momo is mental, which used to make him scary, but they can now see he's ridiculous, a joke. Harris is no fucking joke, and the only reason they didn't hate her more earlier was that they didn't have much to do with her beyond her hymn practices and the occasional crackdown on lining up late. Momo is officially the boss, but Harris is the one who rules the Sixes and Sevens, and 'rules' is definitely the word.

Even if it wasn't raining, they'd be having a shite playtime, because Harris has banned almost everything that they like to do, including football. *She has banned football.* Not completely, only from the playground, but as it's March right now and the pitch is a swimming pool, it's the same difference.

As is usual when the pitch was flooded, they had returned to playing up on the concrete, until Stephen Rennie sliced a shot on the half-volley and smashed a window. Martin has been playing in the same playground since Primary Four, and in that time, despite anything from one to four games of football taking place simultaneously at every interval, this was the first window breakage. A few near things, granted, but only one smashed pane. One, however, was enough. God, she must have been waiting for it, dying for it. In the winter she banned sliding, as she does every year because once upon a time Helen Dunn's big sister Nicola broke her ankle; this on top of banning snowballs 'because you could take someone's eye out'. Which made for a truly miserable January for anyone not *really* excited by building snowmen.

When it thawed, the pitch became its current quagmire, so the game of choice up on the concrete was pinkies, or bar-the-door, or British bulldog as some folk called it. It's a great game for this time of year because all the running keeps you warm when it's so chilly and windy outside. Or rather, it *was* a great game until Jamesy broke his arm and Harris banned it on pain of the belt.

Tig was a wee bit lacking in scope for occupying thirty-odd eleven-year-olds, but they had their resources and thus managed at least temporarily to spice things up. Frisbee-tig: instead of just touching you with his hand, the guy who is 'Het' has to hit you with a frisbee. Current status: banned (burst nose, Gary Hawkins). Ball-tig: the guy who is 'Het' has to hit you with a tennis ball. Current status: banned (see snowballs re potential eye-loss). Two-man hunt: a large-scale game of tig meets hide-and-seek. Current status: banned (burst nose, James Doon, ran into wall while looking backwards at pursuer).

Which had left the old standby, fitba, until Stephen learnt the downside of a highly polished finish to his shiny new Docs. The pitch will dry out some day soon, but for the time being wet playtime is arguably preferable to plain old dry playtime, because at least you get a seat inside away from the cold.

Martin is scribbling on a piece of scrap paper. He watches Harris depart, guessing she'd prefer to stay and use playtime for some more compulsory hymns. He used to think that leading these practices was part of her duty as deputy head, but this week he's realised that it's her obsession. O'Connor is off sick and they've got Harris as a stand-in until she comes back.

Most classes get a different teacher every year as they move up through the school. Some, occasionally, get the same one for two. They have somehow ended up with Soorpuss O'Connor from Primary Five right through to the bitter end, and it says a lot for just how horrible O'Connor is that Harris seems an easier shift. She's distracted, for one thing, always with her head in some folder or other, while O'Connor misses nothing, eyes like a hawk and the screech to match. A change is as good as a rest in as much as it's a rest from O'Connor, but it's not without its price, the greater part of which is that the woman can't go between two school bells without getting everyone to their feet for an enforced rendition of some dirge or other.

Everybody's gone quiet, like they did the last

time she came in to warn them, but it will start to build up again. Martin saw something on telly last night about things called palindromes, which is where a word or phrase is the same backwards, like 'A Toyota' or 'Sit on a potato pan, Otis'. He writes down the phrases he can remember to see if it is true, and is delighted to find it so, especially in the case of the one about Napoleon: 'Able was I ere I saw Elba'. The man on the telly explained that 'ere' meant before, though he didn't explain why Napoleon would be speaking English.

He then tries writing down some classsmates' names backwards, to see whether they come up as anything interesting. Martin writes his own name first, which comes out as Nitram Noskcaj. He is pleased that it is something pronounceable, though is immediately aware of the slagging potential posed by 'nit' and 'caj'. He's never had nits and he never goes cadging for sweets off people, but facts don't always matter much when it comes to abusive labels. He scribbles a few more, mostly running into consonant congestion. Kevin Duffy gives him Yffud Nivek, which makes Martin smile as he sounds it in his head: 'I-Fud'. He keeps that to himself, partly because he doesn't want to throw Kevin to the wolves like that and partly so he's got something up his sleeve the next time Kevin decides to slag him. He tries Jamesy's, which comes out Nood Semaj. This makes him smile over the 'nood' part. He leans over to Jamesy, who is at a table nearby.

'Hey, Jamesy, do you know your name backwards is Nood Semaj?'

'It's whit?' Jamesy asks, smiling.

'Nood Semaj.'

198

'Noodsy Maj,' Jamesy says. 'That's magic. Noodsy Magic! What's your name backwards?' he asks Gary, who is sitting beside him.

'I'm Renrut Eibbor,' says Robbie while Gary is still working his out.

They all start giving it a go now, though Martin knows most of them will be Welsh- or Gaelic-sounding gibberish. Richie comes up with a decent one. 'I am Nayr Drahcir,' he announces in a Dracula voice. 'I come from Transylvania.' Scot mentions that Zoe is Noswal Eoz. 'No swally— maybe she's got a sair throat.'

Nobody asks Martin his, and he doesn't volunteer it.

Jamesy seems delighted, which is a relief. He repeats the name, aware it may have been missed and forgotten by the others in the clamour.

'I'm Nood Semaj. Noodsy Magic.'

'Noodsy,' Richie acknowledges, nodding. 'Aye, that's your new name: Noodsy. Everybody, Jamesy's Noodsy now. Noodsy Magic.'

Martin has noticed that Kevin didn't proffer his reverse name, and once he hears Jamesy officially rechristened, Kevin begins making determined and soon successful attempts to change the subject.

Stephen Rennie comes back in the room, having been out to the toilets.

'Heh, Stevie,' Robbie greets him. 'Jamesy's new name is Noodsy.'

'Noodsy?'

'Aye. Richie came up wi it. His name backwards is Nood Semaj. Noodsy Magic.'

'Good yin.'

'Aye, it's a pure classic,' Robbie adds.

Jamesy looks across at Martin. Jamesy came up

199

with 'Noodsy Magic', and the whole backwards-name thing was Martin's idea, but they both know how the revisionism works, the hierarchy that's taking an increasingly rigid shape. No point trying to correct them. Richie came up with it, that's now official.

The class is changing. It used to be only a couple of folk you'd have trouble with, and everybody else got on, more or less. Now Martin senses they are all jostling for position on the verge of a divide. On one side of it there will be the folk it is cool to be pals with, and on the other those it will be mandatory to slag off. No neutral ground. People aren't quite there yet, but Martin sees it coming. He knows where he's likely to end up, and that's something he can live with, as he doesn't particularly want to be 'in' with many of the guys who will secure places on the other side of the line. But what is more saddening is that he can see people he thought of as friends starting to align themselves away from him because they can see what is up ahead, too.

In this respect, the change to the big school is less to be feared than welcomed, as it will offer the chance of a clean slate. There are two other primaries forming the intake, meaning he'll be split up from many of his old classmates and thrown in with a majority of new ones, who will be able to judge him only on what they find rather than deciding they already know all they need to know about him.

*   *   *

Karen watches the anaesthetist through a window

in the corridor outside the intensive therapy unit. The anaesthetist and a nurse are standing by Robbie's bed, the nurse nodding as the doctor talks, occasionally gesturing to indicate one of the many monitors sited around the station. Also sited around the station are two Dibbles on guard duty. Robbie isn't going anywhere, but there remains the possibility that someone might wish to finish what they started in case he survives to give his version of events. The Dibbles try to keep out of the way, but as is often the case with handless wee shavers, the harder they try, the less they succeed.

Karen just waits. The anaesthetist will come out in her own good time, and will be more amenable to discussion if she doesn't feel anyone breathing down her neck.

Poor Robbie. He was never the most likeable of individuals, but she can't help feeling pity for anyone so helpless as to be linked up to all that kit. She remembers feeling sorry for him once before, also because he was unconscious in another ITU. She didn't see him that time, but just hearing about it seemed very sad. School was a battleground, but the prospect of one of them actually dying had been too truly enormous to comprehend.

'Some state,' says Tom Fisher, the DI from Braeside nick she's roped in for up-to-date local knowledge.

'Aye,' she agrees.

'You knew him, from school, somebody said?' he asks.

'Yeah. Both suspects and one of the victims. But best we file what I know under "Inadmissible".'

'I think there's a statute of limitations on having your pigtails pulled anyway.'

201

'I never had pigtails. That's a slur.'

'But if you did, which one of them *would* have pulled your pigtails?'

'I said "Inadmissible".'

'Humour me.'

'I don't have to. I outrank you. But for what it's worth . . . Hmm, a boy called Kevin Duffy would have pulled my pigtails. Colin Temple would have been trying to see up my skirt as I ran away. Robbie would have sneered at me for crying about it. And Noodsy . . .' She laughs quietly, sadly, and shakes her head.

'What about him?'

'He's the one who would have ended up getting the blame from the teacher.'

'A recurring theme?'

'Don't go there. Like I said, Inadmissible. He's learnt to be a lot cuter since.'

'Aye. Not quite learnt how to avoid the blame for his own shite, though. I've huckled him umpteen times myself. Penny-ante stuff, mainly, but we're not talkin miscarriages of justice here, either.'

'And what about Robbie?'

'Him too, yeah. But the weird thing is, oot the two ay them, I'd have said Robbie was the wan that tried occasionally tae go straight. My impression is that when they've done stuff together, it's Noodsy who's been the driving force. Though obviously I couldnae say either was the brains of the outfit.'

Karen laughs but has to recompose her game face as the anaesthetist finally exits the unit. She knows why they're there and comes across to the chairs to greet them. Sometimes they're so scunnered with the polis hanging around that they

202

act like you're invisible and make out they're off to attend to something else. This is to make it incumbent upon the cops to get their attention and thus underline how much you're interrupting their jobs, and there's usually a large sigh-to-information ratio in the subsequent conversations. This one shouldn't be too bad, however.

'I'm Detective Superintendent Gillespie. This is Detective Inspector Fisher.'

'Kate Lanimer. I'm the ITU consultant on duty.'

Karen specifically doesn't ask, 'How is he?' They hate that, like they weren't going to get on to the subject if you didn't ask.

'Critical but stable?' Karen says instead, eliciting a knowing nod from the doctor. That's what they always tell the press. It's utterly meaningless.

'He survived the surgery,' Dr Lanimer says. 'That's as much as we could have hoped for at this stage, to be honest. He'd lost a lot of blood from the abdominal wound, but obviously it was the head that was the biggest issue. The knife went through his eye and got deflected downwards when it hit the rear of the socket. If it had gone upwards, you'd be talking to a pathologist just now.'

'But the surgeons got it out all right?'

'They got it out, but it's too early to tell regarding the all-right part. Your people took the knife away, though I doubt you'll get any fingerprints off it now, apart from Angus Cooper's.'

'Who's he?' asks Tom.

'Surgeon,' Karen informs him. 'Okay. Thank you, Doctor. Oh, one other thing, has he had any visitors?'

'What, with your boys babysitting him?'

203

'Sure, I just mean, anyone try to visit, anyone asking at reception, that kind of thing.'

'I wouldn't know. But I'll ask around, okay?'

'I'd very much appreciate it.'

'Anybody specific you've got in mind?' Tom asks as the anaesthetist walks briskly away down the corridor.

'No, just interested in case it throws anything up. You know, who cares, who doesn't.'

'Relatives, you mean?'

'For instance, yeah. It would give us an insight into the Turner family dynamic.'

Tom glances briefly to the heavens, suggesting it wasn't exactly the *Little House on the Prairie*.

'Not many left,' he says. 'The mother's deid, Joe's inside and the sister lives in . . . Canada, I'm sure, though she's liable to be back, under the circumstances.'

'I was thinking more about Boma,' Karen says. 'But if he did come calling, would it be out of concern that his wee brother might die, or concern that he might live?'

'Fair question. He was away fishing up in Sutherland, according to his bidey-in partner, when we came round to break the news about his dad and Robbie.'

'I'll bet he's been away fishing a few times when other folk were receiving bad news.'

'And landed nothing but an alibi, sure.'

'Worth having somebody keep an eye on him until we know some more.'

'You got it. Are we done here?'

'Yeah. They've got my number if anything changes.'

They give the Dibbles a wave goodbye and head

204

for the exit.

Making a Stand

'Noodsy Magic. I cannae get over that. That's a pure classic, Richie.'

Aye, gaun yersel Robbie, thinks Scot.

Fud.

Scot has to laugh. The wee shite that was never done calling people sooks has now found his true purpose: he's Chief Bum-Licker to big Richie Ryan, the undisputed title-holder of Best Fighter in Primary Seven (and therefore Best Fighter at St Lizzie's). It's the next-best thing to having mates.

No, maybe shouldn't be so harsh on him. At least Robbie's been making the effort of late to find a more sociable role for himself instead of just skulking about looking for new ways to upset people.

Jamesy looks pleased, at least. The only other nickname Jamesy has ever had is Faw, due to his surname and chronic tendency to injure himself. The sharper observer will have also noted its appropriateness in reflecting Jamesy's unfailing ability to be the one guy who gets caught if he ever steps out of line.

He's done well to append the Magic bit on to Noodsy, even if he's getting no credit for coming up with it, but mainly he'll be pleased with the thumbs-up it confers to be given a handle by one of the big men. Arise, Sir Noodsy.

Poor Martin, though. He's going to get fuckin eaten alive at St Grace's if he's not careful. He's quiet, he's trusting, he's good-natured and, worst of all, he's clever, which will unavoidably single him out. At least he doesn't talk as politely as he once did—that would really paint a target on him, like that poor bastard Timothy Halleran in Heather's year.

Scot will be all right, he reckons. He already knows a lot of the real bampots who are coming from St Gregory's, Braeside's other Catholic primary, due to the catchment areas blurring somewhere around Muirlaw Avenue. This puts him on nodding terms with some, which is an obvious advantage, but not as much as the knowledge to steer clear of certain others. The kids from the bought houses up on the Carnock Brae or across in the even newer Sunnylea estate will mostly be walking in blind. He'll try to give Martin some tips, but information can only go so far. Once the wolves start circling, they have an instinct for who is vulnerable. You can see it already, the way some of them are acting towards him. Colin's getting it too, though he'll probably be in with a better chance up the hill. Colin's fairly quiet and he lives in a bought house as well, so he'll get the snob bit, but he won't draw attention to himself as much as Martin.

Scot looks across at the lassies, wonders if it's going to be easier for them. Probably not. Less chance of a doing, obviously, but they're just as feral and merciless in other ways. Certainly doesn't sound like all peace and harmony when Heather's talking about it. They're all a bit quiet and subdued just now, the lassies. That's because they got their Rubella jag first thing this morning. It's just the lassies that get it, because it's something to

206

do with getting German measles when they're pregnant. A few of them came back weeping a wee bit, but Fat Joanne was howling and Geraldine was near screaming. Scot felt sorry for Geraldine, seeing they must have needed the hypodermic equivalent of a pneumatic drill to get anything into her veins, but lapped up every tear and moan of Joanne's distress. The lassies always went first to Nitty Nora the Heid Explorer and that stupid cow always came back rubbing her arm and telling the boys it was a jag. Well, guess what? This time it really *was*, Chubby-Cheeks! And the boys aren't getting it!

The bell rings and soon enough Harris is back at the blackboard; sooner than usual, in fact, because there are no lines to bring in. Scot doesn't mind so much because it's always maths in the morning, and though it's not the kind of thing you let on in company, he quite enjoys it, and not like folk enjoy art because it's easy. He enjoys it because it's hard, or rather enjoys it most when it's hard. He's a 'Late Developer', it said on his Primary Six report card, which is probably why the others haven't noticed; that and the fact that Helen Dunn always comes top in tests, and that's what they tend to pick up on. Plus, it's all right to be good at *some*thing. It's being good at bloody *every*thing that makes folk think you're a sook.

Karen is sent round to dish out plastic set squares to everybody, which is good news because Scot likes geometry, especially all the stuff about angles. It's also good news that it's Karen, because he knows she'll make sure he gets a decent one and not one of the half-chewed efforts. It's teetering on slagging territory on both sides for the boys and girls to be caught talking to each other, so nobody really does, but you still know which ones like you.

Karen has barely sat down again after doing her rounds when there is a knock at the door, and, without awaiting an answer, in walks Father Wolfe.

Shite.

'Good morning, Mrs Harris, and good morning, children,' he says.

Harris's permascowl gets wiped in an instant and her coupon plays host to this ridiculous, overdone grin, which she turns to the class by way of encouragement. 'Good morning, Father Wolfe,' she says, gesturing with her arms to everybody to raise the volume on their half-hearted greeting. She then clasps her hands like a wee lassie and gazes adoringly as he walks across the room. She fucking worships him. Seriously—she's so far up his arse she can probably see O'Connor's feet.

Scot sighs, knowing the ball's burst. He'd be as well using the set square to flick snotters, because that's the only use he'll get out of it now.

Harris celebrates the visitation by striking up (like she needs an excuse) *Soul of My Saviour,* one of Wolfe's particular favourites. Then she gives him the floor and has a seat behind her desk while the Northern Irish Holy Bigot slabbers his shite.

He must realise that their primary school days are in their twilight and so is offering nuggets of advice for the new journey ahead, all of them variations upon the common theme of staying clear of Protestants. Given that most of the weans will be going home tonight to a Protestant parent and then maybe nicking round to play with their Protestant pals, the gangly Irish fud is farting against thunder, but it's never diminished his

208

gusto. Either he's daft enough to believe this isn't so or he thinks it's all he can do to give them fair warning, after which it's up to them if they want to burn in hell forever along with the teeming ranks of Proddiedom.

He's taking the long-term view, as well. He's done education and moves on to marriage guidance. 'If it comes to the worst and you end up murrying a Pradistant, just remember at least that you must get married in the arms of the Catholic Church. *Nat* a rugistry affice or, *even worse*, the Pradistant Church.'

Well, buggeration. Must tell Lindsay Wagner the game's a bogey. It's the piney-apple or nothing, doll.

And it gets worse, Lindsay, hen. Turns out we're doomed anyway.

'But the sad thing you must bear in mind is that muxed murriages don't work. They're recipes for tension and unhappiness, and as a result the couples always, *always,* end up suparated.'

Harris is shaking her head sadly at this, a look of pained regret on her vinegar-sooking fizzog.

'Miss,' says a girl's voice.

Scot looks over and sees that Karen has her hand up.

'Not just now, Karen,' says Harris quietly.

Wolfe is thus able to continue slabbering shite unabated. Karen, however, doesn't put down her hand.

'That is unless the Pradistant converts to Catholicism, and it's actually a fact that ninety per cent of Pradistant ministers ask for conversion on their deathbeds because, deep down, they know . . .'

'But, miss,' Karen repeats, sounding frustrated.

'Put your hand *down*, Karen.'

This sharpening in tone causes Wolfe to pause, concerned some of his priceless words may be obscured.

Karen jumps into the gap. 'But miss, it's not true,' she says.

'What's not true?' Harris demands, sounding aghast that Karen has had the cheek just to pile in. It's a classic Harris tactic, too: she's not asking because she's interested; she's asking so Karen can dig herself in deeper.

'What he said, miss. Mixed marriages don't always end up getting separated and they're not a recipe for unhappiness. My mum's a Prodisant and her and my dad are fine.'

'*Silence!*' Harris shouts. 'How dare you be so insolent. Get out here. Get out here at once.'

'But I'm telling the truth, miss.'

'*At once,*' Harris repeats. She noisily yanks open a drawer and pulls out her belt, clattering it angrily on to the desk. 'You will *not* contradict Father Wolfe and you will *not* speak out of turn in his presence.'

Karen has got to her feet. Scot has a look at her face. Normally at this point, folk are either shiting it or at least deflated, robbed of whatever energy drove their offence. Karen looks utterly fucking raging.

'Quicker, girl, or woe betide you. And take that insolent look off your face.' She turns to Wolfe, who is now looking like a spare tool. 'I'm very sorry, Father Wolfe, very sorry indeed. And this girl will be apologising as soon as I've finished with her.'

There's the usual silent buzz as Karen reaches the front and the class gets ready for the show. This time, though, it is punctured by another voice, this time a boy's.

'Miss.'

Scot turns, and, to his astonishment, it's Martin. He looks nervous as fuck, but he's got his lips tight together like Scot has seen him when he's going in for a tackle on the pitch.

'Not just now, Martin. Right, Karen, get your hands up and we'll teach you—'

Martin gets to his feet, the sound of his chair scraping the tiles turning Harris's disbelieving head.

'Miss, my dad's not a Catholic either, and him and my mum aren't unhappy.'

Wolfe suddenly looks like someone poured four-star petrol into his diesel brain. 'Well, obviously there will be exceptions,' he splutters, 'but as the expression says, it's the exception that proves the rule.'

'That's a misused expression, though, Father,' counters Martin. 'In the olden days, they used the word "prove" when they meant "test".'

Scot has to put a hand over his mouth to stop himself laughing out loud. This is classic Martin, coming out with precisely the kind of know-it-all thing he gets shite for from the other kids, but right now he's got Wolfe clamped and Harris nearly choking in outraged disbelief. She has to swallow before she can speak, and is about to erupt in summoning Martin to join Karen at the front. However, before she gets her words out, Helen Dunn has stood up, too.

'Miss, my mum is a non-Catholic as well,' she

says, pronouncing every vowel and consonant with her usual precision.

Fuck it, Scot decides, and gets to his feet. Both of his parents are Catholics (or at least his dad used to be) but he wants to show Martin some solidarity; and besides, his dad would be furious if he passed up the chance to get it up 'that jumped-up auld bigot Wolfe'.

'My dad's not a Catholic, either,' he says.

After that, there's a further sound of chairs being pushed back. Scot looks around and sees five others either on their feet or holding up their hands.

Harris is standing there looking horrified as the shite keeps piling higher. She's surveying the weans ranked against her and Scot is confident he can pretty much read her thoughts. If she belts one, she has to belt them all, which is not something she'd normally shrink from, but this isn't a bunch of the usual Braeview bampots caught running riot. Among this group are several good little boys and girls from the bought houses, whose maters and paters are going to be seriously dischuffed when they find out their wee darlings got skelped for the crime of pointing out the truth to a lying bastard.

So, in short, she's fucked, and she knows it.

'Okay,' she says, putting on her harshest woe-betide-you voice. 'Everybody, every one of you. *Sit. Down.*' And before anybody can consider maintaining their defiance, she turns her glare full beam on Karen and says, 'On. You. *Go!*' like the lassie's got no right to be standing there.

You have to hand it to Harris, it is a deft wee manoeuvre. She's executed a complete climbdown but made out she's still the one kicking their arses.

Scot notices that nobody is asked to apologise to Father Wolfe. He wants to suggest that Father Wolfe should apologise to *them*, but reckons it would be wise not to push his luck. Wolfe is still loitering wordless in front of the blackboard, his presence now a lingering embarrassment, like an eggy fart needing a door or window opened to let it out.

'Time for a hymn, I think,' Harris says, trying to fill the void.

Wolfe can't wait for it to finish so he can escape, and Harris seems just as impatient to assist him, cutting the hymn short at an unprecedented single verse and chorus. She escorts him out of the room to have a private word in the corridor. The second the door shuts, everybody immediately starts talking about what just happened.

Scot looks across to Martin and they share a wee knowing grin. 'Awright, Spartacus?' Scot says, hoping Martin'll get it. It was on telly a wet Sunday afternoon only a couple of weeks back, after all.

'*I'm* Martacus,' Martin says.

Scot laughs. Maybe Martin will be all right at St Grace's after all.

*   *   *

They're passing through the reception lobby when Karen hears someone say, 'Excuse me,' amid hurried footsteps behind her. She turns to see one of the ITU nurses holding two sheets of paper.

'You're DS Gillespie?' she asks, addressing Tom.

'No, I am.'

'Sorry. Fax just came through for you.'

'Thanks,' Karen says, taking hold of the printouts. She's been waiting for them impatiently, which was why she rather cheekily passed on the ITU fax number.

'What is it?' Tom asks.

'Robbie's mobile-phone records. Our best bet for sorting out a time frame. Alex, the pathologist, was a bit woolly over the time of death, given the state of the remains. Here we go: Robbie called this number—accompanying note says it's Noodsy's—at sixteen-forty-eight.'

'Noodsy's house or Noodsy's mobile?'

'House. It's a landline prefix.'

'We've got witnesses and sales receipts putting them at B&Q at around six and then again at half-eight. So it sounds like Noodsy could be telling the truth: he gets a call to come and help clean up after the show, then they start their beginners chemistry lesson.'

'Except,' Karen says, pointing to another line on the printed page, 'look at this. Robbie *received* a call from this mobile number at sixteen-twelve.'

'Whose is it?'

'That's the thing: they don't know. Look at the notes here. Says it's a pay-as-you-go account, so it's unidentified. They've cross-referenced it back at the station and it doesn't match any of the known numbers used by Colin Temple or Johnny Turner.'

'I see your point. It's half an hour before he calls Noodsy for help. That means he's either standing over two bodies, and therefore a bit busy to take any calls; or he's imminently about to be involved in a situation that ends with two people dead. Again, not a time you'd be answerin the phone.

214

Cannae say for sure, right enough, because we don't know how long the bodies were cold before he called Noodsy.'

'But what if he didn't?'

Tom's forehead attempts to implode as he wrestles with her apparent illogicality. 'Didn't what?'

'Call Noodsy. What if that number is Noodsy's and *he* called *Robbie*? What if it's all the other way around, and it's Noodsy who was standing over two dead bodies? We only have his word at this stage and Robbie is conveniently out of the picture.'

'We didn't find a mobile on Noodsy, or at his place,' Tom reminds her. 'It would make sense to get rid of it, right enough.'

'Well, leaving aside whether Noodsy would have the sense to get rid of it, not to mention his success rate at getting rid of other things, it's worth looking into.'

'Yeah, but why would Robbie phone his home number later?'

'Again, maybe he didn't.'

More brow-compressions.

'There's a lot going on in that lodge once the two of them are on site,' she explains. 'Noodsy could easily have called his own house with Robbie's mobile while Robbie was throwing up in the bathroom or whatever.'

'But if nobody was home, the call wouldn't have registered. According to this, it lasted two minutes. Noodsy lives alone. He used to live with a woman, but that was—'

'So find out whether he's got an answering machine, or BT 1571, because either of those would do it.'

Tom makes the necessary call while they walk to Karen's car, a journey long enough for her to identify a flaw in her theory large enough for her to wonder whether his effort is worthwhile.

'McGowan's over there the noo,' Tom reports. 'Should be a couple of minutes.'

'Yeah,' she says non-committally.

'What?' Tom asks, picking up on the doubt.

'Hole in the argument. Why would *Robbie* help?'

'Dunno. You've heard the expression thick as thieves.'

'Aye, but I've seldom believed it. The two-short-planks kind of thick is more common in my experience than the bonds-of-fraternity variety. If it's Noodsy who called in Robbie, he's gaunny walk in there and find his dad lying dead on the floor. Okay, Noodsy can tell him Temple killed his dad and he killed Temple, but surely he wouldn't call the guy's own son to help dispose of his body. Nah. I'm havering with this one. Waste of time.'

'You're only havering if you exclude the possibility that Robbie wouldn't be entirely broken-hearted about his old man being bumped off.'

'I'm excluding no possibilities, least of all ones suggesting a motive.'

Tom's mobile rings. 'McGowan,' he relays. 'Noodsy's got 1571, but there's no messages.'

Karen looks at the sheet: proof in black and white that the two-minute call *was* made. 'So either Noodsy's telling the truth and took the call himself—leaving us with the question of who called Robbie at sixteen-twelve—or he let his answering service record two minutes of silence and was then smart enough to delete it.'

216

'What's your instinct telling you?'

'That we still know shag-all. We need to remedy that a.s.a.p. Starting with having the first clue what would put Johnny Turner and Colin Temple in a room together, let alone either of these clowns.'

SAINT GRACE'S

First Year
Mu Cassiopeiae 2,
and Vega

The Contenders

They're in a gym hall, except it's got a carpet, which must be a bastard for burns if you're playing football. Robbie knows it's a gym hall because there are wall-bars all round the joint, and a big foldy-out affair at one side that looks like it would be pure gallus to be swinging from. *He'd* be gallus at it, anyway. There's plenty of them would shite it from being up so high; no chance of getting them dangling from a rope. Total shitebags. His big brothers told him there are three gym halls at St Grace's, but he thought they were talking pish until he clocked this place. It's about the size of the gym/dinner hall at St Lizzie's, so there's no way it can be the only one for a big place like St Grace's.

The place is mobbed, every cunt checking out every cunt else. The whole of First Year's in the hall. There's bits of paper taped up on the wall-bars with the names of each class—1S1, 1S2 and all that—but they're all still clustered with the folk they know from their own primary. Robbie knows a lot of the boys from St Gregory's, but it's all new faces from St Margaret's, because they get bussed in from Carnock on the other side of the Brae. Cunts like Martin and Dominic and Colin will be shiting themselves just now, checking out the hard bastards that might be in their class. Aye, no place to run, poofs. It's not primary anymore. Serious fighting at St Grace's, proper fighting. None of this first-to-greet-is-the-loser-and-that's-it-finished-shite. Cunt goes down on the deck up at St Grace's and it's into his nut, fuckin boot, boot, boot.

Fuckin yes. Or like that gallus fight he saw down the Garages during the summer holidays: Johnny Maxwell getting into Ally Catherwood. Got his head down with one hand and started booting into his face, fuckin yes. Fuckin tons of blood, all over Johnny's boot. There was a big puddle on the concrete, left a stain when it dried in. That's what Robbie's going to dish out when he gets into a fight with some cunt. Get hold of the hair, fuckin head down and boot, boot, boot. His Docs will do some damage, fuckin yes.

There's plenty of them round this hall he could take. No danger. And not just the obvious ones like Martin, or Colin, who he's battered before. Or that wee fanny Paul who thinks he battered Robbie that time just because Robbie didn't fight back. Just didn't feel like it. Wasn't worth his while. No, forget about the poofs and fannies, because you don't get noted for battering them. You have to take some cunt that's already battered some cunt else, and that puts you above whoever they've battered before.

You can tell the good fighters in this room from the way they're standing. Taking no shite, not nervous about who's going to be in their class or nothing. Richie's laughing and cracking jokes, looking like he's been at St Grace's for years, as opposed to nearly pishing his pants because he's afraid to go to the bogs in case he gets his head flushed, like half the other cunts in here. Paddy Beattie as well. Paddy's grown a bit since the end of Primary Seven. He's taller than Richie now; might be able to take him, in fact. Aye, maybe just. Robbie would love to see them fight. It's never been on the cards before because they've never fallen out much, plus Paddy's always kind of accepted Richie was the best fighter, but maybe now he's not so sure. Paddy looks more edgy than Richie today: Richie's all relaxed, but Paddy's eyes are really serious. He's checking out the other big men, you can tell, and he's giving out signals: come ahead if you want it. Aye, Robbie's money is on Paddy to be the one to burst a few faces and let folk know the score early days. The competition could be interesting, though. There's a few game-looking bastards staring back from the St Margaret's mob, plus some reputations to be reckoned with from St Gregory's. He can see Jai Burns and Gerry Lafferty who he knows because they live on the far side of Braeview. Jai is some fighter. Robbie'd love to see him take on Paddy or Richie. Richie's got stocky arms and a stoater of a hook on him, but Jai's meant to be really vicious, meant to have bitten Billy Fraser that time when it looked like he was getting the better of him. After that, Jai fuckin leathered him.

But what's more interesting is the St Gregory's lot Robbie *doesn't* know, because most of them come from the Bottom Scheme, and it's mental as fuck down there. Robbie's big brothers have got pals from that end of the town—and enemies. And to give you an idea, folk from Braeview call you a snob for living in a bought house; but folk from the Bottom Scheme call you a snob for living in Braeview.

Check that one there: big, tall bastard. Robbie thinks he's seen him about the town, all dressed in punk stuff: chains hanging off the trousers, ripped T-shirt and leather jacket. Looks hard as fuck. Robbie's not sure, but he thinks that might be

Kenny Langton, who he's heard mentioned as the best fighter at St Gregory's. Jai Burns might have something to say about that, but the one time they did get into it, Robbie heard it was stopped by the teachers. Jai tells folk he was winning, but that's not what everybody says. Whoever he is, he's definitely the scariest-looking guy in the place, even in his uniform: Docs up to his chin and big long legs for swinging them. Aye, there'll be cunts looking at their class name-lists and fuckin praying his isn't one of them.

Robbie's never liked school before, but St Grace's is going to be fuckin yes.

Changing

It's Wednesday, double period between interval and lunchtime. You call it interval at St Grace's, or the break, *not* playtime. Jesus Christ, not playtime. Can you imagine it? They'll find plenty to nail you for; don't go tossing them freebies.

They're in the changing room, which is why Martin is feeling that wee bit more tense. Actually, the tension level has been at a pretty high minimum since he started at St Grace's on Monday, spiking wee peaks throughout each day: class allocation, first interval, first lunchtime, first venture into the bogs and first period with each new teacher. This is the second PE session, and it's causing as much of a spike as the first, though for different reasons.

Martin was really pleased when he looked at the timetable and saw that you get PE twice a week, two whole double periods, guaranteed. You were meant to get it once a week at primary, but you were lucky if it was once a month because the teachers could seldom be bothered, with O'Connor particularly remiss. She'd use any excuse to ditch it: 'You were all talking too much, so PE's cancelled as punishment'; 'There's a virus going around and exercise tires you out and makes you vulnerable to infection.' Utter shite like that. At St Grace's, it's down there in black and white, and it's real, structured sports with proper kit, not rubbishy 'music and movement' tapes or a shambolic game of rounders. The first module is hockey, with even all the proper leg-pads and face-masks for the keepers. But this also means proper sweat and proper showers, requiring a full change of clothes, including socks and underwear.

He knows some boys are very uncomfortable about the idea of the showers, because you have to go in there in the buff along with everybody else. The closest they had come to that before was the occasional St Lizzie's trip to the baths, where you keep your trunks on in the showers, and there are cubicles to get dried and changed in. Martin doesn't feel particularly awkward about being naked in front of the other boys, though he is a little more self-conscious having seen that some of them have got pubes and far more developed tackle. The showers held only one terror for him yesterday during his first bout of post-PE group-scuddiness, and that was the fear of getting a stauner. This fear wasn't born of likelihood or precedent, but simply through contemplating the sheer enormity of its consequences should it happen. In the event, as he should have

227

anticipated, fear itself made sure it was a physiological impossibility, having roughly the same shrivelling effect as had the water been ice cold.

That accounted for some of the first PE spike, along with the rumours that the male PE teachers were super-strict bad bastards and ninth-dan experts at giving the belt. (Or 'the lash', as it is officially known in St Grace's Secondary argot. Further to be noted is that 'gut laugh' is now as square and thoroughly poofy as flares and cords. Anything funny is now a 'deck laugh', or merely 'a pure deck'; and, verb-wise, you now deck yourself laughing. 'Gemmie' would also appear to be on the road out among means of expressing approval, with 'gallus' the new preferred term of the cognoscenti. They should give out Roneo bulletin sheets, appoint an editor.)

Their teacher is actually all right. Better than all right, though nobody would be in a hurry to mess with him. Mr Blake, his name is. When he came into the changing room yesterday, he did this sergeant-major act, getting them all to their feet, chins up, hands behind their backs, told them they would be starting off with a five-mile 'yomp' through the nearby farm and woodland, and anyone who didn't manage it in less than an hour was getting six of the belt before being made to do it again. 'Or we could have a wee game of hockey.' He'd then made a few jokes and taken the piss out of people, which made everybody relax.

Martin—in common with most of his classmates—has never had a male teacher before this week, apart from Momo, and he's not sure that counts as he was just the heidie, and taught nobody much beyond Advanced Pensioner Carriageway Perambulation. He'd thus feared that they would be a truly intimidating breed, but had, he realises, reckoned without the long-term effects of three years under O'Connor. After her, every male teacher he's encountered so far has been like a favourite uncle. There's another male PE teacher, Mr Cook, who looks like a gorilla: all hair and muscles and a glowering demeanour, but 1S1 and 1S2 got him yesterday and Gary said he was a good laugh, too.

However, Gary said something else that was a match for Martin's PE experience, and that is the source of his current unease. Yesterday, it took Martin less than a couple of minutes to change into his shorts, T-shirt and trainers, but as Gary also reported from his class, it was close to fifteen minutes before the teacher showed up to lead them outside.

Further confirmation comes from Tam McIntosh, sitting three places down the bench. 'The PE teachers have a cuppa tea thegither while we're gettin changed. It's ayeways the same, ma big brer tellt us. They know fine it takes us two minutes tae get ready, but they sit oan their erses for a good quarter ay an hour. They only come up if it gets dead noisy, an that's just because it makes it harder tae concentrate on readin the fuckin paper.'

'That's what I heard as well,' agrees someone else.

Yesterday there was an uncertainty about it, the inhibiting effect of thinking that the teacher could walk into the changing room at any moment. But today Martin—and everybody else—can be sure that adult supervision is, at this moment, finitely but effectively suspended. The PE teachers' 'base' is at the far end of the corridor, thirty or forty yards away, with one boys' and two girls' changing rooms between there and here.

Since Monday, few to none of the fears surrounding the move to the big school have proven to have foundation. In the final few weeks of primary, you'd have got the impression it was going to be heid-flushing by rota throughout every break. Consequently, there were a lot of full bladders on Monday, with most people finally breaking at some point over lunch, but their visits to the boys' bogs proved incident-free. Predictions of small-scale civil war between factions hailing from different primary schools have proven to be complete mince, or in the case of some, mere wishful thinking. However, it's fair to say that so far, on the whole, people have tended to stick with who they know during the intervals.

Here, in this dressing room, is a crucible, a melting pot like nothing his childhood has known. Stripped literally naked, they are all thrown together, ungoverned, without the playground's scope for keeping your distance or flat-out running away. Here, in this dressing room, a different law will prevail: mob rule, the law of the jungle, the devil take the hindmost, Martin can't say which yet. All he knows for certain is that none of them tend to work out too well for the wee timid guy. He also knows that mobs don't rule themselves, that every jungle has its king, and that the devil needs an advocate.

It was a mere matter of arithmetic probability, in combining the pupils from three primary schools

230

and dividing by six, that each first-year class would have a proven hard-case in its number. Therefore, you would have thought it fifty-fifty that any particular class would find itself with just one of those schools' acknowledged Best Fighters. But not 1S5. Not Martin's class. No. Despite those odds, they had ended up with Kenny Langton *and* Chick Dunlop: the respective heavyweight title-holders of St Gregory's and St Margaret's—and, outside of Momo, the two biggest, scariest guys Martin had ever shared a classroom with. In fact, they were probably bigger than Momo; certainly taller than a few of the teachers Martin had encountered so far.

He has heard it speculated that it is inevitable the pair of them will fight, most probably sooner rather than later, in order to stake their claim for the currently vacant First Year overall combined Best Fighter title and all that it will bring. This *definitely* sounds like wishful thinking, Martin reckons, as he is sure it would take something a lot more important than bragging rights to make either of these monsters decide to take their chances with the other. So far, they are showing every sign of becoming big buddies and thus forming a formidable alliance. Martin would have to admit to being among those wishing they would fight, if only because if they did have a battle, there'd at least be scope to keep in with one in order to get protection from the other. His other wish would be that the fight happen on a day when Robbie is off sick, as to that wee shite it would be like missing the World Cup Final. Martin's been split up from his pals Scot and Coco, which was a big disappointment, but getting rid of Robbie is a brammer of a silver lining.

*   *   *

Aldo Dawson, the guy three pegs down from Colin, has his cock out and is having a wank in full view of everyone in the changing room.

The rules have changed.

He's never seen one anything like as big. Actually, come to think of it, he's never seen another one in anything but its resting state, which adds to the shock value, as when his own gets stiff, it merely sticks up. It doesn't *grow* like that. Jesus Christ, it's huge. The guy's got his whole hand around it, jerking it up and down. Now he understands the 'wanker' gesture, as a closed fist around his own would totally envelop the thing and have a couple of fingers to spare.

In Primary Six, Stephen Brogan was having a pee at the far end of the urinal when Janny Johnny came in and wedged the door right to the wall, intending to mop the floor. This had the result that Zoe Lawson saw inside as she was walking past. She saw him from the back, that's all, but *she saw him having a pee*, so that was that, pure slagging for Stephen.

The rules have definitely changed.

'Heh, Micky-boy, you might want tae think aboot movin seats,' says Davie Keenan to Michael McGhee, who is sitting directly opposite Aldo, on the bench against the far wall.

Micky shifts uneasily and slides along the bench closer to Craig Finnegan, who playfully pushes him back towards the imaginary line of fire.

'Micky's just feart he gets a wash,' says Liam

Paterson.

'Aye, very good,' Micky retorts. 'Just cause you managed tae sneak oot wi the family towel this mornin, ya black bastart.'

Lots of them laugh, but Colin doesn't. For one thing, he doesn't consider it safe, as those who laughed all know each other from St Gregory's; and for another, he's still confused and catching up. It used to be that you were fair game if you were considered too posh, from a 'boat hoose', too soft, too smartly turned-out, too *clean*. At St Grace's, those rules have been turned on their heads and most of the terms of abuse seem to centre upon lax personal hygiene and domestic poverty. You get slagged for *being poor*. You get slagged for *being dirty*, or 'black' as the preferred term has it. He can't quite get his head around it, not least because he's seldom observed these exchanges from any position of security against becoming the target.

'Yous don't have a clue,' says Aldo, still giving his wrist a steady-paced workout. 'Yous aw think it's gaunny go shootin across the room like a fireman's hose or hit the ceilin or somethin. Shows you don't have spunk or you'd know. It's no like pish. Just a wee dribble compared tae pish.'

'Ten CC,' says Craig.

'Whit?'

'That's how much. That's why that band's called Ten CC. It's the amount of spunk that comes oot.'

'Is that right?' Aldo asks, fair tickled by it.

'Aye. I read aboot it. There was a band called the Lovin' Spoonful, too—that's what that meant as well.'

'Wonder if we can ask Miss Coleman aboot it

233

when we get tae Section Six?' Aldo says. 'Please, miss, how much spunk comes oot your knob when you shoot your load?'

Everyone is decking themselves. Colin finds it particularly funny, which is perhaps why he ventures a response before his natural caution can restrain him.

'Well, Allan,' he says, putting on a female teacher's voice, 'the best scientific method would be to have a ham-shank into this test-tube, and then we can measure it precisely.'

Aldo laughs, though none of the others had until he started. Colin notes that Robbie has been looking on with interest. He'll be disappointed Aldo reacted well to the joke; more so that Colin has made a positive impact.

'You're a cheeky bastart, Coco,' Aldo says, but he's smiling, thank fuck. 'Fuckin test-tube? A beaker more like.'

Folk have been calling him Coco since Primary Seven. He can't remember how or when it started, or even who said it first. It's good to have a nickname, and he could have done worse, but he can't help feeling that somehow Coco is always going to be a wee guy's name. He's noticed that of all the boys called James, it's always the bigger, stronger, harder ones who get called Jai, and it's a name that needs to be conferred by others. If Noodsy decided to start calling himself Jai, he'd be the only one doing it.

'Liam would just need one of those pipettes,' says Mick.

'You can talk,' Liam retorts. 'Knob like a knot in a hanky.'

'Whit's Section Six?' asks Craig.

'You never seen it yesterday?' asks Mick.

'Woa-ho-ho,' says Aldo delightedly, still leisurely chugging.

Colin assumes Craig must have been sleeping or something. It was the first page everybody turned to as soon as they got their science textbooks, if only to confirm that what they had heard was true. It wasn't up to much, right enough: just line-drawn diagrams, and the woman never even had any fanny-hair. Big disappointment, really, but the laugh was just in seeing sex stuff written down in a school textbook.

'That's the bit where they dae sex education,' Mick tells Craig. 'It looks a pure laugh. The teacher has tae tell ye aboot cocks gettin up fannies an aw that.'

'Looks shite tae me,' Colin ventures, buoyed by his previous success. 'Be better with a scud-book.' He's winging it a bit on this one, as the most he has seen of a scud-book was a fragment of a ripped page his cousin found down the park once. It was sun-bleached and wrinkled from damp, but he'd been able to make out that the photo was of a naked woman with her legs open, though the weathering effect was like looking at it through net curtains.

'Aye,' says Robbie eagerly, making his first contribution. 'Ma brers fun wan doon the Craigy Park.'

Aldo laughs, which is a response Robbie was neither wanting nor expecting.

'How come folk ayeways find scud-books doon the Craigy or up the Carnockside? You never hear somebody sayin their big brer bought wan oot a shop or they fun it in their uncle's hoose. They aye

235

find it at the park. Maybe scud-books grow in parks, like fuckin mushrooms or somethin.'

They all laugh. Robbie joins in. Colin knew he would, even if inside he was raging. Robbie always laughs when the big men crack a joke, no matter if it's on him.

'They did, but,' Robbie insists. 'I got a look at it. The fannies never looked like the picture in Section Six, but.'

Liam leans across, suddenly curious. 'Could you see their baws?' he asks.

'Whit?' responds just about everybody.

'Lassies don't have baws,' a few of them splutteringly point out, barely able to believe their luck that a classmate could have laid himself open like this.

'Well, that's what I thought, but that's what it fuckin says in Section Six. Christ, I had to look for the tits to be sure which diagram was the wummin.'

The hilarity grows, but Colin suspects he's not the only one trying to remember details from a diagram that they only got to glimpse before Miss Coleman called the class to order.

'Fuck's sake, Liam,' says Aldo. 'You've a wee sister. Have you no seen her in the scud?'

'Aye, but she's fuckin nine. Lassies' fannies change when they get aulder.'

'Aye, they get gammon flaps. They don't grow baws.'

'I know *that*. They don't grow *baws* baws. But they get *somethin*. The book says they're called ogaries. I was just wonderin if Robbie saw them in his brers' scud-book.'

Robbie looks a wee bit put-upon now, like he's not sure how to answer this one. Colin wonders if

236

this means he was making it up about the scud-book.

'It was mostly just hair you could see,' he says, a bit of a climbdown. 'That's what I meant aboot different fae Section Six.' He attempts to climb back up again by adding: 'But ma brers say ye get these scud-books fae Denmark that show ye pure everythin.'

'Are they from parks in Denmark?' Colin asks.

They all deck themselves, but he can tell Robbie didn't like this. He's aware Robbie could decide to get nasty about this later but feels strangely safe amid his new classmates' laughter.

'Only wan way tae settle this,' Aldo decides. 'We get Caroline McLaughlin in fae the lassies' changin room and get her scants doon. If any ay them's got a hairy fanny an a set ay ogaries, it's gaunny be her.'

'Aye,' says Liam, 'and if any ay them's got baws, it's gaunny be Margaret-Anne McCall.'

*   *   *

Karen fumbles reluctantly with the buttons on her blouse, feeling more self-conscious today than yesterday, on the first occasion she had to get undressed here in the changing room. She knows it could be worse—the boys apparently don't have separate shower cubicles, and have to get in and out of their underwear in front of each other. She only has to get changed into her shorts and T-shirt, but it still feels very uncomfortable. She doesn't imagine anybody is going to be particularly staring at her; there's much more worth looking at elsewhere, but that in itself is part of the problem.

As they undress, Karen reckons that she'd have been able to tell which of her new classmates would turn out to be wearing a bra even if she had seen them only from the back. They're the ones who are first off with their gear, chatting away as they pop open buttons, and conspicuously facing away from the benches and pegs as they do so. Karen can't help thinking that it's because they want the others to notice, like it's a status symbol. She wonders, conscious of all these willingly displayed over-the-shoulder boulder-holders, does having breasts help you develop confidence and popularity, or does having confidence and popularity help you develop breasts?

That one Caroline, from St Gregory's, had her blouse off in seconds but seems in no hurry to replace it with a gym T-shirt, presumably in case anybody fails to notice not only her bra, but that she's got something to fill it with. Admittedly she's not got quite as much to fill it with as Margaret-Anne, a formidably stocky girl whose own lack of shyness seems less to do with confidence as raw aggression.

Of the bra-wearers, only the fat ones seem huddled, backs turned, reluctant to expose anything. Or the fat ones and Karen, to be precise.

Her mum bought her it for going to the big school, that being the given reason because the obvious one—showing signs of growing breasts—was non-applicable. It seemed bloody unfair. She was always the tallest girl in class, which made her feel awkward and conspicuous, but she had somehow convinced herself that the consolation for this would be that she'd be among the first to mature physically. It was the biggest girls who developed first, wasn't it?

Well, no, apparently not always.

So there she was, still just about the tallest girl in her new class, still awkward, still conspicuous, still flat as a billiard table. She hadn't seen the point of the bra, and had intended to stick with her comfy vests. That was until yesterday's first PE lesson, however. There, amid all that cotton and lace, she could see divisions forming along the vest/bra faultline, and decided that the only thing her classmates would consider more weanish and uncool than a mousy wee short lassie in a vest was an unmissable big tall lassie in a vest. But her self-consciousness yesterday lest anybody spot her in her sleeveless wonder was positively carefree compared to how she feels now about unbuttoning to reveal this itchy and redundant article. She turns to face the wall so that anyone who happens to look can see it only from the back, hoping also that nobody remembers she wasn't wearing one the last time. Her fingers turn to bananas around the buttons, her sudden haste to limit her exposure and get the T-shirt on serving only to make her more clumsy. She wonders if there's any way of getting the T-shirt on and slipping the blouse off beneath it. Not with the length of *these* arms, she reckons.

'Heh, you,' says a voice, gravelly and harsh: Margaret-Anne. 'Carol.'

Karen feels relief that it's not her being addressed, then shudders as she feels a finger tap her shoulder.

'I'm talkin tae you.'

'It's Karen,' she says. She has to turn round, and so pulls her blouse closed again, holding both sides of it tight across her sternum.

'Just wanted tae ask ye a question.'

'Yeah?'

'See if you'd nae feet, would you wear shoes?'

Karen is knocked a little off-stride by the oddness of the query, but is grateful that it's not the challenge or accusation that Margaret-Anne's tone suggested. It's something she'll have to get used to, she reckons: Margaret Anne's got the kind of voice that would make 'Good morning' sound like she was trying to start a fight.

'Eh, no. Course not. How?'

'Cause I was wonderin why you're wearin a bra.'

Stranger on Home Ground

Okay, take two for meeting Scotty. This time, at least, he can't say he's stuck at work, as Martin is meeting him *where* Scotty says he's working today. However, as Martin makes his way there by taxi, he is harbouring doubts about whether Scot is taking the piss. It's Saturday, for one thing, but the main suspicion, once again, is the venue. Is the bastard setting him up on a tour of the sites of ghastly personal memories?

'The Bleachfield Hotel, you say?' the driver turns around to ask. 'Did I hear ye right?'

'Yeah.'

'Nae bother, pal, it's just . . . I'm sure I heard somebody say they were knockin it doon.'

This acts, paradoxically, as an assurance that Scot *will* be there. He is an architect, after all.

'It's aw right. I'm no lookin for a billet,' Martin

240

tells him. As he says the words, he's slightly surprised at what's coming out of his own mouth, a stark contrast to how he'd addressed the cabby on his way to Heathrow just two days earlier. All these years of living in London have softened his accent, but more pertinently rendered much of his colloquial vocabulary dormant. It wasn't a conscious process, more a gradual grinding down. In the capital, as soon as they heard your accent, they seemed to ask you to repeat yourself on a point of principle (though if you told them to go and fuck themselves, they never seemed to have any bother understanding that). However, even down there, any time he finds himself in Scottish company, he instantly reverts to the mother tongue. He's aware he's doing it, too, even though it's not an entirely conscious act. He wonders if it's a kind of politeness, a form of patronising or a sort of social camouflage, like Woody Allen in *Zelig*.

He stood out a mile in the playground when he first started at St Lizzie's because he was about the only kid in the place who pronounced all his consonants and didn't employ a glottal stop. It didn't take long for the transformation to start, much to his mother's initial dismay, but as long as he could demonstrate that he was able to switch it on and off, she generally didn't worry too much.

Last night, talking to JoJo, he had found himself oscillating erratically between one and the other. He had instinctively slipped into his hometown dialect but had consciously reined it back at times. He was partly afraid she'd call him on the discrepancy, slag him for being the polite wee boy who learnt to talk like the others at school. But it had also been partly because he wanted to emphasise his distance from here, and from her. Being a prick and—you were right, JoJo—being a snob.

'Aye,' the driver says, indicating the heavy plant looming between them and their destination. 'Looks like they're tearin the place doon, right enough.'

Twenty years too late, Martin thinks.

He pays the fare and gets out on to the pavement, the hotel car park being blocked off by cones. The Bleachfield is on the outskirts of Paisley, on the road to Carnock and Braeside. The railway to Glasgow runs past to the north, crossing the road over an old iron bridge. There are houses in adjacent blocks, fifties-built bungalows with long front gardens, the better to distance them from the passing traffic and the eyesore on the other side of the carriageway. The residents will probably have a party once the action starts, with everybody dancing to the wrecking-ball swing.

Martin walks up the short driveway towards where the heavy machinery is ranged, and soon clocks Scot in a hard-hat, talking to a burly bloke wearing a luminous yellow jacket and boots with more tread than tractor tyres. It's the burly bloke who notices Martin, then Scot looks to see what's caught his eye. He grins and gives Martin a wave, holding up two fingers to indicate he has to finish talking but won't be long. A few seconds later, the burly bloke nods and walks away. Scot grabs a second hard-hat from the track of a crane and turns to face Martin.

There are a few flecks of grey just visible beneath the hat, and he's got a wee bit extra around the waist, though not much. His face hasn't

242

changed a bit. People always look younger when they smile, even Noodsy yesterday, but in Martin's experience, the ones who smile the most are those whose faces age the least. From that first day at St Lizzie's, Scot had been an ongoing source of cheerfulness and effortless reassurance that whatever you were getting all worked up about simply wasn't worth it. Martin wonders where he'd be today if he hadn't stopped listening. Most of his problems and fuck-ups in life had been down to being in too much of a hurry to get somewhere else, to *be* someone else. Scotty was the one guy who was happy being himself. The trendy crowd at St Grace's were always striving for maturity, desperate to be taken as seriously as possible. Scotty was never striving to reach somewhere life would inescapably take him eventually, and gave the impression seriousness was a major impediment to enjoying life. One look and Martin realises how much he has missed the guy, how wasteful it's been that so many years have gone by with little more than a few emails passing between them.

Martin's instinct is to hug him, but it's easily suppressed. They shake hands and smile, a little awkwardly.

Reputations

'I hope it's a side,' says Chick Dunlop. 'I heard 1S1 and 1S2 played each other when it was their second time at PE.'

'Hockey's pish anyway,' says Kevin Duffy.

'Aye, but at least if it's a side, you're gettin a game, no just borin exercises wi a baw an a stick like yesterday.'

'And you should enjoy it while you can,' says Kenny Langton. 'Because it's meant tae be fuckin rugby next month.'

'Aw fuck, man. Rugby's *really* pish,' Kevin moans 'And have you seen the state of the rugby pitch? Like a fermer's field.'

'That's because it *is* a fermer's field,' Chick informs him. 'Over the summer holidays. Coos shitin all over it an everythin. So be fuckin grateful for a wee game ay hockey the noo.'

'A side'll be a good laugh,' says Tam McIntosh. He's got close-cropped hair, almost like a skinhead or an army recruit. He strikes Martin as a bit of a hard-nut, not remotely wary of his words or behaviour around either the class's two giants or the boys from other schools, though his demeanour is a sight more cheerful than the headcases usually exhibit. 'Did they pick teams, or did 1S1 play 1S2?'

'I think they played each other,' says Chick.

'We should sort oot teams and positions, well,' Tam suggests. 'So's we can give 1S6 a doin. Plus, saves fannyin aboot once we get oot there.'

If we ever get out there, Martin thinks.

'Aye, good shout,' says Kenny.

'Bagsy no me in goals,' says Kevin.

'Bagsy no me neither,' says somebody else.

'Bagsy no me an aw.'

'Hang on,' Kenny says. 'Bagsy nothin. We need a keeper, for fuck's sake. Who's goin in goal?'

'The weest yin,' says Andy Brady, sitting on the opposite bench. 'Him,' he adds, pointing briefly at

Martin but barely looking at him. He makes his suggestion matter-of-factly, like it's simply understood, though there is an unmissable contempt in his dismissiveness. Andy reminds Martin of Robbie. He's scowly and sleekit, seldom smiling.

He is also, more pertinently, surely no taller than Martin, which one of his ex-St Gregory's classmates takes delight in pointing out: 'He's bigger than you, Andy, ya wank,' says Sean Cassidy. 'Same size, anyway.'

'Fuck off, you know what I mean: the poofiest. That's who goes in goals.'

Martin says nothing, feels his cheeks burn, hopes nobody notices.

Kenny Langton has got to his feet and is looking back and forth between Martin and Andy. 'You any good in goals?' he asks Martin, looking him in the face. He doesn't add the expected 'wee man', which tells Martin a lot more about the guy than any of the stuff he's heard.

'Shite,' Martin replies with a smile.

'Nae point in puttin you in goals, then. Well volunteered, Orb, good shout.'

'Me?' Andy cries, outraged. 'Why me? I'm shite as well.'

'Aye, but you're fuckin horrible and everybody hates ye, so there's a good chance the other team'll be tryin tae hit you wi the baw rather than score.'

'Fuck's sake,' he moans, apparently knowing better than to contest the decision further.

'Orb?' someone asks.

'Aye,' says Kenny. 'Orble Andy.'

They're all laughing: the St Elizabeth's and St Margaret's ones because they've never heard

245

this before; the St Gregory's ones because they love hearing it again. All laughing except Andy, naturally.

He stares directly across at Martin and jabs a finger towards him, though keeping his hand close to his stomach, like he doesn't want it widely noted. 'You're fuckin gettin it later,' he says under his breath. He looks like he means it.

'Well, thank fuck it's no me in goals,' announces Tam. 'Ma hauns are still fuckin stingin after gettin the lash.'

'You got the lash?' asks Kenny. 'When? Ya sneaky bastart!' he adds, laughing.

'Just at the interval there.'

'Whit for?'

'Fuckin caught havin a drag.'

'Where?'

'In behind Tech Drawin. Fuckin McGinty caught us, the assistant heidie. I was only gettin a wee puff ay Rab Daly's dowt.'

'I was just away fae there,' says Chick. 'I shared a fag wi some big Third Year lassie. Must have just missed ye.'

'Just missed McGinty, ye mean, ya jammy bastard. He lashed everybody.'

'Is he good at it?' asks Kenny.

'All right. Had worse at St Greggy's, but the cunt gave us four—two on each haun. It's the second yin that's fuckin sair, man.'

'Aye, I've heard they can give ye four at a time up here,' says Kevin.

'Just for really bad hings,' says Tam. 'Cardinal Sins, the cunt says. "And smoking is the worst of them,"' he mimics.

'Maist ay them are pish at givin it, but,' says

Sean. 'Ma big brer says, anyway. Apart fae Kerr, the geography teacher. It's supposed tae be fuckin agony aff him.'

'But he's a wee skinny guy,' says Tam.

'Aye, but he's meant tae have some fuckin brilliant technique. He stretches it or somethin. I don't know. All I've heard is you're best tae keep the right side ay him.'

'So is that Tam the first tae get it, well?' asks Chick. 'Anybody else had it?'

All heads are shaken.

'Congratulations, man,' Chick says. 'First aff the mark.'

'Four nothin,' Tam adds, holding up both hands like he's taking applause.

'Aye, but it's a marathon, no a sprint,' warns Kenny. 'We'll catch up wi ye soon.'

'Come ahead,' says Tam, smiling.

'Naw, but seriously,' insists Chick. 'Let's see who can get the maist lashes.'

'Today?' asks Kenny.

'Naw, let's make it tae the end ay the month.'

'Fuckin brilliant, aye,' agrees Sean.

'Aye, we should all chip in for a prize,' suggests Kenny. 'Get a wee shitey plastic fitba trophy fae the sports shop up the Main Street.'

'That would be gallus,' agrees someone else.

'Aye,' chips in Andy. 'An whoever has the least should get a fuckin doin from everybody as well.'

'Whit? Why?' Chick asks.

'So's everybody has tae join in and wee snobby poofs like Jackson here cannae shite oot it.'

'Whit have ye got against Martin?' asks Sean. 'Have ye finally discovered somebody ye think ye can batter, is that it?'

Eureka, Martin reckons.

'*Martin* Jackson?' Tam suddenly asks. 'That's your name? You're Martin Jackson?'

'Aye,' Martin confirms, a little uneasy at Tam's enthusiasm.

'Why?' asks Kenny, intrigued.

'I heard you fought Boma Turner once,' Tam says.

'Aye, that's right,' confirms Kevin before Martin can respond. 'Marty ended up wi blood all over the place, but.'

'It wasnae exactly—' Martin begins, but is interrupted.

'Fuck's sake, man,' Tam says, laughing. 'Boma's whit? Two years aulder than ye an twice your fuckin size, but ye still . . . Fuck's sake, man. Mental.'

Martin smiles bashfully, wanting the issue to close, wanting the attention to focus elsewhere. He tries again to say what really happened, but the dressing room is now a babble of voices stating variously how much of a scary and vicious bastard Boma Turner is, as well as listing the illustrious names etched alongside Martin's on his list of vanquished opponents.

Martin got a doing from Boma, an absolute doing. It was over in seconds, and he doesn't think he even landed a blow. But this is proof that on St Grace's virgin territory, the reputations game can go both ways. He's already heard via a St Margaret's kid that it was Richie Ryan who once stood up to the deputy heidie and Father Wolfe at St Elizabeth's. Once upon a time it must have got around Braeview that Boma Turner leathered a kid called Martin Jackson, but while the outcome has not been forgotten, it has been remembered as a fight rather than an assault, and it seems that to have fought and lost is better than never to have fought at all.

Martin doesn't know where to look, but happens to catch sight of Andy again. All the threat has drained from his face and he is suddenly very interested in the toggle on his duffle-bag.

Plans

'Sorry again about last night,' Scot says, once they've traded the standard hails and enquiries.

'Don't worry aboot it. Wasnae as bad a place for a pint as I remember.'

'Aye, it's no bad at all. Did you talk to JoJo, then?'

'Briefly,' he says, his guilt at lying massively outweighed by the greater need to keep the truth to himself.

'Briefly?' Scot asks, surprised.

For a paranoid moment, Martin wonders whether he might somehow know something. It's a small town, and JoJo is to discretion what . . . Well, he can think of no equivalent. She's an absolute. 'We were never exactly best buddies,' he offers.

'Yeah, I know, but I thought you might have pumped her for information. She doesnae miss much in this toon.'

In his head Martin hears himself saying: 'Well, I did pump her, just not for information.' He hears Scotty laugh, too, but in his head is where it stays. There's no end of reasons why he can't joke about it, not least the freshness in his mind of the disturbing alacrity with which they went about their act of making hate.

'So what's the Hampden with gettin me to meet you here?' Martin asks. 'First the Railway and now the Bleachfield. Is it a concerted campaign to bring me back down to earth and deflate my metropolitan ego?'

'Naw, and I'm sorry again aboot the prick remark.'

'Don't sweat it. I was bein a prick. I *am* a prick. But what's the script?'

'Well, it looks like I'm gaunny be stuck here all day, an we've got Helen's sister and her man comin over for dinner, so . . .'

'So it's the only chance we're going to get to talk. Helen's sister: Nicola, wasn't it?'

'Well remembered.'

'If I cannae remember background details about the lassie I had a crush on, what can I remember?'

'Let's not go there,' Scot says, a twinkle in his eye. Scot never went chasing the lassies, same as he never went chasing the future. Like everything else, he knew it would all happen when the time was right. 'What's for ye will no go by ye,' as Martin's granny used to say. And what was for Scot turned out to be Helen Dunn. Still, at least it gave a degree of balance to Martin and Scot's relationship: there had to be one thing about him he hated, the jammy swine.

'I could have waited till tomorrow,' Martin says. 'I'm not shooting back. Told the office I'd need a week. I havenae taken any time off in six or seven months, so . . .'

'I wanted to talk to you aboot this before I

250

inevitably end up talkin to the polis.'

'The polis? About what?'

'The hotel. It belonged to Colin.'

Martin feels as daft as the time he realised, after several years of using the end of a kitchen knife, that there was a jaggy bit inside the lid of a tube of tomato puree specifically for piercing the metal cover. 'Of course. It was his dad's.'

'His dad died six years ago. Cancer. Left the hotel to Colin. He was ill a long time, so the place was already on the slide before Coco got hold of it.'

'Wasnae the classiest place to begin with,' Martin observes. 'A dump, in fact. Somebody must have thought that low-rise, cornflake-packet-on-its-side aesthetic looked good once, I suppose. When was it built? Mid-seventies?'

'Sixty-nine.'

'So why's it coming down? Falling apart? Asbestos?'

'I wouldnae be standin here if it was asbestos, no. Coco was sellin it. Sellin the land, rather. There's a consortium who want to build a retail development on the site. Sirius, they're called. That's who's contracted the firm I work for.'

'A supermarket?'

'No, not big enough. You'd need a site this size just for the parking. We're lookin at eight mid-size retail units. What the Yanks call a strip-mall.'

'And your firm are building it.'

'Well, yes and no. We're still at the planning stage. The deal hadnae been finalised before Colin . . .'

Martin nods. Neither of them wants to say it aloud if they can help it. 'But if the deal wasn't

251

finalised, what are the wrecking crew doing here?'

'Jumping the gun, that's what.'

'Surely Colin would have had to . . .'

'Yeah. They're jumping the gun on his command,' Scot confirms. 'He ordered the site be cleared, which is kinda confusing for me, because it's normally the purchaser who has to worry aboot that.'

'Was he trying to sweeten the deal? Speed things up?'

Scot gives him an 'are-you-daft?' look. 'It's not the purchasers he'd have to sweeten. They want the site, and the price had been agreed.'

'So why wasn't it finalised?'

'Well, in this game, it's never as simple as the buyer and seller agreeing a price. There's a complicating factor that's as complicating as you can possibly get. In fact, complicating things is how it justifies its existence.'

'The council,' Martin guesses.

'Give that man a poke of sweeties, Granny. This is classified as a residential area. In order for Colin to sell the site to this consortium, the area would need to be officially rezoned for retail, or mixed-use at least.'

'But there's shops a hundred yards the other side of the railway bridge.'

'Different story between what's already standing and what you want to build. The hotel site, right now, could only be sold for housing; maybe bring in a quarter-mill if you're lucky. To be honest, you'd dae better sellin it as a going concern to a hotel chain who might want to renovate it. But rezoned for retail, it suddenly becomes worth a lot more.'

252

'How much more?'

'The price agreed wasnae a kick in the arse shy of two million.'

Martin whistles. 'For this dump?'

'But only if it gets rezoned,' Scot qualifies. 'This consortium has developed umpteen of these places up and doon the country, and they've several sites under consideration at any given time. They contract the likes of my firm to plan and build them, and we proceed provisionally so that if they get the green light from the council, everything can go ahead as quickly as possible. But it's up to the landowner to procure the rezoning or whatever other permissions are required.'

'And if he doesn't, the game's a bogey?'

'Withoot missin a beat, they'd write it off and move on to pursuin an alternative site.'

'So did Colin not get the green light, or what?'

'The final decision wasnae due until next month, when the planning committee were scheduled to meet. That's what I mean by jumped the gun.'

'Maybe he was pretty confident of getting the nod.'

'Still nothing to be gained. Well, it would allow us to start work quicker if we got the go-ahead, but you're only talkin aboot a couple of weeks. And if the application failed, he's just demolished a standing asset. I mean, Colin never struck me as the most astute businessman, but he wasnae daft.'

'Did you know him quite well, then?' Martin asks, realising he has thus far ignored what Colin's death might mean to Scot.

'Naw, no really. Just to say hello to, you know, if I saw him in the street or whatever. I don't think we'd more than a ten-second conversation since school before this deal came up.'

'And how did he seem? Was he doing okay, I mean?'

'A bit anxious, as you'd expect, considerin he'd be set for life if this came off. But aside fae that, same old Coco, really. Full of himself—and there was more of himself to be full of, if you follow—and a bit sleazy with it, as ever. Out-of-order remarks aboot Helen, you know the script.'

'Sure do,' Martin agrees. 'I met him once on a train when I was a student. He was doin his usual, patronisin me and askin if I'd ever managed to get a girlfriend. Because it pissed me off, I was stupit enough to tell him I was seein this lassie . . . Aboot two minutes later he's askin if I'd done X, Y and Z with her, really fuckin graphic, you know?'

'Aye. He was a wank. I'm sorry the guy's deid an all that, but he was still a wank. He was a bully, as well. Not the way the bampots were bullies, but more subtly. He knew how to intimidate people.'

'And would that include the planning committee, do you think?'

Scot makes a pained expression. 'Any planning application I've been remotely involved with, there's rumours flying around regarding which way it's gaunny go. The higher the stakes, the mair rumours you hear. Somebody always knows somebody who heard fae so-and-so who's related tae thingamyjig. It's all best ignored, but when you're in our position, you cannae help bein interested in how the wind is blowin, especially if it might mean what you're sweatin over isnae gaunny happen anyway.'

'So what way was the wind blowing?'

'Erratically. Back and forth and round in circles.

254

I mean, that's not unusual: you hear it's goin one way fae one guy, then you talk to somebody else and they say the opposite. What was weird in this case was that there seemed to be a consensus, but the consensus kept changing. It was definitely gaunny happen. Then it definitely wasnae. Then it definitely was again. And what I heard was that there was pressure—*serious* pressure—comin from somewhere to block the rezoning.'

'Who from? Somebody on the council?'

'Naebody knows. Or rather, naebody's sayin. And naebody's sayin on what grounds, either. You normally know what the stumblin block is gaunny be: environmental issues, residents' objections, transport infrastructure ramifications. There's been no opposition from the residents because they'd rather have a nice new set of shops on their doorstep than an eyesore of a hotel that pukes pished folk oot on tae their street every night. Environmental impact isnae really applicable in this case. It's a brownfield site, or it will be once these boys are finished. Transport issues are negligible. It's a shopping development aimed principally at passing trade on what's already a trunk road. Much as these things are never plain sailing, I'd still have put my money on it gettin approval. But the word is that people on the committee were being leant on heavily from somewhere.'

Scot glances at the building, towards which a Caterpillar machine is noisily trundling with destructive intent. He lets his thoughts just hang there, loose and unconcluded. There's something more to be said, but he seems uncertain, reluctant to volunteer it. It's almost as though he's inviting

Martin to make his own inferences, but Martin suspects he's assuming too much knowledge.

'Why would someone want to block the rezoning?' he asks. 'Or am I missing something really obvious to you gnarled property-trade veteran types?'

'The Bleachfield was losin money and fallin apart, classic cycle of decline; and Colin, by all accounts, was not the man to arrest that decline. If this proposal hadnae come along, he would have needed to sell the place pretty soon anyway. Maybe even been forced to, given the debts it was racking up. His only other assets were some lodges up by the fishing loch, which I think did turn a small profit, so he's hardly gaunny sell a money-makin concern just to shore up one that's bleedin him dry.'

Martin's starting to see it now. 'So if someone else had their eye on the place, and the rezoning application got the knock-back, then they could pick it up for a bargain shortly thereafter when Colin's got no choice but to flog it. But why would anybody want to buy this dump, and why would they want it so much that they were prepared to go to the bother of nobbling a planning committee?'

Scotty just folds his arms and stares at him, eyebrows raised. It's as though there are things he doesn't want to be heard saying out loud, but amid this also, once again, is that 'are-you-daft?' look.

But Martin now proves he is not. 'Because anybody who can nobble a planning committee into blocking one application can nobble them into approving another. After which the site they got for a song will be worth a whole album.'

'Aye.' Scotty nods. 'Funny you never see that on

thon Sarah Beeny programme. Still doesnae explain why Colin fast-tracked the Cat-tracks here, but it's somethin to think aboot.'

'This is why you relayed Noodsy's request, isn't it?' Martin decides to ask.

'Naw, I did that because Noodsy asked me to, Martin. Simple as that. All the toing and froing on the committee . . . it's not somethin you give a lot of thought to until two folk are lyin deid.'

'Who was it you spoke to at the council?' Martin asks. 'Who's your sources?'

'A few second or even third hand, and one very close to the action. He won't talk to you, though. Especially not *now*.'

'But who is it?'

Scot gives him a sardonic look, like he's saying, 'brace yourself'. 'You remember Pete McGeechy?'

And thus Martin understands what the look was about. 'Pete McGeechy? That guy who would start an argument with himself? He's in local *politics*?'

'*In* local politics? Guy like that was *made* for local politics.'

'Actually, come to think of it, was his dad not involved in the council?'

'Was, aye. Noo he's a fuckin MSP. And meanwhile, back in toytown politics, Junior's heading up the planning committee.'

'Jeez. The mind boggles. The guy got an "F" in his O-Grade tech drawing, if memory serves, and now he's . . .'

'I think it was a "D", but I'd be splittin hairs. Bottom line is the usual monkey-plus-Labour-rosette equation.'

'He was quite pally with Colin back at St Grace's, was he no?'

'Aye. They were still pally, far as I was aware, but that doesnae guarantee you anythin when politics is involved. Or property.'

'So what did he actually say to you about this?'

'It wasnae so much what he said to me as what he wasnae sayin, half the time. I could tell he was feelin the pressure, but there was no way he was for sayin where it was coming from.'

'You suspected threats, something heavy?'

'Not necessarily. See, there's intimidatory pressure and there's brown envelope pressure, and the latter can make folk even more jumpy and paranoid than the first.'

'You saying he's bent?'

'I'm sayin nothin. As the politicos put it, I'm not rulin anythin out and I'm not rulin anythin in. But in either case, there's a massive disincentive to reveal the source. He wouldnae tell me aboot it, so he's sure as fuck no gaunny tell you.'

'True,' Martin concedes. 'But we're neither of us experts at asking the questions.'

'And you know someone who is?'

'We both do,' he says, and reaches for his mobile.

Arts of Vigilance

Sign of the times: Scot's class, 1S4, are waiting outside registration, Mrs Gordon's home Eeks room, and nobody wants to be at the front of the queue. In all other classes throughout the day, you just pile in and wait for the teacher, meaning registration is the only time there's a line anymore, but it's such an unacceptable act of weanishness to be bothered about being first that even the lassie who has ended up there is a good three yards from the door itself. Fat Joanne is these days to be found as near to the back as she can manage, though if you observe her approach, she typically puts almost as much planning and tactical nous into securing a spot at the rear as she used to in hogging the vanguard.

That's not all that's changed about her, right enough. She's not quite as fat, having swapped a few circumferential inches for vertical ones. Plus, maybe she's lost weight due to the fags, as Scot's heard they can have that effect. She's lost her love of telling tales, too, perhaps because doing so would entail actually addressing the teacher with some minor modicum of enthusiasm, and that would come at an extravagant cost to her new image as the Baroness of Bored. She stands around with a permanent petted lip, prime exponent of the Everything's Shite philosophy which seems latterly to be taking the First Year lassies by yawn.

Eleanor has had a stretch, too. There's a joke to be made about bad smells and dirt being associated with growth, but nobody's much inclined to mention these things since she got that bit taller. She was always a bit of a torn-faced creature, but these days she seems simmeringly aggressive, to the extent that Scot once heard Richie Ryan say: 'I'd rather fight her than fuck her, and I wouldnae want tae fight her.'

Scot's standing with Richie and the two JJs: John-Jo and John-James, who are cousins from Carnock, but might as well be twins, and Siamese

259

ones at that. Nobody's sure how much thought and consideration went into grouping the First Years when they put the three primaries together (or whether it was just names in a hat, as suggested by the bampot-cluster that is 1S5), but if this pair had been assigned to different classes it would have required surgery.

Richie's got a bit of bruising around his left eye, the cause of which is standing a few feet away in the shape of Pete McGeechy, himself sporting a bit of swelling around his bottom lip. Pete is keeping his distance, lots of eyes having tracked his approach given that Richie was already in the line when he arrived. They were all waiting to see what, if anything, would happen after what took place final period yesterday in the home Eeks practical area, not so far from where they're standing now. Pete is a gangly and awkward bugger with all the physical grace of a new-born foal and roughly the same elegance about his social skills. He's not a heidbanger, and he's not (normally) violent, but he's got the shortest fuse Scot has ever encountered, and a tendency to interpret the least contentious assertions as grounds for argument. He talks faster than an Irish racing commentator and says everything so pointedly that even when he's agreeing with you, you feel like you're on the back foot.

It seemed inevitable that one day somebody would lamp him, given the sudden aggression he unleashes without much apparent regard for such possible consequences, but surprisingly, it was Pete who gubbed Richie first. Richie, for all his reputation as a fighter, is normally very slow to anger, which is probably why nobody seemed aware there was any trouble brewing before the pair of them suddenly started panelling each other in front of a double-oven.

Neither was available for comment afterwards, fair to say, having been huckled off *tout de suite* to the deputy heidie's office for two of the lash to add to their other injuries. This means that the only light shed upon what led to this dust-up in the dough-school came as Mrs Gordon hauled them apart and demanded just what the hell was going on.

'He slagged my sole mornay,' was Pete's outraged response.

Provocation if ever anyone heard it.

The two JJs are even more restless than usual, which is saying something. They're both marginally taller than Scot, but he's seldom been around anyone who made him feel so comparatively mature or who could give such a consistent impression of being 'wee guys' as this pair. Scot recently saw a David Attenborough programme that included a bit about spider monkeys, and had reckoned that if you stuck a couple of them in St Grace's uniforms, the two JJs could just dog it and nobody would notice much difference. They are boundlessly energetic, relentlessly chirpy, unremittingly mischievous, frequently amusing and although relatively harmless, you often feel like strangling one of them if they're around you for long enough. They seem jumpy and excited, like they're bursting to tell everybody a big secret, and yet edgily nervous and inclined to squabble, as though afraid the other has just said the wrong thing and given something away.

Lots of people are still going past in the

261

corridor, hastening—or not—to their own registration classes. Scot spots Dom Reilly making his way towards the 1S4 group and gives him a wave. Dom's been off the past couple of days, and Scot had assumed he wouldn't be in today either when he didn't see him in the line. John-James breaks away from the group to go forward and greet Dom, then the pair stop and begin speaking rather conspiratorially. Scot is wondering why Dom's two-day absence has elicited such an enthusiastic welcome, then rolls his eyes as he realises: it's given them one more unsuspecting numpty to inflict their latest stupidity on. The conversation they are having out of earshot right now will mainly involve JJ enlisting Dom in 'pretending' that despite being from different schools and indeed different towns, they were big pals before coming to St Grace's.

Dom's slightly confused grin mirrors Scot's own reaction when it was his turn. He couldn't see the point of this pretence, but there was something infectious about the JJs' cheerfulness, so he just went along with it.

'Sure we were mates when we were wee?' John-Jo says, once they have rejoined the line and have, in Scot and Richie, an audience for this wee performance.

'Aye,' agrees Dom.

'Sure our maws know each other, don't they?'

'Aye, that's right.'

'And we used tae play thegether during the summer holidays, you and me and John-James, didn't we, over the Brae and up the dams?'

'Aye.'

'And mind the time we got chased by the farmer

262

because he thought we were chuckin sticks at his sheep?'

'Aye.'

'And we ran intae the woods tae get away,' John-Jo adds, laughing. 'And we aw hid up a tree until he went by in his daft wee motorbike hing.'

'Aye,' agrees Dominic, now laughing a little, too. 'And we were pure shitin ourselves because he had a dog.'

'Aye, and then we fun that stream and went guddlin for baggy minnows, an you got that big yin that was aboot the size ay a trout, an you flipped it up for John-Jo tae catch an he tripped over ye and fell intae the water up tae his knees. You mind all that?'

'Aye.'

'Naw ye don't, you're a fuckin liar. We never met afore we came here. Cannae believe the shite some folk come oot with.'

And everybody decks themselves. Again.

Mrs Gordon should be along any sec. In fact, she's running late, Scot can tell without looking at his watch: the numbers filing through the corridor have thinned out. He sees Danny Doyle coming, walking fast because he's late but trying not to look like he's walking fast because he's one of Boma's mates and therefore too hard to care. He's two years above, but isn't that much bigger than the taller First Years, unlike some of the Third Years who have filled out in the chest and arms and are absolute bears. Nonetheless, he carries himself with a bit of a swagger, that practised hard look on his face as he saunters past the 1S4 queue. He doesn't look at anyone, but it's like he's making a *point* of not looking at anyone, so they can notice

263

how consumed he is by the serious matters of being Third Year and hard.

Scot turns to comment about this wee display to Richie, but is distracted by a sudden flash of movement up ahead. He looks round in time to see Eleanor knock Danny sideways into the wall with a flurry of blows, having launched herself across the corridor as he went past. He falls to the floor, his back to the bare brick, throwing his hands up to protect himself as Eleanor kicks frantically at his head and chest before being pulled away by her pal Moira Gallacher and latter-day smoking buddie Joanne. Danny Doyle gets to his feet, blood seeping from a cut on the cheek where Eleanor must have got him with her nails or a ring. He looks a little dazed for a moment but quickly hares off when he sees Eleanor straining at the leash for some more.

'Aye, you fuckin better run, ya prick,' she screams after him.

'Whit was that aboot?' Richie asks.

'Fuck knows,' Scot replies.

'Must be her bad week,' somebody mutters. This would be funny if the permanently furious Eleanor ever had a good one.

*   *   *

Noodsy is keeping the edgy at the changing-room door, checking along the corridor so he can let his classmates know if Cook is coming. As the period started about five minutes ago, this is only liable to be if Cook hears sufficient racket to put him off his crossword, or in the unprecedented event of him deciding to start the class inside fewer than fifteen

264

minutes. There's always something going on in the changing rooms during this gap—games of run the gauntlet, dummy fighting, not-so-dummy fighting—so somebody usually has to keep the edgy, which is a risky and selfless task, and therefore one never taken on by the big men like Jai Burns and Gerry Lafferty. The risk element comes from the possibility of Cook or Blake or one of the lassies' teachers—Watson and Manacre— clocking you at it; the selfless part being that you miss whatever carry-on you're on edgy duty to protect.

Today it's not such a sacrifice, as they're playing run the gauntlet, which Noodsy is content enough to avoid. This usually involves lobbing some object around—a ball if there is one, but a glove or shoe will do—with whoever fumbles it having to run from one end of the room to the other while his classmates line up on either side to take wallops at him as he goes past. Noodsy has never understood the appeal because he doesn't see the fun side of hitting people and is damn sure there's no fun side to having thirty fists and as many feet flailing at you in a confined space. He's run it a few times and suffered a few nasty ones. To be honest, most folk just send in a token slap, but there are some vicious wee bastards who love the chance of a free hit and consequently give it all they've got. The big men don't run it very often, mainly because folk are seldom brave enough to lob the object at them. They don't exempt themselves if caught out, however, but nobody ever tries to hit them very hard in case it's noted.

Noodsy is thinking about the mirror on his pet budgie's cage right now, and how useful it would be for scoping down the corridor without getting caught. Maybe he should start packing it with his PE kit. For now, however, he's settling for trying to look while exposing as little of his head as possible round the door frame. He hears a door squeak and jumps back in response, but realises it was too close to be from the PE base. It's right next door, in fact. He pops his head out again and sees Dom Reilly doing exactly the same thing, on behalf of 1S4, with whom 1S3 get PE.

You often see somebody else keeping the edgy, though never for the lassies. Not surprising, really, Noodsy thinks. With them all in there stripping off, they wouldn't need much entertainment beyond the chance to stare at each other's tits. That's what he'd be doing if he was a lassie, anyway.

'Awright, Noodsy,' Dom whispers. 'Any chance of a doubley-up edgy?'

This would let Dom go back inside, on the understanding that Noodsy would hammer on the wall to let 1S4 know if Cook was coming.

Noodsy doesn't need to think about it long: he's not missing anything, so it's a cheap way to be owed a favour. 'Aye, gaun yoursel,' he says quietly.

'Cheers, Noodsy.' Dom smiles, then withdraws again.

Noodsy returns to his attempts to minimise his visibility. He wishes he could see how it looks from the other end, but reckons there can't be much more than an inch of his face sticking out. There's no way Cook's going to notice anything from the far end of the corridor, not the first second he comes out of the base, anyway, which is all Noodsy will need. He's got one foot holding the door away from him, so he can get inside in a flash. Just need

266

to watch the door doesn't slam on the way in. Oh, and better not forget to chap for 1S4, either. Perfect edgy technique. Should be on the official syllabus. More tricky than the gymnastics they're doing at the moment, though anything's a major fucking improvement on that country dancing torture they were subjected to last mo—

'You, boy. Blue tracksuit. In the doorway. Get here, now.'

Noodsy just about knocks himself out when he nuts the door frame in sheer fright at the sound of the woman's voice behind him. He turns around slowly and sees Manacre standing just outside the entrance to the main gym hall, ten yards along the corridor in the opposite direction from the base.

Balls.

He walks hurriedly towards her. It doesn't do to be anything less than cooperative, especially if your best bet for a lash-free outcome is to act the innocent eejit. Manacre is tall and skinny, towering over him. He looks at her long arms folded across her chest, can think of nothing but how big a swing they'd manage with a leather belt.

'What are you doing out of the dressing room?'

'Miss . . . miss . . .'

'You know you're supposed to sit and wait until Mr Cook or Mr Blake arrives, don't you?'

Thank fuck, she's not calling him directly on keeping the edgy. Noodsy opts to go with the enthusiastic dafty line. 'Miss, yes, miss, I know, miss. I was just having a wee look to see if Mr Cook was coming, because it's been a wee while, and it's gymnastics, and I really like gymnastics, miss, and . . .'

'What's your name?'

267

'It's James, miss. James Doon. 1S3, miss.'

'Okay, James. I'll turn a blind eye this time, but I don't ever want to see you or anyone else out of that room without permission again. Is that understood?'

Gallus. His heart's beating away, but he can feel the relief. Got away with it, and well played, even if he says so himself.

'Yes, Miss Manacre,' he confirms.

Her face suddenly sharpens and her eyes go all wide.

'Miss *what*?' she demands.

James sees it too late. He should have seen it way back, but he's never spoken to her, seldom even seen her, and never, ever, heard anyone address her. Aye, sure should have seen it and worked it out. She's standing there, tall and skinny, arms folded across her chest. Folded across her *flat* chest.

Manacre, that's all he's ever heard her called. Not Miss Manacre, just Manacre.

Man-Acre. Miss Acre.

Aw, balls.

Two of the lash, coming right up. Yet again.

*   *   *

Karen stops the car at the kerbside in front of Johnny Turner's place, one of a dozen or so large modern houses in what the marketing brochures like to call 'an exclusive development' just off Nether Carnock Road. She played here on her bike when it was a derelict site, rubble and debris from a demolished warehouse appropriated to form an obstacle course of ramps and jumps when

268

BMX was cool. Colin Temple had a proper BMX, she remembers, plus a helmet and elbow pads. She had a Raleigh Commando, its twist-grip gears stuck in third, but it handled the course better than the poor buggers trying to do ramp-jumps on five-speed racers.

There's a wide monoblock driveway leading up to a double garage, in front of which a red Toyota MR2 indicates, as they have heard, that Boma has returned to the family pile—probably to put Papa's affairs in order before the reading of the will. Or to shred some documents and dispose of certain items before the polis get hold of them. Could be either.

'What you smiling about?' Tom asks her.

'Posh digs. I'm just remembering how much abuse Robbie Turner used to dish out to anyone who lived in a "boat hoose".'

'Maybe we've finally got a motive for killing his old man.'

'Sure. "Father, you have brought shame on the family name by your upward mobility, and for committing the ultimate sin of being a fuckin snob, you leave me no choice but to administer the terminal malky."'

'Where did he live when you were a kid?'

'Just round the corner from me and my folks in Braeview. My parents live in Saltcoats now.'

'The Shitey Shore.'

'Aye. Had to get out of Braeview, the battle-zone it was turning into. Funnily enough, they were unable to afford a pad quite like their old near-neighbour managed to bag. Can't think why two working households' incomes should so dramatically diverge, can you?'

269

'Naw. Cannae think why the Braeview scheme should have become a battle-zone, either.'

'He was a labourer back then, Turner,' Karen says. 'That's as much as I knew, other than that he was a hard-case and his weans were murder.'

'Labourer, aye, but with an interest in joinery.'

'An interest?'

'Aye. Specifically fence-work.'

'Oh, you're just a wee joke jukebox today, Detective. But do go on.'

'You should see his file doon the station. The jacket's older than Arthur Montford's. Mostly small-time stuff, to start with. Reset and a few assaults. Then he started doing a bit of debt collection for the late and unlamented Jimmy Meechan.'

'Moving stolen gear and beating folk up for money-lenders,' Karen says. 'That's what being a crook used to amount to round here. And a cooncil hoose in Braeview was as much lifestyle as it paid for. Never used to be drugs in the town. Just wee hard men. Now there's organised and regimented wee hard men. Heroin was something you saw on *Panorama*, cocaine in the movies. Closest thing we had to a drug problem when I lived there was solvent abuse.'

'Hard to turn much of a profit from that,' Tom says. 'Certainly not one to pay this kind of mortgage. Turner's business latterly was ostensibly a security firm, covering building sites and the like. More like a protection racket, considering he knew every thief in the county. But mainly he controlled the drugs in the town for Jimmy Meechan Junior. That's where the real money came from.'

'What about the boys?'

270

'Boma's the right-hand man since Joe got sent doon. Joe was done for murdering—'

'Wullie Minto,' Karen interrupts. 'I remember the case. Minto worked for Bud Hannigan back then. I was on the drug squad in Glasgow at the time.'

'Aye. A big loss to Johnny. Joe was a lot smarter than Boma, a lot more controlled. Just as violent, but dispassionately so. Clinical. Boma's far more volatile, and the vibes were that Johnny didnae trust him the same as he'd trusted Joe.'

'And where does Robbie fit in?'

'He doesnae. Definitely not anointed for a role in the family business. He and the other Turners don't have much to do with each other, especially since the mother died. Bad blood, for sure, but Christ knows what it's about. That's family for you, I guess.'

'Noodsy have much to do with them?'

'Off and on, yeah,' Tom tells her. 'He did security shifts for the firm, a lot of folk do. It provides a legit cover so they can get a paypacket for other services rendered. Noodsy's a career thief, and it's hard to move anything around here without Johnny Turner having something to do with it.'

'What about the Fenwicks? The Turner boys were always having bust-ups with them.'

'I remember there was a Frank Fenwick died of an overdose, be about eight years back. Would that be one of them?'

'The oldest, yeah. There was a Darren and a Harry, and a girl, Eleanor, who was in my class. Bit of a poor soul. Mother was an alcoholic.'

'Aye. Darren Fenwick. That rings a bell. A

271

bampot, but not a player. Fortunately, not all junior hard men turn into master criminals. He moved away, if memory serves. The others I've never heard of, so they must have turned out okay.'

'I hope so,' Karen says, remembering the shite Smelly Elly had to put up with, and the more literal shite that had blemished Honkin Harry's schooldays. She kills the engine. 'Okay, let's go in and pay our respects,' she says.

Games

The JJs are getting changed into their PE kits in what looks like being an abnormally short time. Given that the pair of them are sufficiently distractable as to be easily able to waste ten minutes pulling their sleeves into funny shapes or hanging assorted inappropriate items from the jacket-pegs, they're invariably the last ones to be ready; Christ, sometimes Cook even shows up before they've got their trainers tied. But this morning, they are purposefully—if gigglingly—getting changed with an urgency that has got Scot intrigued. It could simply be that it's gymnastics this morning—never underestimate the attraction of those wall-bars to a pair of spider monkeys—but he doubts it, doubly so when they start urging everyone else to get ready quicker, too. That's usually a sign that somebody wants to maximise the free time before Cook reluctantly decides he'd better do a wee bit of what he's paid for. When the teacher does show up, it's a bit of a give-away that there's been some serious extra-curricular activity

272

if half the class is still standing about in their Ys.

'Right, check this,' says John-James, reaching into his schoolbag, a vinyl Adidas effort that looks like it's being held together by the ink from all the mentions scrawled across every tattered inch. He produces an off-white Tupperware box, of roughly the kind Scot had been erroneously informed was social suicide round these parts, and sets it down on the floor. In practice, he's found that nobody gets slagged for bringing one, but sightings still remain pretty rare at lunchtime. This is because their true disadvantage is that they act as an advertisement to all the gannets and scroungers that you have something in there worth cadging, and they'll hover around you like wasps at a picnic, chanting their endless mantra: 'Gunny gie's some, eh, gaunny, just a wee bit, come on, don't be moolsy, just a wee bit, gaunny eh, don't be a Jew, come on, give us some, you're a pure starver.'

They won't be cadging the contents of this one, however. John-James pulls the lid off and reveals a browny-green, slimy mass that upon first glimpse resembles a freshly laid country pancake. Then part of it moves, and Scot notices that holes have been poked raggedly through the lid.

'Whit the fuck's that?' asks Franky Naylor.

The JJs just stand there giggling, letting the box itself answer the question. Every head turns to look, some leaning forward where they sit, others standing or getting up and walking closer. Then something jumps, and so does everybody in the room.

'It's full ay frogs,' Jai Burns points out. Tch, and some folk would say that boy's thick.

'Fuck's sake, John-James,' Scot says, 'your

273

mammy's good tae you. Nails here's just got Spam rolls for his packed lunch.'

Nails pure decks himself at this.

'Now, now,' says Dom, putting on a stern voice. 'If you're going to be eating in class, I hope you've got enough for everyone.'

'I think we do have enough for everyone,' laughs John-Jo, and it looks like he might be right. There must be eight or nine of the slimy wee bastards in that box, though it's hard to tell because they're crawling all over each other.

'What the fuck did you bring them in here for?' asks Pete, as ever making it sound more of an accusation than an enquiry, like they know he's fatally allergic to them or something.

'We're gaunny sell them,' says John-James. 'Anybody that wants wan for a pet.'

'Or anybody that's forgot their pieces,' says Nails, struggling to say it through his laughter. He's fair taken with the frog-eating theme, but that's Nails for you—laugh at a door shutting.

'How much?' asks Sammy Devlin.

The JJs look at each other. It's obvious they've not thought as far as this part.

'Eh, ten bob each,' John-James suggests.

'Fifty pee?' Sammy recoils. 'Get tae fuck. Talkin aboot a fuckin frog here, no a greyhound.'

'Ten, well,' barters John-Jo, the 80 per cent reduction failing to elicit so much as a batted eyelid from his business partner. Scot thinks it's short odds he picked the new price simply because it was the next coin down.

'Heh, there's an idea,' says Richie.

'What?'

'Greyhounds. Let's race them.'

274

'Gallus.'

'Magic.'

'Mental.'

'We can bet as well,' says Richie.

'Aye,' says Scot. 'I'm puttin ten bob on the green wan.'

'They're all fuckin green, ya stupit cunt,' Jai informs him.

Scot and Nails exchange a look and Nails starts decking himself again.

'Dom, away and keep the edgy,' Jai orders.

'Aw, fuck off, man, I want tae see this.'

'Just dae it, right?' Jai insists.

Dom knows not to push his luck, and heads around the partition that masks the changing room's interior from the door.

The JJs start lifting frogs and placing them in a line next to the door leading to the showers.

'Shite, I think this wan's deid,' John-Jo reports, cupping his palms together. He then turns and throws 'it' at Richie, but there turns out to be nothing in his hands.

'Fuckin bastart, ye,' says Richie, laughing.

There may not have been a dead frog, but the ones on the floor aren't exactly bursting with life.

'They're no movin,' Jai points out.

'That's because naebody's said "Marks, get set, go" yet,' says Scot.

'Naw, they're waitin for the wee rabbit hingmy tae go by,' Richie suggests.

'They're sleepy,' John-James informs them knowledgeably. 'It's March, man. They're just oot ay hibernation.'

'Does that mean we can buy wan next year on HP over the winter and pay the balance when the bastart wakes up?' Sammy asks.

Dom comes back from the door and sits at his place on the bench.

'Thought you were keepin the edgy,' Jai says.

'Noodsy's daein it for 1S3. Says he'll gie us a chap on the wall.'

Scot wonders if it's worth cautioning that whatever Noodsy is up to, he usually gets caught, but he can envisage being ordered on to edgy duty himself as a result, and so opts to keep it zipped.

'Gie them a wee dunt,' Richie suggests, but doesn't look too keen to touch any of them himself.

The JJs crouch down and have a poke at various of the frogs. Most barely respond, but one suddenly leaps about a third of the length of the changing room, prompting laughter and cheers. This success encourages the JJs to keep poking until they get a couple more to take the high road away from their irritating attentions. Scot often has the same inclination, usually by about half-three in the afternoon.

This belated burst of progress concentrates interest upon the contenders. Scot wasn't serious about betting on the outcome, but folk are starting to support individual frogs, cheering whenever their chosen amphibian takes another leap in the right direction.

'I think that wan there's gaunny come steamin through late,' says Jai, pointing to one of the stubbornly inert creatures at the shower-door end of the room. 'He's just pacin himsel.'

This is unusually witty for Jai, whose rare stabs at humour usually centre on threats or descriptions of violence.

'Is it true you can blow them up if you stick a straw up their arses?' Sammy asks during a lull in the action.

This makes Scot sincerely hope Sammy hits the tuck shop hard enough at morning interval to leave him with less than ten pence to spare.

'Aye,' John-Jo says. 'We heard Tommy Higgins did that once.'

'That's right,' John-James confirms. 'Then he threw a pen-knife at it and it burst. Fuckin sin, so it was.'

'He's a pure bastart,' his cousin rounds off.

'Ha-llo,' Dom cheers, as one of the miniature athletes makes a particularly impressive jump. It's more sideways than forwards, landing just underneath the bench next to Pete, but it's only a foot from the partition, which has been denoted as the finish line.

Seeing his own choice overtaken, Richie overcomes his squeamishness and kneels down to give it a tentative prod. It hops not once, but twice in a row ('Gaun yersel, wee man, you're away noo') to reclaim pole position.

'Right, no more touching,' Dom insists. 'Let's see which frog crosses the finish line itself.'

Everybody gathers round, forming a semicircle behind the two leading contestants, calling encouragement. Everybody, that is, except Jai, who's still standing over the frog he's tipping to 'break late'.

'Gaun, wee man.'

'You've got him noo.'

'Don't bottle it.'

'Come on, you cannae lose tae that wee green poof.'

277

'Hurry up, Freddo, or Tommy Higgins is gaunny get ye.'

Somebody starts singing the music from *Chariots of Fire*.

'Gaun, Kermit. It's yours. That bastart's legs have gone.'

Something whizzes overhead. Then there is a slapping sound against the outer wall.

'Zat the edgy?' somebody asks, but it's not.

Scot looks around in time to see the frog just as it falls, leaving a grey-green splatter against the brickwork. They all turn to look at Jai, who has thrown it, as hard as he could by the look of the results.

'See,' he says. 'Tellt yous it would break later.'

'You're a sick cunt,' Richie says, shaking his head. He's not laughing.

'And you owe us two bob,' adds John-James.

'Fuck off,' Jai tells him.

'I'm serious,' says John-James. 'Same as the shops: you break it, you pay for it.'

Jai pushes him roughly against the benches and goes back to sit down next to his gear. Everybody knows this should be the end of it, but there's still a silent tension in the air in case John-James is angry (and suicidal) enough to take it further. The silence turns out to be jammy, because through it they hear a door squeak and Cook's voice as he enters the dressing room next door.

'Fuck, get the frogs,' says John-Jo in a panic. Everybody starts scrambling about the floor frantically, aware of the shite they'll all be facing if Cook walks in and sees all these wee green fuckers skiting about the place. Even Jai gets involved, although his first priority is binning the evidence of

278

his recent wee frogicide.

'The fuck happened tae the edgy?' John-James asks Dom accusingly.

'Fuck knows,' Dom says, but Scot is fairly certain the answer will involve the Noodsy Magic touch.

Jai was right about one thing: it seems the previously inactive frogs were indeed pacing themselves, conserving their energy for hopping about like their lives depended on it just at the point when everybody needed them to sit at peace.

'Well seein the bastarts are full ay fuckin beans noo,' Richie observes.

Cook comes in just as John-James is fitting the lid back on his Tupperware.

'Lunchtime already, is it?' he asks. 'Well maybe I'll just have a wee share of what's in there myself.'

'Wouldnae recommend it, sir,' Richie says. 'Didnae look very appetising.'

'What was it?'

'Frog's legs, sir.'

'Aye, very good. Right, out you come.'

Cook holds open the door and they start piling out, Jai unusually first, possibly motivated by getting away before Cook notices the stain on the wall. John-James checks Cook can't see him behind the partition and quickly wheechs open the Tupperware again. Cook's looking at Scot, so he has to get going and therefore doesn't see what happens next, but Scot would put a tenner on it involving John-James stashing a frog somewhere among Jai's belongings.

*   *   *

Boma knows fine who they are and why they're

279

here, but he makes them produce their badges at the front door, as a matter of habit or a point of principle, and very likely both.

The 2005-vintage Boma is a more muscular beast than its Eighties prototype, but there's still no mistaking the model. He looks as cadaverous as ever, a hollow gauntness about his face, made all the more sinister by his honed bulk beneath, the better to manifest the cruelty behind his eyes. He's lost much of his hair but the difference is minimal because the ingrained image she has of him is with a close-shaved bullet crop. It was around Primary Five, when he threw mud in her friend Helen's face. Karen didn't see the incident, but kept an eye open for the perpetrator thereafter. Safe to assume he's done a lot worse since.

They say they need to talk to him to try to work out what was behind his father's death. They know he's going to tell them nothing, but they have to go ahead with it anyway. It's like a courtship dance. To the outsider, it might look daft and even pointless, but important—if tiny—details could still be communicated.

Boma stands by the fireplace, arms folded, like he's guarding the living room. His eyes look heavy. He's knackered, burdened, and may even have shed a private tear. Right now, though, he's all shaped up and strictly in character. They are enemies and they are in his father's home. Every query is rebuffed, treated as a means of casting aspersions on the dear departed rather than an attempt to understand why he died.

'My da was a victim, no a suspect,' he says several times. He is particularly indignant on this point when they ask if there is any reason he can think of why someone might have wanted his father dead. It's like his defence of the man has to be all the more effusive now, because he wasn't there to watch his back when it really mattered.

Outrage on the issue of who chibbed his wee brother is conspicuously lacking, an observation that causes Karen to notice another omission. Old Johnny liked his family photos. There are several along the ostentatiously grand marble mantelpiece and perched on top of a widescreen TV vast enough to be one model down from a Jumbotron. Still more adorn prominent spots in a display cabinet, others atop floor-standing speakers and the window sills. Siobhan, the only daughter, makes the most appearances, closely followed by the late Mrs Turner. Boma and Joe are well represented too, in images spanning three decades; you could probably date each one fairly accurately by the style—or latterly sponsors—of the Celtic jerseys the boys are wearing in almost every pose. Robbie's face does not appear once.

Karen makes a show of looking at them all, turning to take in the whole room, and then lifting one from a side-table. It's of Siobhan, a wedding photo.

'Your sister must have been the apple of her daddy's eye, eh? Beautiful girl.'

'Whit aboot it?' Boma asks, rendering it close to one syllable.

'She lives abroad now, doesn't she?'

'Aye. Canada. She's flyin back, but. Gets in today, I think. Might be here already.'

'Must have been rough for your dad. Daughter away, then Joe inside. No wonder he's got so many photos. None of Robert, though. Why is that? Or

281

did you take them down?'

'If I say aye, does that mean I reckon he killed my da and I went and stabbed him for it?'

'How could it?' Karen says. 'You were away fishing somewhere. Where was it? Perthshire?'

'Sutherland. But I know how you cunts think.'

'*Do* you think he did it? He and your dad had their issues, didn't they?'

'I don't know what happened. And I never touched any photies.'

'Fair enough.'

Tom picks up a shot of Boma and his dad in Celtic tops and sombreros, arms around each other's shoulders.

'This Seville?'

'Aye,' he says, looking for the first time slightly vulnerable. Well played DI Fisher. 'Put it doon. That's precious noo.'

'Aye, must be,' says Tom, placing it down gently. 'Quite a memory. A European final. Eighty thousand folk. Wonder where that eighty thousand were when Macari was in charge. Lot of folk awfy busy on Saturdays back then.'

'I've always went, thick or thin,' he insists, taking the bait. 'My season ticket is for roughly the same spot where I used tae stand in the auld Jungle. If it's glory-hunters ye want to talk aboot, go tae Ibrox an ask where aw thae cunts came fae after Souness arrived.'

Tom puts up his hands. 'Wasnae havin a go, pal. I'm a Tim myself.'

Karen's mobile rings. She reflexively reaches for the 'Busy' button, but pauses momentarily as she notes the caller. It's Martin Jackson. Maybe the Perry Mason wannabe is calling to bust the case wide open. Mustn't mock too much, right enough. The way it's going so far, anything he's come up with will be an advance on what she has.

Tom continues chatting about football for a few minutes, but Karen knows he's already got what he wants. It's now an exercise in covering his tracks. Boma isn't being seduced by the fellow-Tim line, however. As has been the case all along, he's letting the polis do all the talking, and answering with the utmost bristling, begrudged brevity. Model crook; his father would have been proud.

Her mobile vibrates again, this time receiving a text message. Like the call, it's from Martin, and the bugger *has* come up with something. Isn't that just like the class smart-arse? She scans the lines a couple of times to be sure she's grasped what he's getting at, training and self-discipline working hard to suppress a smile, then turns to Boma.

'Just before we go, Brian, can I just ask you . . . when was it your dad decided to sideline into property development?'

'Property development? I don't have a scooby whit you're talkin aboot,' he says. But before he says it, there is the merest pause, the briefest flash of anxiety, and it's enough to confirm a direct hit. She won't get anything more out of him, she knows, but this will most certainly do to be getting on with.

Exodus

All of First and Second Year are down in the dining hall for Mass because it's a Holiday of

Obligation. Karen wishes that meant it really was a holiday, because at least you'd get a day off school in compensation for having to sit through another service. She thinks it would be fairer if, to balance things out, there were also holidays *from* obligation, so that for every weekday you had to go to Mass, you got a chapel-free Sunday in exchange.

Karen's resentment is compounded by two factors, the first of which is that she's missing double art for this. Talk about unfair. Carol and Michelle in 1S2 are missing single maths and single RE, the jammy cows. Single RE is when any kind of school Mass ought to be scheduled, Karen decides. It's time already allocated to the subject, and it being a single period would keep the service down to a maximum of thirty-five minutes. Right now she's looking at an hour and ten, which means loads of miserable hymns and a long sermon from Father Flynn, during which he's bound to tell them all for the hundredth time about the oppressed people in Poland. Karen's been watching John Craven's *Newsround* since as long as she can remember, and, between that and the annual *Blue Peter* appeals, has been made aware of dire circumstances in Bangladesh, Biafra and Cambodia. She doesn't recall any of the priests ever mentioning these, nor even Poland until they got a Pope from Krakow. Since then, it appears to have become the clergy's number-one international priority.

The second factor is that she has been picked to give a reading. It is her 'reward' for being one of the few in her English class who can read aloud a passage from a book without sounding like a malfunctioning Dalek. Mr Flaherty announced

284

yesterday that it would be her 'honour' to do the first reading, and she's been dreading it ever since, as well as cursing the fact that Flaherty, her English teacher, is also the head of RE. Her *honour*. Aye, right. More like her downfall. What better way to get yourself pegged as one of the goody-goody sooks—and even worse, a holy-holy goody-goody sook—than standing up at the makeshift altar and reading from the Bible in front of two whole year groups. Might as well turn up tomorrow in a habit and wimple.

Karen doesn't have anything against goody-goody sooks because in her experience they don't exist. Helen gets called it just because she's good at her work, and made out to be dead square by folk who don't know the first thing about her. Helen had a tape of *Dirk Wears White Sox* back in primary school when all the professed Adam and the Ants fans in her year were still listening to the *Grease* soundtrack. Okay, it was through her big sister Nicola, but it's the same difference.

What's annoying is that there *are* a few holy-holy sooks—such as Bernadette, who goes to eight o'clock Mass every morning before school; and that Second Year, Francis Devine, who is an altar boy—so Karen detests the idea of anyone thinking she's like that, too.

She hates RE. Hates it. Other folk don't mind it because it's a comparatively easy lesson with no tests and no homework, but Karen would rather be in maths, that's how much she hates RE. It's hard to say exactly why, but a big factor has to be that something about it makes her feel as if she's back in primary school, under that crabbit boot O'Connor or that dried-up old shrew Harris, both

285

of whom would have happily taught nothing *but* RE all day, every day, if all that pesky reading and writing nonsense hadn't got in the way. She likes being at St Grace's, and doesn't spend the whole week looking forward to Friday afternoon like she did at St Elizabeth's. It's the variety of subjects, mainly, as well as little things like being expected to follow a timetable yourself, rather than being shepherded about by a teacher all the time. She especially loves art. There's no wrong answers in art, and the teachers never shout at anybody. Her art teacher is Miss Munro, who is the best teacher Karen has ever had, maybe because she's so unlike any other teacher Karen has ever had. She wears crazy clothes and has beads in her hair and manages to find something to praise or encourage in everybody's work. Karen thinks maybe she'd like to be an art teacher when she grows up.

It's really not fair that she's missing art for this. Karen can't think of anything more boring than Mass, not even *Crossroads*. You just sit there listening to a monotonal babble of words that don't seem to mean anything. The priest reads from the Bible, but it's never any of the interesting bits like you see on telly, such as Moses or Noah's Ark. It's always the First Letter of St Paul to the Boredstiffyins or whatever. Only the Gospel ever has a story she can relate to, but that accounts for about five minutes out of the whole thing.

Having it in the dining hall is even worse than at the church, because it gets really stuffy with so many people crammed into it and you can still smell whatever yuck was for school dinners. Plus you have the likes of Flaherty and the First and Second Year heidie, Mr McGinty, patrolling at the sides on the lookout for misbehaviour, with a zeal that suggests they'd be disappointed if they didn't find any.

Karen isn't getting to sit with her pals, or even well positioned for a bit of people-watching to pass the time. She's right down the front, alongside several teachers, as well as Bernadette, the Holy Wilma who's doing the other reading; Rachel Andrews, who's doing the Bidding Prayers; and Francis Devine, Boy Wonder to Father Flynn's Caped Crusader, though he'll only need the seat when he's not kneeling, ringing bells or jockeying the chalice.

She feels a bit sick, nervous about what she has to do. She's not worried about the possibility of making an arse of herself. She's worried because simply by doing this at all, making an arse of herself is guaranteed.

Father Flynn's got his arms spread wide as he says one of the opening prayers. He likes to go all the way with the postures and showmanship, especially here, perhaps to make up for the fact that there's no stained-glass windows to lend ambience, and that his 'holy altar' had six plates of mince and tatties sitting on it less than an hour ago. 'Let us pray,' he intones, in that half-singing voice, then he pauses, closing his eyes to let you know he's saying some secret priesty-prayer to himself before getting back to ministering to the mortals.

Somebody rifts, unable to resist filling the reverent silence. Quite a few folk giggle, and there are lots of hands over mouths. McGinty is on his feet in a flash, looking around with an angry face to warn the anonymous burper against a repeat.

Then he looks back at Father Flynn, by way of both apology and giving him the nod to proceed.

'Let us pray,' he tries again, followed immediately by another rift. It's a weird one, more like a big belly rumble than an open-mouthed belch. Karen remembers—who could forget?—that assembly at St Lizzie's when Momo was driven even madder than usual by someone farting at will. It was Harry Fenwick who got the blame, but she later learnt it was Rab Daly who had the dubious talent.

McGinty leaps to his feet again. 'Excuse me, Father,' he says, which usually means the stakes have risen and the whole Mass is on hold until he's caught the culprit, or at least blamed somebody he doesn't like anyway. 'Okay,' he says. 'I won't ask who it was, but if it happens again, every last one of you will get a punishment exercise.'

He stands with his hands on his hips, looking round the hall for effect. A third rift punctures the silence and this time he stomps towards the source, which seems to be near the back. Everybody looks round. They'll get told to face the front in a second, they know, but it's automatic. There's some sort of urgent kerfuffle in one of the rows, with one of the boys rummaging in his schoolbag. It looks like James Burns, one of the year's out-and-out headbangers. Before McGinty gets there, Burns gets up and scrambles along the row, where he starts scuffling with John-James (or is it John-Jo? She can never tell which is which). Flaherty approaches from the other side and they wade in to separate the pair, who appear to be wrestling over the smaller one's bag. It ends up a tug-of-war, with the teachers hauling from opposite ends while each pupil hangs on to one strap of the scruffy Adidas holdall.

A rip reports above the sound of the struggle, and a box comes flying out of the bag as the handles tear the manky old thing in two. The box clatters against the head of a girl two seats forward, then a moment later the entire row gets up and starts making for the aisles, some of the girls shrieking as they do so. Karen thinks she sees something green flying through the air, then definitely sees another row spontaneously decide to evacuate.

Within a few seconds, half the hall are on their feet, either to pile out of their rows despite the dire protestations of McGinty and Flaherty, or to get a better look at what improbably appears to be— yup, that's certainly what it looks like; uh-huh, there goes another one—1S3 and 1S4 being attacked by an airborne squadron of frogs.

What follows is probably not the most sacred of spectacles, though maybe it could become a new sacrament: the Cleansing of the Puddocks from the Blessed Dinner Hall. Or maybe she's viewing it the wrong way, and the frogs are God's instrument in cleansing the Consecrated Canteen of unholy toerags such as James Burns and the JJs.

It makes for superb entertainment, far and away the greatest enjoyment she's ever derived from a church service, with the added bonus that it eats heartily into the Mass's possible duration. They'll have to ditch a couple of hymns, maybe, and Father Flynn will have to settle for a fleeting mention of the Poles and his new-found love of *Solidarnosc*, 'the only trade union I've ever heard of bloody priests sticking up for', as her dad has bitterly remarked.

Watching them try to gather the errant green invaders while attempting to deter further hordes of the congregation from fleeing their seats gives her the briefest hope that the teachers will decide the simplest plan is to abandon the whole thing, but deep down she knows there's no chance of that. McGinty and Flaherty are grimly determined that it will be seen through: it's a point of principle, an uncompromising religious crusade. The precedent—and therefore incentive—would be catastrophic. If somebody died in here, they'd still finish the bloody service. So no way they're letting some farcical carry-on put an end to *Holy Mass*.

Farcical, she thinks, yes, but not entirely unbiblical.

Karen looks at the tome in her hand, the bookmark at the reading Father Flynn has chosen, and starts flicking further back.

The place is finally returned to order, minus the amphibian visitors and about as many pupils: the boys to answer, via leather, for what happened; the girls to rein in their hysterics and in a couple of instances give their slime-smeared hair a rinse in the toilets. Father Flynn gets the show back on the road, noticeably cutting down on the pregnant pauses, then calls for the readers to come forward.

Karen knows there'll be trouble, but hazards they'll consider it theologically shaky ground to belt somebody for the crime of reading from the Bible. And besides, it's just too good a chance to resist.

'First reading,' Father Flynn announces, and gestures Karen to the lectern.

'A reading from the book of Exodus,' she says.

290

In the front row, she sees Flaherty's brow furrow with satisfying confusion. 'Then the Lord said to Moses, Go to Pharaoh and say to him, Thus says the Lord, Let My people go, that they may serve Me. But if you refuse to let them go, behold, I will smite your whole territory with frogs . . .'

∗   ∗   ∗

So he's sitting alone again, trying to make one drink last, feeling conspicuous as he always does in such situations: paranoid that everybody is looking, everybody is thinking 'Billy No Mates' or 'Sad Mr Stood-up'. It's a restaurant this time, which makes the effect even worse than the pub. Having a drink on your tod in a bar can at least be open to more generous interpretations: swift one before catching the train, mate running late, quiet wee indulgence with the paper or a book. Sitting on your Jack Jones at a bistro table for two, however, makes you the establishment's conversation piece.

It's to be expected, Martin appreciates. He's done it to others often enough, caught up in meetings and unable even to get so much as a text through to that effect. It must be a dozen times as bad for the polis, with maybe only hospital doctors having it worse. This, he speculates, may be a large part of the reason Karen is divorced. Still, no news is good news, he reckons, checking his watch. She wouldn't call to say she's running late but on her way if she could be here any minute. The only reason to call now would be to cancel altogether, so, dear mobile, be silent.

He can't believe he's feeling so anxious; partly regarding simply whether she's going to show and partly in anticipation of being here with her if and when she does. He was cooler waiting for Becky Soleno, but perhaps that's not as daft as it sounds. If Becky Soleno hadn't shown up, how much would he really have cared? Yeah, she was beautiful and never out of the glossies, but those things didn't make her particularly special to him. Not like Karen Gillespie is special. This is the date his inner fifteen-year-old never had, and nothing Becky or Kara or any of the others had to offer could compete with that.

They've got some very important issues to discuss, obviously, but mostly he's looking forward to catching up. Well, perhaps 'catching up' isn't the term, because that would imply that they had a past relationship worth the name to catch up on. But maybe it is catching up nonetheless: catching up by having the conversations they were never able to because of whatever classroom convention decreed that only the coolest boys and girls could ever talk to each other. Catching up by getting the belated opportunity to find out who each other really is, really was.

This thought unfortunately brings him back to last night, and another conversation with someone he'd never truly spoken to. Was he hoping to bed Karen, too? Go for the hat-trick: three nights, three women, one horny but lost and fucked-up little boy? No. He just wanted to talk, wanted to get to know who Karen really is because back then he never had the chance. With JoJo it was different, something else, some brutal act of mutual catharsis.

So, to be more honest, Martin, you're saying you didn't want to get to know who JoJo really is? You

292

reckoned you already knew all you needed to know and the book was closed? No. Okay, kind of. But what he really wanted last night was for JoJo to find out who *he* really is. That's where all that aggression and resentment, all that frustration was coming from, wasn't it? Uh-huh. Yup. But it wouldn't have happened if it wasn't *mutual* aggression, resentment and frustration.

His drink is just about gone. It was a bottle of Sol, not quite chilled enough, served with the standard affectation of a slice of lime. The lime was about the only thing he really tasted. He could murder a pint of Eighty like he had at the Railway.

His phone rings. It's Karen. Shite.

She isn't going to make it. They just got access to a motherload of Colin's files and documents, and she's going to have to spend the rest of the evening sifting through them. She apologises, says maybe tomorrow. He says he understands, and to remember their deal. She asks what he's going to do with the rest of his Saturday night. He looks at the colourless trickle at the bottom of his bottle and says he doesn't know. He's lying.

Hard Cunts and Nice Guys

Robbie's still got this sound in his ear from when his da leathered him last night. It makes this high-pitched noise that goes *eeeeeeeee*. Sometimes it seems loud, sometimes it's just in the background, but it's fucking afternoon interval now and it's still there.

His maw and da argued about it afterwards, like

293

they always do. Da says he needs to learn to take it, toughen him up like Boma and Joe. (Da doesn't batter them much anymore because they're getting too big and they're liable to hit back.) Maw said Da never hit them anything like he hits Robbie. Da just said: 'Aye, well,' and that seemed to be the end of it.

Robbie *can* take it. He gets a battering off Boma all the time. Not so much Joe, but then Joe's more liable to take shite out on Boma, because Joe's the oldest. Boma's a cunt when he's in a mood. Robbie can take that, and take leatherings off his da, and he reckons that means he could take anything the boys in his year could dish oot, no danger.

He ought to have more of a rep. He's been at St Grace's more than six months, fuck, and he's hardly fought anybody. Some folk don't need to fight much to have cunts feart of them, but nobody's feart of Robbie. Every cunt's feart of Boma and Joe, but none of it seems to have rubbed off. He's sure folk shat it from Boma when he first came to St Grace's, simply because he was Joe's wee brother, but then Boma looks like Joe a lot more than Robbie looks like either of them. Now, obviously Robbie's not the biggest, so he's hardly going to be in there with the likes of Jai and Paddy, but fuck's sake, at the moment he's not fucking quoted, and when you see who is, it gets even worse. Christ, that boy Pete McGeechy, who looks aboot five stone soaking wet, had a fight with Richie Ryan, for fuck's sake, and that's him made now. There's plenty will be keeping their fucking mouths shut who before that would have been happy ripping the pish out of him. No, Robbie needs to make a mark. Needs to be seen panelling some cunt so folk get the fucking message.

That fucking *eeeee* noise, man. Doing his melt in, so it is. Some other cunt needs to be hearing that, so he does.

Question is: who?

Paul McKee leaps to mind. Always does. Unfinished business. If it's all about reputations, about who battered who, then that's a record he really ought to put straight. But, but, but, but, but . . . He'd never admit it to anybody, but when it comes down to brass tacks, he doesn't fancy it. He always came out with some shite about how he never fought back that day against Paul, but the truth was he was feart. There was a look in Paul's eyes, this burning, angry look, that told you how much he wanted it. Robbie's seen his big brothers fight so many guys, and seen the look in their eyes that tells you they're beat, sometimes before they've even started. Even the ones that start all determined, you can see the moment they know they're beat, see the fear, after which they just want to end it soon as, minimise the damage. Paul's look was like the opposite of that, the look Robbie's seen in his brothers' eyes: something mental inside, something that just wanted to hurt you and didn't care what you gave back.

There's plenty of cunts Robbie could take no bother, but there's no point if they don't fight back. Just start leathering into somebody like that and folk don't think you're a fighter, they think you're a heidcase. Plus chances are you'll get one of the real big men knocking fuck out you because you're out of order. That's why Martin Jackson's a non-starter, even though some folk think he must be harder than he looks because they heard he fought

Boma. Total shite. Boma just fucked him for a laugh, like swatting a fly. Robbie'd love to show him up, show what happens when he *really* tries to fight not even Boma, merely Boma's wee brother, but he knows it just won't happen. Martin probably wouldn't fight back, which would make it pointless. Plus Martin's all palsy with Kenny Langton, so there's no fucking way Robbie's just going to go up and start picking on him. Aye, what a fucking disappointment that was, Kenny and Chick: Robbie thought they'd be starting wars but instead they're big mates, and so is every cunt in that class. Kenny and Chick don't even fucking smoke anymore, because it would get them chucked out the school football team. Tight wee fucking unit, that 1S5 mob. Never even fight among themselves, even with Tam McIntosh in there. Big fucking disappointment.

But then there's Coco, isn't there, who he battered in primary. Coco fucking thinks he's it these days. Thinks every cunt's forgotten he was one of the wee poofs just because he hangs about with a different shower up at St Grace's. Smart mouth on him. Joins in if folk are laughing at Robbie. Comes out with all sorts of cheek because he knows Aldo will laugh at it, but that doesn't mean Aldo would protect him. Aldo likes the sight of a good fight as much as anybody.

Aye. Maybe about time a few folk got reminded where Coco stands compared to Robbie.

He sees him across the social area, near the big pile where everybody dumps their bags. Robbie bends down and makes sure the laces on his Docs are tied tight, then walks across.

He just hovers about at first, on the edge of the

conversation. He knows a way in will come soon, and it does when Coco refers to him as 'Turkey'. It was Aldo started that a few weeks back. Robbie fucking hates it, but when it's big Aldo, there's not much you can do. But Aldo saying it doesn't mean every cunt can say it.

'Don't fuckin caw me Turkey, Coco, ya cunt, or I'll batter your fuckin melt in, awright?' Robbie says. He gives him a push in the chest to underline his intentions. A few folk's eyes and ears have perked up. Good. If nothing happens, at least they'll see Robbie laid down the law, and Coco shat it. 'I've fuckin leathered ye afore and I'll dae it again,' he adds, figuring he might as well broadcast the track record seeing as he's got an audience, including folk who never went to St Elizabeth's and so don't know.

'Aye, it was fuckin Primary Three, Turkey,' Coco responds, with a disbelieving, *disrespectful* laugh.

Robbie seizes the chance, pushing Coco again with each question. 'So ye hink ye'd dae better noo, eh? Hink ye'd dae better? Ye want your go? Dae ye? Ye want your fuckin go?'

He's waiting for Coco to push back, because that's his cue: that's an accepted come-ahead that everybody can recognise, no question of Robbie just lamping him unprovoked.

Instead, Coco punches him flush on the the jaw. Robbie doesn't see it coming, only feels the impact, and in that instant knows he's just fucked up on an enormous scale. The image he's had of Coco in his mind, he realises too late, is not the boy he's now fighting, nor has it been for months. He's taller than Robbie now, a good few inches, but the main difference is bulk, muscle, power.

297

He's filled out, stocky, sturdy, like Chick Dunlop, like Kenny Langton. Like Boma. Like Joe.

When Coco hits him, it's not like in fights with other kids before. It's like blows from his brothers or his da. Each one shakes him to the bones, impacts through his whole body, which is why he knew he was beaten after the first.

He can take the blows, he knows, but there's no chance of delivering enough damage in return for that hard-learnt stoicism to help. His own strikes are feeble flails in comparison, like every time he's been daft enough to try to hit back at Boma. And just like Boma, when he looks at Coco, he can see he's enjoying it. Robbie feels fear amid the pain: that fear his brothers' opponents feel when they get that look in their eyes that says they just want it to end. His legs buckle and he falls, though he didn't lose his balance really. That's usually the end. Sometimes fighters keep kicking into the guy when he goes down, but they always get hauled off, either by the boy's mates or by one of the bigger guys doing his Captain Sensible. Robbie can sense the pause, the lull in the noise of the crowd in response to the action stopping, as they wait to see whether the boy on the floor will get up and go in again. Sometimes the other fighter offers a hand to shake: the winner giving the loser a road out, no hard feelings; or offered by the loser, showing he surrenders. His face is sore around both sides of his jaw and he can tell he'll have a huge keeker round his left eye, maybe the right, too. His mouth and nose are all right, though, so at least he doesn't look a total mess. He clambers halfway to his feet, still looking at the floor, not at Coco yet. Coco isn't offering a hand, he can tell, maybe not

298

wanting to let down his guard, and just as likely wanting to give Robbie some more. The *eeeee* noise is louder than ever, the room swimming a bit.

Robbie's about to put out a hand, having no other choice, when a voice—sounds like Aldo, not sure—shouts: 'Get fuckin intae him, Coco.'

A hand grabs his hair at the back of his head. Robbie sees a flash of black leather. Feels something crunch. Feels something wet.

*   *   *

'The first goal was scored by Gunni, the second by Geordie Shaw, the third goal was scored by Paul Lambert, the finest of them all . . .'

The Railway Inn is busy and noisy, but not raucous. The singing is coming from four guys at a wee table, and they're not belting it out or clapping and stamping. Somebody started it and the others have taken up the refrain in a moment of lightly bevvied camaraderie.

'No goals were scored by Celtic, three-nothing was the win, and ye couldnae hear *The Soldier's Song* for *When the Saints Go Marching in.*'

The *Soldier's Song* reference gets a couple of sideways glances, probably from Old Firm fans, who get a bit prickly that they wouldn't be allowed to strike up any of their numbers in places like this. Maybe if they ever tried singing one that was actually about football, they might be given a more indulgent reception, but Martin is straying into the realms of fantasy there.

He's glad the place is lively. It makes him feel more comfortably anonymous. He hasn't seen JoJo so far, and whenever she does put in an appearance, he isn't sure he wants her to see him more distinctly than as a face in the crowd. And yet he does want her to spot him. He just doesn't quite know why.

It's an unease, one he knows will not fade or dissipate on its own.

He feels bad about last night, or perhaps it's more accurate to say he feels bad about this morning and the manner of his leaving. No, he *does* feel bad about last night, too. He fears he mistreated her, little as she was complaining, and much as she was reciprocally mistreating him. He was grudge-fucking some residual totem of a daft wee teenage lassie, but the vessel for that totem was a hard-working woman trying to run a business and raise two kids on her own.

He doesn't even have to close his eyes to see the two of them upstairs last night, and it makes him wince. Does she believe that's what he thinks of her? Because it isn't, and he'd like her to know that. And he'd like her to think he isn't the guy she was grudge-fucking, either.

So essentially it's as you were, repeat scenario. The frustration is the same: that he never got her to see who he really is. That he's a decent guy. A nice guy.

The bloke standing talking to the folk at the next table finally spots a spare pew and takes a seat, unblocking Martin's view of the gantry. He sees JoJo now, realises she could have been there a while. She looks a little flushed but is managing a joke with one of her staff and a punter as she places his order on the bar. It's an old boy, probably been drinking here for decades, aside from in the aberrant hiatus of the pub's Eighties teen meat-market misadventure. JoJo sends him on his way with a sweet smile. She thinks *he's* a nice guy.

Martin never got a smile like that from JoJo in twelve years of knowing her. He used to think being a nice guy ought to have been enough for her—and a few others—to like him, or at least for her not to be nasty to him. But maybe being a nice guy *wasn't* enough. What did it consist of, in JoJo's case, he asks himself? Mere acts of omission, if he's honest: what he didn't say, what he didn't join in with. Nothing more. What did he ever do *for* JoJo that would have made her like him? He tries to recall, comes up blank. So in truth, as it turns out, he was merely a nice guy to some other people. Why should that have counted for anything at her end?

His pint is finished. Part of him wants to leave, tell himself she must have seen him sitting there and that's got to count for something. The greater part of him knows he can't, knows he won't, uncomfortable as this next scene is going to be.

He walks up to the bar and places his empty glass down gently upon it. JoJo doesn't see him yet, but it's going to be her who serves him: the other bar staff are taking orders and she's at the till getting someone his change. He tries to compose the right expression, but can't think what that expression ought to be. Doesn't matter anyway: he's going to look the same to her regardless.

She turns around and seeks her next customer. She looks surprised and a little wary. 'Nae waitress service tonight,' she says. 'And the free drinks for celebrities offer's expired.'

'Aye, you reel them in with your special offers,

301

then they're addicted,' he replies, offering a smile but trying not to seem glib.

She takes a clean glass and pours him a pint. 'Seriously, what are you doing back here?' she asks, sounding ready to muster her defences.

'Should I leave?' he asks, a sudden chasm opening in his stomach as he realises how badly he may have misjudged coming here. It's not a polite gesture but a sincere question: if she says yes, he knows he'll be on the pavement ten seconds from now.

JoJo looks down at the pint she's pouring. She closes her eyes very briefly and shakes her head. He lets the gush of relief out through his nostrils in a silent sigh.

'I cannae talk much,' she says, indicating the throng. 'But pull up a stool if you like. It usually gets quieter about an hour from now. Young ones start heading off for the clubs.'

'I would like that, thanks.'

'I'll get you something to read,' she adds.

Before he can tell her not to go to any trouble, she has grabbed hold of a magazine from under the bar. It's a copy of *Heat*.

He nods, says nothing, takes his licks.

*   *   *

'Fuck, you see that wee guy spurtin up?' Sean says with fascinated wonder.

They're in double science, last class of the day: Sean, Kenny, Tam and Martin along the bench at the front, thus assigned so the teacher could keep a close eye on some of them. Chick would normally be on the stool at the end, but he's off with the flu.

302

Sean, having gone to St Margaret's, doesn't know who 'that wee guy' is, doesn't know the history or the significance of what just occurred. Martin does, and he doesn't share Sean's gleeful awe. He never thought he'd say this, but he feels really sorry for Robbie. Feels kind of sick, in fact, thinking about what he saw: his head going back, the blood coming up like a fountain. It was horrible.

He doesn't like what he saw of Coco either, though maybe before he gets too judgemental, he should ask himself what he thought he'd do in the unlikely event that he ever had Boma Turner in the same situation. Martin doesn't know Coco so well these days, with them being in different classes. They still say hello in the corridor and all that, but they don't hang about together.

'That was mingin, man,' says Kenny. 'Mind you, if they mop it up and give him it hame in the bucket, his mammy can make him his own black puddin!'

They all laugh; even Martin. Kenny is infectious that way. Not as sharp as Scotty, but you end up decking yourself anyway. And sometimes Kenny really comes out with a cracker: not dead witty or anything, but it's all in the timing.

'Right, 1S5,' says Coleman, coming in and closing the door with a bit of a slam to shut them up and bring the class to order. 'Books open at page 78, section 5.2. Jotters open also. Face the front. No talking.' She's putting on her tersest voice, used in conjunction with the slam she has judged necessary to set a full-scale nae-messin tone in light of the amphibian hysteria that's gone on earlier today.

303

She walks to the blackboard and wipes it clean with a duster. 'I want you all to copy this down. There's going to be a diagram, so you'll need a ruler. And remember, the quicker we get through this part, the more time we'll have for the practical work afterwards.' She starts writing on the board, speaking out the words. 'In . . . this . . . country . . . we . . . collect . . .' There's a pause as her hand catches up with the last word.

'Frogs,' says Kenny, using exactly the same volume and register.

Within moments she's wheeching out her belt and calling him to the front while everyone else is close to calling for oxygen.

Kenny doesn't care. He winks at Martin as he goes up. He knew what would happen and knew it was worth it for the gag.

Plus, if he gets the standard two lashes or above, it'll put him clear of Tam McIntosh at the top of the March league table.

Intelligence

JoJo was right about the crowd. It thins out steadily as the hour approaches ten, the demographic lurching dramatically towards the grey. JoJo takes a look at the sparse remaining clusters of drinkers and declares herself temporarily surplus. She grabs a coffee from the espresso machine and invites Martin to join her at a table.

The music has been turned down but it still provides welcome cover for the initial silence.

Martin feels he ought to be the one who breaks it. 'I just wanted to say . . . about this morning—'

'Don't,' she interrupts. 'Just . . . let's not, okay? Whatever it is, consider it said. We both know, I think, don't we?' She doesn't say what they both know, doesn't have to. 'Cannae say I'm not a little embarrassed,' she adds. 'But let's not build it up into something anybody needs to apologise for. I've done plenty I've regretted more.'

'Well, I'm sure I can trump that hand, but best we don't go there.'

She laughs a little. 'You? That nice Martin Jackson boy? Surely not.'

'I'm not as nice as I once was.'

'Aye, but at least you're not as boring, either.'

'Touché.'

She takes a long sip of coffee, looks like she's already thinking about her kip.

'You okay?' he asks. 'You look a bit . . .'

'Knackered? Don't flatter yourself, son, it wasnae you. I had to clean this place today. Eleanor who does the cleaning has been off sick since Tuesday, and that was manageable through the week because she just sent Laura, but Laura cannae do Saturdays and Sundays because the weans arenae in school, so . . . Anyway, bottom line is the buck stops here.'

'Eleanor?' Martin asks. 'As in Fenwick?' He composes his expression to be as neutral as possible so that his query cannot willingly be interpreted as being remotely judgemental or in any way superior.

'Aye. Does that fit your picture?' JoJo sneers, confirming his expression didn't pull off any of the above.

'I'm just asking,' he says. 'Gie's a break. How is she doing these days, apart from not being well at the moment?'

'Better than you're assuming. She cleans this place, but it's a business she's got. She employs four folk, two full time and two part time, but she's a hands-on kinda boss. They do this place, a few offices, some domestic work. She's done all right for herself.'

'I'm glad to hear it.'

'Always a hard worker, Eleanor. She got pregnant at eighteen and nae sign of a father, but she was determined she wasnae gaunny end up like her ma. Did everything she could to raise the lassie properly. She's eighteen now, Gail, at uni down in Newcastle. She's studyin languages. Eleanor was proud as punch when she got in, let me tell you.'

'I can imagine.'

'No need to look so surprised. Eleanor wasnae daft. She just never had much encouragement to believe in herself. I'd like to have seen what your precious grades would have looked like if you grew up in her hoose.'

'You don't need to lecture me on this stuff, JoJo. And my grades weren't "precious", just a means to an end. Do you remember once ever hearing me boast about them? Once?'

'No, Martin, but they were precious to you all the same, because they were the proof of how much smarter you were than everybody else. We both admitted last night that we found our own ways to look doon on each other.'

'And I thought you said this morning that we shouldnae be judged on what we did back then.'

'Aye, but you're still doing it now.'

306

'I'm not, believe me. I'm the last person you need to tell about how your start in life affects your chances. You'd be amazed how many utterly mediocre but successful people I've dealt with in my job, useless numpties who've got where they are because they came from the right background.'

'Boat hooses, do you mean?' she says with a bittersweet smile.

'Safe to say, yeah.'

'And the old school tie.'

'Aye, but what folk don't realise is that the old school tie isnae just about connections. It's about confidence, about being brought up to believe you're entitled to take whatever you want from the world, and you don't need to have gone to Eton for that. Christ, look at Colin. He wasnae the brightest, but he was always determined to get what he wanted because he'd been brought up to believe he was due it and he had confidence by the barra-load.'

'He was brought up to believe other people were mugs, there for him to use and chuck away,' JoJo says, quietly but firmly, like she doesn't want to be overheard dissing the dead but won't stand for revisionism either. 'His mother was nice enough, but his da was a blowhard who thought he was better than everybody else just because he'd made a few bob.'

'I don't remember that about his dad, but I would have been less than ten the few times I met him.'

'Aye. You only knew Colin when he was a wean, before he got big enough to throw his weight around. I knew him later, when he wouldnae have been seen dead hangin about with you. And I knew

307

him as an adult,' she says pointedly. She drains the last of her coffee and puts down the cup.

Martin looks expectantly at her, inviting her to go on. He suspects he's giving her precisely the gratification she wants, but doesn't grudge the price.

'Colin's what you get when somebody's confidence tries to break past the buffers of their limitations,' she says. 'His dad was a balloon who got lucky with a couple of business deals and thought that made him a genius. Colin inherited the delusions and the ego but not the luck or the graft. He was a big, lazy chancer.'

'Was he bent?' Martin asks bluntly.

JoJo shakes her head. 'No. Sleazy, but not bent. I'm not sayin he was particularly honest, either, but if you ask me, he lacked the nous, you know? He would have been bent, but somebody would need to have laid the opportunity on a plate for him.'

'Aye.' Martin nods, thinking of Scot and what he told him of the strip-mall deal pretty much falling into Colin's lap, something JoJo clearly knows nothing about, given her remarks on his absence of luck. 'That sounds like him. The sleazy part, too. I take it he never got married or anything.'

'You must be kiddin. Colin treated women like meat. I don't think he had a steady relationship his whole life. He thought that hotel of his was like a giant bachelor-pad for a never-ending adolescence. Spent all his time just gettin pished and shaggin daft wee lassies who thought he was the life and soul. That's why the Bleachfield went downhill so fast. He tried to hire me to manage the place at one point, but I told him to sling his hook.'

'Was it unsalvageable even then?'

'No idea. I just wouldnae work for or with the man. Never knew how Eleanor could do it, but I suppose he was seldom there when she was workin.'

'Eleanor cleaned the hotel?'

'No, he owned some lodges up the Brae.'

'Yeah, I heard they were more of a successful venture than the Bleachfield.'

'Aye, well, small wonder. More picturesque location than the dual carriageway out of Paisley, and they're meant to be very nice. Wouldnae have been tempted myself, right enough.'

'Not exactly a great escape if it's five minutes up the road?'

'Naw, it wasnae that. Eleanor put me off.'

'How?'

JoJo pauses and her eyes scan from side to side, almost involuntarily, as though reluctant to break Eleanor's confidence, concerned that what she is about to impart might fall into the wrong hands. It is the moment when she seems most removed from Fat Joanne, who so relished telling tales; more so than in her slim figure, more so than in her matured features, more so than when they were naked together.

'Just something she once said. I mentioned that I heard Colin would sometimes offer lodges to folk he knew at cut-price rates or even free for a bit of you-scratch-my-back. Eleanor said she wouldnae stay there if she was paid to. I asked her what she meant, but she clammed up. I got the impression she was feart she'd given somethin away that she didnae want gettin back to Colin.'

'What do you think she meant?'

'No idea, but when it's comin from the person

309

whose business is keepin the place clean, it's not exactly a ringin endorsement.'

'Cannae see the place gettin a great write-up fromVisitScotland either, after what happened.'

'No. Course, I'm forgetting: you're up here on a mission to crack the case before the polis so you can free Noodsy an be the hero of the hour.' JoJo smiles as she says it, but there's a mocking sourness to it, much the same as last night but without the sexual sparring. The old JoJo is back in the house, so Professor Brainbox had better watch his step.

'The polis are everybody's best bet for cracking the case,' Martin says. 'I'm just trying to help.'

'Aye,' she says, nodding sincerely. 'Because that's what you're really doin here tonight, isn't it? Fishin for information. Shouldnae blame you, really. I did say I was the one to ask. I'd just have preferred if you were more up-front about it, instead of kiddin on it was somethin else. I'd have preferred it also if you'd actually asked me what *I* thought, but you're not interested in that. Fat Joanne might accidentally shed some light but she's not got the brains to put two and two together herself.'

'That's bollocks,' he says, keeping his voice low. He considered a more ameliorative reply, but that tone only seems to irritate her. 'I came here because I didn't like the way I'd left things.'

'You came here because you like the idea of yourself as a nice guy and you wanted some kinda absolution for what happened. You never quite got that, so you're makin it worth your while by tappin me for background knowledge.'

Fuck this, he thinks.

'Well, you've never exactly been reluctant to

310

show off what you know, JoJo, have you?'

'Look who's talking.'

'Great comeback. Why don't you call me Professor Brainbox and have done with it.'

'Why don't you call me Fat Joanne and have done with it? You're no more interested in what I've got to say now than—'

'Wait a minute,' he interrupts. 'First I'm tapping you for information and then I'm not listening? Which is it, make up your mind.'

'It's both. You want to know what I can tell you, but you're not interested in hearing what I might have to say.'

'No, this is binary, JoJo, do you understand? One or other, off or on. Can't be both.'

She sneered as he said the word 'binary', and he felt like an utter prick for doing so, but he's struggling to fight his corner here. Now they really are Professor Brainbox and Fat Joanne. He recalls one of the more nauseatingly precocious acts of his schooldays, and it's safe to assume she does, too. It was in Primary Seven, when O'Connor was introducing this particular subject. He told the teacher he'd once read a sentence that would illustrate it, and was invited to write it on the blackboard. 'There are 10 types of people in this world,' he'd written. 'Those who understand binary and those who don't.' He'd been so proud of himself. If somebody had kicked his balls for it, it would have been both just and a mercy.

'It isn't both,' JoJo states precisely. 'There's a difference. Why haven't you asked me what I think?' she demands.

'We'd barely strayed on to the subject when you started getting all—'

311

'Two days you've been here, Martin. Why haven't you asked me what I think about the very subject that brought you back to Braeside?'

He says nothing. He could deflect, deny, come up with something, but what's the point? They both know she's right.

'Must be murder for you, just now,' she says, breaking a grim silence.

'What must?'

'Nobody's allowed to be as clever as you. You resent the success of these numpties you talked aboot because you think they're not as clever as you; and you resented playing second fiddle to folk like me and Colin at school for the exact same reason. So it must be murder bein back in this town and knowin *less* than everybody else, that big brain of yours unable tae come up with all the right answers.'

There is another silence, even bleaker than the last. He decides he'll be the one to fill it. She's just taken him apart so she shouldn't complain if he responds in kind.

'You ought to be careful, there, JoJo,' he says coldly. 'I think your insecurities might be showing. Same as they were the time you ritually slaughtered me in front of everyone way back when.'

This, he knows, will bring the old JoJo fully to the fore. If it's going to end as bitterly as it began, then so be it. At least she won't be able to tell herself all that shite about folk not being who they once were.

JoJo bows her head so he can't see her face. When she raises it again, he'll take both barrels, and then he'll be out of here. She runs a hand through her hair. Here it comes.

But when JoJo sits up straight again, there are tears forming in her eyes, as well as anger that he's seeing this.

'And what if my insecurities *are* showing, Martin?' she asks, just about managing to steady her voice. 'Am I not allowed to feel undervalued as well? Am I not allowed to be pissed off because you're not remotely interested in *me* for who *I* am?'

'I'm about as interested as you've ever been in me.'

She wipes at her eyes and smears her make-up a little. 'Aye, well,' she says. 'I guess you're no as smart as I thought. Nobody at our school was immune to feeling overlooked, Martin. Nobody gets spared the feeling that they're worthless in somebody else's eyes.' She stands up. 'The last train to Glasgow leaves in aboot five minutes,' she informs him, then walks away.

Martin stands up too, in that moment remembering something not quite too late. 'I did ask you what you thought,' he says.

For a moment, he is sure she's going to ignore it and keep walking, but she turns.

'Excuse me?' she asks, folded arms accentuating a defensive hostility.

'I did ask what you thought and you dodged it. I asked what you thought Eleanor meant and you said you didn't know.'

'I didn't know. I *don't* know.'

'You deduced that she was scared she'd given something away, and yet you're claiming you never speculated what that was?'

'Oh, Christ, of course I speculated, but what's

313

that worth to anybody?'

'It's worth something to me. That's why I asked. That's why I'm asking now.'

They stare at each other from a few feet away, a real gun-slinger duel of a stare. She's weighing up many things: face, spite, anger, and the best way to serve all three.

She licks her lips, her tongue just the slightest protrusion between them. 'I think the sleazy bastard had a peep-hole,' she says, then glances at the clock. 'You're gaunny miss your train.'

Third Year
Xi Boötis 2

Solvent Abuse

Thank fuck it's Friday afternoon. Just one double period to go and then home for tea, before the school disco tonight. Should be a laugh. Plus he'll get to see all the lassies dressed up, though seeing is about as much as Robbie will have a chance of. Doesn't matter. The lassies in his year are all fucking cows and snobs anyway. Not like the ones he's heard Boma and Joe talking about. Sounds like the lassies in their years were less tight. Course, Boma and Joe could be talking shite. It wouldn't be the first time.

It's been a long week: the first week back since, you know. First week back after holidays is always slow. This week was like that but worse. After holidays, *everybody*'s trying to get their act together again, not just you. And making it more awkward is the awareness that every cunt must know. A long week, sure, but the two before it were a sight longer, were they not? Aye, and they could have been longer still, could have been shorter, in extreme ways he doesn't like to think about.

The doctors said he was lucky. Didn't feel very fucking lucky. Thousands of cunts sniffing glue every day and this never fucking happens to them, does it? So what's fucking lucky about it? But he knows fine what's fucking lucky about it. He could have ended up like one of those poor bastards on the news. One of the real stories, he means, on the telly news. Not the papers, the *Daily Record* and all that shite, whose take on glue is to keep coming out with pish about some daft cunt attacking

317

somebody because they're on a trip and think he's a fucking werewolf or something. He means the nae-kidding glue stories: pan breid, or a fucking vegetable or something. And all for what? Sniffing solvent out a fucking crisp poke to get a buzz. Fucking pathetic, now he's looking back at it. Probably wouldn't have got into it if he'd been able to get hold of some Woodpecker or Merrydown that first time, but who the fuck's going to serve him? Even the bigger guys, like Tempo and Panda, get big brothers or pay somebody older to buy them their carry-outs.

He remembers the day he first did the glue. He was fed up hearing all the stories from other cunts about getting a carry-out and getting steamboats. He had gone round collecting ginger bottles for the deposits; did it every night of the week until he had enough for a bottle of cider. He gave the money to Boma to buy it for him, but the bastard fucked off with the bottle himself and scudded Robbie in the dish when he complained about it. Not as if he could tell his maw, was it? 'Mammy, your sixteen-year-old has just knocked your fourteen-year-old's kerry-out.' So that was him fucked. No drink and no money. And it's not as if you can knock booze, either, because it's all kept behind the counter at the Paki's, with fucking bars and wire, like a cage. You can knock glue, but. No danger. They're talking about making the shopkeepers demand proof of age before they can buy it, sixteen minimum, same as fags. You don't need proof of age to fucking thieve it, but, do you?

So that was him sorted out for a Friday night: tube of Bostik and a packet of fucking Space Raiders. He remembers the room birling, remembers liking it. Remembers the fucking headache he had the next day as well, but it's amazing how quick you can forget something like that when you're bored out your tits the next night and there's still glue left. He must have done it four or five times before he got 'lucky' and ended up in the Alexandra Infirmary with a fucking tube down his throat. In and out of consciousness for three days. He remembers opening his eyes and it being night-time, blinking and it was day. Remembers folk round the bed before he was sharp enough to make them out properly. Maw and Da arguing, though he couldn't always hear what they were saying. Maw was upset, Da just angry. That was usually the script at home, right enough.

He remembers her having a right go at Da for something he said, but doesn't recall what it was. 'You never treated Joe and Brian like that,' she says.

'Aye well,' Da says back. 'I wonder how no.'

Then she was greeting again, and Robbie fell asleep. Or maybe he just pretended to be asleep.

He got a get-well card from the school. Nurses brought it in to him once he had the tube out and he was sitting upright. They were all busy at somebody else's bed when he opened it, which was just as well, because he wouldn't have wanted anybody to see him. He was greeting, for fuck's sake. Him. He doesn't greet about anything, not even when Boma or his da really stoat him one. But this, fuck. Just kind of snuck up on him, greeting before he even knew it. All the names, man, and wee messages. They must have passed it round the social area, off their own backs, as

319

opposed to something a teacher organised and made every cunt in the class sign. He can tell because it's mostly boys, and it's boys from all the classes, not just 3S6. They've had a whip-round as well: got him a fiver record token.

He doesn't know why it made him greet, but he was pure bubbling like a wee wean. Then he got kind of angry about it. He resented the thought of folk feeling sorry for him, thinking of him as weak or like a fucking spastic or something. Well, he wouldn't be having that. It was nice to get the card, but that didn't mean anybody could take the pish. He would panel the first cunt to say anything out of order, no matter who it was.

But there was no escaping what the card told him about how it looked from the outside: he's been a stupid cunt, and everybody *knows* he's been a stupid cunt. That was the hardest thing about going back to school this week: embarrassment. Knowing every bastard's looking at you and thinking about what happened to you. He's felt it before, back in First Year when Big Tempo broke his nose and burst his mouth. This is far worse, because they're not picturing a fight or all that blood spraying about; they're picturing him splayed out on his bedroom floor with his neb stuck in a crisp poke.

Christ, looking back on it, the fight with Tempo's almost something to be proud of by comparison, considering his stature now. Folk looking at the pair of them these days would think Robbie must have been pretty brave to have a go at all, never mind the outcome. Tempo's mother must have been feeding him Popeye's fucking spinach or something, because he just shot up in height and beefed out in build, too. And like his hammering of Robbie, it didn't go unnoticed. Once folk were talking about it, it was only a matter of time before some hard cunt decided they wanted their go, and the smart money was always going to be on Jai Burns. Jai saw it as a day wasted if he never punched somebody, and he was the one that most wanted the reputation as the hardest in the year, especially with the likes of Kenny, Chick and Richie more interested in the fitba team or winching or whatever. It was a fucking miracle it took him as long as it did to start a fight with Tempo. It happened about halfway through Second Year. He'd had a few attempts, right enough, but Temps never rose to the bait. When it finally happened, it was because Temps was mouthing off, not the other way around. Temps is a mouthy bastard to everybody now, but he'd been careful around Jai up to that point. Robbie reckons Temps knew this was unavoidable and decided just to get it over with when he was feeling up for it. Mr Sullivan and Mr Blake broke it up, but Tempo was knocking fuck out of Jai when they did. Jai tried to make out otherwise to any cunt that would listen, but if Jai believed it himself, he'd have made sure it got finished properly after school, whereas he did fuck-all.

Tempo hasn't fought anybody since. Nobody's fancied noising him up, for one thing, but it's mainly because Temps isn't interested in fighting. He's interested in fanny.

Robbie's got on fine with him since their fight in First Year, which is even more surprising considering they never liked each other before that. It was a bit awkward for a while, as you'd expect, but fair play to Tempo: he could have been a pure cunt about it and he wasn't. Takes the pish a bit, but he does that to everybody. It was Temps who came up with Robbie's new nickname: Turbo. Turbo Turner. Sounds gallus, doesn't it? A proper nickname, like Boma's got. Just as well, too, because Christ knows what some bastard might have saddled him with over the glue-sniffing.

This last period is science, which is usually all right, sometimes a laugh. He's sitting with Noodsy, who he hangs about with a lot these days since Noodsy moved house to just up the back from Robbie's bit. Next to Noodsy is George Sanford, who used to be called George Spamford because he was in the remedial group. General George, they call him now, because he isn't in any O Grade classes, not even arithmetic—just general science, general maths, general English . . .

They get Mr Boyd for science. He's a dozy bastard—literally on a Friday afternoon, because that's the day the teachers hit the pub at lunchtime, and he's the one who gets the most bevvied. He must be pretty puggled first class back in the afternoon, but by the final double period he's ready for sleeping it off, especially if the room's warm and there are no windows open. Even if he doesn't actually nod off, he's not at his most observant, so it's usually an easy shift to wind down the week.

It's raining outside, which is a bugger, because it puts the knackers on their favourite Friday afternoon game of taking it in turns to go out the window. Noodsy started it a few weeks back. Just climbed out because he was bored, went for a walk about and then came back in. Didn't even need

322

anybody to keep the edgy—just keeked in to see what Boyd was up to and then chose his moment to return. What was dead funny was that Boyd must have noticed something was different but couldn't suss out what it was. You could see it in his face after Noodsy came back in. He was like, 'Was that seat not empty a wee minute ago?' Fucking funny as fuck.

It became a game the next Friday when Noodsy did it again, except this time he fucked off with Robbie's jotter. Came back in and told him he'd planked it next to the nearside hockey goals, which meant Robbie had to climb out and get it back before the period was finished and his work was due in for marking. Now they have challenges: one of them planks something at afternoon interval and the others have a race to get outside and find it. Nobody's been caught yet, but fuck knows how not. One time, Boyd went up the back and shut the window because of the draught, with General George still stuck outside. Fair play to GG, though, he just walked back in through the school and right in the door of the class.

Boyd says: 'Where have you been?'

GG goes: 'I was taking that book back to Miss Coleman, like you tellt me,' all put out at the accusation and leaving Boyd standing there looking confused. Aye, he might be in the remedial group, GG, but the cunt's not stupid.

With the rain on, they'll be left with their other favourite pastime, which is stealing school gear. There's not actually much that's worth stealing, not that that's ever stopped anybody, but the kind of pointlessness of it did lead to a new game. Now the idea is to see who can plank the biggest and most stupid thing in somebody else's bag, with extra credit if they leave the place without noticing. Sometimes they notice and go home with it anyway, for a laugh. Science is the best for this game, because it's the class with the most gear, though Robbie wishes they'd got into it back in home Eeks. Secretarial Studies has potential, but the teacher, Miss Hannon, is a bit too sharp-eyed. Shame, really. It's an ambition among them all to get a typewriter out of there, or at least to get one inside some other cunt's bag, just to see the look on his face when he goes to lift it.

Boyd hasn't been to the pub. It's the week afore payday, so that'll be why. Surprisingly, the lesson really flies in. Boyd being more on the ball than usual, he gets round to setting up some experiments for a change, instead of setting them an exercise and snuggling down for a kip. Still, at times like this folk's guards are down, so you have to take advantage. The opportunity arises when it comes time to start dismantling the equipment. Everybody's busy with something or other, plus there's nothing suspicious about being on the other side of the room from your own seat. Folk always sling their jackets and bags in a big pile on the worktops running down either side of the class, and these days if you're seen hovering about them, folk know to check their gear before heading for home. A lot of the stuff has been shifted along to make room for equipment or for folk getting into overhead cupboards, so nobody cottons on when Robbie starts lifting the odd coat or bag. He then makes a point of helping Sean Cassidy put away some beakers, then goes back to his seat. The last few minutes take pure ages because he can't wait for Boyd to give them the nod. He usually lets them get ready to go home a few minutes before the bell, specially on a Friday, but he's still blethering about the experiment as the clock approaches four. Must be only a minute-to when he finally says, 'Pack up.' Everybody jumps for their gear, but Robbie says to Noodsy to stay put a wee minute and watch big Kenny Langton over the other side.

Sean Cassidy nearly ruins it because he picks up his jacket first and finds he needs to unhook a toggle from the shaft, but fortunately his coat was at the top. Kenny lifts up his bag with both handles, finds it snagged, and gives it a real tug. Four coats and two bags rise up into the air like they've come to life, causing some of the lassies to let out a screech. They're all threaded through a four-foot metal clamp-stand, the base of which has been planked inside Kenny's bag. The bag's zipped up just shy of all the way so the shaft pokes out, but he wouldn't have noticed because the first coat was covering the gap.

Kenny's pure pishing himself. Boyd kind of rolls his eyes, but reckons no harm done. He sees this carry-on nearly every week, and there's no way that lazy cunt's making a fuss about something when the Friday bell's about to let him head for the boozer. Kenny's asking around to see who did it. Robbie says nothing, but Noodsy points to him, which Robbie is happy about because in the end he wants the credit.

They're all still laughing about it—and all still trying to disentangle their gear from the clamp-stand—when the bell rings. Robbie reluctantly has to take his eyes off the scene over the other side as he turns round to get his own bag and jacket. He's so distracted by what's going on across the way that he forgets to check nothing's been planked inside, but as soon as he lifts it, he can tell there's too much weight. Tube that he is, he was so busy setting up Kenny that he forgot to be keeping an eye on his own stuff.

Usually, if you've clocked it early, the thing to do is sneak it back out your bag and act like nothing happened, but it's kind of accepted that if the bell's gone, you've either got to leave with whatever it is or at least take it out in plain sight, so that whoever did it gets the laugh. There's a good atmosphere about the place just now, Kenny still pure pishing himself, so Robbie reckons it'll go down well if he paps his bag down on the desk and lets everybody see what's been planked on him.

'Fair dos,' he says, and unzips the holdall.

There's a big litre-tub of glue sitting right in the middle of it.

For a wee second, Robbie feels like he's the only cunt in the room: just him, the table, the bag, and this big fucking tub of glue. It's probably because of the silence: there isn't a sound, everybody shutting right up apart from one lassie still laughing at what went on before, and who hasn't noticed the glue.

Robbie feels like he needs to hold on to the desk or he might fly off it like a wean on a spiderweb roundabout. His throat is swelling, water welling up. He's going to greet. He can't greet. He wants to turn round and look to see which cunt did this, but let's face it, he knows which cunt did this, and he can't let anybody see his eyes. He's not giving the cunt the pleasure. Doesn't want anybody to talk to him just now, either. Anybody talks, especially if they try to say something sympathetic, he's going to greet, and if he greets, man, if he greets . . .

Everybody just starts filing out. Noodsy puts a hand on his shoulder. He goes to say something, 'C'mon Turbo,' or whatever.

Robbie bats his hand away without looking at him. 'Don't fuckin touch us,' he says, his voice like a whisper because he's too choked to talk properly. 'Don't fuckin touch us.'

Noodsy steps away. 'I'll wait ootside.'

Robbie says nothing. He keeps his head down and picks up the glue in both hands, turning his back to carry it to the cabinet as they all leave. Boyd hasn't said anything, give the bastard credit. It's not because he doesn't want a fuss at four on a Friday, either. He knows the score, knows the worst thing he could do is make something of this.

The door closes after the last wean leaves, closing off the sound of everybody blethering. That's the moment he can't hold it in anymore. Boyd's still at his desk, but there's quiet, stillness and Robbie's back is to him, which is why it feels like he's alone. He breaks down, greeting near silently, like coughs or big breaths.

Men and Boys

Martin makes it on to the carriage during the three-second window between the guard's whistle and the doors sliding closed. There's no ticket office anymore, only what used to be the exterior

327

exit stairway affording access to the platforms. Had the office still been open, he wouldn't have made it, but it's safe to assume that would be scant consolation to whatever poor fuckers lost their jobs when the station became unmanned.

He's already dialling Karen's number as the train pulls away. The two-minute dash across the road and up the stairs provides a temporary distraction from what just transpired, the cold of the night and the wind in his face like a bucket of ice-water over his head to wake him up from the warm, smoky fug of the bar. It makes him feel like he's well clear of the place, that he's thoroughly left it—and JoJo—behind, but even as he reaches for the mobile, he can't help feeling that he is merely vindicating everything she said. He's got some information out of her, so now he can move on. Even if that wasn't his sole intention, it's what has happened, and though he's got a promising lead out of it, he feels something uncomfortably close to guilt about passing it on to Karen.

She answers after a single ring, causing him to trip up on his words.

'Ha . . . hi. Hello. That was quick.'

'My reflexes are amazing when I'm desperate for distraction. My eyes are bleeding from looking through these files. I've got all his accounts and business records in front of me, or at least what we believe to be all. Please talk to me. Preferably at length.'

'Anything juicy come up yet?'

'Hardly. His accounts are a shambles, but that's not exactly a red flag when you're talking about a failing business. The only question mark at the moment is a discrepancy over the use of the lodges.'

'What, the fact that they were actually making money?'

'Boom boom. No, it's that a lot of the money looks like it's from corporate hire. There's a series of irregular payments in US dollars, account in the name of AmberCorp, but I cannae find any corresponding record of when these bookings took place. All the stays in the ledger have the rates and payments listed next to them, but AmberCorp never appears.'

'Could be a third-party booking firm. AmberCorp would appear in the accounts, but individual guests' surnames would appear in the records.'

'I suppose. Maybe get someone to look into it, but we're only talking aboot eight grand in total, so it's not got me shouting "Eureka".'

'I thought cops always said "Bingo" when they made the vital connection.'

'We like to vary it from time to time.'

'So those files, the books from Colin's lodges, they list who stayed there and when?'

'Yes. Why, what you got?'

'Did Pete McGeechy ever stay there? Or anyone else on the planning committee? I heard that Colin used to let the lodges to friends at bargain rates, and sometimes gratis to others. The phrase used was "you scratch my back".'

'Let me find the folder. We spoke to McGeechy this afternoon, and Tom Fisher's sniffing around him and the planning committee.'

'What did he say?'

'He said nothing. He talked plenty, but he's an experienced politico. Very good at answering your questions without telling you anything. There was also lots of legal posturing: "not at liberty to reveal" this and "strictly confidential" that. Very considered responses throughout. Very frustrating because it's obvious he's lying but you can't get a credit card between the chinks, you know?'

'Aye, but could you not goad him into losin the rag? Never used to take much.'

'Like I said, he's a smoother operator these days. Christ, where is that folder?' she moans, the strain in her voice causing him to picture her with the receiver tucked awkwardly under her chin as her hands search the paperwork. 'It was right here a minute ago. Let me try this pile. Anyway, he was full of denials about pressure being brought to bear on the planning committee, or rather, he said pressure was always being brought to bear but that was what they were there to evaluate, blah, blah, blah. Cute, too. Didnae claim Johnny Turner had nothin to do with it or say he'd never heard of him or anythin that might come back to bite him on the arse. "Confidential submissions", "can neither confirm nor deny the identities of" . . . You're a lawyer, you know the script.'

'Sure. So what was between the lines of the script?'

'Well, obviously he was hiding something, but he didn't seem especially nervous.'

'He wouldn't be if the two people who'd been squeezing him from opposite sides had just been eliminated.'

'You think Colin was leaning on him? How so?'

'You got the folder yet?'

'Finally, yes. Let me see . . . Hang on, back over the page . . . Yes. McGeechy stayed at the lodges

330

back in January. The rate is written down as complimentary. Oh no, wait a sec. January. That predates the submission of Colin's rezoning application.'

'It doesn't predate the Sirius consortium's approach for the hotel, though. Colin knew he would need him onside.'

'Yeah, but it's not exactly Jonathan Aitken at the Paris Ritz. Plus we'll need to check whether McGeechy declared it anywhere. Even if he didn't, it wouldn't give Colin any means of pushing him. McGeechy would only be vulnerable to accusations of impropriety if he did what Colin *wanted*, so how does that give Colin any leverage?'

'Maybe that's not the kind of impropriety you should be looking for,' Martin suggests.

'Why am I picturing you with your hand up right now?'

'Please, miss, please, miss,' he says. It's supposed to sound good-humoured, even flirty, but as he says it he can only think of JoJo. Binary. *Jesus Christ*.

'You always loved being the one who knows the answer,' Karen says, accurately. 'But don't milk it, Martin, it's getting late.'

So he tells her, without fanfare and without naming his source.

'Where are you?' she asks.

'On a train. I'm a mobile-phone cliché.'

'I mean where exactly?'

'Just going past Nether Carnock.'

'Get off at Paisley.'

'That's what all the Catholic girls say.'

'Don't go there, wee man.'

Party time. Pished the night, oooooh yes. Going to get blootered. Going to get stocious. Going to get steamboats. Wooh-wooh, all aboard. Can't wait. Colin and Panda Beattie and Big Tico Hughes and Matt K-9 and Aldo Daws-Baws, and not forgetting the lassies, not forgetting, no indeed. Tico's got ID says he's eighteen, but if he gets a knockback, there's always K-9's big brother Bongo who's in Sixth Year. They're all coming back to his place—Tempo's Temple—after the disco. That's where the real action's going to be. The school disco's going to be a fucking Smartie party, all the wee daft weans thinking they're on a real night out. All the wee lassies that wouldn't let you do anything and have got hardly any tits anyway eating crisps and drinking Irn-Bru out plastic cups in between dancing to Kim Wilde or some shite, same as they were in First Year. All the wee fannies like Scotty and Marty still going out in their trainers and clothes their mammies bought them, standing round the walls spending all night plucking up the bottle to ask for a dance and then going back with a beamer when they get the inevitable knockback. And all the daft wanks like Keany and Liam with no chance of a carry-out, trying to get pished by putting aspirins in Coke. It's a fucking myth, but he's seen them drink it and then try to convince themselves they're getting a buzz from it. Wanks. Near as bad as that daft bastard Kevin Duffy. Duffle heard about banana joints, but nobody told him you need to get tons of the wee stringy bits and dry them out. According to Aldo, the stupid prick tried to light a whole fucking banana like it was a big cigar. Total tube.

And then, of course, there's Turbo, but the least said, eh? Fucking Turbo. Used to think he was a wee hard man, but now he's a fucking joke. Too stupid to realise he's having the pish ripped out him half the time. Just stands there and takes it because he thinks that means he's in with the boys.

Seriously, it's amazing that all these people are in the same year. There were always folk taller than others, and in some cases nearly a year between folk in the same class because of the March cut-off date, but now, at the tail-end of Third Year, it's like men and boys, young women and wee lassies. He used to hang about with Marty and Scotty at St Lizzie's, but fuck's sake, how could they hang about together now? He doesn't mean to act the big man, and feels bad about slagging them, but they're still just wee boys. Their idea of a carry-out is from the Golden Dragon, they know nothing about fashion and they don't have a clue what music is in these days. They slag off Bowie, for Christ's sake. Just shows they don't have a scoobie, and not just about music, but about being cool. If you don't like Bowie, fair dos, but you should have the suss to keep quiet about it. Tempo's cousin Charlotte is up at Strathclyde Uni. She said everybody's into The Velvet Underground and gave him a tape of some albums. He found them a bit boring, to be honest, but it sounds good to be able to talk about this kind of stuff. That's what the likes of Marty and Scotty don't get; that's how they'll never be in with the boys. They lack maturity.

Going to be time to get ready in a wee while. Seven o'clock the disco starts. What's that like?

Seven! Finishes at half-nine. For a Third and Fourth Year disco! Just shows you: it's so the weans aren't out too late past beddy-byes.

He'll have a shower in a wee bit. Got some nice wet-look gel for his hair when he was in the town last Saturday. Him and Tico went in on the train, then straight across to Union Street. Virgin and HMV are practically next door to each other. That's real record shops, not like the wee pishy one on the Main Street. He got a Japan twelve-inch, *I Second That Emotion*. It was going cheap because it's been out for ages. He wasn't into them before, but K-9's brother Bongo likes them and he's in Sixth Year. K-9 said Bongo might come along tonight, later on, so he'll make sure that song goes on the record player if he does.

He's still got his uniform on the now, but he's already looked out what he'll be wearing. He's got his Bowie trousers, the ones with the double pleat on each thigh, and this peach penny-collar shirt like David Sylvian wears on that poster in Bongo's bedroom. Got that in the town on Saturday as well, with his birthday money.

Mum and Dad are away overnight to stay with Nan and Papa in Perth. They're taking Great Uncle Jim and Auntie Vera with them as well. They're over from Canada for a month, and they've been staying here the last five nights since they arrived at Prestwick. Now it's somebody else's turn to have them, thank fuck. Could hardly get in the bathroom for one or other of them this week, and when he did it was usually honking.

House to himself, oh yes. Nothing mental. If any fucking chancers turn up trying to get in, they'll get told to get to fuck. He's not having the place wrecked. Just a select wee gathering. Cocktails of an evening with chums, eh Jeeves? But before any of that, there's the first reason he couldn't wait for the folks to get in the motor and go: he's got a porno off of Mick Garvie, or, more accurately, Mick's big brother Tommy. He had to laugh when Mick gave him it, thinking back to how Momo used to ask after Tommy because he was 'such a good boy'. Good? He's fucking brilliant, far as Tempo's concerned. He's seen plenty of pornos at other folk's houses, but it's dead frustrating because all you want to do is have a wank. Everybody just sits round and laughs at it, or kids on they're dead cool about it and *don't* have a raging fucking stauner. But that's because the bastards are sharing them round and getting a wee bit of private viewing action once their folks are away to bed, which is an option Tempo's never had because he's got VHS and every other bastard's got Beta.

Fucking peasants, that's the problem. VHS machines are dearer, whereas you practically get a Sanyo Betamax free with every council house. Tempo's dad always buys the best, prides himself on it. 'Never be ashamed to show you've got a bit of money,' he always says. 'Being skint's nothing to be proud of.' Aye, fine, Dad, but that's not helping me get hold of scud-films, is it? There are plenty of VHS pornos under the counter at the video club, but that's still no use. Depending who's on, they can sometimes refuse you if you try to rent an Eighteen, never mind hard-core. But besides that, it would be a pure riddie, renting a porno, especially if it's from one of the women. When you hand over your money, you might as well say: 'Two pound, there you go. I'm away hame for a wank,

335

noo.'

But now, at last, here we go. He closes the blinds and turns on the telly. There's a tape already in the video, so he presses 'Eject'. The machine starts its lengthy process of whines and whirrs. Takes fucking ages to eject a tape, unreal, and near as long when you put one in. Might as well make use of the time, he decides, and nicks upstairs to get some bog roll. Andrex: soft and absorbent three-ply tissues, so your spunk won't soak through and dribble on the carpet. *There's* a catchphrase for their adverts, never mind a fucking Labrador puppy.

He slings the old tape on top of the machine, pushes it a bit too hard so it slides off the back. Get it later, can't wait. He puts in the porno and kneels by the telly for a minute, waiting to picture-search forward through the guff at the start. He doesn't need to, though. The film's not been fully rewound, so it's straight into the action as soon as he changes the telly to channel eight. Fucking amazing, man. Absolutely fucking amazing. There's a bird sucking this guy's boabby, and another bloke at the back shagging her doggy-style. Fantastic, but he wants her to turn over so he can get a better view of it going in and out her fud.

It's stunning, magnificent. He used to think getting a view of Mars through his telescope on a clear night was something to get excited about, but this is a whole other universe of wonder. He sits down on the settee and undoes his trousers. Yes, here we go. They change positions and you get a good look at her gammon flaps as she sits on top of the guy and guides it in. Aw yes, man. This is the best wank ever. Never mind Andrex, it's the Artex that his load's liable to splatter at this rate. Fuck, man, yes. They're changing position again and, Jesus, she's got her ankles practically round her own neck, and, man, the guy's boabby is huge and his arse is a blur, absolutely going for it. Aw, man, what he would give to be doing that to . . . aaaaah . . . aaaaah . . . Aaaaaaah.

Aw.

Yes.

Aw.

Fuckin . . .

He hears the noise of a key hitting the lock on the front door and his mother's voice as it opens. After that, the only thing moving faster than that guy's bare arse is his own as he trips on his unhoisted trousers in his urgency to reach the telly. He falls flat on the floor with a thump as he hears footsteps coming down the hall, as well as two voices: his mum and Uncle Jim. The living-room door is closed, thank fuck, so they don't see him lunge to change the TV channel before getting to his feet and pulling up his trousers.

'It's just us,' his mum says, walking into the room. 'Jim forgot his specs.'

'Oh, right.' Colin nods, standing in front of the telly, beneath which the video is still humming as it continues to play the tape.

'Have you got a sniffle?' she asks.

He's about to ask, 'What?' when he sees the scrunched-up bog roll lying on the carpet next to the settee. He swoops to grab it and instantly shoves it up to his face, where it has the opposite effect of normal, in that it applies something warm and gloopy to his nose rather than removing it.

'Oh, yuck, you *have* got the sniffles,' his mum

337

says. 'For goodness' sake, cover your mouth and nose when you sneeze. I wouldn't want a load of *that* stuff all over my face.'

'Yes, Mum,' he says, and stuffs the bog roll into his pocket as Uncle Jim walks in, clutching his spectacle case.

'That's me got them,' he says. 'You mind and make sure you never dae anythin tae damage your eyesight, Colin, mark my words. What are you daein sitting here with the blinds drawn?'

He looks at the window, beyond which it's broad daylight. 'Eh, there was a glare on the telly. Just for a wee while. Sun's gone now.'

'A glare? Rain hasnae been aff the whole day.'

'It was just for a minute.'

Mum has a look at the telly. 'What are you watching?' she asks, which is when he notices that *Jackanory*'s on. 'You not a bit old for this?'

Her hand is inches from the screen, in touching distance of the control panel. If she's suspicious, one brush of her finger could turn it to channel eight, where the porno is still playing.

'I was watching a tape of the Celtic game from Wednesday night,' he says, thinking quickly of something both plausible and of zero interest to his mum. 'Just finished. I was about to rewind it,' he adds, and quickly squats down to hit the 'Stop' button.

'Aye, some game,' says Jim. 'Here, I wouldnae mind watchin it again, and oor Jock might have missed it. Can we bring the tape up tae Perth?'

Oh, Jesus.

'Eh, I'm pretty sure Papa'll have already seen it.'

'Aye, but I know oor Jock, he'd never get tired of watchin a humpin like that. That first yin, what was

338

it like? The look on the boy's face as he stuck it in, absolutely rammed it in, so he did. And what aboot the tackle? Have you ever seen anything like it?'

'Come on, Colin,' says Mum. 'Give us out the tape, then. Dad's got the engine running.'

Oh, Mother of Christ. He looks for the other tape, the tape that was in the machine. Fuck knows what's on it, as he just made it up about the football, but he can't give them this one. He needs to pull off a fly switch, but how's he going to manage that with the other tape somewhere down behind the telly? Jim's standing over him, as well, waiting as the machine makes its interminable noises, slowly preparing itself to deliver Colin into family damnation.

And then, like a shining light as Mum opens the blinds, there comes salvation when he remembers: 'This'll not play on Papa's machine,' he says.

'Aw, will it no?'

'Naw. This is VHS. Papa's is Betamax.'

'Betamax?'

'Aye, Betamax.'

Thank fuck for Betamax.

*   *   *

'So who told you about this?' Karen asks as they pass the last of the streetlights on the outskirts of town and into the darkness of the country road leading up the far side of the Carnock Braes.

Martin thinks about pleading confidentiality, but reckons more damage could be sustained if Karen finds out later and starts wondering why he would be so coy. 'JoJo told me. I ended up in the Railway Inn tonight, got talking to her.'

'The Railway? But I stood you up in Glasgow. What the hell made you go there?'

'A question I was asking myself very shortly upon my arrival,' he deflects.

'Big JoJo's the landlady there now, isn't she?'

'Yeah. She's not so big these days, though.'

'No, I know. She never really was, especially in secondary. I ran into her a couple of years back, coming out of the pictures in Linwood with her kids. We didn't get to talk long, but she was really pleasant. Genuine, too.'

Martin feels the knot tighten. Pile it on, why don't you. 'Was it not a bit tense? I mean, she was a pure cow to you at St Grace's, was she no?'

'Aye, she's still never forgiven me for stealing her best pal in Primary Five. Come on, Martin, it's so long ago, we're lucky if we can remember what we ever held grudges about. I mean, you and she were hardly each other's favourite either, but presumably you got on fine tonight or we wouldnae be here.'

'Aye,' he says, wincing. 'We got on okay.'

He is surprised to see a second car waiting as they pull into the horseshoe clearing where the four lodges sit along the shore of the fishing loch. Karen clocks his reaction.

'What, you didnae think I was gaunny let a civilian come poking around a crime scene with just me to supervise, did you? Besides, Tom lives near the station and I needed someone to pick up the keys.'

The other cop emerges from a fifth building, a small timber shed built in the same style as the lodges. Karen gives him a wave and kills the engine.

As they walk towards it, Martin can see that the shed serves as a maintenance/storage hut and miniature site office. Linen, towels and domestic supplies are piled on clear-varnished pine shelves against one wall, another wall accommodating outdoor hardware. Across the centre there is also a short counter bearing a telephone, a monitor and a keyboard.

'Bugger of a job being the janny for a whole forest,' Martin says, eyeing up the thick-bristled brush that is standing nearest the door.

'You should leave the gags to your wee pal Scot,' Karen says witheringly. Martin feels his metropolitan confidence ebbing. He remembers JoJo's remark about it being murder everyone else knowing more than him. She was right. Every minute back here is causing his stature to recede towards the starting point of overlooked, schooldays, short-arsed nobody.

Karen does the introductions, her brevity suggesting she has already thoroughly filled in Tom on more than Martin finds comfortable.

'I've been here ten minutes,' Tom says. 'Had a wee look around again. First thing to note is that the buildings are all detached and even this wee doocot doesn't back on to anything, so I don't know where any prospective voyeur might position himself. Ceilings are vaulted, right enough, so we might need to get out the ladders.' He nods towards a pair of extendable aluminium steps hanging lengthways along one wall. 'Needless to say, we'll stay out of Lodge Two,' he adds, eyeing the next building but one.

Martin can't help but turn and look at the scene of the crime. There is, as the polis always say, nothing to see here, but the thought of what went on within its walls gives the lodge an inexplicable aura. He feels sad, and guilty, too. A friend died there. He hadn't been a friend since a very long time ago, but he was once, when they were very young and very innocent, and that's the person he thinks of when he looks at the closed door. The Colin he knew disappeared way back in the early Eighties, but this is when it hits home that he'll never be coming back.

Tom lifts the ladders from their hooks and Martin steps behind the counter to get out of the way.

'Okay, we'll start with Lodge One,' Karen says to Tom. 'You see if you can get into the loft space and I'll have a swatch around below.'

Martin has a look at the PC sitting on the floor. He's pretending to examine it but really it's just somewhere else—other than at Karen—to be looking so that he doesn't appear improperly eager. He's not sure how serious she was about the extent of his permitted involvement here. He'll follow if he's told to, but doesn't want the further slapping down of being ordered to stay put. However, now that he's looking at the computer, he starts to notice something.

'Are you coming, then, or what?' she asks him. 'I brought you along as an extra pair of eyes.'

'Sure,' he says. 'It's just . . . something struck me about this PC. What's it doing in a daft wee shed like this?'

'I think it doubles as the lodges' management office.'

'Aye, but I cannae imagine the places needing this much management. Plus, it's a decent bit of kit.'

'You kidding? The monitor's ancient.'

'All the more reason why the box itself is incongruous. This thing's even got a dock for a removable hard drive. I take it you lot have got the drive itself?'

'No,' says Tom. 'We don't know where it is. The PC itself is password protected. We've got guys who can crack it if need be, but it's not been a priority.'

'Noodsy's pleading ignorance about the removable drive,' Karen says. 'Playing to his strengths, you might argue. But to be fair, it could be anywhere: in Temple's house, in Turner's house, at the bottom of the fishing loch, or in the Clyde under the Erskine Bridge, where Noodsy says they dropped the gun.'

Martin squats down and has a closer look at the rear of the machine, specifically the cables protruding from it.

'ADSL broadband modem—*for a hut*. And look at this cable here, coming up from under the floorboards. It's coaxial, going to the graphics card. AV input.'

'Oh boy,' says Tom.

'AV input?' Karen asks. 'What's that?'

'Audio-visual.'

*　　　*　　　*

Scot comes back into the bedroom carrying a tray with three mugs of tea he nipped downstairs to make while they were waiting for *Manic Miner* to load on the Spectrum. Scot's house is on the way to St Grace's, which is why Martin has arranged to come round here before they go on to the disco, though these days it's a regular Friday night fixture for one of them to be at the other's place. Cass, Sean Cassidy, is here tonight, too. He sometimes comes round to Martin's or Scot's on a Friday as well, but he doesn't have a computer, so they never go round to his. This is fine by Martin, as Cass lives down the Bottom Scheme and Martin has heard a few too many stories of people getting jumped down there to fancy walking back home after dark. Cass loves the games, but his real passion is movies. He is a generous source of Betamax pirates, horror Eighteens a particular speciality, though the copies are often so many generations from the original that it can be hard to know whether you're watching *Friday the 13* or *Fast Times at Ridgemont High*.

'Has it worked?' Scot asks, placing the tray down carefully on the floor. He's talking about the poke for infinite lives that Martin got from a magazine.

'Soon find oot,' Martin says. 'Just let Cass have a go and he'll get killed in nae time.'

'Cheeky bastart,' Cass says, but he's happy enough to take this as a cue to get first shot on the computer. They've got it hooked up to Heather's colour portable. She's away out to the pictures in Paisley with her boyfriend, otherwise they'd be making do with the old black-and-white. Martin passed her at the bus stop on his way here, all made up so she looked much older than any time he's seen her in the corridor at school. Heather's pretty, but Martin can't really think of her that way, as he's known her so long it would be like fancying his big cousin or a youngest auntie; not

344

forgetting the fact that he wouldn't have a chance in a million years. He'd love to be going to the pictures, though, with any girl. Well, not *any* girl, obviously, but, you know, a girlfriend.

Cass bursts out laughing as he reliably guides Miner Willy to an early death in the Central Cavern. They all look to the bottom of the screen as the level restarts, and share in a cheer as it shows three lives intact.

'This game's brilliant,' Cass says. 'Even better than that wan we played at Marty's, *Jetpac*.'

'You were better at *Jetpac*.' Martin laughs, watching Cass snuff it again.

'Wish I hadnae got the cheat code the night of the disco,' Scot says. 'I'll be up tae aboot three in the mornin tryin tae finish this efter I get hame.'

'Me too,' Martin agrees, though in truth he'll be in bed by ten as usual, parents' rules. There are no rules about how early he can get up, right enough, and it's Saturday tomorrow.

'Have you got this game as well, Marty?' Cass asks.

'Aye,' Scot answers. 'It was Marty taped it for me aff his.'

'See, that's what's amazin aboot computer games,' says Cass, shaking his head in apparent wonder. 'The picture's always brilliant: crystal clear, gallus quality even if it's a pirate.'

Scot bursts out laughing. 'Cass, ya tube. It's software, it's machine-code.'

'Aye, but it's still a tape of a tape.'

Scot ejects the tape from the cassette-recorder and holds it in front of Cass, who looks alarmed for a moment until he sees that the game is still playing on the screen.

'It's digital, just a string ay numbers that's on the tape. The numbers don't change no matter how many times you copy them. Videos deteriorate because they're analog recordings.'

'Analog recordings?' Cass retorts. 'Fuck's sake, who's been teachin you the big words?'

Scotty gives him the finger. It's done in fun, but Scotty can be a bit nippy if you allude to him being clever. It's the only thing Martin has ever seen get him riled, as normally Scot just laughs off all the mud-slinging and posturing that goes on at school. You could almost say he's the one guy who really doesn't care what anyone thinks of him . . . as long as they don't think *that*.

'Anna Logue recordings,' says Cass. 'I wouldnae mind wan ay them. She's that wee honey in First Year. Noodsy's wee cousin.'

'Cradle-snatcher,' says Scot.

'Geezabrek. It's only two years' difference. Anyway, lassies ayeways go oot wi guys aulder than them. We'd be in wi a better chance if it was a Second and Third Year disco, no Third and Fourth.'

'Cass,' says Scotty, 'if we were the only guys there, the lassies would dance by themselves.' Martin laughs, wishing it was a joke.

'The wans that think they're dead grown-up wouldnae look at ye, and the rest wouldnae gie ye a dance because they're too feart ay the slaggin.'

This is all true, but Martin doesn't want to agree out loud, as though doing so would break some spell that might yet prove it wrong. It would be great to dance with one of the girls, and surely it isn't totally out of the question. Not a pure ride like Samantha Gerrity or one of JoJo's trendy in-

346

crowd, obviously, but there had to be somebody, surely? It didn't have to mean anything, didn't have to say they were 'going with each other' or imply that he was asking to get off with her. Just a few dances, maybe a decent conversation, a shared smile, some kind of validation that the opposite sex didn't see him as a complete nonentity.

'Aye, you're right. Well, we can dance ourselves. Fuck it.'

'Music'll be shite, though,' says Scotty. 'It'll be all the Human League and that New Romantic synth pish.'

Martin eyes the records and tapes on Scot's shelf. *Plus ça change*, he thinks. He remembers parties at St Lizzie's, Primary Five onwards, everybody bringing their own music, their names etched on the labels and sleeves for claiming them back. There'd usually be about ten copies of the same Abba albums, and in the singles pile a dozen Boney M seven-inches, five of *Do Ya Think I'm Sexy* and at least three of Father Abraham and the Smurfs. Scotty and Martin always brought a stack of punk and New Wave stuff that the fucking teachers would never play.

'Not forgetting Saint David,' Martin adds pointedly.

'Who?' asks Cass.

'Bowie,' Scot explains with a smile. 'As worshipped by the more sophisticated element in our year.'

'Oh, aye.' Cass nods, catching on. 'Tico and Tempo an all that lot. I heard them boastin aboot how they were gettin a kerry-oot the night for later. Headin back tae Tempo's hoose. I think JoJo Milligan and that lot are goin as well.'

347

'Aye, I can just see it,' says Scotty. 'Aboot a dozen ay them in Coco's livin room, passin roon wan bottle ay Woodpecker, tryin to convince themselves they're pished.'

Martin smiles as he hears Scotty call him Coco. Scotty has not once allowed the name 'Tempo' or 'Temps' to cross his lips, even—no, *especially*—when addressing the man himself.

'Actually, they don't need the kerry-oot noo,' Martin suggests. 'If you've heard them, the real work is done. Cause let's face it, the important thing to that shower is talkin aboot it rather than drinkin it.'

'Too right,' Cass agrees.

'Aye, big Coco,' Scotty says, shaking his head. 'Never been the same since he woke up one mornin an found a hair on his baws.'

*   *   *

'The guy had his own private *Big Brother* house going on here,' Karen says. 'Four of them, in fact.'

They're standing in the bedroom area of Lodge One, surveying their haul of hardware. So far they've found a camera behind a wall-mounted two-way mirror facing the double bed, one hidden in the smoke-detector on the ceiling, one peeking neatly through a hole in a black plastic plant pot (complete with plant) and one built into the casing of a (functional) radio/CD player; in addition to two more mirror-disguised lenses raggled into the walls in the bathroom, trained on the jacuzzi and the shower. None of it took much finding; but then the greatest camouflage disguising the cameras was that nobody previously had any cause to look.

348

Nobody other than Eleanor, that is. Martin wonders how much she merely suspected and how much she had found out for sure. What was certain was that if anybody was going to stumble upon this stuff, it would be the cleaner.

'These aren't cheap webcams or pinhole spy gadgets, either,' Tom observes. 'Because they're built into the walls, or housed in fairly sizeable and camouflaged locations, he hasn't needed to economise on size or quality. No grainy images or low frame-rates. As good as camcorder footage, easily.'

'And that's what the broadband is for?' Karen asks. 'So he could watch it all from the comfort of his home?'

'Image quality would be too high for streaming video,' Martin says. 'My guess is it was being written to the removable hard drive, but he could stream a lo-fi version to his house and effectively direct the recording from there: switch feeds depending on where the action was or what view he preferred.'

'Dirty bastard,' Karen says. 'That's absolutely revolting. God, I feel ill. I feel like I need a shower, except I don't think I'm gaunny feel comfortable in my shower from now on, either. The thought of him sitting there at his monitor . . . There's a thought, though: would it record only if he was controlling?'

'There's an infrared spot on the one we found behind the bedroom mirror,' Tom tells her. 'Motion detector. It could well be set to record from that camera by default whenever it's activated, so he didn't miss any action while he was out.'

'So there's a pretty good chance the murders themselves were recorded,' Karen suggests. 'And whoever took the hard drive knew that.'

'The shed was still locked when we first came here after the bodies were found,' Tom says. 'So it's possible it could have been removed before the killings, but you never know.'

'Noodsy and Robbie would have had ample access to Colin's keys,' she says.

'But they may not have been the only ones with a reason to want that hard drive,' Martin points out. 'I've a feeling Pete McGeechy might have had a passing interest in its contents, too.'

The Politics of Dancing

For 'disco', read dining hall with the curtains drawn, though that and some flashing lights were all it took to transform the place. It's amazing how the same space can have such a different atmosphere, Karen thinks: From the babbling chaos of lunchtime, to the enforced solemnity of a Mass, to the charged excitement of tonight's gathering. Still smells of chips under all of the above circumstances, but at least tonight it is cut with the scents of over-applied make-up, hair-spray, perfume and after-shave.

And there *is* excitement; the atmosphere *is* charged. It was pretty much mandatory all week to predict how shite the disco was going to be, and for maximum effect you really had to suggest how unlikely it was that you would even bother going, but she knew fine none of them would miss it. For one thing, despite a lot of big talk from certain quarters about carry-outs and house parties, when you're fourteen or fifteen there isn't much competition on the average Braeside Friday night social calendar. However, the greatest compulsion to attend was never going to be about music or dancing. It's about status. It's about pecking order. It's about sorting the big girls from the wee lassies, the in from the out. That's why the atmosphere is charged, as opposed to simply excited. This isn't a party, for God's sake. Tonight, this dining hall is the board for a very big game. She'd love to say that those who don't know they are playing it are likely to have the best time, but she knows this is wrong for two reasons.

One: it is those who come out ahead tonight who will have the best time.

And two: deep down, everybody knows they're playing it, even those who are aware they are destined to finish bottom. It is a game in which there are no triumphs, only lesser increments of defeat; where the rules are made (and frequently altered) by those already at the top, and never revealed to those beneath.

She had waited outside the building for Ali before going in together. It was more than safety in numbers or mere solidarity, though both of those were undeniable factors. It was about consolidation, maximising the impact of the declaration they were about to make. (There was also the unworthy but inescapable slight fear that the other might back down on their planned dress, but that was moot now.) They both had long coats on, but what was visible above the neck was enough to reassure each other that it was all systems go. They proceeded to the cloakroom to shed their camouflage, then walked downstairs to the dining hall hand-in-hand, giggling, nervous, excited. And now here they are, just inside the door, taking in the room while the room collectively takes in them.

Karen spots Helen standing near the serving hatch, opening a can of Irn-Bru. Karen waves, and Helen just stares back for a confused moment before realising at whom she's staring. She smiles and trots across. They'd told Helen what they were planning to wear, but Karen understands the double-take. When you're used to seeing someone in their uniform, it takes a wee minute to register them looking different. Helen was easier to clock because she's wearing the same jeans and blouse as she did when they all went to the pictures last month. In fact, she wore them to the previous disco, too, and to Michelle's birthday party: they're her going-out clothes. Ali has a slightly wider and marginally cooler selection—though she's eschewing it tonight—simply because she's had a more recent growth spurt, thus necessitating her mum authorising (and indeed supervising, hence *marginally* cooler) some new purchases. Helen is still barely taller than she was in First Year, and her fashion options are further handicapped by the fact that when she does grow out of things, they tend to be replaced by whatever no longer fits her big sister Nicola. Karen shared the same paucity of social wardrobe herself until last weekend's shopping spree, but it wasn't exactly a big-budget blow-out, and the shops concerned were a lot further along Argyle Street than where the likes of JoJo and her pals get their gear.

Helen came along with them too, and offered lots of encouragement as they unearthed their dark gems amid the second-hand jumble, but Ali and Karen couldn't persuade her to buy anything herself. Karen suspected this was principally because Helen didn't have much more than the train fare home in her pocket, things being very tight in their house since her dad was made redundant. However, the explanation she offered in rejecting various suggested items, indeed in rejecting the look the other two were attempting to achieve, was that 'it just wouldn't be me'. And Karen loved her for that. She was right. It wouldn't have been her, and the dining hall right then was wall-to-wall with people trying to be something they were not because they were too scared to be themselves.

You should have seen them all at the same disco this time last year. There was some inexplicable fad for burgundy: burgundy skirts, burgundy trousers, burgundy shirts, burgundy cardigans, burgundy tank tops (!), burgundy jumpers. Girls and boys, dozens of them, all head-to-toe in multiple layers of the same colour. It was kind of an *out-of-school* uniform.

This year there is more diversity among the in-crowd, but there is a shared denominator about their attire, and that is size. It's always big to be in, but these days it's very in to be big. Skirts are long and baggy, their material thick and heavy. Blouses billow, nothing clings. Big shoes are in, too; big, mind, not high, the clumpier the better. Hair is big too, shaggy perms spilling down past padded shoulders. They all talk about Bowie and the New Romantics, but their template appears to be the lassie from the Thompson Twins.

There's a whole host of them on the dance floor, territorially occupying a wide space near the DJ. JoJo, Caroline, Margaret-Anne, Linda, Angela, all that lot. Tony Hughes, Colin Temple and Matthew Cannon are dancing in the same group. It's hard to tell whether any of them are dancing specifically in a pair, but there's a showy confidence about their intermingling. They're really going for it, too, because *Let's Dance* is playing; not merely a song but a sacrament. And if something comes on that they disapprove of, they'll make just as enthusiastic a display of vacating the dance floor, *en masse*.

The dance floor is standing up to it well, Karen thinks, looking at JoJo and Margaret-Anne's less-than-delicate footwork. It's been pretty fortuitous for them that they have sprouted and become the in-crowd at a time when this look is in. Not so long ago, the trendy get-up was ra-ra skirts above the knee and wee, tight cut-off tops that showed your belly-button. Those long blouses hide a multitude of deep-fried sins. JoJo is nothing like as plump since she stretched in height, but she's still not the daintiest of creatures, and it's hard to imagine her ruling the roost among the trendy crowd if she was squeezing herself into a boob-tube and miniskirt.

But Karen remembers she's got the horse before the cart. The trendy crowd make the rules in this game. They are the ones who decide what is cool, whether it be clothes, music or people. So they're not wearing big clothes because big clothes are in. Big clothes are in because they are wearing them.

*   *   *

354

Martin, Scot and Cass are having a rerr terr, dancing together, getting off on that energy rush you get from good music played really loud. Martin hasn't quite broken sweat but he wants to, wants to give it laldy until he has to sit down, breathless and laughing. Truth be told, you couldn't really call it dancing, as much of the time they're just birling and bouncing in a circle with their arms round one another's shoulders. Have to make the most of it while the music's good, before the DJ puts on more Spandau Ballet or Duran Duran and the mature-and-sophisticated mob come strutting their stuff again. It's funny watching them bail out, actually, the demonstrable, grimacing distaste with which they evacuate the dance floor before anybody can make the mistake of thinking they could possibly *like* certain songs. Their fire-drill haste when it's anything by Madness is particularly hilarious, the Nutty Boys and their frivolity being the absolute antithesis of the dispassionate image they want to project, as proven by Madness being the one band that gets the likes of Noodsy, Robbie, GG and the JJs pinballing around the dance floor.

He and Scot are getting a particular kick from the sheer unexpected delight of the DJ owning, never mind playing, the song that's on just now. It's *The Cutter*, by Echo and the Bunnymen, and their singing along with the lyrics has, he is sure, been approvingly noted by Karen Gillespie, Ali Taylor and Helen Dunn. Perhaps even more surprisingly, it was Helen who went to the DJ and asked for it; certainly it was the first song to come on after Martin spotted her leaning over the turntables to talk to him. He feels slightly ashamed that when he saw her doing so, he was expecting something like

Kajagoogoo or Wham!, and angry with himself because it's precisely the sort of wrong assumption he knows people are likely to make of him.

He's having a good time, but there's something gnawing away to prevent his total contentment, something he partly wishes he could just forget about. It's the girls. They're everywhere, and they're all dressed up, hair styled, wearing make-up, wearing perfume. He knows he should just accept it, like Scot says, that guys like him have got no chance, and just concentrate on having fun. They're having fun, aren't they? Great fun, yeah. The music, the energy, the singing. Nearly bounced their way through a window when *Fields of Fire* came on! But he can't help thinking . . . I mean, that was a smile—wasn't it?—from Ali, when she saw that they knew the Echo song. That was definitely a smile, an acknowledgement of something they had in common. See, Scotty? They aren't completely invisible. They aren't treated with total disdain. There are some decent lassies out there. Not everybody is like JoJo and that lot, folk who once had the cheek to call *him* a snob.

Keep the heid, though. There was no point in asking Ali or Karen to dance with him. For one thing, they were both about six inches taller than Martin, which just looked and felt wrong. Even if they had the decency to say yes, it would still be mutually embarrassing: they'd look silly and he'd look like he was being patronised. And more pertinently, he'd never have the nerve, because the pair of them look a class above tonight; not just above him, but above everybody, as far as he's concerned. They're wearing ankle-length, long-sleeved black dresses that look like costumes from

356

some Gothic vampire movie. Ali's is velvet with black frilly cuffs, and Karen's is made from two layers of material—like a doily tablecloth draped over shiny silk—that reminds him of Auntie Mhairi's living-room curtains. They've both got their hair sticking up like Sylvester the Cat after jamming his fingers in the mains, and they have heavy black make-up around their eyes.

Martin noticed the looks they were getting when they made their entrance, the traded smirks and pointed fingers, but thinks jealousy played a part. And if the others weren't jealous, they ought to have been. The pair of them were about the sexiest thing he had ever seen in the flesh, like two magnificent visitors from a more interesting world whom it was a rare and fleeting treasure to behold. Scotty had made a gag about them—'She's alive. *Alive!'*—but that was because Scotty made a gag about everything. It wasn't that he didn't think they looked amazing; though, to be frank, Martin didn't care. If Auld Nick had walked in right then and offered the exchange of getting off with either of them, then the cloven-hoofed bastard would have left very shortly afterwards, one soul to the good.

No, Karen and Ali were only marginally less of a non-starter than bloody JoJo or Samantha Gerrity. But what about Helen? There was definitely eye-contact a couple of times during that last song. Helen is a lot like him, when he thinks about it: condemned as a 'brainy wan', overlooked for being behind in the physical-development stakes, and just too bloody friendly and affable to be anything but scorned by the in-crowd. He'd always thought she was quite pretty, but she doesn't give the impression she sees herself as hot stuff like some he could mention. Certainly not a clothes horse. In fact, if he is being strictly honest, her clothes are arguably even less cool than his. And, okay, he knows he is hardly the pick of what is on offer tonight, but nor is he the worst. Helen Dunn. It's a thought, isn't it? He used to walk home with her when he was wee, and they got on fine then, didn't they? And wouldn't it be great? All those things he wanted: a girl to dance with, talk to, share a smile. They already had one out of three.

Or is he kidding himself, and cruising for the humiliation of another knock-back that would just ruin the rest of what is otherwise shaping up to be a fun night? Aye, Scotty is probably right. Stop torturing yourself, pal. Accept it.

However, the more he looks at her, the more he wants to dance with her, and the more he thinks it's worth the risk. But at the same time, the more he looks at her, the prettier she gets; and the prettier she gets, the less he fancies his chances. Nah. Leave it. Scotty is right. Probably.

*   *   *

Karen, Ali and Helen are having a seat at the side and sharing round a can of juice when Karen sees JoJo and Margaret-Anne heading in their direction. They're probably on their way to the toilets, but they've chosen this route for a reason. She knows they're about to get some lip, but takes it as a compliment, because, at other discos and parties, in Karen's experience, that crowd normally make a point of acting like you're not even there. So serve it up, JoJo. Let us know we've pissed you off.

'Hi, Karen, hi, Alison, hello Helen,' says JoJo, her voice all fake nicey-nicey, she and Margaret-Anne sharing a smirk that is drippingly patronising.

'Hi,' she and Ali both mumble disinterestedly. Helen says, 'Hello,' and smiles, because that's Helen.

'Like your gear,' JoJo says, with a grin that is intended to convey her delight at seeing them kitted out in such a supposedly embarrassing get-up. 'It's really . . . different.'

And yours is really, really *the same*, she doesn't reply. 'Thanks,' she says instead, in a tone that means 'Fuck you.'

'You enjoying yourself?' Margaret-Anne asks Helen, in that foghorn rasp of hers that makes everything she says sound like a threat.

'Yes,' says Helen.

'Saw you up askin for music,' Margaret-Anne adds.

'What kind of music do you like, Helen?' asks JoJo.

Karen can feel her hackles rise, her mouth turning to acid. Leave her alone, she's thinking. Pick on someone your own size. Bitches. They're not asking because they're interested. They're asking because they want to shoot her down and they like it best if you give them the ammunition yourself. Karen clocked them a few times on the dance floor, looking she, Ali and Helen up and down: the two freakshows being bad enough, but compounding their status by dancing with their square wee-lassie pal. That's why they're picking on Helen now: anything they can laugh at Helen for is a slagging for this pair who still hang about with her.

'Echo and the Bunnymen,' says Helen.

'Bunnyman? Is that him oot *The Magic Roundabout*?' Margaret-Anne barks.

'What else?' presses JoJo.

'Bauhaus,' Helen replies, biting her lip a little. Helen's sweet, but she's not fucking stupid, and she knows what's going on here.

'Bow-wows?' says Margaret-Anne. 'Bunnies and Bow-wows!' This is at the sophisticated end of what passes for Margaret-Anne's sense of humour.

'Bauhaus,' Helen restates, more firmly.

'Never heard of them,' says JoJo dismissively. 'What do they sing, then?'

'*She's in Parties, Bela Lugosi's Dead, Ziggy Stardust*,' Helen suggests, emphasising this last song by way of implying it ought to ring a few bells.

'Bunny, Bow-wow and Ziggy,' says Margaret-Anne, laughing.

'Never heard of that, either,' sniffs JoJo.

'Oh, yeah, that's right,' says Karen. 'You're Bowie fans. *Big* Bowie fans, obviously.'

'Aye, what aboot it?' demands JoJo.

'Nothing,' Karen replies; she, Ali and Helen sharing a smile, which JoJo doesn't like one bit. Knowing she's being got at but being too daft to work out precisely how has probably been a major source of frustration throughout her life.

'Bela Lugosi's dead, did you say?' JoJo asks. 'That's a shame, isn't it? Cause if he was here wi Boris Karloff, it would be the only chance yous had of gettin asked up for a dance.'

'Aye,' affirms Margaret-Anne as they walk off. 'Fuckin lez-beans.'

A little later, the three of them are up dancing again, but nobody has said much for a while. After JoJo and Margaret left, Ali finished off the can and suggested they get back on the floor, to which Karen and Helen instantly agreed. Normally it would take a decent record starting up for them to make their move, but on this occasion they'd have got up even if it was *The Birdy Song*. They needed to get away from the silence that was growing in the wake of the wee visit they had just endured. Sure, they swapped a few 'cow's and 'just ignore them's, but it had left a sour taste, being so blatantly got at, especially the nasty way they'd singled out Helen.

Helen's acting like she's all caught up in the dancing, pretending it didn't bother her, but Karen knows otherwise. She's innocent but she's not naïve. Helen knows about the game, same as everyone else, and knows she just took a hit. It'll pass, though. Just keep dancing. The sting will wear off. Don't let those cows ruin your fun.

Karen sees Scot Connolly up talking to the DJ. She sits in front of him in O Grade maths. She's seen his books and jotters, the names of bands lovingly etched on every spare inch of their wallpaper coverings. Karen isn't familiar with half of them, but a lot of the names are ones she's heard Nicola mention. Helen and Nicola don't have a lot of pocket money for buying records, but they listen to Janice Long and then John Peel on the radio all night in their room, and make tapes off it, too.

The DJ puts on one she does know, a song by

Stiff Little Fingers. She sees Scot dancing with Martin Jackson and Sean Cassidy, just jumping around having a good time together like she and her pals. She also sees JoJo and that lot at the side, not dancing but making a point of watching. Part of her wishes she and Ali and Helen could just turn around and start dancing with Scot, Martin and Sean, all in a group, giving their own stiff little fingers to the sneering in-crowd at the side. It's not going to happen, though. JoJo and that lot would just love it too much anyway: them dancing with three wee guys still in trainers, Sean in his tracky bottoms, too.

She smiles at them, though, and they smile back, apart from Martin. He is smiling, but she doesn't catch his eye because he keeps looking at Helen. Karen wonders if he fancies her. The thought tickles her a bit, but she knows she can't say anything to Helen, because the girl would be mortified.

They dance another couple of numbers and then decide to take a seat. It's mostly guys on the floor just now, because another Madness song has started. Scot, Martin and Sean are sitting this one out, too. They're over against the far wall, laughing about something, but Martin is still stealing looks at Helen, who seemingly remains oblivious.

The Madness number finishes, replaced by Tears for Fears, then Wah!, which gets Scot and Sean up, but not Martin. He stays seated for a minute, still taking frequent gawps over at Helen. Karen smiles to herself and looks away, notices Christine Morton from Fourth Year dancing with Kenny Langton. It's unusual for girls to be with younger guys, but Kenny is taller than half the staff, and, she'd have to admit, quite good looking, as well as extremely charming when he's not acting the clown. When she looks across again, Martin has gone. Then two dancers unblock her view and reveal, to her great discomfort, that he is heading across the floor towards Helen.

Oh, God. Oh, no.

He stands in front of where Helen is seated. Karen can see his right hand tremble as it hangs by his side, his face all but drained of colour, poor bastard. He tries to smile, but his nervousness just makes him look temporarily palsied.

He asks Helen to dance. It takes two attempts because his voice sort of dries up halfway through the first. Helen becomes instantly as pale as Martin. Her eyes bulge and she physically shrinks in her chair. She looks panicked. She shakes her head then suddenly gets up and walks—almost runs—towards the exit. Karen and Ali exchange a look across the empty seat and get up to follow her. Karen tries to offer Martin a wee look of . . . she doesn't know what, just *something*, but he's staring at the floor, probably wishing it would open up and swallow him.

Poor bastard. He didn't know what he was walking into. He put Helen on the spot and gave her no choice. He shouldn't take it personally. It's just the dictates of the game. Down on the hockey pitch, when Karen whacks it as hard as she can away from her goal, it's not because she has anything against the ball.

Bonds and Confederacies

It's a less polished Pete McGeechy who sits across from them in the interview room, and not just because he's meeting them on their turf. The fact that it's not long after four in the morning plays a part. Soon as they found the right DVD in Temple's house, she had somebody go pick him up. She figured as she was going to be up all night anyway, she might as well make it work for her; guys like that are far less composed when you haul them out of bed in the wee small hours. He really wouldn't be looking forward to the missus asking him what it was all about, either.

It was quite a collection Temple had amassed, though fortunately she hadn't needed to cue through any great quantity of other people's violated intimacies in order to find what she was looking for. Something as crucial as the McGeechy disc was never going to be just lined up on the shelf next to the rest, and nor was there likely to be only the one copy. Tom found one hidden in the ice compartment of the fridge at almost the same time as Spiers located another taped to the underside of a drawer in Temple's bedside cabinet. No sign of the removable hard drive, but this was plenty for now.

He's slumped on the other side of the table from Karen and Tom, looking tired, beaten, angry and bewildered, which is pretty much how they want him. The DVD sits between them in a transparent case. McGeechy's eyes seldom leave it for long.

'So, Peter,' Karen says. 'Are you "at liberty to

364

reveal" a wee bit more now? Because it certainly looks like Colin Temple was.'

He closes his bloodshot eyes and sighs deeply, putting both hands to his head, revealing two large sweat-rings under his arms despite his shirt being on him for less than half an hour. Karen keeps herself from smiling as she recognises all the signs. Stick a fork in him: he's ready.

'When did he hit you with this?' she asks.

'Later than you'd think,' McGeechy says. He laughs bitterly. 'I thought we were friends. Not big pals, but still in touch, the odd pint, you know? So I never thought much about it when he offered me the lodge.'

'For free?' Karen asks pointedly.

'Aye. Christ, I knew he'd want a favour back at some point, but I was fine with that. There's a difference between doing somebody a favour and doing something corrupt. He said the place wasnae booked the now, would be empty anyway. Perfect for a fly wee night away.'

'From the wife,' Tom adds.

McGeechy says nothing, just gives another small sigh, shakes his head a little. It must all look so foolish now. It always does after you're caught. 'This was before he submitted the application.'

'We know.'

'Once he had, in the back of my mind I thought . . . but no. He even said to me, something along the lines of: "Look, that wee favour with the lodge, I hope you don't think this is what I'm lookin for back, hope it doesnae put you in an awkward spot," that kinna thing. I'm like: "No, it's fine, I've declared it, it's all above board." Things looked like leaning in the application's favour anyway.

365

There's always a few rumbles from folk, sometimes just to remind you they're there or to let you know that if they back this, they'll expect your cooperation on something else. That's politics. But as these things go, it looked like plain sailing.'

'Until another party declared an interest,' Karen suggests.

'Aye,' he confirms grimly, 'Johnny Turner. Although I didnae know right away it was Johnny Turner. Folk were getting leaned on in various ways. I won't name names, but I'm pretty sure money changed hands in some cases. In others the incentive was staying out of the Royal Alexandra. Johnny Turner knows some bad, bad people. Jimmy Meechan's mob. But then, you know all that.'

'All too well. Were you intimidated personally?'

McGeechy looks involuntarily around himself, like he's scared of being overheard. That's a yes before he even speaks. 'I'm just a fuckin town planner. I didn't want my fuckin legs broken.'

'Why didn't you tell the police?'

'See above.'

'Fair enough.'

'Anyway, it was when word started getting about that the application would be rejected that Colin played his ace. He let me know the footage would be freely copied and passed around if I didnae swing the application back his way. The phrase he used, which I have no difficulty in recollecting, was that "half of Renfrewshire is gaunny be wankin themselves or pishin themselves".'

'Charming. But you're only one guy. Turner had nobbled a few people on the committee, you just said.'

'That's what I tried to tell Colin. That was my problem, he told me right back. He knew how these things work. If you make one person desperate enough, they can prevail upon the rest. Obviously the rest were reluctant to cross Johnny Turner, but Colin said he could guarantee Turner would be oot the equation if permission was granted.'

'What did he mean?'

'He wouldn't say.'

'Didn't you want a bit more assurance before you put yourself on a collision course with Johnny Turner?'

'I considered that the lesser of two evils. I'd have taken the broken legs before I let that fuckin video get out.'

'Sure. Can't envisage it enhancing your political career very much.'

'Not unless you're Cicciolina,' Tom suggests.

'And I guess your wife wouldnae be too pleased, either.'

'Well, for Christ's sake, that's who I was trying to protect. I don't even like to think what this would do to her.'

'Maybe you should have thought about it a bit more back then,' says Karen.

'Who thinks about stuff like this, for fuck's sake?' McGeechy volubly protests, more resembling the volcanically indignant boy she remembers. 'Christ, have you actually watched the fuckin thing?'

'I did you the courtesy of looking only at as much as was necessary to know we had the right DVD. We'll only watch more if there's any information you don't give us. Such as who was the

367

girl?'

'Who was the . . . ? Christ, don't you fuckin eejits get it? There *was* no girl. It was my *wife.*'

There is a reeling silence for a moment as Karen and Tom take this one in. Fortunately, the more familiarly fired-up McGeechy is determined to fill it.

'Do you think if I was havin it away with somebody, I'd do it five miles up the road in a place belongin tae somebody as lewd and sleazy as Colin fuckin Temple? It was just meant tae be a quiet wee night away at a time we were both feelin a bit snowed-under with the January blues.'

'But if that's the case, then Temple's the one who would be liable to prosecution if this video emerged.'

'It was his zero option,' McGeechy says. 'You know the situation he was in financially. So basically he was saying that if he ended up fucked, he was fucking us too, so I'd better make sure it never came to that.'

'But if you were the ones who were violated by this,' Karen begins, but does not get any further before McGeechy blusters over her.

'Look, being the victim doesnae save you in politics. Embarrassment is poison, no matter how little it's your fault. But I couldn't care less aboot that. It was my wife. She's a primary-school teacher, for fuck's sake. School boards are even less forgiving than voters. "Yes, tough break, Mrs McGeechy, not your fault, *but* . . ." And Christ, if you knew what the job meant to her. She didn't do that well in school, didn't make the most of herself. Ended up with a bad crowd. But by the time I started going out with her, she had become determined to clean up her act. She went to night school and got her Highers, then after we got married six years back, I paid the way so she could give up work and go to teacher-training college. Her job means everything,' he implores. 'Do you understand?'

Karen nods, saying nothing for a moment to let the temperature cool. 'What's her name?' she asks softly, having let the silence grow long enough.

'Anna,' he replies, clearing his throat before he speaks, attempting to regain his composure. Despite pulling himself together, and despite the pause Karen granted him, he looks less certain of himself than ever.

'Anna what?'

'McGeechy. She took my name.'

'I meant what was her maiden name? Did she go to our school?'

'She was a couple of years below. You wouldn't have known her.'

'What was her name anyway?'

'Logue.'

Karen casts her mind back. He's right. She didn't know the girl, but she does remember the name. More importantly, she also remembers why. 'So what happened next?' she asks. 'What did you do?'

'I moved mountains,' he says. 'I lobbied, I hustled, I threatened, I sweated blood. Short version: I turned the committee around. Unfortunately, this didnae take long in gettin back to Johnny Turner, who was, it would be fair to say, somewhat disappointed.'

'I'll bet. What did he do in response?'

'Had me bundled into a car one night and

dragged oot to the middle of nowhere for a wee chat. Tea and crumpets, you know the kind of thing,' he says bitterly, his mouth trembling slightly as he speaks. Not a favourite memory. 'Prior to that, I had no idea how much pain can be inflicted on parts of the human body withoot leavin a mark. Turner guessed Temple had something on me, some leverage, and he made me tell him what it was. I could tell he understood that Colin's threat was greater than his, because it affected more than just me. I said if he could guarantee that the video disappeared, I'd make sure the application sank.'

'When exactly was this?' Tom asks.

'Couple of weeks ago. I never heard anythin for a few days and started to get really worried, because I realised there was a big hole in my deal. If he got hold of just one copy of the DVD and released it to the right people, he could have torpedoed the rezoning application in one blow. I'd be fatally compromised as head of the committee, and Colin would be facin prosecution. But I was wrong. Guys like Turner always see a bigger picture. He also saw a bigger flaw.'

'Which was what?'

'There was no way of knowing how many copies existed, and Colin only needed to hang on to one.'

'And what was the bigger picture?'

'A very dirty one. Turner called me up last Sunday and said he had it all sorted. I asked when I'd be getting my DVDs, which was when he told me I wouldn't, and why. But he said he could guarantee Colin would be keepin them to himself.'

'How?'

'He put a few things together. Reckoned Colin wouldnae have fitted all that kit just to snare me,

370

and that he wouldnae be using it just for his own amusement. He got someone to do a bit of diggin on the internet and it turns oot Colin's been floggin this footage to a porn outfit in America.'

'Online feeds?' Tom asks. 'Hell of a risk in the global village.'

'No,' McGeechy says. 'Voyeur DVDs, sold mail-order, and only shipping within the US, so there was little chance of some bloke in Paisley loggin on to a porn site and seein himself in action.'

'AmberCorp,' says Karen.

'What?'

'He received payments in US dollars from a firm called AmberCorp.'

'Well, I doubt Turner knew that part, but he knew enough to put Colin in jail and see him sued from arsehole to Elderslie. Turner was using this to get him to drop the rezoning application, and to agree to sell the hotel to him—at a pretty fuckin preferential rate, I'd guess. Plus, of course, to keep me onside, Turner said he'd let Colin know that if my DVD ever saw the light of day, then so would everybody else's.'

'So Turner had already informed Temple he knew all this?' Karen asks.

'Aye. He said he had broken the bad news, and they were meeting in a couple of days so Colin could put pen to paper. Next I heard about either of them, they were both dead.'

*　　　*　　　*

The DJ's just put on *One Step Beyond*, but Noodsy practically has to drag Turbo up to join in. Normally he'd be first out there and going pure

371

mental, but he's not himself the night. Or more like he is himself, as in himself from a few years back: the old Robbie. He keeps drifting off into a dwam, getting that cold look in his eyes, anger and hate, thon psycho way he used to be all the time. It was the glue that did it, Noodsy knows. Not the glue that put him in hospital, the glue that was put in his bag this afternoon, in front of everybody. That was fucking sick.

Noodsy doesn't know who done it—he was busy with a wee bit of business of his own during science today—but he knows it wasn't something that was done for a laugh, which just went too far or got took the wrong way. It was meant to be vicious. Everybody knows Turbo could have died, and you don't fucking joke about that. Not that way, anyroads. Noodsy can imagine somebody like Kenny Langton mentioning it in a funny way to make light of it and cheer Turbo up, but that's not what this was about. This was done to make everybody *but* Turbo laugh, and it was done anonymously.

Normally with pranks like that, half the laugh is in everybody knowing what's coming, so most of the guys are in on it. Noodsy doesn't believe that could have been the case today, because there's no way Kenny would have let it happen if he knew. So some bastard did it purely for spite, but Noodsy can't work out who. Turbo's made no shortage of enemies in his time, Noodsy among them, but he's never been quite the same since Tempo battered him, and that was nearly two years back. You'd think if somebody hated him that much, he'd have done something about it before now, and to his face. Noodsy supposes the person with the best

372

idea who did it is Turbo, but he doesn't want to ask. Like the glue-sniffing itself, it feels wrong to bring it up, like picking somebody else's scab.

Turbo perks up a bit once he starts cutting about the dance floor, which is just as well, as Noodsy reckons it's important that they both get noticed. Turbo's at his best when you keep him busy, keep him involved in stuff. It's when he's idle he's most in danger of getting thon broody way, and that's when the old Robbie threatens to make a reappearance. Noodsy puts the tip of his thumb in his mouth and mimes playing a sax, like he does when they're listening to this song at his hoose. Turbo responds like he hoped, kidding on he's playing a trumpet. Then they do that thing from the Madness videos where the boy with the sax ducks just as the one with the trumpet swings it round over his heid. Mr Kerr, the geography teacher, clocks them doing it and has a laugh.

Result.

The song ends and some other shite comes on, gets all the trendy crowd up. Noodsy feels butterflies in his belly. It's an exciting night, one he's been looking forward to. There's a buzz about the place. Everybody checking out everybody else. A lot of the lassies are looking really nice, some you really wouldn't be expecting to, either. Tico and Aldo and K-9 and that lot are kitted out flash, as you'd imagine. They're dancing with lassies, lucky bastards, trying to make out they're dead cool about it, but they'll be having butterflies as well, hoping they can get off with somebody later.

Big Temps was dancing with that lot earlier, but now he's dancing with Eleanor. She's a lot different these days. You'd hardly recognise her

373

from what she used to be like, apart from the scowl. In fact, you'd hardly recognise her tonight from what she looked like in class earlier on. There's some lassies at the disco you can tell only get done up with make-up and that for occasions like this, but others look so comfortable in their glad rags that you can hardly picture them back in their uniforms. Eleanor's one of the latter. To say she's cleaned up her act would be the understatement of the year. No more Smelly Elly, no more greasy hair and clothes that never saw the inside of a washing machine.

This transformation has come about, according to Noodsy's maw, 'since she became auld enough to look after hersel—because her mammy never did'. Noodsy's maw has told him a few things he wishes he'd known before, because now he feels a bit guilty about how everybody carried on. Eleanor's maw's an alky. Eleanor's da just walked out on them when she was a baby. That's how the Fenwicks were always skint. Mrs Fenwick's 'a deid loss, poor soul', Noodsy's maw says. 'There's been other men aboot the hoose, but maistly neerdowells.'

Eleanor works weekends at the frozen-food place in Nether Carnock, stocking freezers and mopping floors. That's where Noodsy and his maw saw her recently, and what prompted these wee, belated revelations. 'Pulling hersel up by the bootstraps, that lassie,' said his maw.

But not everybody is as charitable or admiring about her as Noodsy's maw. Folk don't like to let you live down your past too easily round here, and while Eleanor might look different, there's plenty of folk still look at her like she's shite off their shoe. Tempo isn't up dancing with her because of any romantic shite. See, Eleanor hangs about with a lot of older guys and the rumour is she's been shagged off some of them. That's why Tempo's turning on the charm—he'll be hoping for a wee bit more than any of JoJo's pals would let him away with.

Noodsy knows he's got no chance for a couple of years yet when it comes to that game, but he's got his sights set on scoring tonight just the same.

*   *   *

'Quite the little chatterbox this time around, wasn't he?' Tom observes dryly as they watch McGeechy make his way out to a waiting unmarked car.

'Obviously a morning person,' Karen replies. 'And a sharp one, too. He talked plenty, but on the whole he didn't tell us anything he knew we couldn't deduce now that we're aware of the video and how Colin made it.'

'You think he's still holding back?'

'I think he's smart enough to realise there's nothing to gain but suspicion by withholding information that the polis are going to find out anyway. He was knocked sideways by us turning up with the DVD, but he regrouped. Only really lost it around the subject of his wife.'

'Understandably so.'

'More understandably than you know, Tom.'

'How's that?'

'He said it himself: guys like Turner always see a bigger picture. If Turner's shakedown of Temple had all worked out, McGeechy would still be in the same boat. Instead of Colin Temple dangling the

375

DVD over him, it would be Johnny Turner. That's an even worse prospect if you ask me, because unlike Temple, Turner would have nothing to fear by way of legal comeback if he deployed his "zero option", because *he* didnae make the recording. Plus, as he also said, there'd never be any way of accounting for all the copies. Until now, all we've had are reasons why Turner and Temple might want rid of each other. Now we've got somebody whose problems would be solved if he could get rid of both. Somebody who knew they were meeting up and would therefore be conveniently in the same place at the same time.'

'He didn't know where or when they were meeting, though.'

'No,' Karen corrects. 'He never *said* he knew those things. Big difference.'

'True. So what's the script with the wife?'

'He lost it when he was talking about her, which was understandable, as you said. But once he calmed down, it struck me that he seemed more rattled than ever.'

'Scared he'd given something away while his emotions had the better of him? But you cooled everything down at that point. Why didn't you keep the pressure on?'

'I did, in a way. I asked him his wife's name. And I had to ask several times before he would give me it. Anna Logue.'

'You know her? Knew her?'

'Knew the name, knew the face. As McGeechy said, she was a couple of years below us, so I was only aware of her because she was the cousin of somebody in my class.'

'Who?'

'James Doon.'

*   *   *

'Time we went for a single fish,' Noodsy says.

'I've just been two minutes ago,' says Turbo.

'I know, ya daft bastart. I mean it's time we *went.*'

Another Madness single has just finished; *Baggy Trousers* this time. Noodsy made a pest of himself to the DJ until he caved in and played it just to get rid of him. Daft bugger would have no idea that getting a record played was just a fringe benefit. Making a pest of himself was the true point of the exercise. Same as doing that wee routine that made Mr Kerr laugh. It was about getting noticed, about giving the impression they were busy having the time of their lives.

Noodsy has learnt a lot about impressions. He's learnt the hard way about how the folk in charge only need a wee bit of information in order to make up their minds, and how no amount of contradictory evidence will then change them.

'Aye, awright,' Turbo agrees, though he's not exactly jumping at the prospect.

He's been a bit funny about the whole thing. Noodsy reckons it's mainly to do with the mood he's in after the glue carry-on, but there's other stuff as well. He's definitely not happy about Boma and Joe being involved, even less so that it was Noodsy's idea to talk to them, but he didn't see how else they could make it work. There are weird vibes in that house between those brothers, so there are. They give Turbo a right fucking hard time, but that's why Noodsy thought he'd be happier for the chance to get on the right side of them.

To be fair, he did spring this on Turbo kind of at the last minute, but Noodsy wasn't sure himself whether he would go through with it. If Boma and Joe hadn't been home when he went round to Turbo's bit, Noodsy would have said nothing, probably. Just kept the idea for another time, or forgot about it altogether.

It's kind of weird, it being Noodsy who's had to chivvy Turbo along, considering it was Turbo who got Noodsy started on knocking stuff. He remembers that first time at the Paki shop on a Saturday afternoon in Second Year. He was starving, they both were, neither of them due in for their tea for ages. He was always hungry these days. Must be because of growing. Turbo only had enough money for a packet of Polo Mints, while Noodsy never had a bean. Turbo said he'd buy the mints as a distraction while Noodsy knocked some chocolate. He said no at first. He was shiting it about getting caught, but more because of his maw finding out than about the shopkeeper or the polis. Maw was always going on about honesty, how low it was to steal stuff. And Noodsy agreed. But he was branded a thief on his first day at primary school, and he's been picking up the blame for shite ever since. Nobody ever listened, they all made up their minds. *Vee-lan. Bawd igg. James Doon! What are you doing rummaging about in there?* So if he was taking the shite for it anyway, he might as well get a free fucking Ritter Sport for his troubles. Honesty had got him fuck-all.

They leave the dinner hall and go up the stairs, then hang about in the corridor for a wee minute to make sure nobody's coming, before going right outside. The school's built on a slope, so it's on three levels, but all the main entrances are in the middle tier, apart from fire exits. The staff aren't daft enough to be wanting dozens of unsupervised weans stoating about the place on a Friday night, so they've locked the big barrier doors that cut across the main inside thoroughfare. This cuts off access to most of the classrooms, including the whole of the top floor. On the mid-level, the staircase down to the dining hall is open, obviously, plus there's access to the First and Second Year bogs and cloakrooms. You can get to the Third-to-Sixth-Year bogs and social area through the fire doors, but the lights are off and there's a paper sign taped to the wall saying: 'Out of Bounds!'

They've been playing these daft games for ages, about knocking stupid stuff from the classrooms. It's pish-easy, but it's useless as well, which got Noodsy to thinking there must be some more valuable gear worth libbing from the place. Then, as luck would have it, his RE class got taken to the lecture theatre to watch some minging film about abortion, and that's when he realised: same as burglars when they tanned your house, the top merchandise to go after was the video. Or, in this case, two videos, and both VHS as well.

Noodsy doesn't have a video anymore. They used to have a Betamax on rental, but it had to go back after his da got laid off again. He'd love to knock one from the school and bring it home, but you can't see his maw and da believing him if he said he just found it, eh? Naw. Especially when it's going to be all over the town that the school's machines got tanned. Kind of hard to get home

379

with one under your arm and not get noticed, too. All of which is why he needed to bring in Boma and Joe. Noodsy reckons he can get the machines out of the building, but he needs somebody to move them after that, move them in more ways than one.

Noodsy leads the way round the back, along the outside wall, until they get to their science classroom, and a window that's had more traffic through it recently than half the corridors. That's what Noodsy was busy with this afternoon—while Turbo was farting about with a clamp-stand and some bawsack was planking glue in Turbo's bag— undoing the window lock at the top, then wedging a wee bit of a broken ruler between the frame and the sill. The windows are meant to be locked when they're closed, but the teachers and the janny are only liable to check if they notice one still open. That's why Noodsy's only opened it enough to get the ruler through and no more. It's enough, though. The ruler's still in place and the window's not locked.

They wait there a wee minute until they see the motor: Joe's pal Benzy's Allegro. It pulls up on the back road that goes past the school, just trees and fields along it, and no houses. The headlights flash, then go off altogether.

Right.

They're both giggling a wee bit as they climb in. Turbo's looking a lot more into it now, which is not surprising, because it's some buzz. Better than anything he could've hoped for off the glue, that's for sure. It's like being nervous and really excited at the same time. His heart's pounding, his stomach's burling but he can't keep the smile off his face. There's a wee moment of concern as they approach the door, in case it's been locked from the outside, but it opens no bother. Come to think of it, the only doors Noodsy's ever seen the staff locking up with keys are the tuck shop and the school offices, in both cases because there's money sometimes kept there.

It's right weird walking through the place with nobody about and the lights off. The corridor's practically pitch dark, with just a wee glimmer of the exterior lighting coming through glass panels in some of the classroom doors. They go upstairs to the top level, and it gets a bit brighter as they approach the gallery. This is the bit that looks down into the big social area. The overhead fluorescents are off down there, but there are two storeys of tall windows to let in the orange glow from the school yard and the car park. The lecture theatre's at the end of this, after it becomes a closed corridor again. Noodsy and Turbo have been whispering to each other up to this point, but now they have to zip it altogether. They're getting close to the corridors that are open downstairs, plus there's only an unlocked fire door separating those from the social area.

They walk on the soft soles of their trainers; it's definitely not a night for Docs. They're just about all the way across the gallery bit when somebody makes a moaning noise and Noodsy nearly jumps over the railing. He turns and looks at Turbo, and he can tell he shat it as well. Then they take a careful look over the side at what's below.

There's two folk sitting in one of the big window-alcoves, their legs dangling over the brickwork, their top halves merged in the shadows.

Noodsy holds his breath, feart any noise will make them look up, but after a second or so he realises he could be playing a mouth organ and they'd still not notice, as they're too wrapped up in getting off with each other.

It's Temps and Eleanor. Aye, called that one right. They're kissing away, and that dirty bastard Tempo's feeling one of her tits.

Noodsy turns to see Turbo's expression, so's they can have a quiet wee laugh, but he looks all serious. Could be jealous, Noodsy supposes. It's a laugh to be watching, but he knows he'd prefer to be the one doing it. Not that either of them fancies Eleanor, but who wouldn't want a feel of a nice pair of diddies?

Aw, here we go, check this. Temps's hand goes down to her thigh for a wee minute, then he tries to slip it under her skirt, but she pushes it away. He plonks it back on her tit instead, then starts kissing her neck. She puts her heid back and Noodsy panics for a second, till he sees that her eyes are closed. Then the hand goes for the legs again, and this time it's a different story. She even shifts in her seat so she can hitch her skirt up a wee bit, and opens her legs as Tempo's hand disappears out of sight.

Noodsy nearly hurdles the barrier again when Turbo taps him on the shoulder. He looks even more serious, pissed off in fact. Then Noodsy remembers: he'll not want to keep Boma and Joe waiting. Plus, the quicker they're back on the dance floor, the tighter their alibi. Noodsy reluctantly pulls himself away from the spectacle and follows Turbo to the lecture theatre. It's safe to turn on the lights because there are no windows

382

in here. When he does, he sees that they're a video short. There's one that sits on a trolley, underneath a portable telly, and the whole shebang is away somewhere. It'll be in one of the classrooms, but they've no time to start searching. It would take all fucking night. The other video's there, but. It's a big, heavy bastard of a thing, and not exactly state-of-the-art. Right enough, he can remember it sitting there since First Year, probably the first video he ever watched anything on, so it must have been an early model. Still works fine, but, and that's the main issue. It'll be less of a pay-out, just tanning the one machine, but on the plus side, it takes the both of them to carry this fucking thing, so maybe coming back for the other one would have been a risk too far.

It takes them no time to get back to the science block, because their eyes are more used to the dark, plus there was no waiting around spying on Temps and Eleanor. They could still hear them as they passed, right enough, loads of slurping and heavy breathing. Lucky bastard, getting to feel her fanny and everything. Bet Temps wouldn't have gone near it a couple of years back, but.

They go back into their science class, where Joe and Boma are already waiting at the window.

'It's just the wan,' Turbo says as they approach. 'The other yin wasnae there.'

'Fuck's sake,' Boma grunts, looking all angry.

'Better than nothin,' says Joe, leaning in over the worktop. 'Gie us it oot.'

'Hing on,' Noodsy says, and lowers his side of the video to the floor so that Turbo has to do the same.

'Whit ye daein?' Turbo and Joe both ask.

383

'Money first,' says Noodsy. He's heard Turbo talk enough about his brothers to know if they don't get paid before they hand over the goods, then they'll never see a penny.

'We've got to flog it first,' says Joe.

'Aye, and you'll get a sight more than you're payin me, so cough up or this stays where it is.'

'Watch your mooth or I'll come in there an leather ye, ya wee cunt,' warns Boma.

'Shut up, Boma,' says Joe. 'Naw, fair dos,' he tells Noodsy. 'Here's twenty.' He holds up two tenners.

'It was fifty for the pair. Hauf ay fifty's twenty-five.'

'Cannae fault your arithmetic, son, but twenty's all you're gettin. Take it or leave it.'

Noodsy takes it, handing a tenner to Turbo, then they pass out the video. It's better than nothing, but a tenner still seems a shite return for his grand plan.

They watch Boma and Joe run towards the fence, Benzy getting out the car to help. Turbo climbs on to the worktop, readying to climb out the window, but Noodsy stays where he is.

'You comin, well?' Turbo asks.

'I want to see if there's anythin else worth havin afore we go.'

'Aye, right enough.' Turbo nods. 'Need to be quick, but.'

'I know. We'll just check the science base upstairs. Bound to be somethin worth floggin in there, eh?'

'Fuck knows, but seein we're here . . .'

Noodsy doesn't have a scoob what they could expect to find in there, to be honest, but he thought of it because it's nearby and it's where all the gear for experiments is kept. He's always wanted a snoop round it, and he'll never have a better chance.

When they get upstairs, they find it's really just a glorified cupboard: mostly shelves, drawers and cabinets but with a double sink built into the worktop down one side. The shelves are pure stowed, jars of chemicals and boxes of stuff. There's potassium in paraffin. He remembers that was quite exciting back in First Year, seeing it stoat about when it got dropped into water and then exploding at the end, but there's nothing leaps out at him as worth knocking. Well, the van de Graff generator would be a pish laugh to have in the house, but he doesn't think he could fit it down his jooks for taking home unnoticed after the disco.

Turbo's opened a cupboard and found a wee scalpel set with spare blades in wee foil packs. He sticks it in his back pocket.

'Whit ye daein wi that?'

'Worth carryin aboot in case ye ever get jumped. That would fuckin show them: *kweesh, kweesh, kweesh*,' he says, doing a wee stabbing motion with his hand.

'Aye, an if ye fall doon on it, ye'll cut your arse open. Put it back.'

'Fuck off. It's mines noo.'

Noodsy doesn't argue. He just hopes Boma doesn't ever get hold of the thing. He opens a couple of drawers, finds nothing but Bunsen burners in one and some daft wee trolleys in another. He's heard Scot Connolly talk about them, thinks it's something they use in O Grade physics. Then he notices that a big black leather

385

thing on a nearby worktop isn't a box, as he had assumed, but a covered cage. He pulls the drape away and sees that it's the school guinea pig, Bubbles, or whatever its name is. He remembers Coleman had it in their class once, but can't remember why. He was too busy watching the thing to pay attention to what she was sayin. He'd really wanted a wee shot of it, but it was only one of the lassies that got to touch it.

He opens the cage.

'Whit ye daein?' Turbo asks.

'I just want to haud it a wee minute.'

'Ye daft? Come on. There's fuck all in here. Let's go.'

'Let me just clap it a wee bit,' Noodsy says, reaching his hand in through the gap as the guinea pig scurries into the far corner of the cage.

Then the wee bastard lunges forward and sinks its teeth into Noodsy's index finger.

'Aaaaayaaaa, bastart,' he shouts, and pulls his hand back, but the wee fucker's still attached.

'Fuck's sake, be quiet,' Turbo urges.

It's fucking agony. Noodsy's shaking his hand, but Bubbles won't let go. He grabs hold of the thing and tries to pull it, but that's even sorer and lets him know how hard the vicious wee shite is biting down. Then in a fit of either inspiration or desperation, he sticks his hand in the sink and turns on the tap. This causes the wee bastard to let go, then skite about on the porcelain because it can't get a grip with its feet. There's blood dripping from his finger.

'Christ. Need tae get this wrapped with somethin.'

'I fuckin tellt ye tae lea it alane,' Turbo says, not

exactly bowling him over with sympathy.

'There must be plasters or something in here,' Noodsy says, still running the tap with his injured finger under it.

'Take this the noo,' says Turbo, and hands him a big roll of kitchen paper. 'I'll keep lookin.'

Noodsy rips off a length and wraps it round his finger. Bubbles is huddled up in the corner furthest from the running water.

'Need to get that back in the cage,' Noodsy says.

'Aye, right. I'm no fuckin touchin it.'

'Cannae leave it, but. It'll no be able tae eat.'

'Has it no eaten enough?'

'Very fuckin funny.'

'Oot the way,' Turbo says. He nudges Noodsy aside and puts a big biology textbook into the sink, forming a ramp. 'He can make his ain way back. We better go.'

'I still need a plaster,' Noodsy says, opening another door. This one takes a bit of a yank, and it turns out it's because it's actually a big fridge. 'Eeuuh,' he says.

'Whit?'

Noodsy opens the door further so Turbo can see in. There's a set of lungs and a windpipe sitting in a tray, for a demonstration you get in Second Year. Noodsy can't recall if they were from a cow or a sheep, but he does remember he nearly spewed his ring from the smell. He shuts the fridge and tries another drawer, where, thank fuck, there's a big packet of Elastoplasts. He bins the kitchen paper and sorts himself out with a couple of plasters. All the while Turbo's standing there with thon blank look on his coupon, like he's back in Robbie mode. Then his face becomes determined as he opens the door and lifts the tray out of the fridge.

'Whit the fuck ye daein?' Noodsy asks, but Turbo doesn't answer.

He walks out the door; no, runs is more like it. Noodsy goes after him, but he's slow because he's still trying to sort out the plasters. He heads along the main upstairs corridor, back the way they came earlier. Turbo's got a head start, so Noodsy's just got through the swing doors in time to see him tipping the lungs out over the side of the gallery. Turbo doesn't look; just immediately starts walking back towards Noodsy as shouts, screams and then the sound of somebody puking come from below. Turbo's face is horrible, his expression worse than anything the old Robbie ever showed: a storm of anger and hatred, but something scared and confused as well. He barges past, through the swing doors, starting to run. They both know they have to get back out and into the disco again sharpish.

Noodsy doesn't speak until they're on the stairs, far enough for nobody else to hear. 'Whit the fuck was that for?' he asks.

'It was for the fuckin glue in ma bag, that's whit it was fuckin for.'

'The glue in . . .? But it couldnae have been Tempo. He's no in oor science class.'

Then Turbo says it, just as Noodsy works it out. 'Naw, but that fuckin slut is.'

The Fool

Martin closes his phone and drops it on to the bedsheets as his head slumps back against the pillow, knocked flat by what Karen had to say. The ball is well and truly on the slates, or on the flat bitumen roof even, and he can't get it back for Noodsy like Noodsy got it back for him. Two things remain consistent from then to now, however. One is that Noodsy's been the one who got himself in trouble. The other is that despite knowing it wasn't his fault, Martin feels like shite about it. Christ, at least back in primary school his role was little more than incidental, the ball simply coming off him last. These past few days, he's been doing whatever he could to uncover the murderer's trail, only to find the trail led back to Noodsy all along.

Karen was right: we're none of us the people we used to be; except for, as his experience with JoJo proved, the ways in which we are still *entirely* the people we used to be. Martin would never have believed Noodsy had it in him to hurt anybody, but then who would have believed Martin had it in him to attack Boma Turner? Regardless of the result (and that was the point—in that blind moment he was utterly regardless of the result), he had launched himself at the nastiest, scariest bastard in the school, completely possessed by a compulsion to protect and avenge a wronged, innocent girl. That was how far he was prepared to go when he was nine, just for a girl he was walking home from school. How far would Noodsy be prepared to go for his wee cousin? How far would Pete McGeechy be prepared to go for his wife?

He feels like a tube. Like JoJo said, he hated being here without being the one with all the answers, and the only ones he found merely contradicted what he had hoped to prove. He looks at the alarm clock. It's just after one on Sunday afternoon. Time to draw a line and beat a quiet, inauspicious retreat. He can be on a flight inside two hours, home to his flat by teatime, back at work on Monday morning like he was never away.

His mobile rings again. He picks it up and flips open the display. It's Scot. He has half a mind to divert the call to voice-mail, slip away without any further entanglements. However, if there has been one good thing to come out of this wee misadventure, it's been seeing Scotty again, and all too briefly at that. So he answers: 'Hi, Scot, how you doin?'

'I'm awright, how are you? You sound fucked. Heavy night, was it?'

'Oh aye,' he says grimly. 'Restaurant, pub, two different women, dirty videos, you name it.'

'Seriously, mate, what's up? You sound like you've got one foot in.'

Martin tells him. 'The game's a bogey,' he says in conclusion.

Scotty is silent a moment, then clears his throat and speaks. 'Well, I'm no sure if this means the fat lady's still in make-up or whit, but there's somethin you ought to know. I'm at the Bleachfield again.'

'Don't you get a day off?'

'Normally, aye, but the demolition guys don't— not when there's double-bubble to be had. Colin had booked up-front for them to press right on

390

until it was done. Anyway, I got a call from the foreman aboot an hour ago. Christ, you should see this place; there's polis everywhere.'

'What's happened?'

Scotty pauses again to swallow before telling him: 'They've found a body.'

'What, in the hotel?'

'Naw, the hotel's rubble noo. In the foundations, the concrete. Been there since it was built. Male, they reckon. I don't know anythin more than that, but I thought, you know, it could hardly be a coincidence. Colin's in a desperate hurry to get this place demolished. Johnny Turner's equally desperate to stop it. Wants to *buy* the place, as it turns oot.'

'Colin told Pete he could guarantee Turner would be out of the picture if the committee gave him the green light,' Martin says. 'They both *knew* there was a body to uncover. That's what this was really all about.'

'How Johnny Turner knew is pretty easy to work oot,' Scotty opines. 'But how the fuck Colin knew is a different story altogether. Don't suppose you've any bright ideas on that? Or on who the poor bugger was?'

'No,' Martin admits. 'But I do know somebody who might.'

*   *   *

'Fuck her, Marty, she's just a stupit wee lassie. Never bother. Forget aboot it. Mon, we'll go up an ask for the Pistols. The DJ's got *Pretty Vacant*, I saw it. We'll get that on then go fuckin mental.'

Forget about it. Easy for Scotty to say. It wasn't

him who just got KB-ed. Martin has to share about five classes with Helen and umpteen more with folk who just witnessed that train crash. Easy for Scotty to say, aye. But not as easy as 'I told you so', which he would be well within his rights to come out with. Why didn't he just leave it; why didn't he just enjoy the carry-on with his pals? God, he wishes he could wind time back five minutes. What a fucking mess. So much damage—weeks', months' worth of grief—self-inflicted in a reckless matter of seconds.

Girls, he now knows, are just not worth this.

'C'mon, Marty,' Scot urges, nodding towards the dance floor.

'In a wee minute,' he says. 'You two go ahead. I'm gaunny go to the bogs, then maybe get a can.'

He doesn't feel in need of either, but he can't be on the dance floor right now; can't be where everyone can look at him. He can't go to the toilets either, he realises, at least until he's seen Helen return, because he most definitely can't afford to pass her in the corridor.

Fuck. *Fuck*.

He wanders disconsolately over to join the queue at the serving hatch. He waits and gets himself a can of Irn-Bru and a Mars bar and finds a quiet spot to consume them. He unwraps the chocolate and remembers Scotty talking earlier about the miniature variety: 'Fun-size Mars bars? I've never understood that, mysel. Wee totey things. Whit's fun aboot that? My idea of fun-size would be roughly the dimensions of ma bed.' But nothing's funny right now. Not since he threw himself to the wolves, again, just like when he asked Diane Murray at the Christmas disco. The music seems hollow now, too, even though it's *Pretty Vacant*. It's lost that magic energy. It's just background noise.

Scotty will be looking for him to join in, but he still doesn't feel like it. He finishes his drink and walks over to put the can in a bin. That's when he sees Linda Ogilvie walking in his direction. At first he's sure she's just on her way to put something in the bin too, but he catches her eye and realises it's him she's heading for. Linda is one of JoJo's crowd, so this, like JoJo herself, is not going to be pretty.

He feels a lump in his throat, hopes to Christ he doesn't fill up.

'Martin,' she says, 'c'mere a minute,' and beckons him against the wall. This is odd, as slaggings are best conducted in the widest possible field of vision. 'I need to ask you something,' she goes on.

'What?' he asks tersely.

'Will you dance with JoJo?'

'Aye, right, very good,' he says. So it *is* a slagging, but a very private and horribly self-indulgent one.

'No, I'm not messin,' she insists. 'And don't worry, she's not askin you to go oot with her or anythin, just to ask her up.'

She must think he came up the Clyde in a banana boat.

'Pish,' he declares.

'I mean it.'

'How come? She doesnae even like me. I'm no stupit. In fact, I'm the brainy wan, remember?'

'She does like you. You just don't know her. JoJo's a good laugh. Christ, you've probably barely spoken to her since yous were at St Elizabeth's.'

393

This, he realises, is true. He can't remember having exchanged any words with her in years. He's exchanged a few with Helen, polite but functionary, and that doesn't seem to have done much to aid his standing.

'Well if she hasnae spoken to me since primary, why the hell would she want me to dance with her, when she's got Tico and K-9 and that lot?'

'She heard what happened. That's how she wants *you* to go up an ask *her*—not just for a dance, but so that snobby wee cow Helen sees ye daein it.'

Okay, so *now* we're getting to something plausible.

'Come on, she's waitin,' Linda implores.

Martin considers it. He doesn't think Helen's a snobby wee cow. He thinks Scotty's right: she's a stupit wee lassie who 'wouldnae gie ye a dance because they're too feart ay the slaggin'. He doesn't hold it against her; he knows the score. Nor does he want to be the instrument of JoJo's vindictiveness.

But then, maybe it's not about vindictiveness. He just admitted to himself that he doesn't know JoJo any better than he knows Helen. He wouldn't expect either of them to fancy him, but perhaps he was wrong in assuming which one would have the decency to give him a dance and the maturity to understand that it didn't mean anything in some giggly Primary Five kind of way. JoJo and her pals all dance with boys they're not going with. If JoJo's got a point she wants to score over Helen, perhaps it's to show the supposedly nice girl that the reputedly bitchy one can still teach her a lesson on how to behave.

Martin glances across, sees JoJo standing at the

394

side next to Caroline and some boys from Fourth Year. He fancies her about as much as he can imagine is reciprocated, but she's still a very different creature from the Fat Joanne he used to know. Anyway, it's not about fancying anybody, that's the point, and surprisingly she's one of the few who gets it. Plus, once he's danced with her, it should open a few doors, break down some barriers. At the very least it will erase the shame of Helen's knock-back, and if he's really lucky, he could end up dancing with her yet. It's a new beginning, really. They'll all be sitting their O Grades next year, some of them even leaving school shortly after that. They're not daft wee boys and stupit wee lassies anymore, but on the cusp of becoming young men and women. So maybe it's about time they all started acting more grown up.

'Aye, okay,' he says.

Linda beams. 'There she's there,' she says redundantly. 'On you go.'

'Now?'

'She's waitin. That's how she's no up dancin just now.'

'Okay then.'

He feels nervous, but not anything like as much as when he approached Helen. There seems nothing to lose this time. He passes Helen, dancing with Karen and Ali, and must confess he hopes she is looking as he walks up to where JoJo is standing with her back to him. He taps her on the shoulder and she turns around. Up this close he sees that she is not that much taller than him, maybe only an inch or two, and that could be down to her footwear. He smiles, feeling himself get a bit of a riddie because it's all contrived. Her expression is feigned surprise mixed with impatient expectation.

'Eh, JoJo, would you like to dance?' he asks.

JoJo's eyes widen with delight. Martin feels his smile get involuntarily broader and his riddie involuntarily redder.

Then she bursts out laughing and so do all her pals. 'Ah-haaaa! He fell for it. Whit a slaggin! As if I'd dance with Professor Brainbox! Ah-ha-ha-ha!'

And so on.

Martin says nothing. He swallows, stands his ground for a moment. He knows they want him to run off at this point, and not doing so is about the only counter-measure he can manage.

It doesn't sting as much as the knock-back from Helen. It's as though the humiliation is tempered by his disdain for those laughing at him. It's also tempered by there being something familiar and thoroughly unsurprising about it. In his head he briefly pictures Lucy swiping the football away, yet again, just as Charlie Brown is about to kick it.

*   *   *

She's standing in the St Grace's dining hall, mere feet away from where she humiliated him on that horrible, bitter night. Just like then, there is music playing and teenagers dancing all across the floor, the non-participants lining the walls alongside the same blue plastic chairs. Just as then, JoJo is standing among a group of her female peers, though in this instance they are fellow mothers, here to observe or perhaps assist at their daughters' Sunday afternoon dance class.

She sees him approach and instinctively folds her arms.

396

He stops, indicating he wants to speak to her away from the others' hearing. This time, at least, he won't be asking in front of everybody.

JoJo says something to the woman next to her and briskly walks towards Martin.

'I need your help,' he says.

She makes to reply, but he presses on before she can say anything.

'I'm lost here,' he goes on. 'I've got umpteen jumbled pieces of a puzzle I can't put together and a shitload of questions I'm not smart enough to answer. I'm not here because I'm desperate, Joanne. I'm here because I believe you're the one person who can work it all out.'

Her arms remain folded, her lips pursed in testy distrust. She looks him in the eye and he hopes she sees the very sincerity she'd have slaughtered him for two decades earlier. Then, finally, she sighs, the furrow in her brow softening just a little. 'Okay, Professor,' she says. 'Seeing as you asked nicely. But not here. Music's too loud. Come with me.'

So he follows her out of the dining hall; past where Karen incensed the priest with her reading about the plague of frogs; up the stairs leading into the main school building; past the spot where Colin burst Robbie's nose; past the alcove where Colin and Eleanor were hit by a sheep's lung dropped by a mystery assailant; to a long bench in the Third-to-Sixth-Year social area, where they sit down together.

And with watery spring sunshine flooding through the windows and glass double doors, that's where they talk.

Fifth Year
Delta Pavonis

Dreams of Flight

'I don't know why we're even botherin goin to this shite,' Martin says. They're standing in Martin's living room, eyes on the window as they await the mini cab that's taking them to the Bleachfield Hotel for the Fifth and Sixth Year Dance. It's also known as 'the leaving dance', though with very few exceptions that only refers to the Sixth Years. Hardly anybody will be leaving after Fifth Year; even fewer than left after Fourth. Robbie Turner's still here, for fuck's sake. Dreams of academe? Don't fucking think so. Eleanor Fenwick's still here, and staying on for Sixth Year, too, he's been told.

Martin's even heard the teachers remark upon it: folk are clinging on, doing one Higher or resitting O Grades, when in the past they would have been off like a shot as soon as they were legally allowed. But that was when there was still such a concept as a job. This is 1985. You don't even get apprenticeships: you get YOP schemes, which in more civilised ages used to be known less euphemistically as serfdom. Nobody wants to leave school, it seems. Nobody except Martin. For him it really is a leaving dance, or maybe it should be a leaving-a-vapour-trail dance. He's counting the minutes, never mind the days.

For the others, Christ, it must seem like a ringing endorsement of St Grace's as an educational establishment, despite their exam results tending to suggest otherwise. But it's not just the fear of unemployment that's keeping a lot

401

of them in the classrooms. Folk like Tempo, Tico, JoJo, Margaret-Anne: they would never admit it, but deep down they all know this will be the last time they get to be kings and queens of the castle. Bunch of fucking nonentities who have been allowed to feel like big shots in this tiny wee world just because they were that bit taller, matured that bit faster, or had big brothers and sisters who let them hang on their coat-tails.

'Aye, get yoursel into the party mood,' Scotty says, laughing.

'I mean it. We should go somewhere else. Get the taxi to take us up the West End, Byres Road or somewhere instead.'

'Don't be a tube. We've paid for oor tickets, and just cause we're all dressed up doesnae mean we'd get served in a real pub.'

Served. The magic word, the defining rite of status in the Fifth Year tribe and the second-most compelling factor in deciding where the leaving dance would be held. The most compelling factor was that Temps all but hijacked the student council with the sole agenda of securing the gig for his dad's dump of a hotel. His guarantee that a blind eye would be turned by bar staff to the Fifth Year contingent being seventeen at the oldest (and many not even that) was, naturally, a key plank in his argument, but only if you overlooked the fact that the two other hotels in contention—both of which had hosted the dance previously—could be relied upon for the same profit-boosting laxity. And as it happened, most people did overlook that fact, because Tempo was going to get what he wanted one way or another. He pressured, cajoled and outright bullied any dissent out of the way, with Martin having his own contribution to the debate effectively invalidated at one particularly mortifying student council meeting.

'Nae offence, Martin, but you're no really very qualified to comment on this. We're talkin aboot organisin a party with a real bar, an that's no exactly your area of expertise, is it? You've never been at anythin like that, have ye? See, most of *us* have. We were all at K-9's eighteenth. Do you think you'd have got past the door? Naw. So leave this tae the folk that know what they're talkin aboot.'

Ah, yes: Matt Cannon's eighteenth, at Toledo Junction in Paisley. That was the highest currency these days, the true badge of honour. If you'd been at that, if you'd been past the door, and if you'd been served at the bar, you were a man, my son.

What was most galling about Tempo's railroading of his single agenda was that he'd had nothing to do with the student council or anything of the sort before. The teachers always landed anything 'voluntary' on the same reliably dutiful and responsible individuals, such as himself, Scotty, Helen Dunn, Karen Gillespie and Pete McGeechy. Come Fifth Year, however, not only had Colin decided to take an interest in the student council, but so had several of his mates and their female counterparts. Their attitude was like: 'Okay, kiddies, the big boys and girls are taking over. There's a party to organise, and we can't leave something as important as that to dweebs like you. Run along, now.'

They weren't remotely interested in any other aspect of the council: just making sure the big night was on their terms (choice of DJ, dress code, no meal, just dancing), and in Tempo's case

403

principally that the venue was the Bleachfield.

Thus Martin and Scot were standing there in suits, awaiting transport to a place where you'd normally look overdressed if you weren't covered in sick.

'Dressed up, aye,' Martin says. 'That's hackin me aff as well. We're dressed like *them*: two more fuckin Bowie clones. Where's your tie, by the way?'

'In my pocket. I'll put it on in a minute.'

'Don't see why we all have to wear suits and ties anyway.'

'Cause it's no a fuckin school disco, Marty. I'd have thought you of all folk would be grateful for that.'

'Oh, cheers. Give me a few digs while I'm on the floor, why don't ye?'

Scotty's laughing again. Martin feels he's got serious points to make, but he might as well tell them to the wall. Once Scotty's decided he's not taking you seriously, it's hopeless.

'It's so we're all glammed up,' Scot suggests. 'See each other in a different light, something like that, I don't know. Fun, Martin, remember?'

'Aye. Fun's what I'm gaunny have when I get out of here and go to university. Proper discos, proper music, proper *style*.'

'Whit, you're saying *you*'ve got style now?'

'Naw, but there'll be folk there who have. And I mean their own style. As opposed to folk that think a visit to Chelsea Girl or Concept Man of a Saturday puts them up on a fuckin catwalk.'

'Aye, fair enough. But don't start on Simple Minds again right now, I cannae handle it.'

Martin has to laugh. His catwalk remark had indeed triggered his next intended rant—about the music they'd be stuck with tonight—and Scotty read it like a telegram. *Up on the Catwalk*: Simple Minds. The appositely named band of no-choice for those who preferred their 'taste' dictated by what so-and-so's big brother said was 'dead cool the noo, by the way'.

'Okay,' Martin says. 'But you do know that's what we're in for: three hours of—'

'Marty, I warned you . . .'

'Okay, okay.'

'The music doesnae matter. Would you lighten up? It's just gaunny be a laugh. A few bevvies, a few dances.'

'A few dances? With who?'

'With anybody and everybody. That's whit these things are like. Heather was at two ay them, said they were really cool, mellow, like. As I says, it's no a school disco.'

'Aye, and it isnae the prom in a fuckin teen movie, either. They're still the same up-themselves bitches and daft wee lassies they always were.'

'Mince, Marty. It's you that's in the huff with everybody, not the other way round. Lighten up, for fuck's sake. This could be a historic night. Might end up with the love of your life and you don't even know it.'

'I don't think Phoebe Cates is going. And is that what you think: that you're gaunny get aff wi somebody the night just cause it's the big dance?'

'I *think* . . . I'm gaunny enjoy mysel, Martin. That's the purpose ay the fuckin exercise. Can you get thon big brain ay yours to process such a primitive concept?'

Martin smiles and shrugs. 'Just aboot.'

'Good.'

405

'You puttin that tie on yet? The taxi'll be here any second.'

'Aye, right enough,' Scot says. He reaches into his inside pocket, from which he produces a leather bootlace tie with a spread-eagle clip and spiralling metal loops at each end.

'Ya fly bastard,' Martin says, with mild outrage and not a little envy.

'Don't worry,' Scot tells him, dipping into his pocket again. 'I got you one as well. Get that deid kipper aff your chest. Come on.'

*   *   *

Karen's frustration is growing by the second. She's trying to raise the temperature without losing her temper, but it's a delicate balance, and so far she's succeeded only in making Noodsy lose his. Normally that would be an intended outcome of her calculated affectations, but right now it's not yielding anything that supports her thesis.

'I've got fuck-all tae dae wi Pete McGeechy,' Noodsy growls at her. 'Or rather, Pete McGeechy makes damn sure he's got fuck-all tae dae wi me. Aye, he married my cousin Anna. So fuck. I only see her at funerals. That's the way they baith like it. I'm the crooked end ay the family, remember? Don't want me in the picture, dae they?'

This is hopeless. She's tried to trip him up by seeing if she can get him to betray some knowledge of the video footage or the cameras, things that haven't been mentioned to him by the police and that he only ought to know about if he was indeed in cahoots with McGeechy or even with Johnny Turner. Nothing. Not a glimmer. Either he's a lot

406

smarter than she ever gave him credit for or he really knows nothing about this stuff.

Okay, Karen girl, Occam's Razor time.

Noodsy was never smart. He might be shrewder and more streetwise these days, but not smart. Armed with this much information, she's wheedled plenty out of far brighter guys than him. If it yet turns out he did outwit her, she's resigning forthwith, because it would mean she can't do this job anymore.

She hears a knock at the interview-room door and turns around to see Tom peering through the narrow window. He beckons with his fingers. She stops the tape and excuses herself. Noodsy just glowers as she exits into the corridor.

'Save me, Tom, I'm sinking here.'

'Your wish is my command.'

'What?'

'Just got a call from the Southern General. Robbie Turner is awake and off his ventilator.'

'Thank Christ. On every possible level, thank Christ.'

'Got those CCTV captures I was waiting for as well; email came in about ten minutes ago.'

'And?'

Tom just nods.

'How's the quality?'

'Good enough. Shall we?' he asks, gesticulating towards the exit.

'One minute,' she says. 'I'm going to pass on the good news first.'

She opens the door. Noodsy has his head in his hands as she walks in. He does that any time he's left alone; it's like he's scared it'll fall off and roll away. He glances up and sighs. He looks knackered, but he's mustering whatever he's got left for repelling one more assault.

She doesn't turn on the tape just yet. It can't record what he's about to tell her anyway; it's his expression that is going to say it all.

'Robbie's awake,' she says. 'And talking.'

Noodsy's eyes brighten, the way she imagines they must have when Martin Jackson walked in.

'Thank Christ,' he says.

'Yeah, that's what I said, too.'

Written in Blood

This is fuckin yes. Best time Robbie has had since he can remember. He was nervous as fuck about coming, wasn't sure until right up to the last minute whether he'd even bother in case he ended up standing about like a tool, as welcome as diarrhoea in a bedpan, but no, it's well worth it. The dance floor is kind of wee and the function suite's a bit cramped for this many folk, but the atmosphere is brilliant. Folk are being really cool for a change. He's been talking away to everybody, lassies as well, and he's even dancing with them. He's up on the floor right now, dancing with Zoe Lawson, and that's as well as dancing with Alison Taylor, Karen Gillespie and even Samantha Gerrity. It's not like that means he's in with a shout of getting off with any of them, especially not a pure doll like Samantha, but that's the whole point. That's what's brilliant about it. It's dead friendly.

He wishes it had always been more like this.

Look at Zoe there, for instance. He can remember her from their very first day at primary, when she burst a carton of milk, but he can't remember having a conversation with her in the whole twelve years since. That's probably true of just about every lassie here for most of the guys, but it's not the lassies that are making him feel kind of regretful. He's had plenty of conversations with the guys here, but he's starting to wish he'd been less of a cunt during most of them. Not be long until they all move on, and that'll be that, all over. Then what chance has he of seeing half of them again? Martin Jackson's leaving this year, away to uni. Not much odds of seeing him again, that's for sure, and Martin'll not give him the time of day if he ever does. Can't blame him, right enough. Martin never did anything bad to any cunt, but he still got given a lot of shite.

One more year and then that'll be *everybody* away. Robbie's not very sure he'll be staying on after the summer, either. It's been hard enough at home over him staying on for Fifth Year. Can't see the old man wearing it if he says he wants a sixth.

Maybe he'll get lucky and find a job. That way he could move out the house, get away from the family. It's been fucking murder lately. Ma and Da fighting all the time, and what makes it worse is he now knows what it is they've always been fighting about. It all came out last summer, when he said he wanted to stay on and do Higher History because he got a 'B' for his O Grade. He didn't let on to anybody, in case they made out he was a poof, but he was well chuffed at getting a 'B'. He also got 'C's in Arith and Geography.

Da—aye, right: 'Da'—said no chance. Wanted

409

him out the house soon as he was sixteen, never mind out the school. Said it was time for him to support himself. Ma pointed out there was no way of supporting himself if there were no fucking jobs, and he'd be in with a better shout of getting one later if he'd more exams. And that's when Da lost the place and said it: 'I've supported that useless wee cunt for sixteen fuckin years an he's no even mine.'

Aye, that was a champagne fucking moment.

However, tell the truth, when Da finally came out with it, Robbie realised it was something he'd suspected deep down for a long, long time. Just never got round to admitting it to himself. Not as if there hadn't been plenty of fucking clues down the years. But there you are, that was it finally in the open.

He'd since asked his ma millions of times who his real da was, but she wouldn't tell him. 'Just leave it,' she'd always say. *Leave it?* This was his fucking father he was talking about. Did she really expect him to shrug his shoulders and quit asking? Probably not, but she wasn't fucking telling, that was for sure, and she got really upset if he pushed it too hard. Da leathered him for it once, absolutely knocked fuck out him. He saw Ma was upset, and even though she wouldn't say what was wrong, Da guessed. Told Robbie never to ask her again, so that was always the risk he was running.

Atmosphere in the house has been fucking awful ever since; worse than usual recently. He can't see himself getting his Higher history. He didn't think he did well in either paper. Hardly studied in the run-up because he couldn't bear to be in the house. Realistically, he can't see himself being able to

410

come back and resit it next year. That's why he's lapping this up the now: he knows it's the end.

Scot Connolly appears alongside him, dancing with Helen Dunn. Robbie might end up dancing with Helen in a minute, because there's a lot of that been happening: you just swap over and dance with whoever. That's how he ended up getting a dance off Samantha. Mind you, he might not get a swap off Scotty, as now he thinks about it, he's not seen either of this pair dancing with anybody else since really early on.

The song changes and Zoe starts dancing with big Tico Hughes, who was behind Robbie dancing with Margaret-Anne. This leaves Robbie with her as a partner, and it kind of says it all about tonight that she just smiles and gets on with it. Margaret-Anne can be a right torn-faced bitch, and if anybody was going to give him a knock-back, she'd be the one. Well, maybe not just her. There's Eleanor as well. That would be the ultimate test, wouldn't it? He can see her close by, now that he's facing the other way. She's with Kenny Langton, and she's smiling, probably because Kenny's coming out with all his jokes as usual. Robbie's glad she's smiling, but. It's a fucking sin for her, what happened. Her ma killed herself. Took a fucking overdose. Left a note, they said, then washed down a bottle of sleeping tablets with a half-bottle of vodka. It was about a month ago. Eleanor's not been back at school since. Missed her exams and everything. Nobody knew whether she'd come along tonight, but maybe it's a way of breaking herself back in gently. He's tried not to look out for her, because he knows everybody'll be doing that, and he of all folk understands what it

411

feels like to be the subject of their fascination.

He'd like to talk to her, but, to let her know he's been there as well, and that he knows how hard it is when every cunt's tiptoeing round you but unable to keep their eyes off you.

He wants to say sorry as well. All that shite between them, it was fuck-all to do with him and her. It was all about fucking Boma and Joe—mostly Boma—and how much they hated the Fenwick boys. He and Eleanor were just caught in the middle, and he feels like he ought to say something about it. This feels like the kind of night for things like that. Everybody's getting on, acting like adults, treating each other with a wee bit of respect. Tempo's still acting like Charlie Big Balls, because it's his da's gaff, but other than that, nobody's holding any grudges.

Aye, he thinks. That's what times like this are for.

He moves along a bit as he dances, Margaret-Anne staying close, following his lead, then he positions himself so that he's got his back to Kenny.

The record starts fading and another one begins. He taps Kenny's shoulder and he turns round.

'Awright, Robbie?' Kenny says with a big grin, then flashes his gnashers at Margaret-Anne, stepping in to be her new partner.

Robbie side-steps to let him pass, then finds himself face-to-face with Eleanor in the centre of the dance floor. Linda Ogilvie's to his left, dancing with Matt Cannon; and Big Tempo's on the right, dancing with JoJo.

Colin is getting a semi here, which is a worry. He knows these trousers with the double pleat look cool-as, because he saw Don Johnson wearing a pair just like them on *Miami Vice*, but if his cock doesn't cool the jets in a minute, it's going to be really fucking obvious. Would have been all right if he'd just worn Ys instead of these boxer shorts, but the boxers look a sight more sexy if they're all you've got on, and he's set fair to be seen in just that condition not too many hours from now. That's why he's getting a semi, in fact. It's quite a bouncy record that's on—*Waterfront* (the DJ's been told: plenty Simple Minds and Bowie or he'll not be getting another gig at the Bleachfield)—and between the sight of JoJo's tits jiggling about in that low-cut dress and his own unsupported tackle swinging free, it's difficult to think about anything else.

He's been buttering up JoJo for a few weeks now, and this is when it's all planned to pay off. He's the main man here tonight, everybody knows it; it's practically his party, and he's got a room ready upstairs.

Embarrassing to relate, Tempo's never done it, and that seriously needs to be put right, which is why he's been working hard and carefully on this. Ideally, he'd have lined up somebody that's definitely done it already, because that would be a surer bet. Unfortunately, most of the ones who he knows have done it are either spoken for or total dogs. He doesn't know whether JoJo's done it or not, but she always talks big about sex, so he reckoned she would be a good shout. If she hasn't done it, then it'll probably be a worry to her that most of her pals have, because JoJo always likes to be the one in the know. Plus, she's not the bonniest of that crowd, still a bit on the plump side, so he's accurately predicted she'd be flattered he was paying her so much attention; in fact, semi-officially going out together. So far he's had a finger up her and she's given him a wank, so he's betting that now she's the one on the arm of the star of the show tonight, she'll reckon her ship's come in. And he'll be sailing that ship right upstairs and on to that king-size.

* * *

Robbie smiles at Eleanor, trying to look apologetic, trying to look friendly.

Eleanor smiles too, for about a second, the second it takes for it to register who she's dancing with, who she's looking at. Then her face just sort of crumbles. She stares at him, not dancing, not moving. He's expecting a mouthful, or her to turn away, but she just stands there, looking at him, staring at him, and there's this look in her eyes, this sadness.

He sees her mouth start to tremble. She raises her arms. For a fraction of a second he thinks, incredibly, that she's about to hug him, but then she collapses into tears. And he means collapses. She puts her hands to her face, then her legs go wobbly and she slumps to the floor on her knees.

JoJo's right in there like a shot, helping her up and leading her away, right out the room. Robbie should have been the one to lift her, to help her, but he felt unable to move, like he was stuck in a

414

silent glass box with everything still going on around it. He was paralysed in the moment because he saw exactly what Eleanor saw, saw what had knocked her down, what her dead ma must have told her in that note before she went.

Did Boma and Joe know as well, all this time, he wonders? No. Specially not Boma. Cunt would never have been able to keep his mouth shut. All he'd have known was that his da hated the Fenwicks, was never done slagging them and especially their no-good father who walked out on the whole sorry bunch.

* * *

'I took her out to the car park for some air,' says JoJo. 'Took her to the toilets first, but they were mobbed. We sat on the steps to the fire escape and she just poured it all out. We weren't big pals or anythin back then—no enemies either, we got on okay—but no exactly confidantes, you know? I think it just needed to come out. She needed to tell somebody, and I was the first person on hand to take an interest.'

'I had no idea,' Martin says. 'I don't think anybody did. We all just assumed she broke down because it was too big an occasion for her to be in the middle of after her mum died. I don't think anyone thought Robbie's part was anything more than incidental. In fact, I don't think anybody else today would have been able to tell me who Eleanor was dancing with when it happened.'

'And that's where you'd be wrong again, Professor.'

415

*   *   *

Colin stands next to JoJo as she helps Eleanor to her feet. He's offering an arm to help support the lassie, but JoJo shakes her head and puts out a hand, gesturing him to leave them alone.

'I'm takin her oot,' JoJo says. 'Just leave us the now.'

He nods and steps out of the way. Around him there are couples and groups still dancing, oblivious to what just happened, or maybe in some cases politely pretending they never saw it. There's plenty more being less sensitive or discreet: heads turned, fingers tapping shoulders, hands cupped to ears. And then there's Robbie: standing like it's a massive game of sticky statues and he's the only one who thinks the music's stopped.

Colin, similarly bereft of his dance partner, taps Robbie on the arm to break the spell and leads him off to a seat at the side. Nobody is looking at them: whatever happened, Eleanor's the one it happened to, while Robbie and Colin are just two guys leaving the dance floor. But something did happen to Robbie, Colin can see. He looks totally spooked, white as a ghost, his eyes focusing somewhere that isn't in this room.

And suddenly something clicks into place. The secret fragment of childhood history that Colin has always carried, jagged and anomalous, transforms from a baffling isolated shard to the piece that completes a larger puzzle.

It's Primary Four, St Lizzie's. Playtime. Colin has left the game of Colditz early because he needs a pee and wants to go before the bell rings. Plus he was stuck being a Jerry. He walks into the boys'

416

toilets and sees a sight he will never forget.

Boma Turner is booting at the door to one of the stalls, repeatedly bringing his right foot to bear upon the side of the lock, furious, determined grunts issuing from his mouth with each kick. Fairly miraculously, the lock holds out against this onslaught. Boma then gives the door a charge with his shoulder but is again rebuffed. In response, he lets out a guttural roar that starts as frustration but becomes like a war-cry as he takes another runny and scrambles his way over the top of the cubicle.

Colin then sees the door shudder further, accompanied by more thumps and, this time, yelps of pain and panic.

He hears Boma's voice, low and breathless now: 'This is for what your bastart da done tae ma maw,' followed by more blows, more cries. Then the lock snaps back and the door opens just enough for Harry Fenwick to hurl himself through the gap before Boma can pull it closed again. He sprawls on the floor, his trousers tripping him around his knees. Colin sees shite all over Harry's legs before he hauls them up and scrambles for the exit, clutching his waistband.

Boma steps out and watches Harry run, then turns to look straight at Colin. 'You say anyhin tae any cunt an you're next,' Boma says quietly, walking to the sinks where he calmly proceeds to wash his hands.

Colin shakes his head rapidly. He can't find the words to state his acknowledgement.

'Now get yoursel tae fuck.'

Colin told nobody the truth about the legendary incident, at first through fear of Boma, and later out of shame that he had been so cowardly as to

417

hide it for so long.

Boma would have been ten, maybe eleven. Chances were he didn't know precisely what Harry's da had done to his mammy; and, like Colin, was probably under the mistaken impression that the Fenwicks' da was whatever man was then living with their mother. There would likely have been some conversation or argument between Boma's parents, overheard and half understood, about which all he knew for sure was that his da was really angry. Like Colin, Boma himself at that point probably assumed this outrage to have involved Harry's da somehow hurting Mrs Turner.

As far as Colin understood, Joe Turner and the older Fenwicks had already crossed swords, so with no way of knowing how historical Mrs Turner's injury to be, he was under the impression it was part of an ongoing greater animosity, rather than the cause of it. They were the two bampot families of the scheme, so it was inevitable that their boys would be laying rival claim to being kings of the midden. That, Colin assumed, and not whatever Boma had referred to in the toilets, accounted for the mutual hatred between the Fenwicks and the Turners in later years: such as Eleanor putting the glue in Robbie's schoolbag, and Boma dropping animal guts on Colin and Eleanor that time he was getting off with her. Boma wasn't at the disco, but soon afterwards it was common knowledge that he had been the one who broke into the school that night and stole the video. Colin therefore had no doubt about what else he'd done, though he'd never felt much inclined to dig him up about it.

Once Colin was older, on the rare and

uncomfortable occasions he had cause to remember the incident in the toilets, his teenage fixations made him imagine Mr Fenwick's transgression must have been something darker, like rape. Tonight, though, seeing Eleanor break down and Robbie freeze, he understands not only what it truly was, but *when* it truly was.

Eleanor's mum killed herself a few weeks back. Left a note, they said.

Colin thinks of Boma and Joe, how Robbie never looked much like them. And now, after years of it literally staring him in the face, he realises who Robbie *does* resemble.

*　　　*　　　*

'Did Robbie already know by that point?' Martin asks. 'Christ, I'm saying that, but . . . I should be asking you if Robbie even knows *now*.'

'He knows,' JoJo says, nodding. 'I don't know when or how exactly he found out, but I do know they faced up to it together shortly after. Eleanor says they met a few times over that summer. Must have been hard, specially given how much they'd hated each other, but family's family: they were brother and sister, or half-brother and -sister anyway.'

'Must have been easier for Robbie to forgive than the other way around,' Martin suggests.

'Maybe,' JoJo demurs. 'Eleanor knew she was no saint either.'

'Hard to believe Robbie would want another sibling, given how he got on with his brothers.'

'He got on okay with the women, I think: his mum, his big sister. Having a sister who was

419

nothing to do with Johnny Turner must have seemed a good thing.'

'So is it common knowledge now?'

'No. I mean, there's folk who know, but it's not mentioned aloud, you know?'

'And Robbie and Eleanor, are they close?'

'Not really. Eleanor kept him at arm's length. Robbie was always a bit of a shambles, as you know, though Eleanor told me any time he had money he tried to help out with Gail. He also tried to track down their father, but got nowhere. Spent money on agencies and stuff, but nobody really knew where to begin. Eleanor's mum wasnae around to ask, and Eleanor knew nothing because Charlie Fenwick disappeared before she was even one. That was 1969.'

'The year the Bleachfield was built,' Martin says.

JoJo nods and gives him a penetrating look. 'You worked it oot yet, Sherlock?'

'Oh yeah.'

'Aye, well, so did Colin, would be my guess. At roughly the point when Johnny Turner became determined to stop him demolishing the hotel.'

'But how did Colin know Charlie Fenwick was Robbie's father?'

JoJo sighs and an uncharacteristically vulnerable, regretful look plays across her face.

'You told him,' he guesses.

She winces a little and briefly closes her eyes. 'It wasn't quite like that,' she says. 'It was . . . That was the night . . .' Her words falter and she has to swallow and sniff as a few tears form. Martin puts his hand into his pocket and produces a tissue. She doesn't take it, but does hold the proffered hand.

*   *   *

It's getting late, close to midnight. The bar closed half an hour ago, which is a good thing, considering how pissed certain folk look. Karen thinks they ought to run a sweepstake on who pukes first out of John-Jo, John-James, Tam McIntosh, Liam Paterson and James Doon. She'd give evens on a dead-heat between the Carnock Cousins, as they did everything together. Kenny Langton looked pretty blitzed, too, she thought earlier, but that turned out to be just the way he was dancing.

It's winding down: slow numbers from the DJ, the dance floor left to a few genuine couples and two of the guys having a slow waltz as a carry-on. Helen is still out there with Scot Connolly. Karen came here with Helen and Alison in Karen's mum's car, but she and Alison have hardly spoken to the lassie for the past two hours. Karen's delighted for her, though: she's positively radiating. Helen looked good tonight anyway, if a little self-conscious about being so glammed-up, and seemed to grow into her dress once she started dancing with a few guys. However, it was after she danced with Scot, and then went off to a table with him and talked and laughed and talked and laughed that she really started to glow.

Helen has actually confided recently that she fancies Scot; that she's *always* liked him, in fact, even though she was often a wee bit intimidated by his mischievousness and that perceptively wicked tongue of his. Karen's always liked him, too, and for precisely the reasons Helen found intimidating. She's always liked his pal Martin as well, but

421

neither of them ever seemed suitable as boyfriend material. They're the kind of guy she wishes she could have been better friends with, but that's about it. Both too short to be anything more, for one thing, and just too damn boyish. They look the part tonight, though. Those bootlace ties are a cute touch; just enough of a hint of dissent without it being any kind of attention-seeking protest. She can tell Martin is delighted to be dressed just that bit more individually. She of all people can identify with the buzz of walking into company like this and making a statement about yourself. However, the statement Martin seems keenest to make these days is 'Cheerio'. The tie seems more a Scot thing, she estimates. He's the cheeky one. It's not intended as a protest, just a wee bit of good-humoured devilment.

Karen's had a good time. It's been great to see everybody away from the snake-pit that school always turns into. There's a lot of goodwill in the air tonight, and not a little regret. Plenty of people here won't be seeing so much of each other in future, and it's taken an occasion like this to make them realise that might be a bad thing. The only sour note she's aware of—apart from poor Eleanor having to leave—is that Martin walked off the dance floor to the bar rather than dance with JoJo when they ended up together. He didn't do it demonstratively, but he still did it. JoJo would never admit it in a million years, but Karen could tell she was hurt. Some might say she had it coming, but for Christ's sake, not tonight. This was a night for putting all that shite behind you. Martin was leaving anyway, why burn bridges? She thought he was more magnanimous; thought he had more class. Thought he was a nicer guy.

Karen won't be leaving this year; she's in no hurry. She doesn't have a scooby what she wants to do, and the best way to defer a decision on that is to go to college. A sixth year and a couple more Highers won't hurt, especially as she's none too confident about that second maths paper she sat. She hasn't really known what she wanted to do for years; and being the Bionic Woman probably doesn't count. She once thought she wanted to be an art teacher, but the truth was she just wanted to be *her* art teacher, or even just dress like her. She also thought about becoming a polis, as it's one of the few jobs where being a comparatively tall female is seen as an advantage. She blew it off, though, on the grounds that nobody ever tells her anything. JoJo Milligan: *that*'s who should become a cop.

The thought makes Karen look around for her, but there's no sign. She saw JoJo leave the function suite with Colin Temple, with whom she'd been dancing for most of the night. Karen's kind of surprised he would be out of the room for longer than it took to have a pee, as he seemed intent upon milking every moment. Colin's been acting like the whole event is *his* party, the hotel the site of his own personal triumph. She wonders what spell JoJo has cast to be honoured with so much personal attention.

$$*\qquad*\qquad*$$

'That was the night I . . . you know, lost my . . .' JoJo swallows again and nods in lieu of saying it.

Martin nods, too, so that she can continue.

423

'To Colin . . . with Colin, in fact. I'm pretty sure it was his first time as well. Anyway, part of his seduction that night was to act all sensitive and concerned, askin aboot Eleanor. I didnae really tell him what I knew . . . Some of the things he said . . . it was like he knew already. Okay, maybe I joined a few dots, but he had most of the picture drawn. I don't know how, but the main thing is he *did* know, and he's known for twenty years. So when Johnny Turner started comin over heavy about the hotel, Colin also must have realised what happened to Charlie Fenwick.'

'Scot said Johnny might even have worked as a labourer when they were building the place.'

'That would be aboot right, aye.'

'And Colin reckoned that once the hotel was demolished and the body found, Johnny Turner would be removed from the equation.'

'Aye,' JoJo agrees. 'Forcibly, by the polis. But I guess he didnae work it oot quite soon enough, otherwise he wouldnae have bothered leanin on Pete McGeechy.'

'Or, knowing Colin, it was belt-and-braces. He needed Pete to guarantee the planning permission, especially after Johnny Turner nobbled the committee. Johnny being lifted for murder wouldn't necessarily undo the damage he'd already done to the planning application. So he blackmailed Pete, but then it backfired and presented Turner with a winning hand, which he chose to play just days before Colin knew the demolition would take him out of the game . . .'

*   *   *

424

Colin hears the car before he sees it. That's always how it is out here: so quiet, just the chirping of the birds and the rustle of wind in the branches. Sometimes you can even hear the waves lapping on the fishing loch. The sound of an engine and the crunch of tyres on dust and bark is like a roar by comparison, even two or three hundred yards away through the trees. He doesn't need to see the car anyway to know who it is. Nobody happens along here in passing. The single-track road leads only in and out. It's a dead end.

He lifts his new, second mobile and makes the call for which it was anonymously purchased. It's a simple act, and yet so difficult. He knows it will make the rest easier, though, or at least reduce the dilemma of choice. Making this call will set everything in motion; will make it harder to shite out of it and decide he'll just take his losses on the chin instead when it comes to the real moment.

'I need you to meet me here at the lodges as soon as possible,' he says. 'It's really important. And I need you to come alone, because it's sensitive. It's about your dad.'

The black BMW pulls into view, coming around the side of the end lodge and rolling into the horseshoe with a stated lack of hurry. Colin sees him through the windscreen. He's alone, thank fuck. It would still work if Boma was with him— arguably even better—but it would be twice as tricky.

Johnny Turner gets out of the car slowly, again underlining a lack of haste, like he's out for a stroll in the woods. He's got a briefcase with him. Cunt probably bought it for the occasion, acting the businessman. Can't imagine him having much call

425

for it the rest of the time, or the suit. He's a fucking site labourer turned crook inside whatever he's wearing. The threads just make him look like he's due in court.

Colin is standing in the doorway of Lodge Two. Turner holds up the case and points enquiringly towards the shed.

'In your wee office?' he asks, smiling, like he's a fucking rep here to do a sub on some linen supplies.

'Naw, just come on through here,' Colin tells him. He's just locked the hut, having shut down the PC so it doesn't record anything.

Turner follows him into the lodge, where Colin gestures towards the low coffee table and sofa in the sitting area.

'Let's make this brief, I've things to get on with,' Turner says, the smug bastard acting like this is all routine, in order to more subtly rub it in. He places the briefcase down on the coffee table with near ceremonial delicacy, bending over to open the catches.

Colin has never been sure he'd be able to go through with this, hasn't slept since he decided it was his only way out. The moment is almost upon him. This was when he feared, even expected, that he'd falter, but he feels different when he sees the paperwork being laid out in front of him, and with such self-satisfied relish.

Two million quid. That's what he'd be signing away.

'Do you need a pen, son?' Turner asks, holding up a bookie's biro, which, like the briefcase, he must also have chosen and brought specifically for the occasion.

426

'It's all right, I've got my own,' Colin says, then pulls out the gun from inside his jacket and shoots Turner through the centre of his forehead.

*   *   *

'So the unidentified mobile that phoned Robbie must have been Colin's,' Martin suggests. 'He needed somebody to blame for Turner's death, somebody he could then also kill and make it look like suicide. Who better than Robbie, who is known to hate Johnny anyway?'

'Who better indeed?' muses JoJo, a concerned, concentrated look on her face as she speaks.

'A few days later, Charlie Fenwick's body would be uncovered and the story would come out: Johnny murdered Charlie in 1969 after he had an affair with his wife. Colin can tell the polis he told Robbie about Johnny's interest in stopping the demolition and Robbie drew his own conclusions. It would then look like Robbie killed Johnny in revenge for his real dad's murder, but then couldn't face what he'd done and killed himself.'

JoJo nods sincerely to convey that she's buying his theory, but there's still a furrow of doubt along her brow; caused, he knows, by the one remaining question neither of them can answer.

'So how come it's Colin who ends up dead?'

The Black Hole

'He's able to talk, but not for long,' Dr Lanimer says. 'He's agreed to speak to you, against my

427

advice, I should state, so if I think he's getting distressed, I'm warning you now, I'll be asking— and expecting—you to leave.'

'That's understood, Doctor,' Karen assures her. She can see Robbie through the window. He's still wired up to various machines, but the ventilator is no longer one of them. He looks very pale and very small.

'I'll take you through, then,' Dr Lanimer says.

'Thanks.'

Dr Lanimer leads them to Robbie's station, stepping aside to let them through, but remaining at the foot of the bed. Robbie is lying flat on his back, but turns his head slightly to face Karen when she takes a seat next to him.

'Hello, Robert,' she says. 'I'm—'

'Karen Gillespie,' he says, his voice a hoarse croak. 'Jesus.'

'Well remembered.'

'Nothing wrang with this eye,' he says. 'Or my memory.'

'Glad to hear it. Though it's Detective Superintendent Gillespie now.'

'Congratulations.'

'How you doing?'

'Been better. Could be worse. How's Noodsy? He awright, or did Boma get him as well?'

'Boma did this to you?'

'Aye. He heard me and Noodsy got lifted tryin tae steal that ololeum stuff. He knew his auld man was missin, so when he heard aboot the bodies, he went mental. Have you got him?'

'It's in hand,' Karen says.

'Good. What aboot Noodsy?'

'He's in custody. You want to tell us what

happened?'

'What did he say happened?'

'Let's hear your story first, and we'll play spot-the-difference later.'

'Am I under arrest?' Robbie looks at Karen and then to Dr Lanimer.

Karen shakes her head. 'All in good time. You're not going anywhere, are you?'

'Do I need a lawyer?'

'We're just having a wee chat the now.'

'I think I should have a lawyer.'

'This isn't a formal statement we're taking. We just want to hear your version of what happened. Who killed your father, Robbie?'

'Johnny Turner.'

'Yes. Who killed him?'

'Naw, you're no gettin it. Johnny Turner killed my father.'

Karen and Tom look at each other. '*What?*' they both ask.

Robbie nods, as much as the wires, tubes, bandages and his obvious discomfort will allow. 'Johnny Turner killed my father,' he repeats calmly. '*Colin Temple* killed Johnny Turner.'

Karen almost trips over her words, so many questions threatening to spill out that she only just manages to prioritise the most important one. 'And who killed Colin Temple?'

*   *   *

Colin doesn't know how long he's been standing there when he hears the second car pull up outside. He hasn't moved since he pulled the trigger and Johnny fell, other than to lower his outstretched arm. Even that stayed in place for a long time, until sheer fatigue from the weight of the gun tugged it down. He hasn't looked at anything else either, hasn't taken his eyes from the mess on the floor: three spheres gaping unblinkingly back at him. Two of them are Johnny's astonished open eyes. The third comprises two concentric circles, powder burn framing the entry wound like a ring around a planet.

His own planet, his own world, no longer exists. It was swallowed by the black hole in Johnny's head, from which he knows it can never return.

He hears soft footsteps, the sound of a voice.

'Colin?'

Oh, God. Oh, no. Oh, no. Please, no.

He can't do this.

He must do this.

'In here,' he responds, though his own voice sounds miles away, sounds like someone else's. It's not his anymore. He's not him anymore.

*   *   *

'He's staunin there wi a gun,' Robbie says. 'I never saw it was in his hand until I was practically in the door. That's when I saw Johnny. I cannae mind what I says. My heid was, ye know, just . . . naewhere. That's when he tellt me Johnny killed my real da, an that's how he'd disappeared in 1969. He was in some state, could hardly talk for greetin. Said Johnny was tryin tae stop him demolishin the hotel because that's where the body was buried. So we're baith just staunin there for . . . Christ, felt like ages . . . And eventually I says, ye know,

430

"Fuck's sake, whit ye gaunny dae noo?" That's when he pointed the gun at me, tellt me tae get doon on ma knees. I worked oot the script pretty fuckin sharpish at that point, believe me.'

Robbie sighs, closes his eyes for a second, opens them again. 'I'd like tae be able tae say I made a grab for the gun or whatever, but the truth is I was helpless. Couldnae move, couldnae think, couldnae even speak. I was doon on the floor, an he was right next tae me, the gun at my heid. I wanted tae look at him, but I couldnae even dae that. I just closed my eyes. We were like that for ages, or that's what it felt like. Then all of a sudden he just says: "I'm sorry."'

*   *   *

Colin has the gun inches from the head of this trembling, terrified figure cowering on the floor. He's done it once, he tells himself. He can do it again. He *has* to do it again. That was different, though. That was Johnny. That was the man who was going to take everything away from him. This is somebody he's known since he was not even five years old; somebody he saw every day of his childhood.

Johnny has taken everything away from him anyway. There is no way back. There is no escaping this.

He can see the arrest, the cameras, the papers, the trial, the van, the cell.

There is no way back.

He puts the gun to his own head.

'I'm sorry,' he says.

431

We Can Be Brave Again

There's half a dozen Dibbles round Boma's house in case it has leaked that Robbie is awake and the bastard's planning to make a run for it. From the sight of the car in the drive and the sound of a telly inside, Karen can safely conclude that this won't be the case. She walks up to the front door and rings the bell.

'What are you grinning about?' Tom asks.

'It's moments like this that keep me doing this job,' she replies.

Boma comes to the door in his stocking soles, Y-fronts and a Celtic top. 'The fuck yous want noo?' he snarls.

'To arrest you,' Karen says. 'For the attempted murder of Robert Turner. He's feeling better, by the way.'

'Whit?' Boma splutters, his eyes flashing briefly with shock before he pulls it together and restores his game face. 'This is harassment. I was in Sutherland. I tellt ye. I've got somebody up there can corroborate.'

'Can he corroborate this?' Tom asks, and holds up a sheaf of computer printouts. 'These are still images from CCTV footage taken at Celtic Park on Wednesday night. That's you there in your usual seat, in roughly the same spot you used to stand in the old Jungle, as I believe you put it.'

If it is at all possible, Boma looks even more pallid and cadaverous than usual as this sinks in.

'Hey, Brian,' Karen says. 'Do you remember you chucked mud in my pal Helen's face back at

432

primary school?'

'Dae I fuck. Whit ye talkin aboot?'

Karen looks him in the eye and smiles broadly. 'Because I do,' she says. 'Okay boys, cuff this piece of shite.'

*   *   *

This time, Noodsy really does hug Martin. They're on the steps of the police station, a taxi waiting to take Noodsy home. Noodsy is in tears, and just clings on to Martin for a while before he can compose himself enough to speak.

'Thanks man,' he says, sniffing. Martin almost expects to see him wipe his nose with his sleeve like he saw him do a thousand times at St Elizabeth's. 'You're the fuckin' man, Marty. I knew you'd come through for me. You were always the smartest guy I knew. I owe ye forever, mate. I owe ye forever.'

'It was a team effort, Noodsy,' Martin replies. 'Karen played her part, remember, and I should inform you that you owe Scotty quite a few pints as well. But the real brains of the outfit was JoJo.'

Noodsy nods enthusiastically. 'I owe yous all.'

'You don't owe me anythin, except to keep your nose clean from here on in.'

'Aw, nae danger, seriously,' he insists. 'This was a big fuckin wake-up call for me, man. Lot ay time tae dae some heavy thinkin these last few days. I'm playin it straight fae noo. I know a second chance when I'm lookin at it.'

'Glad to hear it.'

'Whit aboot Robbie? Is he in the clear, then?'

'Same as yourself, there's still the conspiracy-to-

433

pervert charge, but they cannae make a case for the murders. Karen said there's no way the Procurator Fiscal would touch it. Plenty of circumstantial evidence, but no motive. His explanation might be uncorroborated, but it's the only one that ties everything else together and makes any sense. You're both still looking at custodial terms.'

'Ach, six months, probably. Jakey sentence. Canter. Specially considerin I thought I was for the big ticket. All-day pass. And dae ye know what scared me most aboot that?'

'What?'

'The feelin that it was always due me: tae get done for somethin I never did. It's been happenin tae me since my first day at school. That auld ratbag Lanegan pulled me up for stealin money aff some boy. Wouldnae listen when I tried tae tell her Colin had given us it. That was me branded a thief for life. *Vee-lan*,' he mimics. 'Remember?'

'Aye. How could I forget?'

Noodsy raps him on the head. 'Bawd igg.'

'What ever happened to Momo?' Martin asks. '*Is he still living?*'

Noodsy laughs. 'I think he ended up in Calderpark Zoo. Or mibbae they returned him to the wild. Fuck knows.'

*   *   *

Martin watches the taxi drive off as he walks away, heading in the direction of the railway station, Noodsy giving him a last wave through the rear window. He smiles to himself, all those memories coming back, right to that first day. Poor Colin. He did give Noodsy that money, but Martin had no idea Noodsy had ended up in trouble for it. Bastard of a coincidence some other kid had money taken off him the same day.

Then it hits him: there was no other kid, just Colin. He gave out all those coins like he was paying for their books, a wee wean with no concept of what the money was worth. Went home, probably got asked by his mummy where his cash went. Realises he's screwed up and tells a big fib: a bad boy took it from me. Mummy tells the infant headmistress and suddenly Noodsy's a thief for life.

Jesus.

It set Colin on a certain path too, Martin realises. He became quite the arch manipulator as the years went on. Learnt how to use peer pressure, learnt how to isolate people, learnt how to influence the pack. But the incident with the coins was what first taught him how people would believe a story if you presented it properly; how the blame could be shifted from yourself if you picked the right person to shift it to.

That was how he came up with his plan to make it look like someone else had murdered Johnny before committing suicide. He chose someone with a plausible motive, but that only covered the first part.

Martin has to stop walking as it strikes him that Colin would not have chosen Robbie as the ideal candidate for the second. There was someone else, someone with an identical motive, but someone who might almost be expected to die a suicide. Someone whose own mother had killed herself. Someone who, despite being the lodges' cleaner, was conveniently ill and thus out of the picture for several days while all the corpse-disposal was going on. Someone whom Robbie felt loyalty towards. Someone who knew she could turn to him in the most acute crisis, such as being stuck at a murder scene with two dead bodies and an apparent motive for killing one of them. Someone who, he is certain, also owned a pay-as-you-go mobile phone. And someone with keys to the hut in order to remove that hard drive.

He thinks of JoJo at the school today, that concentrated, slightly worried look on her face. 'Who better indeed?' she had asked. A question to which she had already worked out the correct answer.

*   *   *

He waits until it's late, almost closing time, then takes a seat at the bar and orders a pint. He drinks it slowly as JoJo sees out the last customers and eventually the rest of the staff. He thinks about Colin, better able to mourn him now that he knows the truth. Thinks not about what Colin became, and definitely not about what he contemplated but couldn't see through to conclusion. Instead, he thinks about those younger days. He thinks about the games they played: Colditz and pinkies, two-man hunt, best man fall, Colin's killertine. He thinks about those endless football matches, Colin's goalkeeping feats on the soft grass. And he thinks about the last time he heard Colin talk innocently about his passions, before his later enthusiasms set him on a different path. Must have been early Second Year. It stands out because it

436

was after the onset of Colin's new-found stature, and thus rare—and kind of precious—that they ended up in such an involved conversation. Colin was talking about the stars, something he had done quite a few times at St Lizzie's too, though Martin assumed he had by this point abandoned his nine-year-old stated ambition of being an astronomer. Colin knew everything about the sky. He had even got this huge telescope for his Christmas in Primary Five.

'The most amazin thing aboot the stars', he said, 'is the distance, and the time it takes their light tae reach Earth. If a star's twenty light years away, then the illumination generated by the events happenin right now—the fires and explosions—won't shine on us for another two decades.'

The staff run off the till, fill the glass-washer, empty the ashtrays, turn off the music. JoJo switches it back on once the last of them has gone, puts on a CD, then fills herself a large glass of wine and takes a seat next to Martin.

'You're a fly one,' he says softly.

'Fly? How?'

'It was Eleanor at the lodges, wasn't it? Not Robbie. Why didn't you tell me?'

JoJo takes a sip of wine and looks him in the eye over the rim as she swallows. 'So Professor Brainbox worked out the answer yet again,' she says.

'Took me longer than you, though. But don't worry. I'm not going to tell the teacher.'

'Well, if you're smart enough to solve the big question, you must know the answer to the one you just asked.'

'I guess. You figured the polis have got a

437

solution everybody's happy with, so you're protecting Eleanor from a whole load of grief.'

'I'm protecting Robbie, too,' she says.

'Robbie? How?'

'It's a hell of a thing he's done for Eleanor. I don't want that taken away from him.'

Martin nods. 'That's . . . You're really the sweetest girl, JoJo,' he says. 'I mean it.'

'I liked it when you called me Joanne.'

'Okay. Joanne.' He takes a sip of his pint and places it down very carefully on the bartop so that his fingers just brush against hers. 'I've got one last question for you,' he says.

'What?'

Martin stands up and glances over his shoulder at the empty room. There's a slow song playing on the stereo, some old soul number from 1985.

'Would you like to dance?'

JoJo takes his hand and smiles.

'I'd love to.'

Glossary

afore Earlier than the time when.
auld Advanced in years.
ay Pertaining to.
baith Affecting or involving one as well as the other.
bampot A somewhat combustible individual.
baw A spherical object.
beamer Ruddy-cheeked display of embarrassment. See also **riddie**.
birling Motion inclined to induce disorientation.
blooter A hearty and full-blooded strike. See also **lamp**, **scud**, **skelp**, **stoat**.
boat hoose Evidence of upward mobility; a privately owned dwelling.
bogey, the game's a Declaration of despair; resignation that all is lost.
brammer An impressive specimen. See also **stoater**.
brer A male sibling.
bubbling Prolonged and self-pitying bout of tearfulness.
bunnet A fetching item of headgear.
cadge To solicit charitable donations of money or more often confectionary.
cheenies Treasured orbs in the possession of the male.
chook, is it Expression of profound scepticism.
clamped Rendered lost for words.
clap To stroke affectionately. 'Ken them? I've clapped their dug!'
coupon One's visage.

439

crabbit Of foul humour. See certain Scottish broadsheet literary critics.

da Patriarchal head of the household.

dae To effect, perform or carry out an activity.

deck An incident considered sufficiently amusing as to imagine one rendered horizontal with laughter. See also **gut**, **pish**.

deid Expired, no longer with us, snuffed out, passed on, ceased to be.

diddies Protruberant milk-producing glandular organs situated on the chest of the human female and certain other mammals. See also Greenock Morton FC.

dowt The end of a cigarette, much coveted by impoverished but aspiring apprentice smokers.

dug Four-legged domesticated flesh-eating and leg-humping mammal of the wolf-descended genus Canis familiaris.

dunt A small, controlled blow.

dwam A state of foggy befuddlement.

edgy, the Look-out duty, usually in cover of nefarious deeds.

eejit One not blessed with ample intelligence. See Old Firm supporters.

eppy Paroxysms of uncontained anger.

erse The posterior, buttocks or anus. Used by Old Firm supporters to accommodate the brain.

fae Used to indicate a starting point.

fanny The female pudenda. Term of abuse for particularly whiny and snivelling individuals. See also certain Scottish broadsheet literary critics.

feart In a state of anxiety.

fitba Popular team sport known in some quarters as 'soccer', invented and given to the world by the Scots. English claims to have invented it rest on

440

their having the first Football Association, which proves only that they invented football bureaucracy. Thanks a pantload, guys. You form yet another bloody committee and a hundred years later, we had to put up with Jim Farry.

fly Sharp-witted and elusive.

fud See **fanny**. And yet again, see certain Scottish broadsheet literary critics.

fullsy-roundsies Challenging skipping-rope technique, not for dilettantes. Comparison: see **shoe-shaggy**.

gallus Term of glowing approval. Derives from description of that which is cheerfully bursting with self-confidence. The word comes from 'gallows', coined at at the hanging of a Glasgow thief and murderer known as Gentleman Jim, who had remained his smiling, cocksure and witty self right up until the drop.

gaun yersel Shout of encouragement, insinuating the recipient needs no assistance to perform his attempted feat. Literally 'go on yourself'.

geezabrek Invoked to wish for peace or better fortune.

gemme A match or playful diversion. One might request to join by entreating: 'Geezagemme'.

gemmie Most enjoyable, highly approved.

gie To transfer possession of something.

ginger Generic term for carbonated minerals. Despite billions of dollars spent on brand recognition and advertising, in Glasgow, Coke, Pepsi, Seven-Up and Sprite are all referred to as 'ginger'.

greeting Tearful outpouring of grief.

gub The human mouth, usually referring to a large and loud one.

gubbed Soundly beaten, inferring the resultant metaphorical closing of the aforementioned large and loud gub whose outpourings occasioned the gubbing.

guddle A state of frantic unco-ordination.

guddling A subtle means of angling practised without a rod or net.

gut An incident considered sufficiently amusing as to imagine one's innards rent asunder by laughter. See also **deck, pish**.

hame Where the heart is.

haun The end of the forelimb on human beings, monkeys etc utilising opposable thumbs in order to grasp objects. Also the appendages dragged along the ground at the end of Old Firm supporters' sleeves.

heid Uppermost division of the human body, containing the brains, except in the case of Old Firm supporters. See **erse**.

heidie The headmaster.

hing An inanimate object as distinguished from a living being.

hingmy All-purpose procrastinatory term for that which one cannot quite think of the name of yet. Equivalent of the French truc.

honking Emitting a foul odour; poorly thought of. See St Mirren 2001–04.

huckled Arrested or apprehended by agents of authority. See also **lifted**.

humping The act of coitus. Also a convincing and comprehensive victory. See Celtic 0–St Mirren 3, April 1991, or St Mirren 3–Rangers 0, October 1983.

jakey Homeless indigent partial to Buckfast and superlager.

jakey sentence An undaunting custodial term, like those commonly conferred on the above.

jammy Enjoying extreme good fortune. See Rangers 1–St Mirren 0, Scottish Cup semi-final replay 1983.

jinky Swift-footed and elusive.

jobbie Malodorous human waste product. See the performance of Brian McGinlay as referee, Scottish Cup semi-final replay 1983.

jooks Outer garment extending from the waist to the ankles.

kb-ed Rejected. Knocked back.

keech See **jobbie**.

keek To glimpse briefly or surreptitiously.

keeker A black eye, rendering one able only to keek.

kerry-oot A cargo of alcoholic refreshments purchased from an off-licence to be transported elsewhere for consumption.

knock To take without consent or permission and with no intention of returning it.

lamp To strike out using one's fist. See also **blooter**, **scud**, **skelp** and **stoat**.

lash Leather tawse used for administering corporal punishment in Scottish schools. Outlawed in the 1980s less on humanitarian grounds than upon the belated realisation that the weans were having competitions to see who could get the most lashes.

lavvy Water closet.

leather To bring considerable force to bear upon an object or person. See also **malky**, **panelling**.

lifted See **huckled**. That Lighthouse Family song never quite hit the same note north of the border.

lugs Organs of hearing and equilibrium in humans,

Old Firm supporters and other vertebrates.

ma Female parent of a child or offspring.

maist To the greatest degree or extent.

malky An act or instrument of extreme violence. See also **leather**, **panelling**.

maw see **ma**.

mention Succinct and economical graffito stating simply one's name.

mibbae Perhaps.

minging See **honking**.

mockit In a state of very poor cleanliness. See also Greenock.

moolsy Selfish, ungenerous, disinclined to share one's sweeties with half a dozen cadgers who wouldn't give you the steam off their shite if it was the other way around.

morra (the) The day after today.

nae Denoting the absence of something, such as the likelihood of an Old Firm supporter winning Mastermind: 'Nae chance.'

neb Nose.

noggin See **heid**.

numpty See **eejit**.

old firm Ingenious idiot-identification scheme which tags halfwits, criminals, thugs and assorted neerdowells voluntarily in blue or green-and-white garments, making them easier for the rest of us to avoid.

Paisley, to get off at To practice coitus interruptus.

pan breid A soft loaf made with refined white flour. Also rhyming slang for deceased.

panelling A brutal and inrestrained violent assault. See also **leather**, **malky**.

pish Urine; urinary function. Also an incident considered sufficiently amusing as to imagine one rendered incontinent by laughter. See also **deck**, **gut**, and Morton blowing promotion in 2004.

porteed, you're a Early playground declaration of intent to bring the authorities to bear upon a transgressor.

poke A paper bag.

polis Organisation employed to harass and intimidate under-twelves.

proddy Member of the Protestant or Presbyterian faiths, or one perceived to be so due to non-attendance of a Catholic school.

puddock A frog ('Aye, it's a braw bird, the puddock').

riddie See **beamer**.

sair Painful.

sclaff Poorly executed strike of a ball failing to make clean or well-directed contact. See Jose Quitongo.

scoobie A clue, or inkling.

scud In a state of undress. Also, to strike something with dull force. See also **blooter**, **lamp**, **skelp** and **stoat**.

scud book A magazine celebrating the female form.

self-reference See **self-reference**.

shite See **keech**, **jobbie**, and certain Scottish broadsheet literary critics.

shoe-shaggy Undemanding novice level of skipping ropes, swinging back and forth without describing full circles. Comparison: see **fullsy roundsies**.

side A proper match contested by two teams, as opposed to a kick-about or a game of crossy or three-and-in.

single fish Serving of battered fish without chips

which rather confusingly includes two fish. Also rhyming slang for urinary function.

skelp To strike or slap. See also **blooter**, **lamp**, **scud** and **stoat**.

skitter Diarrhoea; also anything watery, weak and poorly formed.

skoosh A task or prospect one expects to be less than taxing. Also a soft drink, usually uncarbonated.

snotters Mucous discharge.

sook The act of, or one given to acts of sycophancy or ostentatious obedience.

square go Pugilistic unarmed combat, with both parties ready and willing participants.

steamboats An advanced state of refreshment. See **stocious**.

staun To stand.

stauner When one's member chooses independently to stand.

stoat See **skelp**, **scud**, **lamp**, etc.

stoater See **brammer**.

stocious See **steamboats**.

stowed Crammed to capacity.

swatch A brief glance.

tanned Subject to an act of robbery.

thae Those.

thon That.

tight Descriptive of a young lady of robust moral virtue, who probably has nae tits anyway.

toe A strike at a football making up in brute power what it lacks in accuracy and panache.

wan The singular; one.

weans Children.

winching The romantic pursuit of young ladies.

wrang The opposite of right. See Brian McGinlay's

decision to award Sandy Clark a goal in the 1983 Scottish Cup semi-final replay when the ball failed to come within two feet of the goal line. See also Brian McGinlay's failure to award St Mirren any one of three stonewall penalties during the same match.

yin The singular. See also **wan**.

yins Multiples of the singular.